RAVE REVIEWS FOR BARBARA DAWSON SMITH!

HER SECRET AFFAIR

"Fast-paced, intricately plotted and filled with intriguing characters . . . Smith blends the elements of romance and mystery well. But most of all, the warring wills and sexual tension between Justin and the sensuous Isabel sizzles throughout."

—Publishers Weekly

"Barbara Dawson Smith cleverly merges old-fashioned Gothic suspense with a seductive romance all packed into an alluring setting . . . This one will keep you up all night, and you'll see why Ms. Smith is so respected for her ability to create a new and different story each and every time."

—Romantic Times (Exceptional rating)

"Ms. Smith's books are always a pleasure to read. She conjures remarkable characters and a wondrous love story. I was most impressed with the honesty of thought, word, deed, and sexual desire between the hero and heroine . . . Ms. Smith's name on the cover is synonymous with spellbinding reading."

—Rendezvous

"HER SECRET AFFAIR is Regency romance at its most inventive . . . Barbara Dawson Smith has demonstrated again why her novels are eagerly awaited."

—CompuServe Romance Reviews

More . . .

ONCE UPON A SCANDAL

NEVER A LADY

"Timeless romance that will keep you turning the pages."
—KAT MARTIN

"It's time for the rest of the world to discover what Barbara Dawson Smith's fans have known all along—this is a can't-miss author."
—*RomEx Reviews*

"A treasure of a romance . . . a story that only a novelist of Ms. Smith's immense talent could create. Barbara Dawson Smith continues to be a refreshing, powerful voice of the genre. A must-read."
—*Romantic Times* (Exceptional rating)

"A brilliant and daring tale."
—*Affaire de Coeur*

"This is a multi-faceted story with deep secrets and many forks in the road to true happiness. Ms. Smith constructs a passion-filled story draped in suspense and danger. An action-filled story set in the Regency period."
—*Rendezvous*

"NEVER A LADY is an outstanding Regency historical that keeps the reader in suspense right up to the end . . . the sexual tension is beautifully handled . . . a winner! Barbara Dawson Smith is a romance writer to watch!"
—*Romance Forever*

"NEVER A LADY is a fantastic read!"
—*The Reader's Voice*

**St. Martin's Paperbacks Titles
by Barbara Dawson Smith**

*A Glimpse of Heaven
Never a Lady
Once Upon a Scandal
Her Secret Affair
Too Wicked to Love*

Too Wicked To Love

Barbara Dawson Smith

St. Martin's Paperbacks

TOO WICKED TO LOVE

Copyright © 1999 by Barbara Dawson Smith.

ISBN: 0-312-96893-0

Printed in the United States of America

St. Martin's Paperbacks edition / April 1999

10 9 8 7 6 5 4 3 2 1

To Jennifer Enderlin, an editor of superior skill,
keen insight, and great enthusiasm.
Your work is appreciated!

Acknowledgment

As always, a big thanks goes to four fine ladies who cleverly pinpoint where the manuscript needs work, who patiently listen to me whine, and who gently convince me to fix it anyway: Joyce Bell, Christina Dodd, Betty Traylor Gyenes, and Susan Wiggs.

And thanks to Connie Brockway for managing to get in the last word, as always.

Too
Wicked
To Love

Chapter 1

Wessex, England
Late April 1816

For only the second time in her life, Miss Jane Mayhew found herself facing a naked man.

At least she presumed he was naked beneath the rumpled sheets. Entwined with a giggling blonde in the four-poster bed, he turned toward the doorway with more irritation than abashment.

Then he sat up, the covers falling to his waist, the gray light of morning bathing his athletic form. "What the deuce—Jane?"

She refused to avert her eyes from that shocking display of muscled chest. She would not let him intimidate her as he had done so many years ago. To regain her equilibrium, Jane had only to consider the bundle that had been left on her doorstep that morning. "Lord Chasebourne, I demand a word with you. Immediately."

"Good God. Has your cottage burned down?"

"Of course not. It's another matter. One of vital importance."

He relaxed a little. "Then if you've come looking for lessons," he drawled, "you'll have to wait your turn." One of his hands moved beneath the counterpane, doing heaven

1

knew what to the blonde, who tittered unashamedly. "You may return at a more suitable hour."

"Don't be absurd," Jane snapped. "I shall remain here until you grant me an audience. In private." For emphasis—and because her legs were trembling from her own audacity—she lowered herself to a gold-fringed ottoman and sat rigidly upright. She planted the point of her umbrella between her sturdy half-boots, which were muddy from her march across the moors.

Never in her life had she behaved so boldly. She far preferred her books to confronting irredeemable London rakes. But drastic circumstances called for drastic measures.

Ethan—Lord Chasebourne—stared at Jane. His dark, chiseled features had matured into a godlike handsomeness. She remembered him as a wild, unruly lad who chased the girls and made them squeal. Just as the blond strumpet squealed when he idly fondled her. All the while, he kept his gaze on Jane.

She would not shiver under the chill of those obsidian eyes. Into the silence, the mantel clock ticked and a flurry of raindrops struck the windows. Abruptly he slapped his bed partner on her bottom. "Run along now," he murmured silkily. "We'll finish later."

"But Chase, darling—"

"Go," he stated.

Pouting, the blonde snatched up a frilly pink robe that lay rumpled on the carpet. Jane glimpsed a pair of astonishingly huge bosoms before jerking her gaze to the silver crest that adorned the blue canopy. Out of the corner of her eye, she saw the woman blow him a kiss and then saunter out of the bedroom, leaving a waft of heavy perfume.

Jane had heard about such women. Fallen women. Women who thought nothing of sharing a man's bed.

A tiny pang nibbled at Jane's aplomb. Once, just once, she would like to be lush and pretty, rather than too tall, too angular, too plain. She'd like to have fair hair and red lips and astonishingly huge—She stopped that absurd thought. She didn't want to attract a man like this one. It mortified her to recall that at one time she had secretly fancied herself in love with Ethan Sinclair, then heir to the fifth Earl of Chasebourne.

She hadn't seen him in years, but he hadn't changed. If anything, he had sunk lower in her estimation.

Now the sixth earl, her childhood nemesis lounged in bed, his skin swarthy against the white pillows, the sheets riding scandalously low on his hips. He casually clasped his hands behind his head, as if receiving angry spinsters in his bedchamber were nothing new to him. She forced herself to meet his direct gaze. Really, it was ridiculous to feel this flush of mortified fascination. She had cared for her father in his final illness, and no aspect of the male anatomy was unknown to her.

Ethan regarded her with condescension. "Still poking your nose where you're not wanted? May I suggest that in the future, you send your calling card with my footman rather than barging into my bedchamber and spoiling a most pleasurable morning."

She sat stiff and straight, her gloved fingers gripping the ivory handle of the umbrella. "Pilcher refused to deliver my message. I was obliged to take matters into my own hands."

"Still the same bossy female, too. Apparently no one has ever told you that a woman wins favor with men through deference and submissiveness."

"I am not here to seek your favor," Jane retorted. "Nor am I one of your mutton-witted hussies."

"So whose mutton-witted hussy are you?" He laughed at his own jest. "Don't tell me. I don't want to know."

She didn't like the queer tightening in her stomach when he looked her up and down, one dark eyebrow cocked. Nor did she appreciate the amusement that quirked the corners of his mouth. It made her feel gauche and unpolished, as if he were privy to a mystery she could never know.

And he was. She could never fathom the depravity of a

man reputed to be the greatest lover in all England. A man who'd had the audacity to divorce his wife for *her* adultery.

A man whose exploits had made him shirk his responsibilities.

Jane sprang to her feet and stalked to the foot of the bed. "Enough of this idle conversation. I've come here for an extremely important purpose—"

"Whatever your complaint is, it can wait until I've dressed. Now kindly have the courtesy to take yourself downstairs."

"No." Jane would not be put off. If she left now, he would go prowling after his harlot. Men like him were weak, venal creatures, and Jane might not see him again for hours. "You will heed what I have to say—"

"Suit yourself, then."

Ethan threw back the covers and rose from the bed. She noticed two facts in rapid succession. First, he had grown much taller; he was one of the few men to tower over her. Second, he was built nothing like her ailing old father.

The breath stuck in her throat. Her fingers clenched convulsively around the handle of the umbrella. Despite her better intentions, a flaming heat scalded her cheeks and sped through her body. She spun around, fixing her gaze on a closed mahogany writing desk.

His chuckle increased her embarrassment. "Something wrong, Miss Maypole?"

She wanted to cringe at that hated old nickname. But she was no longer a too lanky adolescent, afraid to offend the boy she secretly adored. "I am Miss Mayhew to you, sir."

"I do beg your pardon," he said from somewhere behind her.

He didn't sound sorry in the least.

She heard the slap of his bare feet as he moved toward the dressing room. The hinges of a clothes press squeaked. A drawer slammed. She imagined him pulling a linen shirt over that magnificent torso, stepping into a pair of tight breeches—

Jane halted her runaway thoughts. She felt overly warm in her high-necked gown. It wasn't like her to waste time on wicked speculation. Especially not when she had an injustice to rectify.

"Lord Chasebourne." Her voice came out thin and raspy, and she spoke louder so that he could hear. "Lord Chasebourne, I am determined to tell you why I am here."

"Tell away," he called.

"Just this morning, the most intolerable situation has come to my attention." Jane welcomed the outrage that imbued her with the courage to swing back toward him. "I wish you to know that I will not permit your abandonment of Marianne."

He stepped out of the dressing room. His shirt flaps hanging down to his fawn breeches, he fastened his cuffs with silver links. "Marianne?"

The sight of him half-clothed was every bit as daunting as his former nudity. With his dark mussed hair and half-opened shirt, he looked like the prince of depravity. She swallowed. "Don't pretend ignorance. Surely you recall her existence."

He shot her a distracted glance. "There was Mary, Countess of Barclay, but that was years ago. And Marian Phillips, the actress. However, our liaison lasted only one night, so she can hardly cry abandonment."

"Enough about your women," Jane snapped. "The world already knows you are a cad in the worst degree. A bounder extraordinaire. A—"

"A rake, a rogue, and a scapegrace," he finished with a droll grin, ticking off the names on his long fingers. "A knave and a blackguard, too."

"This is no occasion for levity. You will do right by Marianne. It is your duty."

Snatching up a starched cravat, he strolled to the pier glass between the tall windows. "Where is the chit, then?" he asked in a jaded tone. "I shall pay handsomely to get her—and you—out of my life."

"Pay!" Jane marched forward and glowered at his reflection in the mirror. "You will do more than issue a bank draft, Ethan Sinclair. You shall behave as a man of honor. If you do one thing right in your misbegotten life, you will take care of your own infant—"

"Wait a moment." He swung around, his cravat half-tied, the ends dangling. "You're saying Marianne is a *baby.*"

"Of course she is. And you shall take charge of her care immediately."

Those impenetrable brown eyes studied Jane. Then he threw back his head and roared with laughter. "No infants for me, thank you. I prefer my females experienced."

"This is not a matter for jesting."

"Well, she can't be mine. I've taken scrupulous care not to sire any bastards."

It was on the tip of Jane's tongue to ask how. She had only a hazy notion of the manner in which children were conceived, yet surely if preventive methods were available there would be no unwanted babies born. "Marianne *is* your byblow. She must be." Digging into the pocket tied to her loose skirt, Jane walked to him and dropped an object into his hand. "Here's the proof."

He looked down at the gold signet ring embossed with a *C* entwined with holly leaves. Jane knew he had inherited the seal upon his father's death some ten years ago. "This has been missing for at least six months or more," he mused, rotating it between his fingers. "Where the devil did you find it?"

"Inside Marianne's swaddling blanket along with a notecard bearing her name. She was left on my doorstep early this morning."

A lump constricted Jane's throat. She had opened the door of the cottage to go on her daily walk and almost stumbled over the basket with its bundle of slumbering baby, set on the stoop like a gift from the fairies. Falling to her knees, Jane had gazed in awe at the tiny eyelashes, the button nose, the rosebud mouth. With trembling hands, she had lifted the baby from the basket and cuddled her close, an indescribable joy rising in her. . . .

"And you didn't see anyone running away?" Ethan asked. "Or perhaps hiding in the bushes?"

She gave him a withering look. "No. But it was obviously one of *your* women."

"Then explain why the baby wasn't left on *my* doorstep."

"It's simple. The mother was afraid to confront you. *I* am not."

"Utter nonsense." Ethan slid the ring onto his finger, then pivoted away to finish tying his cravat. "She'd have come straight to me for help. I treat my women well. They each receive a fine gift when our liaison ends."

"Well, one of them received an additional gift—nine months later."

He chuckled. "That's a Banbury tale. My guess is that this child is the offspring of a shepherd or farmer who wants her to have a better life. You should have a look around the area, see who's lately been *enciente*."

"The swaddling blanket was of the finest quality. And Marianne's name was written in a lady's fine hand."

"Show me this notecard," he said in a scoffing tone. "I'll see if I recognize the penmanship."

"I didn't bring it with me." Jane could grudgingly accept that he hadn't known about the infant. But not this willful lack of concern. "The baby is undeniably yours."

"*You'd* like to think so. Someone is playing a nasty trick on you, that's all."

"No, *you* are trying to shirk your obligations." Jane regarded him in disgust. For all his masterfully male features, he was living proof that physical beauty went only skin deep. "I can't imagine why I thought you'd want your own baby. What more could one expect of a divorced man?"

His good humor vanished, leaving his face hard and cold. "Have a care what you say, Miss Maypole."

She didn't care. "Furthermore, I would never have thought you could fall so low," she said, tasting the bitter remnants of old illusions. "You should be ashamed of yourself, denying support to a helpless infant, withholding your guardianship to a little girl who didn't ask to be born a bastard. Whether you like it or not, she *is* your daughter. And you, Ethan Sinclair, are a worthless excuse for a man."

His hostile stare unnerved her. His hands tightened into fists at his sides. For one startling instant, she sensed a darkness in him, deep and black and dangerous. And too profound for a shallow rake. Abruptly he said, "Where is this child? I wish to see her."

"She is presently at Mayhew Cottage, napping in the care of my Aunt Wilhelmina." Still unsettled by the impression of hidden depths in him, Jane took a shaky breath. "And do not think for one moment that because we are women, *we* should watch over Marianne instead of you."

"Consider your obligation ended, then. You may deliver the infant to my housekeeper. She will see to her welfare." All sardonic politeness, Ethan strode to the bedroom door and held it open. "Good day, Miss Mayhew."

In a daze, Jane descended the grand staircase with its wide marble steps. The coolness of the wrought-metal railing penetrated her threadbare glove. She should be feeling triumphant—or at least relieved that she had accomplished her mission. But instead, misgivings churned in her stomach.

During her time upstairs, the drawing room doors had been opened. Several housemaids were cleaning the spacious chamber. One swept ashes from the rug, while another piled glassware onto a tray and toted it to the scullery. A third servant hurried upstairs with a frilly corset that had been discarded on the floor. Along with the scent of beeswax, the air reeked from tobacco and spirits.

Jane pursed her lips in distaste. Obviously, Ethan Sinclair

had hosted a wild debauchery the previous evening.

So much for his suitability as a father.

She shuddered to imagine sweet little Marianne being raised in such an immoral environment. And therein lay the crux of Jane's dilemma. Had she been wrong to come here, to demand that Ethan assume his paternal role? Would he show any love to his illegitimate daughter, or simply banish her to the dubious care of servants?

Was *she* the one abandoning Marianne?

Pursued by doubts, Jane fled out the front door. She paused beneath the huge portico and gazed past the formal gardens to the vast, windswept moor, half-hidden by the misting rain. She had come here on a moral mission, to make Ethan shoulder responsibility for his sins. It was only fitting he grow up, after all. Like her, he was fast approaching twenty-seven.

Unlike her, he had yet to assume the sober maturity of an adult. Deliver Marianne into the hands of a *housekeeper,* indeed.

Now Jane realized her lapse of judgment. She could not—she *would* not—bring a child to this dissipated household. A house where he fornicated, where he kept unchaste women and strutted around *naked.*

She snapped open her black umbrella. Instead of taking the path that led to home, she marched down the graveled drive, heading toward the gatehouse and the main road to the village.

She had another plan for Marianne's future.

"Damn the meddlesome bitch," Ethan muttered under his breath.

Standing by the library window to catch the meager light of late morning, he glowered down through his spectacles at the legal document that had been delivered to him only moments ago. The single brief paragraph stated that he would relinquish forever all rights to the foundling named Marianne and sign her over into the wardship of one Jane

Agatha Mayhew, of Mayhew Cottage, Wessex.

Ethan tried to fathom why he felt so infuriated. He was being spared the nuisance of assuming responsibility for a baby who was in all likelihood not of his blood. His anger must stem from the fact that Jane had ruined his morning—and now proceeded to withdraw the reason for doing so. Without so much as an apology, she had invaded his house and pecked at his good humor until he bled from a rare attack of conscience.

You, Ethan Sinclair, are a worthless excuse for a man.

A cough broke the silence. "M'lord?" ventured old Grigsby, the village solicitor. Tugging at his gray forelock, the gaunt little man shifted from one foot to the other. "If ye wish the wording to be altered, I should be happy to do so."

"Everything looks in proper order."

"Then if we might proceed, yer lordship." Grigsby respectfully pulled out the chair at the mahogany secretaire. "Miss Mayhew requested I wait while ye sign the document. We'll require two witnesses, of course."

"Of course."

Fighting the urge to rip the document into shreds, Ethan stalked to the bellrope and rang for a footman. Jane was doing him a favor. There was no need to feel so disgruntled about giving up his right to claim a baby.

But what if Marianne *was* his?

The possibility nagged like a sore tooth. It was the one question he could not ignore. The one question he could not answer satisfactorily, though he assured himself it couldn't be true. He treated his women well, never made false promises of undying love, and scrupulously avoided virgins and spinsters. He left his lovers satisfied, with an expensive parting gift to ease the loss of his attentions. Any of his women would have felt free to approach him had she later discovered herself pregnant. None of them would have left a baby on the doorstep of his self-righteous neighbor.

Unless someone wanted revenge on him. Someone who knew him well enough to realize that Miss Jane Mayhew would cause him trouble. Grimacing, he thought of one female who would play such a trick on him. . . .

The footman entered, and Ethan snapped out instructions to fetch his clerk and his steward. Within moments the men were assembled in the library and Ethan seated himself at the opened secretaire.

He snatched a pen from the silver cup and dipped it into the inkpot. His hand hovered over the document.

You, Ethan Sinclair, are a worthless excuse for a man.

The rebuke galled him. Age had not improved Miss Jane Mayhew. She'd glared like a governess straight out of a boy's worst nightmare. Her shapeless gown of muddy black had a collar so high he wondered that she didn't choke. A knob of mousy brown hair had protruded from the back of her head. Though her eyes were a tolerable shade of gray-blue, her features were plain, her skin sallow, her shoulders militantly squared. She possessed nothing of the feminine softness he liked in a woman.

And she was as bossy as ever. He would never forget the time she had caught him in the stables with a comely maid and scolded him for taking advantage of a servant, regardless that the giggling girl had enticed *him*.

Yet Jane Mayhew, despite her flaws, would make a far better parent than he would. He didn't need her harsh truths to know that.

In angry black strokes, he scrawled his name across the document.

Even as he did so, a commotion came from the corridor: voices and the tap of feminine footsteps. Irritated, Ethan snatched off his spectacles and turned around to order the library door closed. But the words halted in his throat as an exquisite woman glided into the room.

A drift of expensive perfume preceded her. Draped in a gown of peach silk that hugged her slim figure, Lady Rosalind looked more like a girl than a woman in her middle years. Her tawny, upswept hair and dainty features glowed as lovely as ever.

Stopping before him, she opened her arms wide. "Ethan, dearest," she said, smiling. "It seems *forever* since last I saw you. Do give me a kiss."

He reluctantly rose from the desk and touched his lips to her smooth cheek. She could not have chosen a worse time to reappear in his life. "Hello, Mother."

"Oh, my," she said, gazing from him to the other men. "Have I interrupted a business meeting?"

"Yes," Ethan said bluntly. He stood in front of the secretaire to block her view of the document lying there. "I should be obliged if you would await me in the drawing room. I'll only be a moment."

"Ah, you're sounding as stuffy as your father used to be. Now, we haven't seen each other since autumn, and I wish to tell you all about the delights of Italy. Not to mention, learn all *your* news." She made a little shooing motion with her fine-boned hand. "You men may return later."

Gritting his teeth, Ethan dismissed them. As the clerk and secretary headed out the door, Mr. Grigsby picked up the document. "I'll deliver this to Miss Mayhew, your lordship." He blew on the signature, then rolled the paper into a tube.

"Miss Mayhew?" Lady Rosalind asked, looking sharply at Ethan. "What business have you with that unpleasant old maid Wilhelmina?"

He didn't correct her mistake. "It's nothing. A minor legal matter."

The diminutive solicitor hadn't taken two steps when Lady Rosalind plucked the paper out of his gnarled hand. Before Ethan could stop her, she unrolled the document and frowned down at it. "Oh, *Jane* Mayhew. My dear friend Susan's daughter. I always thought it a shame poor Jane lost her mother at so young an age . . . what's this? Jane has found a baby?" Her blue eyes rounded, Lady Rosalind looked up at Ethan. "*Your* baby?"

He held out his hand. "Give that paper back to me."

Lady Rosalind clutched it to her breast. "At long last, a child. And you would give her away, just like that?"

The shock and disappointment on her elegant features stabbed into him. He felt like a boy again, scolded for peering into the ladies' retiring chamber at one of her soirées. He resented the rebuke from a featherbrained socialite who had breezed in and out of his childhood on a whim. "It's doubtful she's mine."

"Bah, I know your reputation," his mother said, not disapprovingly. "If Marianne is your only offspring, I should be surprised. But you will not give away my granddaughter like an unwanted stable cat." Turning from him, she glided to the hearth and dropped the document into the flames.

Momentarily stunned, Ethan sprang after her. Too late. When he snatched at the paper, the edges were already curling to black, and he succeeded only in burning his forefinger and thumb. "Damn it, Mother!"

"Kindly refrain from cursing." Lady Rosalind watched as he shook his stinging digits. With a snap of her own fingers, she directed him to the door. "Come, Ethan. You and I are going to visit my granddaughter."

☞ Chapter 2 ☜

Marianne had a fine set of lungs. It dismayed Jane to learn just how piercing a wail one infant could emit.

Cuddling her close, Jane paced the length of the kitchen. Marianne had looked beautiful in slumber, with fine black eyelashes, plump cheeks, and a sweet little mouth, as physically perfect a creation as one would expect of a Chase-bourne. Now, however, that cherubic face shone red with fury. As she'd done several times already, she turned her head and rooted against Jane's bosom, then sobbed all the louder.

Jane felt horribly inadequate, and a lump clogged her throat. "Shhh, darling," she murmured. "The milk is warming. If you'll just be patient."

"Oh, I don't know how much more of this my nerves can bear," Aunt Willy said plaintively. She reclined in a chair by the hearth, fanning her jowly face with a black-edged handkerchief. "I daresay you stuck a pin in her when you . . ."

"Changed her nappy? I assure you, I was very careful." Frustrated, Jane held on to her temper with effort. "She's hungry, that's all."

"You ought to have let that Crockett girl suckle her."

"Lucy Crockett is filthy. I won't have her anywhere near Marianne." Jane shuddered to recall the only nursing

14

mother in the village: a slovenly innkeeper's wife who stank of musty sweat and stale liquor. Jane had promptly sent her packing.

"I simply do not understand why that baby was left here, of all places," Aunt Willy complained. "It is Lord Chasebourne who ought to assume guardianship of the child, not us. Oh, what a vile sort he has turned out to be! And divorced, no less! It is a blessing no one saw you visit there."

Her aunt would suffer heart palpitations if she knew Jane had stormed into his bedchamber and seen him naked. Feeling hot color at the memory, Jane ended the pointless quarrel. "That is precisely why I am keeping her. Here, you hold Marianne while I prepare her bottle."

"Me?" Aunt Willy recoiled, fumbling vainly on the table for her flask of restorative. Her graying brown curls jiggled as she shook her head vigorously. *"I've* no affinity for babies."

"You came to live here when I was an infant. Surely that gives you some experience."

"But your dear father—God rest his soul—hired a *nursemaid* to care for you. And of course *I* never married due to my exceedingly delicate constitution—"

"You'll survive a few minutes." Desperate, Jane pressed the crying infant to that broad, maidenly bosom. Aunt Willy's arms came up automatically to clutch the squalling parcel.

"Oh, mercy!" The older woman sat rigidly straight, staring down in wide-eyed fright at Marianne. "Mercy me!"

Too harried to coddle her aunt as she usually did, Jane dashed to the hearth and dipped her little finger into the pan of milk. She snatched it back. Too hot.

Wrapping the corner of her apron around the handle, she carried the pan to the long table and added a dash of chilled milk from the crock, stirring until the temperature seemed right. Then she poured the milk into a brown glass jar and used a bit of twine to tie on the new teat. If this method worked for orphaned lambs, it ought to work for human babies, too.

It had better work.

She rescued Marianne from Aunt Willy, who promptly snatched up her flask and took a long drink, then squawked about her ordeal. Paying no heed, Jane nestled the baby in the crook of her arm and gently inserted the teat into that toothless, howling mouth.

The crying died to a gurgle. Tiny lips closed around the makeshift nipple and sucked. Once, twice, thrice. Oh sweet, blessed child.

But Jane relaxed too soon.

Marianne spat out the teat, turned her head away, and screeched louder than ever. Jane coaxed her, but the baby refused again and again. Milk squirted over Jane's bosom. She bit back a sob of failure. Then a tiny flailing arm connected with the bottle and sent it crashing to the floor.

It shattered on the stone flags. Liquid drenched the bottom of Jane's gown.

"Good gracious!" Aunt Willy moaned. "Whatever shall we do *now*?"

Jane had no answer. Bowing her head, she hugged the unhappy infant. The tears she'd been fighting coursed down her cheeks. She wanted nothing more than to sink to the floor and bawl along with the baby. She felt useless, ineffectual as a woman, a poor excuse for a mother.

The door hinges squeaked. A male voice drawled, "There's no use crying over spilt milk. Or so goes the old adage."

Aunt Willy let out a maidenly screech. Jane froze. Blinking to clear her watery vision, she stared aghast at Lord Chasebourne.

Ethan Sinclair lounged against the door frame, a gorgeously groomed gentleman in fawn breeches and forest-green coat, the snowy white cravat setting off his swarthy skin and pirate eyes. His elegance made her all the more aware of her own rumpled appearance. Her hair hung in hanks around her face, her everyday black gown reeked of milk, and she jiggled a squalling baby in her arms.

His baby.

Instantly hostile, she clutched Marianne close. "You're supposed to be at home," she accused. "Mr. Grigsby is coming to see you."

His mouth hardened into a grimace. "That's precisely why I'm here."

A woman glided out of the shadowed corridor. "It's why we're both here."

Jane had been so focused on Ethan that she hadn't noticed his companion. Her tawny-gold hair was fashioned in an artful cascade of curls that Jane could never duplicate if she lived to be a thousand. Clad in peach-colored silk, she looked too slim and lovely to be the mother of anyone, let alone a full-grown man. Jane's throat went dry as she recognized the dowager countess—her godmother, though Lady Rosalind had always regarded the role with carefree negligence.

"My lady! I heard you were abroad."

Lady Rosalind's smile seemed almost pained as she listened to the baby's squall. "Oh, I've been back for a few days. I wouldn't miss the Season for all the world."

"Dear Rosalind," Aunt Willy put in. "Forgive me if I don't rise. My lumbago, you know."

"Dear Wilhelmina. I wouldn't dream of asking you to trouble yourself on my behalf." Lady Rosalind glided closer, stepping daintily around the broken bottle. In a silly, nonsense voice, she added, "And who is this fussy little darling?"

For one horrified moment, Jane wondered what to say.

Then the countess continued. "Is this my new granddaughter?"

Lady Rosalind knew.

Jane's heart sank lower. She looked at Ethan, who glowered in the doorway, clearly wanting nothing to do with this disastrous scene caused by the fruit of his philandering.

If he'd seen Grigsby and signed the paper, why was he here?

A sharp fear pierced Jane's bosom. He must not have signed. He must have come to claim Marianne, after all.

"My goodness, you do have a temper," Lady Rosalind was saying in that absurd, singsong tone that seemed to come naturally to her. "We heard you all the way to the front step. You look to be at least two months old . . . and quite well cared for. Oh, look at those pretty blue eyes." She aimed a telling glance at her son. "Your papa had blue eyes when he was born. I wonder if yours will turn as dark as his."

She tickled Marianne beneath her small chin. Marianne blinked at the newcomer. For the space of a few seconds, the sobs slowed, but the lull was only temporary. She sucked in a breath and wailed again.

"She's hungry," Jane said in despair. "I tried to feed her a bottle, but—well, you can see what happened."

Lady Rosalind tilted her head in a thoughtful pose and raised her voice above the noise. "Have you looked for a wet nurse?"

"Yes, I sent out my cook, Mrs. Evershed. But she hasn't yet found anyone suitable."

"You should have brought the child to my housekeeper, as I instructed you," Ethan said from his stance by the door. "Obviously, you know nothing about mothering an infant."

His superior expression made Jane feel all the more inadequate. She resented him for it. She had done her best for *his* child, and this was her thanks?

She marched across the kitchen. "You know so much. Perhaps *you* can do better than I."

She thrust the fretful baby at him, and he caught Marianne awkwardly. His dark brows rising in horror, he held her away from himself, as if he expected her to bite.

"Afraid she'll piddle on your pristine coat?" Jane taunted.

"Don't play games with me," he snapped. "I never said *I* knew anything about babies."

"Then you shouldn't have come here, spouting advice. You ought to have signed that legal paper and stayed with your little blond tart."

His mother coughed delicately.

Mortified at her own shrewishness, Jane said hastily, "I'm sorry, my lady. I didn't mean to offend you."

"It is no matter," she said with a regal wave of her hand. "I am aware of my son's . . . interests."

Ethan strode to Lady Rosalind. "Here, Mother. *You* hold her."

Laughing, she shook her head. "You need the chance to meet your new daughter."

"She is *not* my daughter," he ground out.

Even as he spoke, Ethan wished to God he could be certain of his claim. Loath to look at the child, he aimed his most lordly scowl at Lady Rosalind. She only smiled sweetly and crossed her arms when he would have passed her the baby.

All three women assumed an identical pose, arms folded across their bosoms. His mother beamed like a proud grandmama. In the chair by the fire, Wilhelmina waved a handkerchief at her florid face. Standing between the two of them, Jane returned his scowl. Wisps of loose brown hair lent a curious softness to her obstinate features. Her expression glowed with zeal. She wanted to punish him, to force him to accept this child.

Damned self-rightous spinster.

Gritting his teeth against panic, Ethan looked for a safe place to lay down the screeching infant. Not on the table; she might roll off. Nor any of the other countertops. The wood box? Too hard. Upstairs, then.

Yes. In one of the bedrooms.

She squirmed like a trout caught in a net. Fearing he might drop her, he gingerly tucked the baby into the crook of his arm. She felt sturdier than he would have expected of so small a creature. Still, she was better left to someone qualified in child-rearing, someone who could abide this caterwauling. Then, just as he pivoted toward the door, something remarkable happened.

Marianne ceased crying.

She took a few shuddering breaths and fell silent. Egads, had he given her the coup de grace?

Alarmed, he frowned down to find her watery blue eyes intent on him, a faintly quizzical expression on her dainty face. Tears spiked her fine dark lashes. The noonday light played over her pert nose, the damp rosy cheeks, the quivering mouth. Her milky scent drifted to him. She looked helpless and trusting, utterly innocent.

An inexplicable tenderness clenched his chest. Without thinking, he stroked his finger over her smooth skin, and the satiny texture of it awed him. He felt the disturbing urge to protect her, a feeling he resisted with all the force of suspicion.

Marianne.

Who had named her? Who had abandoned this little girl on a neighbor's doorstep? More importantly, *was* Marianne truly his?

The baby awkwardly worked one tiny fist into her mouth. She sucked noisily for a moment; then she wriggled against him and resumed crying.

Powerless as he'd never been with any female, he swung toward the three watching women. "There must be a nursing mother somewhere in the district."

"Oh, this is horrid," Wilhelmina cried out. "The poor thing will die!"

"Hush," Jane snapped, as if she feared just that. "My cook found one prospect. But she was unsuitable, and I refuse to foster Marianne, anyway."

"Good God," he exploded. "Will you let her starve, then? She doesn't belong to you."

He immediately regretted his harshness. Jane's lower lip trembled, and for a moment she looked as vulnerable as the baby. Out of the blue, he wondered if she had ever wanted to marry and bear children of her own. Strange to think of tart-tongued Jane as a woman with feelings and desires outside of her dusty books. But his untimely flash of compassion vanished the instant she opened her mouth.

"She isn't yours, either, by your own admission," she stated. "So you should sign that paper. And for now, you may hand her back and go on your merry way."

Skirt swishing, she advanced on him. Perversely, he kept Marianne snug against him. "This morning, you were certain she was mine. So certain you couldn't wait to tell me."

He relished seeing the pink color leap into her cheeks. So the bold Miss Mayhew could blush, after all. "I changed my mind," she said, her gaze disapproving. "Marianne doesn't belong with a dissolute rake like you. I won't have her corrupted by your wicked ways."

"Never fear, then. I corrupt only females *over* the age of eighteen."

Those gray-blue irises widened, and her cheeks deepened to a rosy hue. The sight intrigued him. Had she ever experienced sexual desire? Did she ever lie in the darkness of her own bed and long to be seduced?

Not Jane. She was too stridently opinionated to yield to any man.

"If I may suggest a solution," Lady Rosalind said. "While wintering in Italy, I found a maid who has the most cunning skill at hairdressing." She primped at her reflection in a shiny tin platter standing on the sideboard. "No one in all the Continent can match Gianetta's ability to fashion the perfect ringlets, or to choose the perfect bonnet for the occasion. And her talent at sewing, why it is unparalleled—"

"What is your point, Mother?" Ethan broke in, his patience thinned by Marianne's incessant wailing. He walked up and down in a vain, instinctive effort to calm her.

"If you would kindly refrain from interrupting, I shall explain. There was one condition to my employing Gianetta.

She has a daughter of eighteen months whom she refused to leave behind. If she weans the child, perhaps Gianetta is capable of nursing Marianne.''

"Where is she?"

"Why, she's unpacking my trunks at Chasebourne Manor. But I warn you, I shall still require her services as a lady's maid."

"If she can feed Marianne," he said grimly, striding toward the door, "I'll reward her so handsomely she'll never want to leave your employ.''

The haunting notes of a lullaby drifted through the boudoir.

Though adept at ancient Greek, Latin, Gaelic, and more obscure old languages, Jane had never studied Italian and she didn't understand the words of the song. But she did comprehend the smacking sounds of contentment made by a suckling baby.

In a pink-striped wing chair by the hearth sat Gianetta with her bodice drawn down, Marianne held to her plump breast. The voluptuous, dark-haired girl had taken instantly to the baby, crooning in rapid Italian, fussing over her with the instincts of a mother. What a blessing it had been when Marianne had stopped crying.

What a relief to know that she would not starve.

Jane knew she ought to leave the pair in privacy, as Lady Rosalind and Ethan had done. Yet she lingered, unable to shake the irrational fear that letting Marianne out of her sight would be the next step to losing her.

Anxious at the thought, Jane put her hand to her throat, where she could feel the oval lump of the locket hidden beneath her high neckline. The keepsake was all she had left of her own mother. Inside nestled a finely detailed miniature of the lovely, dark-haired lady who had died at Jane's birth. Had she ever come here to visit all those years ago? She had been Lady Rosalind's good friend.

Her godmother's boudoir was a long, elegant room lined with armoires and clothes presses and gilt-framed mirrors.

A pattern of roses and vines trailed over the plush carpet. Painted cherubs cavorted on the high ceiling, lit by the late afternoon light. The rich scents of perfume and powder drifted through the air.

In the elaborate setting, Jane felt appropriately awestruck. Her own room at home was a utilitarian chamber with a plain wooden bedstead, a writing desk, and wall hooks for her three gowns—one for church, one for housecleaning, and one for visiting, which she wore now. All three were black in deference to her father's death the previous year. The monotony of her garb had never bothered Jane until today.

Today, she stared in fascination at the pink-ribboned corset lying in the opened traveling trunk. She felt the shocking urge to try on a pair of sinfully sheer stockings, along with a wispy chemise. Just once, she would like to feel the softness of silk against her skin, the pleasure of wearing a slim-fitting gown instead of the practical garments sewn by her aunt. But such fripperies as these were suitable only for fashionable women like Lady Rosalind.

Women like the blonde who had shared Ethan's bed. Women who flirted and teased, who danced at *ton* balls, and wintered on the Continent. Women who bore illegitimate babies and left them for others to raise.

Miss Jane Mayhew always slept alone, had tended her ailing father while other girls went off to London for their first Season, and had never once left the desolate downs of Wessex. It was only fitting that she wear sensible, durable undergarments of bleached linen. Only reasonable that she take charge of an infant no one wanted.

"Mees?"

Jane started, realizing that Gianetta was motioning to her. She had ceased nursing and held the baby to her now-closed bodice. As Jane walked closer, the foreign woman pressed her finger to her lips.

Miracle of miracles, Marianne had fallen asleep. A droplet of milk glistened at the corner of her mouth. Her tiny hand was splayed over the mound of Gianetta's bosom as if to jealously guard her milk supply.

Reaching down, Jane gathered the baby into her arms. Marianne stirred slightly and sighed in her sleep. A rush of tenderness inundated Jane. How amazing that she could care so deeply for a child she had never known existed before this morning. She had been dressed for her customary early morning hike across the downs when she opened the door and practically stumbled over the basket.

For a moment she had believed the infant an exquisite porcelain doll, her tiny features rendered with beautiful precision, from the fine eyelashes to the sweetly bowed lips. Then Jane had reverently touched the warm, smooth skin, and she had thought the baby a gift from heaven, the child she had always longed for in her most secret dreams. . . .

But now a jarring realization destroyed her fantasy. Marianne couldn't live in Mayhew Cottage, as Jane had envisioned. Not while the baby's food supply resided in Ethan's household.

The full impact of that dilemma shook Jane. What would happen when Lady Rosalind returned to London? Certainly she wouldn't rusticate long in the wilds of Wessex while the Season was in full swing. And Jane very much doubted Ethan's mother would agree to leave behind her treasured maid. Jane might have to say good-bye to Marianne.

Her arms tightened around the baby. She mustn't let herself worry about that—yet. Better she should find a cradle and prepare the nursery. She had no right to issue orders in this household, but the unusual circumstances demanded unorthodox action. If she did not firmly establish a place for herself in Marianne's life, Ethan might well deny her access to the baby.

The thought chilled Jane. She must not allow Marianne to be raised in this amoral setting, with a father who hosted wild revels and entertained a procession of fallen women in his bed. She couldn't depend on Lady Rosalind, either, because the countess had a habit of running off to the Continent or getting caught up in her own amusements. Heaven knew, Jane had observed enough of that neglect during Ethan's childhood.

It was up to Jane to be Marianne's caretaker. And she would begin right now.

Giving Marianne back to Gianetta, Jane went into the dimly lit bedroom dominated by a canopied bed. The carpet muffled her footsteps.

She halted abruptly.

By the outer doorway, Lady Rosalind stood in whispered conversation with her son. It was not a pleasant exchange, judging by the way he furrowed his fingers through his dark hair. Pouting prettily, Lady Rosalind rested her hands on her slender hips. It looked as if she were lecturing him— and he wasn't cooperating.

Jane meant to tactfully withdraw. But Lady Rosalind motioned her closer. ''You had better tell her, Ethan,'' she said in a disapproving tone. ''Jane deserves to know what you've decided.''

Jane's heart skipped a beat. She hastened toward them. ''Decided?''

Ethan regarded her in that faintly superior manner. ''I intend to find the baby's mother. To that purpose, I'm leaving in the morning for London. And I'm taking Marianne with me.''

⌒ *Chapter 3* ⌒

"You can't take Marianne away," Jane said. "I won't let you."

Silhouetted against the bank of windows, she had the air of a warrior queen. Her pose was militant, her shoulders squared and her hands gripped at her sides. In the watery afternoon light, her scraped-back brown hair had a coppery tinge at odds with her prim appearance, and Ethan could detect her scent of soap and milk.

Sour milk.

He grimaced. "May I remind you, it was *your* wish that I assume responsibility for the child."

"That was before I realized just how unfit a father you would make. It is best that you leave Marianne with me."

"And how, pray, will you feed her?" Returning her insult, he lowered his gaze to her bosom, where the ill-fitting, high-necked gown hinted at two milkless bumps. From out of nowhere came the memory of a time long ago, when he had attempted to peer down her dress from the vantage point of a tree limb. He had fallen into a bramble bush instead and spent the rest of the day pulling burrs from his backside. Jane had laughed herself silly.

She wasn't laughing now. Crossing her arms over her inadequate breasts, she said, "Gianetta will feed the baby."

Lady Rosalind stepped out from behind him. "Oh,

dear," she said. "I'm returning to London, too, and Gianetta simply must go with me. Who else would arrange my hair so cunningly?" She patted her tawny curls.

Jane's hope flagged. "But my lady . . . perhaps Gianetta could remain here. It's only for a few months, until Marianne is weaned."

"That is quite impossible," Lady Rosalind said gently. "I am sorry." Turning away, she studied her reflection in a gilt-framed mirror.

The despair in Jane's expression stirred a reluctant twinge of conscience in Ethan. Finding a baby must have been the most excitement she'd had in her life since that tree incident when they were twelve. "I'm sorry, too," he said. "But surely you can see there's no other way."

The glimmer of emotion vanished, leaving a more familiar scorn made plain by her curled lip and elevated chin. She looked down her nose at him. "Yes, there *is* a way. I shall go to London, too. Someone has to watch the baby."

God forbid. The thought of Jane scowling at his table, chiding him for staying out late, was enough to wither a man. "I intend to hire an experienced nursemaid," he said. "So you may rest assured the baby will have the best of care."

Jane took a step closer. "Nevertheless, I *am* going with you."

Deciding a little charm might succeed where harshness had failed, he crossed the bedroom and took her by the elbow, coaxing her toward the outer door. "Come now, Jane. You did a good deed in rescuing Marianne. But you wouldn't want to uproot yourself, to leave all your books behind, to trade your quiet and orderly life for the sins of the city."

She dug her heels into the carpet. "That's precisely why I need to go—to protect Marianne from your immoral influence."

"She will be perfectly safe at all times. I give you my

solemn vow. And should I find out she isn't mine, then certainly you may claim her.''

Jane uttered an outraged gasp. Pulling out of his grasp, she pivoted to face him. ''See? That's what I mean. You don't really care about her. If you did, it wouldn't matter who fathered her.''

''Sentimental nonsense,'' he muttered, his good humor vanishing. ''I've no obligation to support another man's bastard.''

''Which makes *me* the better guardian. I don't care whose child she is.''

''I'll said I'll do right by her,'' he growled. ''*If* she's mine.''

''And if she's not, will you leave her at an orphanage? Abandon her at a baby farm—''

A sharp clapping of hands interrupted Jane.

''Enough quarreling,'' Lady Rosalind said, her slim figure framed by the mirror where she'd been primping. ''Really, one would think you two were still ten years old. Jane, I do like your idea about accompanying us to London, though. It's an excellent compromise.''

Jane's sulky expression brightened. ''Oh, my lady. Thank you.''

''She's not coming with us,'' Ethan objected.

''But Jane does have a point. Marianne needs a mother, not just a nursemaid.''

He focused his dark turmoil on Lady Rosalind. ''Curious. The nursemaid arrangement suited me when I was growing up.''

His mother shrugged one silk-clad shoulder. ''That was an entirely different situation. Your dear departed father believed a boy shouldn't be coddled by his mother. Be that as it may, however, I do have a solution to our present dilemma.''

Ethan didn't trust the faint smile that played on her mouth as she glanced from him to Jane. His mother was up to no good; he would wager his fortune on that. ''The solution," he stated, "is that Jane stays here in Wessex. Where she belongs."

Lady Rosalind lifted her hand in an airy motion that nullified his order. "Don't be a bully, Ethan. Jane *is* my godchild, after all, and I've neglected my duty toward her for far too long." Looking at Jane, she deepened her smile. "So I hereby invite her to London for the Season."

Her nose pressed to the window, Jane absorbed the sights of the city as the coach advanced through a congestion of carriages and drays. Never in her life had she seen so many buildings crowded together. At Lady Rosalind's insistence, Gianetta and Marianne traveled in the baggage coach, while Ethan had ridden on ahead, a tall, handsome gentleman on a fine chestnut gelding. He had scarcely spoken a word to Jane since their quarrel, except to examine the notecard left with Marianne and to say flatly that he didn't recognize the penmanship.

Jane had glimpsed an unsettling anger in him, far more than one would expect of an irredeemable rake. He resented her interference, that much was clear. And so she had prudently elected to stay out of his path. At least for the moment.

Now, she occupied herself with viewing London for the first time. She'd had a hazy expectation of rich palaces with half-naked women lounging on the windowsills. However, the southern approach to the city was a warren of narrow alleys and dusty yards, littered with clothing strung out to dry. Children swarmed the byways, dirty and barefoot, their mothers watching from doorways. The tang of coal smoke pervaded the air.

The coach rattled over a tall bridge spanning the great slate-gray river, and the dilapidated houses gave way to finer neighborhoods. There were an amazing number of people here, too, from street sellers to strolling ladies, ragtag beggars to refined lords. Here at last were the fancy town houses and wide cobbled streets, the elegant shops with bow windows displaying stationery and boots and jewelry.

"London is so drab compared to Rome," Lady Rosalind said on a sigh. Wearing a mint-green bonnet that complemented her fair curls, she clasped her small, gloved hands to her traveling cloak. "But no other city in the world can match London for its glorious parties."

Aware of staring like a bumpkin, Jane sat back against the crimson velvet cushions. "Is it really true that people dance till dawn? It seems utterly mad to miss a good night's sleep."

Lady Rosalind laughed. "Ah, just wait until you waltz in the arms of a man you admire. *Then* you shall understand."

Wistful longing proved stronger than common sense, and Jane pictured herself whirling around a ballroom with Ethan. His grip would be firm and warm, and she would relish his male scent. He would flash his teeth in that easy grin, and she would melt like a smitten girl. . . .

"Jane never learned to dance," Aunt Willy said, adjusting her ruffled spinster's cap. "And I see no reason why she should start now. Why, she is twenty-six years old and long past the bloom of youth."

"Is she?" Lady Rosalind said, smiling thoughtfully. "I wonder."

Jane pictured what Lady Rosalind surely saw: a too-tall woman wearing a black merino cape buttoned to the chin and an out-of-fashion black bonnet framing her unremarkable features. She had never felt quite comfortable in social settings. "You can't really mean to introduce me to society," she said. "You only said so because you knew how much I wanted to be with Marianne."

"Certainly I'm delighted that you adore my granddaughter." Lady Rosalind's blue eyes shone bright with gaiety. "But you'll have your evenings free to attend parties. It's an experience every young lady should enjoy."

"Jane is too sensible for frivolities," Aunt Willy said.

"That is the reason I've consented to staying in the same house as his lordship. Jane's reputation needn't suffer since she has been long on the shelf. She is no silly young girl."

Jane felt a perverse desire to protest, to admit that sometimes she tired of her staid life. What new experiences awaited her in London? Ethan had wanted to keep Jane and the baby in a separate residence, but Lady Rosalind refused to part with her maid, and Gianetta could not be expected to dash back and forth in between feedings. Her mistress might need her to mend a gown or fashion a hairdo.

"Were it not for her ladyship's kind patronage," she reminded her aunt, "we would not have come to London at all."

"Humph." Aunt Willy took a sip from her silver flask of restorative. "I don't see why we had to travel all this way on a whim. It disrupts my routine. Already I have pains in my chest from breathing the noxious air."

"Do try not to breathe, then," Lady Rosalind said cheerfully. "Ah, here we are, home at last."

The coach rolled to a stop and the footman let down the step. As Jane emerged onto the cobbled drive, she blinked in amazement at the house spread out before her. Now here was a palace—or perhaps a castle. Built of Portland stone, the grand edifice occupied the entire side of a square. At either end rose a turreted tower, and Jane could almost imagine knights and ladies strolling along the battlements. Seldom did she feel dwarfed, but the tall columned portico with its ornate pediment gave her the sense of a mouse approaching the throne room of a king. She had known Ethan was wealthy, but not to such an ostentatious degree.

"Come inside," Lady Rosalind invited. When Jane would have waited for the baggage coach, the countess took her by the arm and led her up the broad marble steps and past a blue-liveried footman, who held open the massive door. "Gianetta will bring the baby. Now where is that errant son of mine?"

A rather severe-looking woman with a hook nose stood

waiting inside the hall. "His lordship arrived well over an hour ago, m'lady. Then he set out again in the phaeton not ten minutes past."

"Probably gone to his club, the wretch," Lady Rosalind said, handing her cloak to the footman. "I do hope he returns in time for dinner. Jane, this is Mrs. Crenshaw, our housekeeper. Miss Jane Mayhew will be staying here for the Season. Along with her aunt, Miss Wilhelmina Mayhew."

"His lordship mentioned as much." Mrs. Crenshaw's keen gray eyes swept over Jane, and Jane sensed that she'd been assessed and compartmentalized, though she wasn't exactly sure what that appraisal meant. Certainly she had to be very different from the women Ethan usually brought to his house. Or did he entertain his lovers elsewhere?

Jane compressed her lips. That had better be the case.

Huffing and puffing, Aunt Willy caught up to them. Her white cap framed her florid cheeks. "Far too many steps you have here. It is all very grand, but most impractical. I shall need a cup of tea to refresh myself."

"Then you must allow a footman to escort you. Crenshaw will show Jane to her room." Lady Rosalind spoke over her shoulder as she glided toward the great curving staircase. "Dinner is at eight. I've a special guest coming, so don't be late."

"This way, Miss Mayhew."

Mrs. Crenshaw led the way, her footsteps tapping on the black-and-white checkerboard marble of the floor. Trailing her, Jane peered up at the high ceiling, where an enormous crystal chandelier caught the last rays of afternoon light from the beveled fan window over the door. Rainbow prisms scattered along the white walls and created the aura of a fairyland castle.

Awe tingled through her, though she sternly told herself not to be too impressed by the splendor. Monetary wealth did not define the greatness of a man. Still, she admired the white and gold balustrade, the Grecian plasterwork along the cornices, the wide marble steps. It was a vast difference from her two-story cottage in Wessex, where floor-to-ceiling stacks of books were the primary decoration.

Upstairs, Mrs. Crenshaw paused at a fork in the passageway and inclined her graying head toward the other direction, where a broad corridor was lit by a window at the far end. "There be the master's apartments. His lordship doesn't care for people to wander in this wing. Most especially not in the tower room above his bedchamber."

"Why is that?"

"It is not for me to question his lordship's orders," Mrs. Crenshaw said with a sniff. "Suffice to say, he will allow no housemaids or footmen to intrude there. Only myself, once a week, to clean."

"What manner of room is it? What does he do there?"

"Forgive me, but I am not at liberty to say more." With a twitch of her dark skirt, Mrs. Crenshaw headed into the west wing.

Jane walked slowly, her curiosity piqued. That tower chamber had to be where he seduced his women. She had read once about an Eastern seraglio, and her mind conjured a room lit by a hundred burning candles, the air heavy with incense, the wide bed draped in silks and pillows. Like a pasha, he would strut into the room, discard his robe, and guide his lover in acts so depraved no moral woman could even imagine them. . . .

"Here we are, Miss Mayhew." The housekeeper stood by an open door, one gaunt arm extended toward the room.

Blushing at her wayward thoughts, Jane entered a bedchamber decorated in soothing peach and blue. A coal fire crackled on the grate beneath a cream marble chimneypiece. The windows framed a view of the square with its tall green trees, giving the illusion of being in the country. Untying the strings of her bonnet, she took it off and then hesitated, unsure where in this pristine room to deposit her sadly outmoded headgear.

Mrs. Crenshaw took the bonnet, holding it at arm's

length as she bore it into the dressing room. Upon emerging, she said, "Your trunk should be delivered shortly. I'll send a maid to unpack for you."

"I'm sure I can manage by myself." Jane couldn't bear for anyone, not even a servant, to appraise her meager wardrobe. "But please, before you go. Where is Marianne?"

"Marianne?"

"The baby." Jane stopped before adding *Lord Chasebourne's daughter.* How had he explained the sudden presence of his natural child?

Mrs. Crenshaw's blank face gave no clue to her thoughts. Clearly she was loyal to a fault. "She will be staying in the nursery, directly above here. I must say, it is exceedingly kind of his lordship and his mother to take in the foundling." Bowing, the housekeeper left the room.

Jane tore off her cloak and tossed it on the bed. It was exceedingly *clever* of his lordship to present himself as a benevolent protector. As if anyone would believe such a tall tale about a divorced man and a renowned rakehell.

Where had he gone so quickly? To seek out the baby's mother?

Jane tamped down her impatience. She had intended to accompany him, to judge for herself if he'd found the mother who had abandoned Marianne. Jane didn't trust him to handle the matter properly. He would likely return the baby without question.

To the woman who'd left her on a stranger's doorstep.

Half an hour later, after unpacking and changing into her best black gown, Jane found her way upstairs. She couldn't rest until she knew Marianne had settled well into her new home. The nursery was a bright, sunny room, complete with miniature table and chairs, a rocking horse, and books lining the walls. A faintly musty scent pervaded the air; clearly no child had occupied these rooms for many years.

Jane pictured Ethan here, a mischievous boy, prone to

playing tricks. At least he'd done so to *her*. Once he'd hid in an alleyway of the village, stuck his foot out as she walked past, and tripped her so she landed in a mud puddle, her book flying into the rutted road, where it was run over by a farmer's cart. Although Ethan had rescued the mangled book, presenting it to her with a flourish, he'd had the audacity to laugh.

Silly of her to remember that now. She had no interest in Ethan, only his child.

Hearing voices, she hastened through another doorway and found herself in a bedchamber with cheerful, yellow-striped wallpaper. Two strapping workmen were moving a fancy, gilt-painted cradle into the corner. A housemaid stood ready to polish the baby's bed.

Jiggling Marianne in one arm and her own one-and-a-half-year-old girl in the other, Gianetta directed the workmen in English interspersed with Italian. "*Attento!* You weel break. Ah, good, that ees good."

Jane gathered the baby into her arms. She breathed in her clean scent, overjoyed at the way Marianne studied her with expressive blue eyes, her lips parting in a toothless grin. Something warm and fierce curled inside Jane. Already the infant knew her, loved her. No one must take her away.

Especially not a man with a bad reputation.

"Did Marianne sleep on the journey here?" Jane asked Gianetta.

The dark-haired woman nodded vigorously. "Two girls, so good. Mine, she ees sleepy still." Laughing, she kissed her shy little daughter, who sucked her forefinger and stared at Jane with velvet brown eyes.

"You may put her for a nap," Jane said. "I'll watch Marianne for now."

The Italian woman scurried away, crooning to her daughter. While the workmen departed and the housemaid cleaned, Jane sat down with the baby on the window seat. Marianne gurgled contentedly in contrast to her crying the previous day. Talking nonsense to her, Jane decided she was happier right here than dancing with a royal duke. At dusk, when the shadows grew long, Gianetta returned and Jane reluctantly handed Marianne back, for the infant had begun fretting in hunger.

With a guilty start, Jane realized it must be past time for dinner. She patted her taut bun, making sure every hair was secured. Finding a stairway, she made her way down to the first-floor reception rooms. She wandered around for a bit, searching for a dining room, awed by the sumptuous chambers.

In a green and gold drawing room so enormous it could have swallowed Jane's entire cottage, she found the small gathering of people. Aunt Willy sat on a chair by the hearth, conversing with Lady Rosalind and a distinguished older gentleman in a dark blue suit and a stiff cravat.

Where was Ethan?

Then Jane spied him at a sideboard, pouring a tumbler of dark liquor. Drinking spirits, of course. She might have guessed. Clad in charcoal-gray, his white neckcloth a startling contrast to his bronzed skin, he looked every inch the sinfully attractive rake. He turned, saw her, and lifted his glass with an insolent grin.

She pursed her lips. So he was back. Where had he been for the past few hours? Had he found the baby's mother? Jane had a few words to say to him on the matter.

"Ah, here's my dear godchild at last." Smiling, Lady Rosalind swooped across the fleur-de-lis carpet to guide Jane to the stranger. He stood up as they approached, and Lady Rosalind said in a soft voice quite unlike her usual playful tone, "You remember my friend, Lady Susan, don't you, Peter? Well, this is Susan's daughter, Miss Jane Mayhew."

His thin gray brows drew together. He had keen, ruddy features and an imposing manner which radiated the innate confidence of the nobility. "I recall Lady Susan wed a scholar who took her off to the country."

"Yes, a neighbor of mine. Jane, this is the Duke of Kellisham."

Jane had only a hazy notion of the proper protocol, but something seemed to be expected of her, so she extended her hand. "Your Grace, I'm happy to meet you."

He frowned at her hand, then gallantly brought it to his lips. "A pleasure, Miss Mayhew. You are newly arrived in town?"

She suspected belatedly that she ought to have curtsied. Feeling gauche, she said, "Yes. We are here at Lady Rosalind's kind invitation. . . ." She paused, wondering what—if anything—he knew about Marianne.

"We have come to the city on a moment's notice," Aunt Willy said. "And for a more havey-cavey purpose, I cannot imagine—"

Lady Rosalind broke in. "Now that we are all gathered here, His Grace and I have an announcement to make before we go in to dinner." She smiled at him, and he gazed at her with a befuddled rapture on his stately features.

Then he cleared his throat and looked around the small party. "I am most pleased to say that Lady Rosalind has done me the great honor of agreeing to be my wife."

The fire snapped into the silence. Jane blinked in surprise. Had Ethan known of the impending nuptials? She turned to study him.

Giving his mother a hard, assessing stare, he strolled to the mantelpiece. Something dark flashed in his eyes, and he took a long swallow from his glass. Jane knew him well enough to see that he was displeased by the news. She tried to fathom why. Did he not consider Lady Rosalind's chosen partner good enough for her? The duke seemed a fine, upstanding man, perhaps the ideal influence to tame her wild spirit.

Unwilling to let Ethan's ill-mannered behavior spoil the occasion, Jane hastened to Lady Rosalind and hugged her, then stepped back. "I'm so delighted for you. Have you set a wedding date?"

She laughed gaily. "We are hoping for the early part of June. Tomorrow, we shall settle it with the pastor of Saint George's."

"How well you've kept your secret, Rosalind," Aunt Willy said almost accusingly. "To think, you've only been back in England for a few days and already you have such felicitous news."

"Oh, but Peter and I have known each other for many years," Lady Rosalind said, clinging to his arm while casting an adoring glance at him. "We corresponded often while I was abroad."

"In truth, I made my offer in a letter," he said in a gruff voice. "I begged Rosalind to come home and make me the happiest of men. And so she has."

They smiled into each other's eyes, and their bliss caused a tightening in Jane's breast. How wonderful it must be to know the love and devotion of a man. To look forward to a life of shared contentment. To be the most important woman in the world to him.

Her gaze stole to Ethan. He had failed at marriage with his bride, Lady Portia. Only the previous year, Jane had heard the shocking story bandied about the neighborhood back home, that he had caught Lady Portia dallying with his valet. Ethan had sued her lover in court on grounds of adultery, then used the conviction to obtain a bill of divorcement in Parliament. It had been whispered that Lord Chasebourne liked his assignations, but he had condemned his wife for the same immoral behavior.

His actions seemed so heartless, so cruel, that Jane wondered if she really knew him.

He went to the sideboard and poured glasses of sherry for each of them. "If I may propose a toast," he said, holding up his glass. "To the bride-to-be and her esteemed groom."

Whatever his objections, he concealed them behind a mask of charm. With the way he smiled, his teeth a flash of white in his swarthy face, one might have thought him pleased by the betrothal.

But during dinner, Jane noticed the way he watched the joyful couple, his gaze narrowed ever so slightly. Could it be the jealousy of a son wanting to keep his mother true to the memory of his father?

After a rich meal of roast beef and asparagus, Lady Rosalind said suddenly, "Ethan, I nearly forgot. I've only just heard the news about Lord Byron leaving England. What a tragic tale, that he would abandon his wife and daughter."

"Good riddance," Ethan drawled. "There's one less poet foisting his flowery sentiment on the masses."

Jane frowned at his flippant remark. "Lord Byron is a superb poet," she objected. "I've read all of his works."

"You?" His droll gaze swept over her. "You don't seem the sort to enjoy romantic tripe. It would put any intelligent woman to sleep."

It was both compliment and insult, and before Jane could form a suitable retort, Aunt Willy cleared her throat.

"Speaking of sleep, I vow I shall welcome my rest tonight," the older woman said, sagging in her chair. "Such a long journey we've had."

The party broke apart, Ethan excusing himself, saying he intended to go out.

In the corridor, Jane hastened after him, her half-boots tapping on the marble floor. "Ethan—Lord Chasebourne, wait." She stifled her proclivity to address him by his given name. It reminded her too painfully of the boy she had once secretly adored and the witless girl she had been.

Pivoting toward her, he placed his hands on his hips, pushing back his coat to reveal his trim waist and hips. "If it's more literary commentary, I must beg you to take pity and desist."

Jane pursed her lips. She had more important concerns on her mind. "You were surprised, weren't you, by your mother's engagement?"

He shrugged. "Nothing my mother does surprises me."

"Why do you disapprove of her marrying the duke?"

"I never said I disapproved."

"You glowered at them. Just for a moment. Though I don't suppose anyone else noticed."

He grunted. Jane persisted, determined to understand him. "Well, I think it's wonderful that Kellisham adores her. He certainly proved his love by staying true to her for so many months." When she paused, Ethan merely arched one eyebrow, so Jane went on. "She must be lonely since your father's death—when was it? Ten years ago?"

"Nine." He withdrew a silver pocket watch, glanced at it, then snapped shut the lid. "If you mean only to spout sentiment, then pray excuse me. I have plans for the evening."

"With whom?" she blurted out.

He shook his head. "Jane. Must you always pester me with rude questions?"

She hated the superior way he regarded her, his hint of amusement in him. "Then I'll ask again until you answer me. I wish to know if you went in search of Marianne's mother this afternoon. And if you will do so tonight as well."

His dark eyes bored into her. He stood tall enough that she had to lift her chin in order to hold his gaze. Reaching out, he patted her on the crown of her head as if she were a child. "It's late, Miss Maypole. So run along to bed and stay out of the affairs of men."

Turning, he strode down the wide passageway, heading for the grand staircase. His decisive steps rang out like a challenge.

Her hand jerked toward a blue and white vase on a nearby pedestal. She wanted to heave it at him, to crash it over his patronizing head.

Even as her fingers brushed the cool porcelain, she forced herself to think. He had not answered her question. Which meant he must be intending to confront the woman he suspected of abandoning the baby. Surely he would have denied it otherwise.

Jane clenched her hand in the folds of her skirt. She couldn't let him dump Marianne on a woman who clearly didn't want her.

And since he refused to cooperate, she would have to resort to subterfuge.

☙ *Chapter 4* ❧

Jane hastened to the staircase railing and peered down into the entry hall. The huge chandelier hung in darkness, and the candles in the wall sconces cast a flickering illumination over Ethan, his shadow towering on the wall. He addressed a footman in blue livery at the front door. "Have the barouche brought round," he said, his deep voice echoing in the vast room.

"Aye, m'lord." Bowing, the footman headed down the corridor.

Without looking up, Ethan disappeared into one of the ground-floor rooms. While the horses were harnessed and the carriage delivered from the stables, he would wait there, no doubt. She had ten minutes—perhaps a little more—before he would depart.

Retreating down the passageway, Jane found a door cleverly hidden in the white paneling. She went into the dimly lit, utilitarian shaft designed for the servants and raced down the wooden staircase to the ground floor. She emerged into a spacious corridor and guessed the way toward the rear of the house. For a few frustrating minutes she feared she was lost; then she entered a music room with a pianoforte, the ivory keys glistening like teeth in the shadows. A pair of glass doors led out onto a loggia that spanned the length of a small, formal garden. Going outside, she paused beside a stone pillar and spied the stables beyond the darkened trees.

Jane stepped quickly toward a wooden gate in the brick wall. A cold mist hung in the air, and she shivered, wishing she had taken the time to fetch her shawl. But certainly she was accustomed to long, brisk walks on the windswept downs, and a little London chill would do her no harm.

She heard the voices before spying the men. A pair of grooms, one tall and bandy-legged, the other short and stocky, chatted by the carriage house as they hitched a pair of horses to the barouche. Jane's foot struck a pebble and sent it skittering down the path. It sounded like a pistol shot, and she froze in the gloom beneath a spreading oak. Luckily, one of the gray horses snorted at that moment, shaking its silvery mane, the harness jingling.

Jane slowly let out her breath. Knowing she had only a few moments to spare, she crept closer, keeping a hedge of clipped boxwoods in between herself and the men. She was thankful for her black garb as she worked her way around toward the rear of the carriage.

Torchlight illuminated the brick stable and a stretch of open yard. Indecisive, she hid behind a bush. Although it was only a few steps, the fancy equipage might have been a hundred miles distant.

Footsteps thudded on the packed earth and a burly coachman rounded the corner of the carriage house. "Damp night, eh?" he said in a rumbling voice that carried to Jane.

"Aye," said the bandy-legged man. "Better 'ope 'is lordship don't tarry too long in 'is lady's bed an' leave ye sittin' out in the cold."

"Wonder which one 'e'll visit tonight?" said the short man. "The blonde 'e took to Wessex last week 'ad a prime set o' udders."

The two grooms chuckled. Taking advantage of their tasteless humor and inattention, Jane dashed across the short distance to the rear of the carriage. She halted there, her heart pounding, her body plastered to the sleek cab. The air smelled of leather and horses.

"Quit yammering about yer betters," snapped the coachman. "Tend to yer duties lest ye find yerselfs back in the gutter."

Their mirth died amid a raspy clearing of throats and a sudden flurry of activity. Leather creaked and feet shuffled. Jane knew she didn't have much time left. She eased to the edge of the carriage, her palm damp on the large iron wheel as she stole a look toward the front.

The grooms were busy with the horses and the coachman had gone back into the carriage house. This was her chance! She tiptoed to the far side and quietly unlatched the door. Bless heaven, the hinges had been oiled. She dared not lower the step, but her long legs served her well as she clambered inside. With the utmost caution, she drew the door shut.

Jane crouched in the dark interior, bracing herself for a hue and cry. None came. After a few moments, her heart ceased slamming against her ribs. Touching her mother's locket for good luck, she felt her way to the long bench seat and sank against the velvet cushions.

Just in time.

The vehicle rocked—the coachman must have climbed aboard. She heard the slap of reins and the clopping of hooves, then felt the slight sway of movement. The shadowy gardens slid slowly past. As the front of the house came into view, the barouche stopped.

Ethan emerged from the doorway. The torches cast stark light over him, giving his features a sinister, almost malevolent aspect. In his black cloak, he looked more demon than mortal.

Jane deliberately unclenched her fingers by degrees. He was only a man, and a rather worthless one at that. She positioned herself in the darkest corner and sat very still as the footman opened the door. Ethan paused a moment to snap out an address to the coachman. Then he ducked his head into the cab.

She knew the moment he caught sight of her. He stood with one foot on the step, his large form blocking the light. He stared at her.

She stared back.

"One moment," he growled at the coachman, then stepped inside, shutting the door behind him. Flicking his scarlet-lined cape to the side, he seated himself opposite her. "So, Jane. I should not be surprised."

He slapped a pair of kidskin gloves against his palm. His male scent, dark and seductive, eddied to her. She was conscious of his powerful presence and her own precarious position. The closeness of the interior emphasized how much larger he was than she. Their knees almost touched, and she forced herself not to recoil lest he see it as a sign of weakness.

"I am going with you," she stated. "*If* you intend to call on Marianne's mother, that is."

"Perhaps I'm off to a night of sin and depravity. Will you accompany me into the gaming hells and brothels, I wonder?"

His mocking words shivered over her skin. "Tell me the truth about where we're going."

"There is no *we*. *You* may get out of my carriage."

She swallowed her pride for Marianne's sake. "Ethan, please. I want to question the woman who abandoned Marianne. Because you can't just hand back a helpless child where she isn't wanted. How do you know she'll be loved and properly cared for?"

"You might trust my judgment."

"Hah. You haven't shown much judgment in regard to women. Look at what happened with your own wife."

Jane feared she'd gone too far. She couldn't read his expression in the darkness of the carriage, but she could feel a strange force emanating from him, thickening the cool night air. Yet when he spoke, his voice was controlled.

"May I point out," he said, "that gently bred ladies do not pay calls on fallen women. So leave this matter to me."

She stubbornly shook her head. "If you want me out of here, you'll have to toss me onto the pavement. But you shan't do that. Making a scene in public would ruin your image as Lord Charming."

He regarded her for another long, uncomfortable moment. "You know me so well," he said, his tone conveying that he'd lost interest in the quarrel. He rapped on the roof, and the barouche set off at a gently rocking pace.

Jane released a breath, the tension sliding away and leaving her limp. Her ploy had worked! She had been correct about his purpose tonight.

Or had she? What if he really *did* mean to visit a house of ill repute? Would he abandon her in the carriage while he engaged in revelry? Yes, she could believe that of him.

He frowned out the window at the passing scenery. An occasional street lamp flashed in the darkness, briefly illuminating his strong features. His intense expression was unlike the debaucher who had nary a serious thought rattling in his empty skull. He looked introverted and secretive, as if he were plotting a nefarious deed.

"Where are we heading?" she asked.

"You'll find out soon enough."

His ambiguous answer only increased her uneasiness. "You aren't really taking me to a cesspool of sin, are you?"

He gave a snort of laughter. "Cesspool of sin? Did you make that up yourself?"

"It's a phrase used by Reverend Gillespie in the pulpit," she said stiffly. "You'd know so if ever you attended services at our parish church."

"That squinty old goat wouldn't know a cesspool from the Sistine Chapel."

Jane felt a perverse bubble of humor, but stifled it in time. "Just answer my question. *Are* we going to a brothel?"

She forced out the question she'd been afraid to face. "Is Marianne's mother . . . a whore?"

Through the shadows, his features took on a hard edge. "Enough questions."

"At least give me her name. Tell me about her background, her character. Could she have been forced to give up her baby because she had no money to support her?"

"You wanted to decide for yourself. And so you shall."

He fell silent, and she sat back in frustration, wondering at the wicked life he had led. Back when they were children, he had been a daredevil and a prankster, always landing himself in trouble with his stern father. And then once Ethan had gone away to school, she had seen him only in the summers and on holidays. As he grew older, he'd fallen in with bad company, and she remembered when he was nearly twenty, having one friend in particular who shared his wild proclivities.

Once, she'd had to jump out of the way as they raced their phaetons along the dirt road to the village, a squealing lady clinging to them on the high perch, their horses thundering past, the wheels rattling, leaving a trail of dust and laughter. Captain Lord John Randall, Jane remembered, had died at Waterloo.

"Ethan, I've never expressed my condolences."

His gaze pierced her through the darkness. "Condolences?"

"On the death of Captain Randall. I heard the news, and I'm very sorry. I know you were particular friends."

For a moment there was only the hollow clopping of the horses' hooves. On his thigh, Ethan's fingers tightened into a fist, though his expression remained bland. "Ah, well. One less shallow rake to tempt the ladies onto a path of sin."

His callousness shocked Jane. "Captain Randall died a hero. Surely you don't think I would denigrate him."

"Frankly, I don't care who you malign so long as you keep your opinions to yourself."

Unable to wrest another word from him, she turned her attention out the window and saw the city veiled by mist. Now and then, the carriage lights illuminated a lone person trudging along the curbstone. They had left the wealthy neighborhood with its stately squares and broad avenues, and these row houses huddled close like old maiden aunts cozying up for a gossip.

At the end of the block, the barouche slowed as if the coachman were searching for a number. Ethan peered out, then signaled him to a stop. A footman let down the step, glancing in startlement at Jane as she emerged onto the cracked pavement. When a flurry of cold droplets sprinkled her face, she crossed her arms and fought back a shiver.

Ethan removed one of the brass lamps from the front of the barouche and used it to light their path to a red brick dwelling. The white paint on the door was peeling and the ram's-head knocker appeared dull and unpolished. He rapped hard, the sound shattering the stillness of the night.

Jane huddled beneath the shelter of the porch. Misgivings prodded her again, anticipation jumping in her stomach. Ethan had come here to meet one of his paramours. He had swept her into his arms and kissed her. . . .

She tried to imagine the kissing. Would it be a firm pressure or a tender brush of lips? How long did a kiss last? Did the woman pull away first or let her partner determine the duration? And where did one put one's hands?

She stole a glance at Ethan, at his hard masculine mouth, and felt a curious warm ache within herself. He wore that distracted, inner-focused look again. She was glad he seemed unaware of her presence. How embarrassing if he guessed her wanton speculation.

How ridiculous of her to care about his opinion. They had led entirely different lives, she with her quiet pursuits in the country and he pursuing loose women who lived in seedy houses like this one.

With a rattling of the knob, the door opened and a mob-capped head peeped out. The servant girl could not have been more than twelve, and she hid behind the door as if fearing they were robbers. She turned her saucer eyes from Jane to Ethan. "Guv'nor?"

"I should like to see your mistress," he said. "Tell her that Chasebourne has come to call."

The girl hesitated, then allowed them into a small, dark entry hall. She scuttled off to a room down a corridor, from which a faint glow emanated.

By the light of the lantern which Ethan set down on a table, Jane could see the dingy striped wallpaper and the lack of furnishings. Straight ahead, a narrow staircase with steep wooden steps led to the upper floors. Strange, she had expected a decadent scene decorated with plush velvet draperies and statues of naked women, an atmosphere reeking of erotic perfume, not this sad, musty odor of neglect.

Was this where Marianne had been born? Did her mother lack the means to keep her? Jane resisted a flash of sympathy. The woman might have gone to Ethan for funds rather than abandon a helpless baby.

The maidservant returned, her shoes making no sound on the bare floor, her little shoulders hunched as if she feared a scolding. She bobbed a curtsy. "This way, m'lord. M'lady awaits ye."

Ethan motioned to Jane to precede him. Girding herself to confront another of his painted whores, Jane marched after the girl, who upon leading them to the lighted doorway faded like a wraith into the gloom of the passage.

Jane found herself in a drawing room furnished in shabby gentility with a single chaise and a few scattered chairs. A coal fire hissed on the grate. At a table nearby, a woman sat playing a solitary card game, a crystal glass of wine at her elbow. She had blond, upswept hair that emphasized her swanlike throat and creamy bosom. Her fine, patrician features and violet eyes were as beautiful as they were familiar.

Jane froze. She recalled the exact moment, five years earlier, when she had first seen this woman in an open landau on a summer day, her laughter coasting on the warm breeze. Jane had lurked behind the hedgerow all morning, feeling foolish and heartsore, yet unable to force herself to go home and spare herself the ordeal. So she had waited by a gap in the shrubbery, her legs cramped, until at last the coach rattled past, carrying Ethan and his bride to their country home.

How fiercely she had envied Lady Portia that day.

A few days later, there had been a small party for the neighbors when Jane had been introduced to his new wife. But Portia had had eyes only for Ethan, clinging to his arm and whispering in his ear. . . .

Now, Jane felt staggered by the shock of seeing Portia again. Why had Ethan come to visit the wife he had cast aside? Surely he couldn't believe *her* to be Marianne's mother.

Jane flashed a bewildered glance at him. He stood behind her, his arms at his sides, his gaze on his former wife.

"Portia," he said, with a crisp nod.

"Why, Ethan. What a lovely surprise." Holding the deck of cards, Lady Portia smiled tentatively, as if she were unsure of him. "Forgive me for not rising, but I've been out shopping all day and my feet ache dreadfully."

"Don't trouble yourself on my account."

"Oh, but I do wish to welcome you properly—both of you." She cast a curious glance at Jane, and Jane felt like a bedraggled crow facing a sleek white dove. "Perhaps you would like refreshment. Shall I ring for tea?"

"Never mind that." He took Jane by the upper arm and propelled her forward, close enough to detect Portia's light, flowery fragrance. "You remember Miss Jane Mayhew."

A slight frown marred Portia's smooth features as she looked Jane up and down. "Mayhew? The name isn't familiar to me."

"We met only briefly," Jane offered. "Shortly after your wedding, there was a party . . . in Wessex."

"Ah, you're one of the *neighbors*." Portia leaned forward, holding the cards to her bosom, the firelight glowing on her generous breasts. "You must forgive me my feeble memory. I confess that at the time, my mind must have been on the honeymoon . . . and my dearest husband." She gazed wistfully at Ethan, but his features remained cool and reserved.

"Don't pretend to have forgotten Miss Mayhew," he stated. "In truth, you went to her house only a few days ago."

Tilting her head to the side, Portia blinked her long lashes. "I beg your pardon?"

"Leave off the pretense. It should be simple enough to ascertain if you left London for a few days. And that you traveled to Wessex and left your little gift on Miss Mayhew's doorstep."

"Gift? Honestly, Ethan, I don't know what you are rattling on about."

"Does Smollett know what you've done? Or have you tired of him and moved on to someone else?"

Portia's eyes rounded to deep, soulful pools. Then she looked down at her card game, selected a card from the deck, and placed it onto the ones spread out on the table. "George has gone out for the evening," she said in a small, subdued voice. "He didn't wish to leave me alone, but I insisted."

"And where has he gone? To gamble away your money?"

"How dare you cast stones. He may be of common birth, but he is far more the gentleman than you ever were."

In a sudden movement, Ethan swept the cards aside. A few fluttered to the floor as he flattened his palms on the table and stared into her face. "I don't give a bloody damn if he worships at your feet. I only want the truth from you—for once in your wretched life."

His rude behavior astonished Jane. "For pity's sake. You haven't even explained what you're accusing her of." Without giving him the chance to do so, she whirled toward

Portia. "My lady, a few mornings ago, a baby was left on my doorstep, an infant perhaps two months of age. I found Lord Chasebourne's ring tucked into the swaddling blanket. That led me to determine the girl is his natural daughter."

"Bloody nonsense," he said. "Someone wanted to cause trouble for me. Someone who knew Miss Mayhew would raise a ruckus. And that someone was you, Portia."

Lady Portia's lips parted as if she couldn't find the words to deny his charge. Then suddenly she arched her neck and laughed, her merriment ringing like a bright bell in the shabby room. "Oh, what a priceless tale. To think I must declare myself utterly innocent in the matter."

"Innocent?" Ethan snapped. "You must have borne Smollett's bastard. And you saw this as a convenient way to rid yourself of an unwanted burden."

Jane gasped. "How can you speak so cruelly—"

Lady Portia held up a fine white hand to silence her. "It's quite all right, Miss Mayhew. The truth is on my side. Ethan, the baby obviously belongs to one of your many *other* women."

"May I remind you, madam, I need only make a few inquiries among your acquaintances to prove your duplicity."

Lady Portia smiled serenely. "You'll have a difficult time, I'm afraid. You see, I could not possibly have given birth two months ago."

She rose from her chair, a graceful figure in pale blue silk. And Jane saw what the table and the dim firelight had hidden: beneath the high waist of her gown, her midsection swelled in a gentle, unmistakable mound.

Lady Portia was pregnant.

⌢ *Chapter 5* ⌢

Jane leashed her temper only until they stepped out onto the front stoop and closed the door. "You behaved insufferably," she hissed. "You might at least have wished her well, instead of dragging me out of there. The poor woman has lost everything—husband, home, reputation. And you only added to her misery by treating her like a common harlot."

In the glow of the carriage lamp, Ethan appeared unrepentent. "Stay out of what you don't know, Jane."

"I know what I see. And I know that you won a bill of divorcement because Lady Portia strayed from your marriage vows." Jane took a breath of mist-laden air, though it did little to cool her indignation. "But surely *you* were as much to blame as she was. It shouldn't be permissible for a husband to have affairs, either."

For a moment she feared she'd spoken too recklessly. His eyes narrowing, he bared his teeth like a dark and dangerous night creature. "That is precisely why I shall never make the mistake of marrying again."

He thrust the lamp into her hand. As her fingers grasped the curved iron handle, he wheeled around and went to the barouche that waited at the curbstone. He growled an order to the coachman; then to her astonishment he strode away down the pavement, his footsteps ringing out until he vanished into the murky mist.

Jane walked slowly from the porch, the cold damp seeping into her bones. Why did she fancy she had heard pain in his voice? It must be her imagination, her unwillingness to give up her foolish, juvenile infatuation for him. She didn't know Ethan Sinclair anymore. Certainly he was no longer the impish boy who had once made faces at her in church. Nor was he the charming rogue who accumulated women as one might collect butterflies.

He was an arrogant knave who cared only for his own pleasures.

And yet she had heard pain underlying his bitter words: *I shall never make the mistake of marrying again.*

"Miss?" said the coachman. " 'Is lordship wishes me to escort ye back to Chasebourne House."

The footman held open the door of the barouche, and droplets of cold rain spattered her face. The air smelled of soot and rubbish. Shivering, she resisted the idea of scuttling back to the safety of her room; she felt compelled to understand the man Ethan had become. And she might never have a better opportunity.

"I'll be a little while longer," she told the servant. "Please wait here."

Then she turned around and marched back toward the town house.

Ethan landed a punch into the long leather sack. His fist dented the sawdust filling, and he welcomed the jolt that shot up his arm.

The boxing gymnasium was empty tonight. Abandoned weight bars lay along the wall, and the smell of sweat lingered in the air. Except for the light from a single lamp, shadows enveloped the cavernous room and the vacant boxing ring where, in daytime, gentlemen wagered colossal sums on prize fights. Ethan often came here for exercise in the afternoon, but now there was no sound except for the echo of his repeated blows. The proprietor had grudgingly admitted him, then vanished to his gin bottle upstairs.

Ethan let out his frustration on the punching bag. He was still angry at himself for permitting Jane to witness that scene. What a bloody fool he'd been to think she might take his side. He knew how Portia ingratiated herself to others, how she made herself appear the tragic heroine in a melodrama. He knew too that her blond beauty masked an amoral hussy. It had taken him four years to learn that galling truth, and he could not expect a mere acquaintance to grasp her character at a glance. Portia played her part too well.

You were as much to blame as she was.

Yes, there was truth in that statement, but not for the reason Jane believed. He had kept a part of himself inviolate. There were aspects about himself that Portia had never known—that no one knew. Would his marriage have survived if he had been more honest? Or if he had disregarded her desire to delay pregnancy? By the time he'd caught her in bed with his valet, their marriage had become a cold, lifeless duty.

You were as much to blame as she was.

To hell with Jane Mayhew and her sweeping opinions. She had made up her mind, and nothing he said could change it. And now he had stupidly given her more ammunition in her war to prove him an unfit father.

He landed another hard punch, and a trickle of sweat rolled down his bare chest. If indeed he *was* Marianne's father. He had been so certain about Portia's guilt that he hadn't given a thought to any other women. Who the devil had abandoned the child?

Even as he mulled over the possibilities, the door opened and a trio of laughing people sauntered into the darkened gymnasium, a pair of gentlemen with a red-haired slattern clinging to them.

Ethan scowled, recognizing the men. Under ordinary circumstances he might have welcomed the company. But he was in no mood to trade witticisms with a couple of fops. With any luck, they would heed his glare and leave.

The taller of the two poked the stout one in the ribs. Then they ambled straight toward Ethan.

"Please don't weep." Perched beside her on the faded brown cushions of the chaise, Jane passed a handkerchief to Lady Portia.

Portia dabbed at her wet cheeks, the square of plain linen looking incongruous in her fine-boned fingers. The tears lent a sheen to her soulful eyes. Her skin tinted gold by the light of the fire, she had the aura of a melancholy Madonna.

"You've been so kind," Portia said, sniffling daintily. "No other gentlewoman has cared to hear the events that led up to my divorce. Indeed, I am shunned whenever I go out in public. *Shunned*, when I was once the most celebrated debutante in England. And it is all because Chasebourne spurned me."

Jane stifled the impulse to point out that Portia had chosen to travel down a wicked path. The poor woman didn't need any more criticism. She had been an unhappy wife driven into the arms of another man. "I am sorry. Truly I am."

"Your good will means so much to me. Oh, Jane, do you know what the cut direct means?"

"No . . . I don't think so."

"It means that should I happen to encounter a former acquaintance on the street, she—or he—will look straight past me and refuse to acknowledge my presence. It is as if I am no more than a lamppost . . . or the lowliest of servants. I have been cut even by those who once counted me among their dearest friends."

"I'm very sorry," Jane said again, knowing that words were inadequate to ease the pain. "It is most un-Christian of them."

"It is the way of society. The *ton* can be so cruel to those women who have taken even a single misstep. So unmerciful to one poor female who has paid for her error with the loss of all status and privilege.'' Portia bowed her head, the firelight painting her slender white neck. "And the most unforgiving of them all is Ethan.''

Something stabbed at Jane, and this time she could not deny the inexplicable urge to defend him. "You did betray your vows to him.''

"Only after years of enduring *his* affairs. Oh, I cannot count the number of times I waited in vain for him at home while he dallied with other women. I craved his affections, but he could not even be bothered to give me a child. A *child,* Jane. That was all I ever wanted, all I prayed to have. My own child to comfort me in my lonely hours.'' She hugged her swollen belly. "But for the last three years of our marriage, he refused to share my bed.''

Touching the familiar shape of the locket beneath her high-necked gown, Jane swallowed her shock at the confession. How could Ethan have done that? Ignored this beautiful, fragile woman?

It was unseemly for a lady to refer to the most intimate aspect of wedlock. And to a mere acquaintance. Yet Portia had no other female in whom to confide.

"You cannot imagine the nightmare my marriage had become. That is why I sought love wherever I could find it.'' Portia's eyes were as big and soft as pansies. "Oh, dear Jane, I feel that we are friends now, aren't we?''

"Certainly.''

"Then if I tell you more, I may trust in your complete confidence.''

Her forwardness of manner made Jane uneasy. Yet she pushed away her misgivings and nodded. "Yes, of course.''

"I made a terrible mistake in dallying with George Smollet. I didn't wish to admit this to Ethan, but . . .''

"What is it?''

"The truth is, George is gone. He's run off with the last of my funds.''

"No,'' Jane breathed. "Are you sure?''

Portia nodded forlornly. "He's fled to the Continent. And I suppose it is all for the best. He put on the airs of a gentleman, but beneath it all, he was a commoner and unsuited to a lady of my delicate sensibilities."

"But . . . you're to bear his child."

"Alas, yes." Portia lowered her gaze to the twisted handkerchief in her hands. "I am mortified to confess, we were living in sin. He has taken everything from me—*everything*! I am in dire need of funds. Ethan granted me only a paltry amount."

"Have you no parents or relations you might turn to?"

"They have all forsaken me in my hour of need. I have no one. No one at all."

Sympathy tugged at Jane's heart. "If only I could help, but I'm afraid I have only a tiny annuity left to me by my father. You see, we've something in common. My mother's family cut her off without a penny when she married a poor scholar."

"Please, I don't mean to beg money from *you*. Heaven knows, I've more pride than that." Portia grasped Jane's hand suddenly, her fingers cool and clinging. "But there is another way that you might assist me."

Discomfitted, Jane wanted to draw away, but held herself still. "What is that?"

"Dare I say it—Nay, I cannot."

"Say it, *please*. If I can help you, I will."

"All right, then." Portia drew a deep breath, and her eyes shone with desperate purpose. "I must have a private audience with Ethan, to plead my case. And you must convince him to receive me."

"Ho there, Chasebourne," the shorter man hailed. "What luck, can it be our favorite gamester? We were passing by and saw the light."

His companion goosed the tawdry redhead, and she let out a squeal. "We were out having a bit of fun." Their approaching footsteps echoed in the empty gymnasium.

"Keeble. Duxbury." Hiding his irritation, Ethan flashed a smile at the dandies. Their faces were familiar to him from many a late-night session across the green baize of dice and card tables. "What brings you two out to prowl the back streets of Covent Garden?"

"Fate, obviously." Keeble glanced at Duxbury, and they sniggered as if sharing a private jest. "Mind if we chat a while?"

"Surely you have better things to do tonight." Ethan looked pointedly at the prostitute.

"Aw, we like your company, too," Duxbury said.

Both men dragged over chairs, scraping the wooden floor, and sat down beneath the glare of the lamp, Duxbury pulling the tittering whore onto his lap and petting her bottom. Feeling a jab of suspicion, Ethan rubbed his aching knuckles. Those two were up to no good. He hoped to God he was wrong about their purpose.

A notorious gossip, Viscount Keeble was short and rotund, his cravat and collar points high enough to choke him. He styled his brown hair in Grecian waves, though with his habit of tugging at it to cover his bald spot, the result resembled a bird's nest. "We'd just heard you were back in town," Keeble said in a jovial tone. "Didn't we, Ducks?"

"You were the talk of the Barclays' ball tonight," said the Honorable James Duxbury, his blue eyes avid in his baby face. "Though a more deadly dull herd of cows I cannot imagine. There wasn't a female present I'd dance with, let alone lure into a darkened room."

"However, the evening wasn't a complete waste," Keeble said.

"Right-o," Duxbury agreed. "We found us this bit of fluff not half a mile from here." He thrust his hand beneath the woman's skirt, and she squealed again, slapping playfully at him, then draping her arms around his neck.

"Not her, you dolt," Keeble said. "It so happens we intercepted a rather nasty rumor. Not that I'm one to pass along unfounded gossip."

"Then pray, don't start now," Ethan said in a hard tone. Turning away, he thrust his fist at the leather bag in a rapid punch.

The viscount cleared his throat. "Yes, well, a man should know what people are whispering behind his back. And I feel it my moral obligation to relay the lies they are saying about *you*."

"What is it now? I trust it isn't about the harem of slave girls at my country estate. I did so wish to keep that a secret."

"A harem?" Duxbury quit fondling the whore and stared wide-eyed at Ethan. "Truly? You have all the luck."

"Never mind that," Keeble snapped. He worked his pasty features into a caricature of concern. "This concerns a young woman living in your house, Ethan. Along with an infant. People are saying she bore your love child. And that you'd flaunt the two of them in the face of society."

Flexing his fists, Ethan felt a cold tightening inside himself. He'd expected talk to fly, but not so quickly. The aristocracy liked to believe the worst—especially of a man who had disregarded their petty rules.

But Jane, the mother of his child? What a jest. She likely wore iron underdrawers to bed. "The woman is a friend of the family whom my mother is sponsoring this Season. And the child is merely a foundling, my ward."

"Most extraordinary," Keeble said, with a narrow-eyed look that showed his skepticism. "Who is the mother, then? And the father?"

Ethan gave a cool shrug. "No one knows."

"Why haven't you sent the little nipper to a foundling hospital?"

"I've reformed," Ethan said glibly. "You may spread the word that henceforth, the Earl of Chasebourne shall be a model citizen and a doer of good deeds."

Both men hooted with mirth. "Oh-ho, that'll be the day," said Duxbury, laughing so hard he half fell off his chair, the whore clinging to him. "You, a decent chap."

Keeble wheezed, his plump cheeks turning red. "Better I should believe in a skinny Prinny."

The quip set them off again, and Ethan bared his teeth in a smile, though he didn't find their incredulity all *that* amusing. Was it so impossible to credit that he could change his ways?

Not that he meant to do anything of the kind, of course. Hedonism was too enjoyable a life to renounce.

Keeble wiped his eyes on his plum-colored sleeve. "Ah, you are a wit, Chase, old boy. But the truth now. *Is* the infant yours?"

"Do tell," encouraged Duxbury. "Your secret is safe with us."

Both men regarded Ethan with sly expectancy.

He gritted his teeth. He would sooner emblazon the story across tomorrow's newsheets than tell these tattlemongers. The memory flashed to him of Marianne's small, swaddled form, her tiny fists waving, her blue eyes gazing up at him in utter trust. *Trust*.

God help her if she ended up with him as a father.

"Marianne is an orphan," he stated. "And you may send anyone who says otherwise straight to me."

⇐ Chapter 6 ⇒

The news spread with amazing swiftness.

The following afternoon, Jane sat in the cavernous green and gold reception room, listening as Lady Rosalind fielded polite queries from a procession of genteel callers. Aunt Willie had taken to her chamber with a sick headache and a bottle of restorative. Jane eyed the doorway longingly, wishing she too could escape. But it seemed churlish to abandon her hostess, who obviously thrived on scandal.

Lady Rosalind presided from a gilded chair, poured endless cups of tea, and held court like a queen. To everyone, she praised her son for sheltering an orphaned infant. "It is admirable of a man to provide for those of lesser fortune," she confided to a small group of ladies. "I am so very proud of Chasebourne's kind and generous heart."

There were nods and sighs and smiles all around. Half the women present looked dreamy-eyed at the mere mention of his name. Unlike Lady Portia, disgrace had not cost him his status. Even a *divorced* earl was considered a good catch.

"Where *is* Lord Chasebourne today?" Lady Bagwell asked. A stout woman with a dark fringe of hair dusting her upper lip, she glanced at the milling guests as if she expected the master of the house to be lurking behind a chair or drapery.

"Oh, he's off doing what men do," Lady Rosalind said with a vague wave of her hand. "Business matters, you know."

Jane knew that to be a fib. According to the housekeeper, his lordship remained in his rooms and was not to be disturbed. He was probably nursing a headache from his late night out, she thought sourly.

Thinking of her conversation with Lady Portia the previous evening, Jane shifted in her chair. As soon as he deigned to show his face, she intended to have a word with the self-indulgent dastard.

"My dear Fanny and I did so hope to pay our respects to his lordship," said Lady Bagwell. She turned to her daughter. "Isn't that so?"

A pink-cheeked brunette, Fanny kept her gaze trained on her gloved hands. "Yes, Mama."

"I am sorry," Lady Rosalind said, her voice filled with a proper note of regret, though her blue eyes were lively. "In his absence, allow me to introduce you to Miss Mayhew, who is newly arrived from Wessex. She's the daughter of my dear departed friend Lady Susan Spencer."

"You are in mourning for your mother, Miss Mayhew?" asked the dowager, cutting a glance at Jane's drab black dress.

"No, ma'am, she died shortly after my birth," Jane said. "It was my father who died last year."

"And now the dear girl is ready to brighten her wardrobe," Lady Rosalind chirped. "That is why she's come to London, so that we may visit the modiste and purchase the very latest in fashion for her."

"Purchase?" Jane stuttered. "I never said I—"

"Oh, I do adore shopping," Lady Rosalind broke in. "We shall have such fun, you and I, just wait and see. It will be like outfitting my own daughter." Wistfulness touched her fine features, but only for a moment; then she focused her attention across the room and a smile transformed her face. "Ah, Kellisham is here. Pray excuse me, ladies." A vision in blue silk, the countess glided toward the doorway, where the duke stood chatting with a sober-faced young man.

Jane sat very still, her fingers taut around the smooth gilt arms of her chair. Did Lady Rosalind not realize that Jane lacked the means to pay for extravagant clothing? Papa had left only a tiny annuity, enough for her and Aunt Willy to get by if they practiced stringent economies and Jane supplemented their income by doing copy work for her father's colleagues. That left nothing for frivolities. Jane would have to tell her ladyship so.

Yet just for a moment she fancied herself wearing a gown of soft azure silk, her hair curled and shining, as she gracefully descended the grand staircase to an enthralled crowd of guests. In the far shadows would stand a man in an elegant dark suit, his gaze intent on her, as if she were the only woman in the room, Iseult to his Tristan. He would thrust his way through the assembly and before any other gentleman could grasp her gloved hand, he would claim her for his own. She would lift her gaze to his handsome face, and her heart would flutter madly when she saw that her mystery admirer was none other than—

". . . Lord Chasebourne."

"Yes," Jane blurted, then realized she had heard only part of what Lady Bagwell had said. "Or rather, I beg your pardon?"

"I asked if you were neighbor to Lord Chasebourne."

"Oh. Yes. I am." There was a long silence in which Lady Bagwell waited expectantly and Jane heard the chattering of the other guests nearby. Unaccustomed to small talk, she fumbled for something to add. "I . . . live in a cottage there. It is pleasant to take walks upon the downs."

"A cottage?" Lady Bagwell's sniff conveyed her ill opinion. "Was your father no gentleman, then?"

Jane stiffened. "He was an eminent scholar of medieval and pre-medieval writings. He did a new translation of *Beowulf*. And if you would but read his essay on monastery documents of the first millenium, you would realize the vital contribution he made to our knowledge of the Dark Ages.''

"Indeed.'' Lady Bagwell's lip was so curled it was hard to imagine how the woman managed to sip her tea. "And did he never seek a husband for you?''

Jane looked away to the window, which showed a glimpse of green trees in the square. The truth was, Hector Mayhew had been too engrossed in his books to notice his daughter had grown up. Or perhaps he'd believed her to be content in her duties. She *had* been happy to be useful. As his assistant, she'd spent hours looking up obscure references in dusty old tomes, days copying over his crabbed handwriting into readable text.

Then he had fallen ill, and any chance she might have had to learn the social graces had vanished into an endless round of mixing medicines and reading aloud to him. Not that she had minded; she had thrived on the work. But since his death, she had been aware of a vague discontent . . . at least until she had found Marianne.

"I don't suppose either of us thought a husband was important,'' she murmured.

"Not important? Why, there is nothing more essential to a woman's happiness than marrying well. Isn't that so, Fanny?''

"Yes, Mama,'' said her daughter, who sat as still as a little pink mouse.

Lady Bagwell leaned forward, her moustachioed lip twitching as she whispered, "Fanny will wed no less than an earl. She has been groomed from the cradle to become a countess at the very least.'' Her ladyship's gray marble eyes seemed to hold a warning, a warning Jane didn't quite fathom. Surely the woman didn't think *Jane* had designs on any earls . . . or that one earl in particular would view her as a desirable mate.

Jane stifled the mad urge to laugh. How could Lady Bagwell imagine such an absurdity?

All of a sudden, Lady Bagwell gripped her daughter's white arm, hissing into her ear, "The Duke of Kellisham approaches, with his nephew Robert. But never mind the nephew. You must charm His Grace."

Like a trained spaniel, Fanny sprang from the chair and sank into a deep curtsy.

Arm entwined with his, Lady Rosalind led the duke forward. Trailing them was a studious young man with meticulously combed brown hair that failed to conceal his jug ears. Lady Rosalind made the introductions, deftly seating Robert beside Fanny. The two slid glances at one another, blushed and pretended disinterest, before stealing a second look. All the while, Lady Bagwell tried to encourage conversation between the distinguished duke and her daughter.

Lady Rosalind linked arms with Jane. "Your Grace, if you will excuse us, Jane and I shall take a turn around the room."

He made a courtly bow. "Of course."

The moment they were out of earshot, Lady Rosalind leaned close in a waft of violet perfume, whispering, "Robert and Fanny make a well-matched pair, don't you think? It is deliciously amusing that Old Baggy has designs on Kellisham as a son-in-law instead."

"Why didn't you tell them of your engagement?"

"We're saving the announcement for my ball next week. I did mention the ball, didn't I?"

"No, my lady."

"I mean for it to be the most outrageously magnificent party of the Season." She squeezed Jane's arm, and her eyes sparkled with the same mysterious facets as her sapphire brooch. "Oh, how perfectly things are proceeding."

"Things?"

A Mona Lisa smile tilting her lips, Lady Rosalind scanned the throng of visitors. "Why, yes, no one has dared to criticize Ethan for settling Marianne in his house. That is absolutely necessary if she is to be accepted someday. Meanwhile, we shall scarcely have a moment to breathe,

what with all the preparations for the party. It will be a
brilliant time for you to make your formal debut into society.''

''Me?'' Mired in dread and longing, Jane halted near the
massive double doors. ''My lady, about the new gowns. I
cannot afford them.''

''Pish-posh. We'll send the bills to Chasebourne.''

''To Ethan?'' The very idea mortified Jane. ''*No*. Absolutely *not*.''

''Oh, he shan't blink an eye at the expense,'' Lady Rosalind said with an airy wave. ''He never questions my purchases, but if it makes you more comfortable, we simply
won't tell him the things are for you.''

''But . . . that's dishonest. And besides, *I'll* know.'' No
doubt he bought clothing for women all the time. Lewd
women who wore fine silk stockings with frilly garters and
heaven knew what else. Or little else.

''My dear Jane, it is one of the functions of men to pay
our expenses. Besides, I am your godmother, am I not? It
is my duty to see that you are dressed appropriately.''

''A godmother's purpose is to care for the needs of the
soul.''

''Then that settles it. One can hardly pray when one's
body is ill clothed.'' The countess peered across the drawing room, and her complacent expression changed into a
frown. ''Good gracious. Kellisham looks positively thunderous. I daresay Old Baggy must have mentioned Marianne to him.'' Releasing Jane's arm, she started to walk
away, then turned back. ''Oh, by the by, my son ordered
the carriage for half an hour hence. It seems the rogue
means for us to entertain his callers while he goes off to
who knows where.'' Her silk skirts rustling, she walked
toward her fiancé.

Jane's heart lurched. If Lady Rosalind meant to distract
her from quarreling about clothes, then she certainly had
succeeded.

After glancing around to make sure no one noticed, Jane

slipped out the doors of the drawing room and ran with unladylike haste toward the grand staircase. She mounted the steps, her shoes scuffing softly on the marble, her hands gripping her stiff black skirt to keep from tripping. She followed the wide corridor, and instead of turning toward the guest wing, she headed for the master's chambers.

It was a relief to escape the judgmental gazes and covert disapproval; that must be why she felt this curious lightness, this exhilaration as if she had outrun a storm on the moor. The aroma of lemon wax perfumed the hushed air. A tall window at the end of the corridor released a silvery stream of daylight along the rich burgundy carpet.

She stopped before a white door framed by gilded woodwork. Ethan's apartments. Mrs. Crenshaw had warned her never to venture here.

No, *warned* was too dramatic a word. *Informed,* then. Jane had been informed of his order. But she could not be swayed by petty rules when the well-being of a child was at stake.

Girding herself for battle, she glanced up and down the empty passageway before rapping on the door. She admonished herself to be firm with Ethan, to make him tell her what she needed to know. And then she would tell *him* a thing or two.

The door opened. She found herself facing a short, perfectly groomed man with the narrow face of a whippet. His impassive gaze politely regarded her. "May I direct you somewhere, Miss . . . Mayhew?"

Undoubtedly, Ethan's valet knew her identity from hearing gossip in the servants' hall. "I'm not lost," she said. "I must speak to Lord Chasebourne immediately. Has he left yet?"

"I shall have to check on his whereabouts. If he is still here, I will give him your message."

"You don't understand," she said, angling up her chin to peer over his head and into the bedroom. Through the slender crack, she glimpsed only the bright panes of a window in the far wall. "It's urgent that I see him. Right this minute."

"I will convey your request. Good day."

The valet stepped back to shut the door. Desperate, she jammed her black leather shoe into the opening. "I know he's in there. So let me see him."

Huffy with outrage, the valet held the door almost shut. "This is highly irregular. Please remember this is a gentleman's bedchamber."

"Ethan, are you there?" she called, then said to the valet, "Tell him I shan't be put off." Spurred by the thought of Marianne being returned to the mother who didn't want her, Jane pressed her shoulder to the wooden panel and pushed hard. For a moment she and the valet engaged in a ludicrous struggle for domination.

Ethan's voice rumbled from somewhere inside the room. "Oh, let her in, Wilson. It's only Jane."

Only Jane.

The words deflated her, but just for an instant. She'd been right to guess he was avoiding her, the cowardly rogue.

Expecting a vulgar, crimson-draped bedroom trimmed in gaudy gold, she was surprised when she found herself in a pleasant chamber done in pale blue and silver. His mother must have done the decorating. The counterpane on the four-poster was drawn tidily over a hill of pillows. Several books were strewn on the bedside table, and a wing chair waited near the unlit hearth, close enough for the master to prop his feet on the fender if he liked. The effect was comfortable and inviting, not at all like a lover's lair.

Of course, she reminded herself, it was the tower room above this one where he entertained his women. Did that nondescript door in the corner hide the secret stairway to his den of depravity?

Ethan stood before a silver-framed pier glass. He was fussing with his neckcloth, and Wilson scurried over to help him arrange the white folds. The earl wore no coat or waistcoat, only a pair of leg-hugging fawn breeches and a white shirt. With his every move, the cloth brushed against powerful muscles. Her stomach did a little tumble, twisting itself into an annoying knot. She had the irksome urge to slide her arms around his lean waist, press her cheek to his strong back, and absorb his heat and scent.

She hated this effect he had on her, the wretch. She wasn't a lovelorn girl anymore. She was a woman with a life of her own, independent of any man.

Their gazes met in the mirror. As he fastened a diamond stickpin in his cravat, he watched her with an air of enjoyment, as he might regard a jester in a troupe of traveling players. "So, Miss Maypole. Invading my bedchamber is fast becoming a habit with you."

"I would like to speak to you in private."

"So would a lot of women." He flashed her a wolfish grin, his eyes dark with deviltry. "Of course, it's not the speaking that interests them."

"Well, unlike *them*, I wish to conduct a serious conversation with you. If you are capable of it."

"There's a first time for everything." Turning to the valet, Ethan inclined his head. Wilson vanished into the dressing room, shutting the door.

Ethan sauntered across the room and threw himself into the wing chair, both legs stretched out as he gazed up at her, his hands behind his head. "It was risky of you to come here. If anyone finds out you're alone with me, you shall be ruined." He looked her up and down. "And it's a pity to be ruined without at least having some pleasure of it."

She had the disturbing notion that he could see right through her gown. Just like that time she'd caught him in a tree, peering down into her dress. Fighting the urge to cross her arms, she held her hands rigidly at her sides. "I had no choice. You were planning to leave without me again."

He shrugged, not denying it. "Men are free to do as they

like," he said, his grin rakish. "It's you ladies who require chaperones."

"A practice you tend to abuse. After all, a husband can betray his wife, but *she* dare not do the same."

His smile died a hard death. "Have a care how you form your opinions. Judgments should be based on facts, not conjecture."

Her throat felt like parched earth. Jane told herself she had a duty to help one of her own gender fight this predator male. "I know more than you think. After you left, I went back and visited with Lady Portia."

His muscles seemed to tense, though he remained slouched in the chair. "The devil you did. What did she tell you?"

"That George Smollett has gambled away all her funds. That he ran off and left her." *That you had all but ignored your wife, flaunting your affairs with other women.* Jane twisted her fingers together, uneasy in her role of intermediary. "She wants you to know that she repents her mistake and wishes she could make it up to you."

"Does she."

His granite features didn't offer any encouragement. "I know she must have angered you," Jane went on doggedly. "But I do believe she is truly sorry."

The muffled rattle of carriage wheels came from the street. Ethan's eyes were narrowed to slits, hiding his thoughts. "Let me make one thing clear," he said. "I will not discuss Portia with you. Not now. Not ever."

"But you ought to at least go and talk to her—"

"The topic is closed." His voice was congenial, but with a keen edge. "If that is all you've come here to say, then be gone."

Jane felt a rush of frustration and fought it by taking a deep breath. She would have to bide her time for now. "No, that isn't everything. I wish to discuss Marianne's mother."

"Ah. You're never without a crusade."

"I deserve to know the name of every woman who might have left Marianne on my doorstep. I don't care how long the list is, I intend to investigate each and every one of them."

"Then ask me nicely. Vinegar won't catch you many flies, or however the old saying goes."

He was laughing at her again, she could tell by the slight crinkling at the corners of his dark eyes. The sight stirred that bothersome tension in the pit of her stomach. "*Please* name the women," she said on a note of sarcasm. "In fact, if you have paper and pen, I shall take notes."

She marched briskly toward a small writing desk, seated herself in the chair, and reached for a sheaf of paper that was tucked into a cubbyhole. Before she could pull it halfway out, Ethan slapped his hand down.

His very large, very male hand.

Jane jerked her head up to see him looming over her. She had not even heard him cross the bedroom.

He stood close to her, his face hovering just inches from hers. Never in her life had she swooned, but his intimidating presence made her feel light-headed, piercingly aware of him. She could see each spiky black lash on his eyelids, the faintness of stubble on his smooth-shaven jaw, the small pale scar on his brow where he'd once fallen from that tree. She could smell him, too, a dizzying combination of cologne and deep, mysterious masculinity. Swallowing with difficulty, she wondered if his skin tasted of exotic spices.

He scooped up the papers, and she had a glimpse of bold black penmanship, a series of short lines with many of them slashed through and rewritten. It didn't resemble a letter. It looked rather like . . . a *list*.

A list of potential mothers?

He took the top sheet and rolled it into a tube. The rest of the papers were blank, and he left them on the desk. Pivoting away, he strode to the mantelpiece and stuck the roll into a blue Grecian urn, where the end protruded tantalizingly.

He resumed his seat. Only then did his hard mahogany eyes focus on her. "Next time you're in a man's bedroom," he said, his silky voice holding an underlying menace, "ask permission before you use his things."

Jane ordered her heart to cease racing, her hands to stop quivering. With exaggerated civility, she said, "Please, may I borrow a pen, m'lord?"

"Help yourself."

She busied herself with selecting a quill from the silver penholder. The very first one was beautifully sharpened— by his efficient valet, no doubt. She uncapped the inkwell and dipped the quill tip into the black liquid. "So. Who are these women?"

"Miss Aurora Darling. Lady Esler. Miss Diana Russell. And Viscountess Greeley." He rattled off the names as if he'd memorized them.

Jane scribbled madly, her pen scratching into the silence. When he didn't speak further, she looked up at him. "You may continue."

"That's all."

"*Four* women?" She couldn't keep the surprise from her voice. She had expected him to list at least a dozen names or more. "Sometimes babies are born early or late. Are you certain you took that into consideration?"

He arched an amused eyebrow. "I'm not a half-wit, Jane."

She glanced at the rolled paper sticking out of the blue vase. There *had* been quite a lot of strike-outs. Perhaps he had eliminated some women for various reasons. If, for instance, he'd seen one of his former lovers a few months ago, he could be reasonably certain she wasn't the mother. Yes, that made sense.

Even if his cooperation did not.

⌒ *Chapter 7* ⌒

It didn't look like a brothel.

Located in a quiet residential district, the town house was sandwiched in a row of pale stone dwellings. The modest white door and columned porch made the house indistinguishable from its neighbors. Lace curtains shrouded the windows, both upstairs and down, and had Jane not known better, she might have thought it the residence of a respectable family.

She ascended the three granite steps and stood by a fluted column while Ethan lifted the brass knocker and rapped. In sudden trepidation, she regretted her boldness in coming here. She should retreat to the barouche. She should let Ethan interview Miss Aurora Darling. Jane had seen enough of his wicked women to last a lifetime.

But there was Marianne to consider.

With a rush of tenderness, Jane imagined the infant, cooing in her cradle back in the nursery. Someone had to settle the baby's future, to make sure she had the best possible home. And Jane couldn't trust Ethan not to relinquish the baby on a whim.

"They must be asleep," he said, knocking again.

"Surely not. It's the middle of the afternoon."

"Work all night, sleep all day." Cocking one eyebrow,

he peered closely at her. "Good God, Miss Maypole. Is that a blush I see?"

She willed away the depraved curiosity that made her wonder what exactly these women did throughout the long nights. "I doubt you would recognize a blush if you saw one."

"Quite true," he said unrepentantly. "In my circle, one doesn't encounter many virgins."

"In my circle, it is the scoundrels who are in blessedly short supply."

"Touché."

The door swung open. A short, round woman filled the opening, her enormous breasts bulging from the bodice of a red silk dressing gown. She had untidy ginger hair and smears of black cosmetic beneath her hazel eyes. The sullen tightness of her mouth eased into a smile. "Holy Mother of God. Why, m'lord Chasebourne, isn't it? We haven't seen you in many months."

"Hello, Miss Minnie," he said, kissing her plump hand. "I trust you've been a naughty girl in my absence."

Minnie batted her eyelashes. "Never a dull moment here, that's for certain."

"I'd like to visit with Aurora Darling. Is she available?"

" 'Tis a mite early for company. If you'll come back in the evening, we'd be happy to accommodate you." With frank curiosity, the whore scrutinized Jane in her high-necked mourning gown, and her eyes narrowed in suspicion. "You haven't gone religious on us, have you, m'lord? We've had enough with preachers knocking on our door in hopes of redeeming us."

Ethan let out a hoot of laughter. "No, I'm here on another matter entirely. So do be a love and fetch Aurora. Here's something for your trouble." He took a sovereign from his pocket and pressed it into Minnie's fleshy hand.

Clutching the gold coin in her fist, she opened the door wider and shooed them inside. "Come in. Make yourselves comfortable while I run upstairs." She did just that, heading for the staircase in the foyer, her slippered feet slapping on the wooden risers.

Jane followed Ethan into a parlor. Here at last was gaudy decadence: pink draperies trimmed in gold fringe, plush maroon couches, statues of gods and goddesses showing an alarming amount of flesh. Even the air smelled carnal with a trace of rich perfume. She averted her gaze from a painting above the mantelpiece of half-clothed warriors romping with naked nymphs. Secretly, she longed to examine the scene more closely, but she was too aware of Ethan settling in a gilt-armed chair, his long legs stretched out, crossed at his booted ankles.

"So," he said, "does the place meet with your disapproval?"

"Quite. Though *you* look perfectly at home."

"Stop glowering and sit down. I promise, you won't absorb any loose morals from the furniture."

Jane perched on the edge of a gold-braided chair. "If I were worried about that, I should be more concerned about living in *your* house."

He pretended to wince. "I can always depend on you, Jane, to put me in my proper place. It's hard to imagine there was a time when you liked me."

She tensed, fighting the rush of memories. "Liked you?" she said on a scornful laugh. "You must have been dreaming."

"Perhaps *liked* is the wrong word. *Fascinated* would be more apt. You spent your time spying on me, looking for ways to get me into trouble."

"I didn't."

"You did. Once you tattled to my father that I'd gone down into the tin mine at Denby."

"Only because I thought you were stuck there and going to die."

"And there was the time I was kissing Eliza Fairchild behind the church. You threw a clod of dirt at us."

"Be pleased I didn't tell the vicar. You were desecrating a cemetery."

"Not desecrating. *Con*secrating." One corner of his mouth tipped upward into that detestable grin. "Enlightened people don't deny their passions. They use their bodies for the purpose God intended them."

A retort sprang to her tongue, but she couldn't voice it. Lowering her gaze, she stared at her entwined fingers in her lap. What in heaven was she doing, discussing intimate acts with a rake, in a brothel, no less? And why, by all that was holy, did her mind throb with the image of lying beneath him, his body covering hers, his mouth stealing kisses. . . .

"*Now* you're blushing," he said.

The amused satisfaction in his tone infuriated her. She jerked up her chin. "You mistake the flush of fury. I'm thinking of the babies who are born to those carelessly indulging their passions. I'm thinking of Marianne being left on a doorstep because no one wanted her."

The gleam disappeared from his eyes, leaving them as opaque as darkened glass. "She's a fortunate child, having so staunch an advocate as you."

Fortunate.

That was not the answer Jane had expected, nor did she appreciate the pleasure his praise aroused deep inside herself. Of course, he merely meant to catch her off guard and deflect her anger. Before she could point that out, the tapping of footsteps distracted her, and a woman glided into the parlor.

She was a statue come to life, a slim, curvaceous goddess with copper-tinted brown curls cascading around her shoulders. Her creamy skin made a pleasing contrast to her rose-hued gown, and a pink boa looped her neck, the feathers fluttering against her generous bosom. Her mouth was impossibly red, her lashes thick and dark, as if enhanced by a subtle application of cosmetics. From a distance, she appeared no older than Jane, but as she drew nearer, the fine lines at the corners of her eyes became discernible.

Jane tried to hide her unseemly curiosity. Here was a woman who sold her body to men. It was her profession, her calling in life. Having a baby in the house would certainly put a damper on her nightly activities.

"Ethan," she said, smiling, her hands outstretched. A waft of musky perfume preceded her. "What a delightful surprise."

Rising from his chair, Ethan kissed her cheek. "My dear Aurora. I hope I didn't awaken you."

"Gracious, no. I was drinking my tea." Her warm expression turned wary as she glanced at Jane. "And who have we here?"

"Miss Jane Mayhew." His eyes narrowing, he studied Aurora. "She's a neighbor of mine."

To Jane, Aurora said apologetically, "Please don't think me unwelcoming, but his lordship should know better than to escort a lady to a house such as this one."

"Miss Mayhew understands the risks," Ethan said. "And surely you can guess why we've come, Aurora."

"I'm sure I cannot. Perhaps you should explain yourself."

He watched her intently. "A few days ago, a parcel was left on Miss Mayhew's doorstep. I wondered if it had been delivered by you."

"By *me*?" She laughed in a puzzled manner and glanced at Jane. "I am quite certain I've never before set eyes on Miss Mayhew. I wouldn't even know the number of her town house."

"Not a town house. Her cottage in Wessex."

"Wessex! Well, that settles it," Aurora said with an air of finality. "I haven't left the city in weeks. And then only to go to Oxfordshire. . . ." She looked away, her expression contemplative. There was something odd about her manner, something almost furtive.

Jane searched for a resemblance. Like Marianne, Aurora Darling had delicate features. Unlike Marianne, she had dark coloring. Deciding to be blunt, Jane asked, "Do you also deny giving birth to a baby two months ago?"

Those sherry-brown eyes fastened on her in shock. "A baby, Miss Mayhew? Are you saying . . . someone left *an infant* at your door?"

Jane nodded. "A ring was tucked into her swaddling blanket—a signet ring belonging to Lord Chasebourne. That led me to believe he was the father. We are trying now to determine the mother's identity."

Aurora sank into a chair, the gauzy dress drifting like a rosy cloud around her slender form. "*Her*. It is a girl, then."

"Yes."

"The poor child. But why would she have been left with you and not with her father?"

"That is what I intend to find out," Ethan said, his voice uncustomarily grim. "A year ago, you and I enjoyed a liaison. You must tell me the truth now. Did you or did you not bear my daughter?"

On the mantelpiece, an ormolu clock ticked into the silence. Aurora Darling sat very still, gazing not at him, but at the cold hearth. A frown knitted her fine brow, and Jane could have sworn she looked guilty.

Abruptly, the older woman rose and went to the window. In the sunlight, her lovely profile took on a somber aspect. "No, I did not, but I cannot expect you to take my word for that. Instead, I implore you to listen while I tell you something very few people know. It is a secret shared only by the women in this house and . . . well, you needn't know who else."

"I want the whole story," Ethan warned. "Not any half-truths."

Her lips curved into a sad little smile. Then she drew a deep breath and nodded. "It is really quite simple: I too have a daughter born out of wedlock. But she is most definitely not yours."

Jane sat on the edge of her chair. Never in her uneventful

life had she heard such a riveting confession.

"Her name is Venus Isabel," Aurora added huskily, looking out the window. "She's nearly twelve years old and lives with a governess in Oxfordshire. I visit her whenever I can, and sometimes she comes here—of course we do no entertaining during her visit. Someday . . . someday I hope to leave London and go to live with her, so that we may be together always." She swung to face them, her eyes sheened with tears, the daylight forming a nimbus around her. "So you see, Ethan, if I'd borne your baby, I would have kept her. I could never give away my own child. *Never.*"

Jane's heart went out to Aurora. Surely no one could fabricate the emotion in her voice, the spill of tears down her cheeks. This woman could not have abandoned Marianne.

Ethan crossed the parlor, gathered Aurora to him, and stroked her slender back. His deep voice murmured words of consolation. Jane felt uncomfortable, as if she were spying on a private moment. Yet she remained rooted to her chair.

A year ago, he and Aurora Darling had been lovers. This was the sort of woman he desired, a pretty, petite beauty who wept on his broad shoulder. How amazingly tender he could be, how considerate of her sorrow. It was a side to him that Jane had never seen, and the insight only enhanced the mystery of him.

Oh, to be held close like that, to feel a man's arms encircle her, to hear him whisper words of wanting. To go upstairs with him to the seclusion of a bedchamber. . . .

Jane's heart pounded madly, and she scolded herself for an appalling lack of decency. She didn't want an affair; she didn't wish to become like this woman who had lost her morals, who could not even live with her own child. Besides, Jane had been alone with Ethan in his bedroom twice already and nothing untoward had happened. The reason was quite simple. He would never, ever look at her in *that* way.

But the fantasy lingered like a physical ache inside her. If only she had the chance to be so wicked.

Just once.

"Wicked," Lady Rosalind proclaimed with satisfaction. "That gown will make you look positively wicked."

Jane stared doubtfully at the drawing in the small fashion book *La Belle Assemblée*. They sat at a table beneath an enormous domed skylight in the linen-draper's shop. Colorful bolts of fabric lined the columned walls, along with trays containing all manner of trimmings, from ribbons to buttons to lace. The pleasant aroma of newly spun cloth mingled with the expensive scents worn by the few customers strolling the spacious room.

She focused her attention on the open book. The gown under consideration had a scooped neck cut scandalously low in the front. The short puffed sleeves were barely more than a wisp of gauze. The skirt descended from the bosom to skim the dainty figure of the model. It was raiment for Aurora Darling—or Lady Portia.

Not a rustic who preferred books to parties.

For once, Jane's imagination failed her. She could only picture herself looking like a giraffe in that gown, loping across the dance floor as if it were an African savannah.

"It is all wrong for me," she said. "Since my funds will stretch to only one gown, it makes sense to choose a more practical style."

"Practical, bah. You need a positively splendid evening dress for my betrothal ball." Rising, Lady Rosalind went to the display of fabrics and fingered a bolt of sea-foam green. "I wonder if this silk would do."

"It looks far too dear. A tweed or bombazine would wear better—"

"What an excellent choice, my lady," the proprietor of the shop said, hastening toward them. A haughty man with a stiff white neckcloth and a mop of brown curls, he bowed to the countess.

"Thank you," Lady Rosalind said. "But I am thinking perhaps my godchild needs a more vivid hue to enhance her strong coloring."

The man considered, looking from the bolt of cloth to Jane, his upper lip curled slightly. "Yes. Yes, you are indeed observant, my lady. I have the very thing that will suit." Searching through the bolts of fabric, he drew down a swath of forest-green gauze. "Might I suggest this, with the sea-foam silk as an underskirt?"

Lady Rosalind clapped her gloved hands. "Wonderful! Send both to Madame Rochelle's dressmaking establishment on Bond Street."

"How much will it cost?" Jane asked.

The proprietor ignored her, his groveling attention focused on Lady Rosalind. "As you wish, my lady. And may I suggest some additional cloths? We have a celestial-blue muslin for evening wear. And a gold angola suitable for a shawl. It goes well with this sprigged poplin for a walking dress."

"We'll take a length of those, and that primrose silk, too. Oh, and twenty yards of white cambric." Lowering her voice, she mouthed to Jane, "One can never have enough pretty undergarments, you know."

"It's all too much," Jane whispered, rising in a panic from her chair. "I can't possibly pay for it. I thought we'd agreed—"

"Never mind, we can settle up later. I can't have my godchild running around in rags."

Jane glanced down at her plain black serge. Her best dress wasn't so awful, was it? There were no patches or worn places, except of course for the frayed hem, but that portion, she'd turned under and resewn. She had hoped no one would notice the skirt was now an inch too short.

Intending to be firm with Lady Rosalind, she followed the countess to a long table, where she and the fawning proprietor were deep in conversation over a box of buttons. "My lady, I appreciate your thoughtfulness," Jane said, "but I will purchase the materials for only one gown. *One*."

"Pish-posh. Touch this beautiful silk and tell me you don't wish to wear it." She grasped Jane's hand and guided it over the length of sea-foam silk.

The cool softness felt like a caress to Jane's fingertips, and a little tremor of yearning coursed through her. The fabric was deliciously sensual compared to the stiff serge. Jane could imagine the silk draping her skin, clinging to her body, whispering as she danced at the ball. . . .

Clad in a garment paid for by the Earl of Chasebourne.

She snatched back her hand. "It doesn't suit me. I'm sorry, my lady."

The corners of Lady Rosalind's mouth turned down in hurt. "My dear girl, consider it a gift," she said. "Surely you cannot deny me the pleasure of dressing you."

"Shall I put it on Lord Chasebourne's account, then?" the proprietor asked.

"Yes—"

"No," Jane said, not caring if she was rude. "Sir, you are not under any circumstances to do so."

Lady Rosalind threw up her hands. "Oh, all right, stubborn girl. You win. But I can't say I understand you."

Jane felt satisfied, but it was a cold victory. She would plead a headache on the night of the ball, and no one would be the wiser. She hadn't come to London to dance, anyway. She had come for Marianne's sake. It was best she remember that.

She turned to examine a bolt of sturdy gray cotton. And in doing so, she missed seeing Lady Rosalind wink at the proprietor.

In the garden behind Chasebourne House, Jane sat in the shade of a pear tree. The perfume of its blossoms filled the late afternoon air. Across the pathway, a bumblebee buzzed the rosebushes, a fat black and yellow form drifting from one red bloom to another.

Jane felt drunk with contentment. After that disagreeable shopping expedition, she reveled in the warmth of the spring day. Beside her on the blanket lay Marianne, seemingly fascinated by the play of light and shadow in the leaves overhead. The baby gurgled and cooed, her voice as soft and sweet as the breeze that soughed through the branches.

Tenderly, Jane stroked the angel-fine hair that peeked from beneath the white bonnet. Those plump cheeks gave proof to Gianetta's frequent feedings. The pink swaddling clothes made Marianne look like a newborn princess in a fairy tale. Jane's throat caught. This baby was so precious, so innocent. Someone had to guide her through life. Someone had to give her a firm moral backbone. For heaven's sake, someone had to take her from the nursery for outings, too. Who else besides Jane cared enough to bother?

Yes, she had to admit that her life here in London had turned out better than she'd anticipated. Besides her time spent with the baby, she had discovered Ethan's library with its treasure trove of books. It was difficult to believe a frivolous rake could have accumulated all those volumes, everything from poetry and philosophy to history and novels. She could only conclude that his father or grandfather had followed intellectual pursuits.

The scrape of footsteps on the flagstones alerted her, and she sat straight up against the trunk of the pear tree. Shading her eyes with the edge of her hand, she looked toward the house with its pillared loggia and tall windows. Her heart did a little tumble when she spied Ethan striding down the garden path, the sunlight gleaming on his black hair. He wore a butternut-brown coat and dark breeches, and discreet gold buttons glinted on his waistcoat.

He looked around and spied her, coming forward until he stopped a few feet away. He cast a guarded glance at the baby. "You sent for me, Jane," he said, in an imperious tone that stated his displeasure at being summoned like a servant.

Jane refused to be intimidated. "I hoped you might wish to join us out here. It's a fine day."

"Your note said you had something urgent to tell me."

"I do. I thought you should know that Marianne reached for her rattle today."

"Her rattle."

"Yes." Jane picked up the silver toy and held it near the infant. "Look, princess. Look what Auntie Jane has for you."

Those blue eyes shifted from their study of the leaves. Marianne blinked at the shiny object; then her chubby arm darted out and her hand swatted awkwardly at the rattle.

"See?" Jane said proudly. "She's trying to grab it."

"She wants you to get it out of her face," he said.

"No, she's only just realizing that she can touch things. Isn't it wonderful?"

He made a noncommital sound deep in his chest. But he hunkered down on the other side of the baby, took the rattle from Jane, and moved it in front of Marianne. Her eyes followed the gleaming toy, and once again, she batted at it. This time, her tiny fingers briefly curled around the handle before it slipped from her grasp.

"Well. Will you look at that?" Ethan murmured, a note of surprise softening his gruff voice. He continued to play the game with Marianne, shifting the rattle here and there, while she managed to make contact with it each time.

A tender tension squeezed Jane's chest. Would he make a good father? Or an indifferent one, willing to acknowledge his daughter only when forced to do so? She wished to heaven she knew the answer.

Perhaps she shouldn't have tricked Ethan into coming out here. Perhaps she shouldn't encourage him to form a paternal bond with Marianne. He could take the baby from her; he could claim Marianne as his own. He could send Jane back to her lonely cottage in Wessex. . . .

Choked by bittersweet fear, she wanted to snatch the rattle from his hand. Then she noticed the ink stain on his middle finger.

The sight struck her as so peculiar that without thinking, she reached out and touched the blemish to make certain it was real. In that quick touch, the warm strength of his flesh seemed to sear up her arm and into her bosom. To cover her confusion, she said, "How strange . . . my own finger looks like that after I've copied manuscripts all day."

His face seemed to darken, or perhaps it was just a cloud passing over the sun. He tossed down the rattle. "I've been going over estate business."

"But don't you have a secretary who records the accounts and pens letters for you?"

"He was busy with other matters today."

Something didn't ring true. She watched him closely, dissatisfied with his explanation. Had Ethan been writing letters? Did it have something to do with Marianne's mother? "You didn't come from your office," she said slowly. "Mrs. Crenshaw told me you were in the tower room, and you didn't wish to be disturbed."

"So you sent your *urgent* message via a footman." Scowling, he pushed to his feet. "Next time, don't bother me over trivialities."

"Marianne isn't trivial. She's your *daughter*."

"That remains to be seen."

Jane decided not to press the issue. "When shall we interview the next of your women?"

A muscle jumped in his jaw; Jane could see that, though she remained on the blanket, looking up at his towering form. Clearly he still resented her interference.

"This evening," he said shortly. "Be ready at ten o'clock."

"So late? I usually retire by then."

"I can always go alone."

She shot to her feet and looked straight into his eyes. "I'll be there."

"I'm sure you will."

A sparrow twittered from the top of the brick wall surrounding the garden. Marianne cooed in accompaniment, making contented baby sounds. The gentle breeze ruffled Ethan's hair, causing a lock to fall rakishly onto his brow. The intensity of his eyes fascinated Jane, the sunlight picking out golden flecks in the deep, dense brown.

What was he hiding from her?

Just then, the murmur of voices came from the house. Jane saw Lady Rosalind stepping down from the loggia, accompanied by the Duke of Kellisham. They made an attractive couple, the countess with her youthful figure and tawny-gold hair, and the duke so tall and distinguished.

"Bloody hell," Ethan cursed under his breath.

"What's the matter?" Jane whispered. "Why don't you approve of the duke?"

He ignored her questions. Crouching down, he scooped up the baby, pink blanket and all. "Make haste and take her back up to the nursery," he said in an undertone. "I'll distract them."

He tried to thrust Marianne at her, but Jane crossed her arms, outraged by his order. "You can't hide her away like a bit of rubbish. She's your daughter. She has every right to be out here, enjoying the sunshine—"

"Damn your stubbornness, they've seen us."

Sure enough, the duke now propelled Lady Rosalind toward the rose garden. The countess looked worried, and from the movement of her lips and the way she clung to his arm, it appeared she was trying to reason with him. He shook his head, stalking forward in grim-faced disapproval.

The duke halted before them and nodded to Jane. "Miss Mayhew." Then he glowered at Ethan. "So this is the infant. Your byblow."

Ethan's features took on that cool mask. "Her name is Marianne. Would you care to hold her?" He indicated the swaddled baby, who yawned, showing her tiny pink gums. "After all, she'll soon be your granddaughter."

The duke held his arms rigidly at his sides. "You must have gone utterly mad. Have you no shame, bringing such a child into your own home?"

"So long as she might be mine, I must provide for her."

With the ease of an experienced father, Ethan held Marianne in the crook of his arm. Jane realized belatedly that she had been wrong to think he meant to hide the baby. He had foreseen this confrontation and wanted to protect his daughter.

"I've told everyone that Marianne is an orphan," Lady Rosalind said in a conciliatory tone. "I explained that to you, Peter. You saw for yourself during visiting hour yesterday that people were beginning to accept it."

"Orphan, bah. No one really believes that Banbury tale."

"Then we must *make* them believe." She flashed a glance at the baby, who yawned again, sleepy-eyed and content against Ethan's coat. "I do think it is admirable of Ethan to accept his duty toward his child."

"Let him send her to the country, then," the duke stated. "Hire an army of nursemaids if necessary. But don't flaunt her before all the *ton.*"

"He isn't flaunting her." Jane could no longer hold her tongue. "For once, he is behaving honorably. And if narrow-minded people like you wish to believe otherwise, then I say, let them."

Silence fell over the gathering. The wind rustled the leaves of the pear tree and sent a white blossom tumbling across the walkway. Lady Rosalind looked more anxious than ever, peering up at the duke's thunderous expression. Jane knew she'd been rude, but she held her chin high, unwilling to apologize for speaking the truth.

"*Once,* Jane?" Ethan said. He cast a droll, sidelong glance at her. "Only *once* have I acted with honor? If I search my memory, I'm certain to find it is twice at the least, perhaps even thrice."

His jest snapped the tension. A bell-like laugh rang from

Lady Rosalind. "There, you see?" she told the duke. "Even Jane believes my son is doing the proper thing. The gossip will die down eventually."

"A lady of Miss Mayhew's background can know little of scandalmongers," the duke said gruffly. "But *you* know, Rosalind. You know how easily a person's good name can be ruined. As it is, Chasebourne has a less-than-stellar reputation."

"Oh, but surely you cannot blame him for the divorce," Lady Rosalind said. "The guilt of that woman is a matter of public record. We can be thankful she didn't saddle him with a child not of his blood."

Portia. They were speaking of Lady Portia, Jane thought. In dismay, she realized she'd nearly forgotten her promise to help Ethan's former wife.

"Certainly a nobleman must secure the succession of his line," Kellisham allowed. "But it is wrong to publicly acknowledge his illegitimate issue. And that is precisely why—"

"You must cease interfering in my affairs," Ethan finished. Cuddling the baby, he gave the duke a hard stare. "If I choose to house my child under my roof, then it is no one's decision but my own."

"Young man, you also have a duty to the women under your care. By your actions, they will be judged."

"My mother is an expert at handling social disasters," Ethan said. "She doesn't need protection. Isn't that right, Mother?"

His words sounded more accusation than praise, and Jane wondered at the veiled look that passed between mother and son.

"Don't be disrespectful, Chasebourne," the duke snapped. "I will not tolerate it."

"It's all right, Peter," Lady Rosalind said, stroking his sleeve as if he were a stallion to be gentled. "Ethan only means that I won't stand for nonsense from small-minded gossips."

"Your Grace, could *you* not lend your support to Lord Chasebourne?" Jane suggested. "Could you not deny the rumors for the sake of Lady Rosalind? Surely people would heed your word."

"An excellent point," Lady Rosalind said with delight. "No one would dare to disagree with you, Peter."

"I will not lie," he said stonily. "The child is not an orphan."

"No one is asking you to *lie,* darling. Only to refer to Marianne as a foundling." The countess gave a little laugh. "And that is certainly the case since she was *found* on Jane's doorstep."

"I hardly think—"

She briefly placed her fingers over his lips: "If you use that fierce stare of yours, you are sure to forestall any further questions."

"Rosalind, it is not proper to mislead people—"

"But it *is* proper to protect your beloved." Pressing her cheek to his sleeve and gazing up at him, she smiled, all charm and sensuality. "Surely you would do your best for me. Please?"

He compressed his lips, as if he were fighting an inner battle. Gradually, his harsh expression gave way to a besotted warmth. His gaze focused fully on her, and they might have been the only two people in the world.

Jane's heart melted. She glanced at Ethan, to see if he too rejoiced in their accord. But he stood glowering, the breeze lifting a lock of his hair.

The duke raised Lady Rosalind's hand to his lips. "It shall be as you wish, my dear." To her son, he gave a slight bow. "Chasebourne, it seems I must be your advocate in this."

"The devil's advocate," Ethan said.

The two men exchanged a flinty glare, then the duke and Lady Rosalind strolled away, the countess casting one last intense look over her shoulder at her son. Or had that glance been aimed at her little granddaughter?

His face devoid of emotion, Ethan passed the now-slumbering baby to Jane. The warm weight of her thrilled Jane, and she could not resist bending close to inhale the sweet, distinctive scent of powder and soap. When she lifted her head, she noticed Ethan watching his mother and Kellisham go back into the house.

"Why do you disapprove of your mother marrying the duke?"

He grimaced. "You've seen what a puritan Kellisham is. He's wrong for her. And she's only marrying him for the exalted status he'll bring her."

Jane let out a huff of disbelief. "That isn't true. Haven't you seen how they gaze at each other? It's clearly a love match."

"Love. And what does a dried-up spinster know of love?"

His words hit like a fist to her heart. For an instant, she couldn't breathe, couldn't think past the pain gripping her breast. Before he could realize the effect of his words on her, she hurled back, "What does an unconscionable rogue know of love, either?"

That moody darkness descended over his stark male features. "Not much, it would seem." He lifted his hand, and she thought for one pulse-pounding instant that he meant to caress her. Instead, he gently stroked his forefinger over the baby's rosy cheek. "Not much at all."

⌐ *Chapter 8* ⌐

Lady Esler held up a sweetmeat while the fuzzy white poodle danced on its spindly hind legs. The widow of the Marquess of Esler, Eleanor had flame-colored hair, sparkling brown eyes, and a fondness for animals, as proven by the two tabby cats asleep on the hearth rug and the many paintings of horses on the drawing room walls. Crooning nonsense to the dog, she leaned forward, giving her guests an unashamed look down her bodice.

With the coolness of a connoisseur, Ethan appreciated the view. Eleanor made a voluptuous contrast to Jane, who sat primly upright in her chair, her gloved hands folded in her lap. He knew exactly what Jane was thinking. That he chose his women by their physical attributes. That he was a lecher, a walking phallus who possessed no skills outside the bedchamber.

He didn't know why her assumption annoyed him so much lately. He never mistreated his women; in truth, he lavished attention on them. And when the liaison ended, he always left a generous gift. It was no wonder Eleanor had welcomed him tonight with open arms.

She dropped the treat and the dog snatched it in midair. "There, my little Snowball, you've earned your reward, dancing for Mama."

"You'll make him sick," Ethan observed.

"Oh, don't be a scold. We used to have such fun together." An impish smile illuminated her fine, freckled features so that she looked like a spoiled child rather than a
widow of two-and-thirty. To Jane, she murmured, "He is
a very naughty man, you know."

"So I have heard," Jane said disdainfully.

"Watch out if he entices you into a dark room. He is
liable to take all sorts of wicked liberties."

Ethan snorted to himself at the absurdity of Eleanor's
chatter. He'd like to do that just once, to corner Jane and
see if he could infuse some warmth into that frigid body.
Would darkness ease her inhibitions?

Hardly. Jane looked typically strict, her lips pinched together, her hair scraped into a no-nonsense knob atop her
head. The only loose aspect about her was that sack mas-
querading as a gown. The only hint of emotion was the
fervent gleam of longing in her eyes.

Longing?

No. That gleam had nothing to do with ardor; it was a
trick of the candlelight. Miss Jane Mayhew had never entertained a carnal thought in her life. She likely occupied
her mind with recitations of virtues. Or a list of his sins.

Jane said, "Lady Esler, if you will allow me to explain
why we are here—"

"Please do! Especially if it is in regard to the startling
news I heard at the Herringtons' rout last night." Eleanor
turned to Ethan. "Forgive me for being blunt, Chase, but
do you really keep your love child hidden away in your
nursery?"

With effort, Ethan maintained his smile. He despised the
notion of people gossiping about Marianne as if she were
a carnival amusement. "I'll tell you the truth, if you agree
to do likewise," he said. "Do we have a pact?"

"Of course. I'll never reveal what you say to another
soul, cross my heart." For good measure, Eleanor solemnly
traced an X over her lavish bosom.

"The gossip is true, then," he said, watching her intently

for signs of subterfuge. "The child might be mine."

"Might be?"

"The infant's parentage is in question. But I'm hoping you can shed light on the matter. It's your turn now, so tell me all you know of her."

"Her? Who?"

"The baby, of course."

Eleanor frowned. "Why, what else would *I* know?"

"Quite a lot, perhaps. Beginning with the fact that you bore Marianne in secret and then left her on Miss Mayhew's doorstep."

"Left her? *I?* You think *I* am her mother?" The bewildered expression changed into a sorrowful look that tugged down the corners of her generous mouth. Patting her lap, Eleanor invited the poodle to sit with her. She slipped her arms around the animal, and both mistress and beast regarded Ethan with liquid brown eyes. "Oh, Chase," she said in a subdued voice unlike her earlier exuberance. "How I wish it were true."

"Can you prove that it isn't?"

"Unfortunately, yes." She cuddled the dog, pressing her cheek to his curly white coat. "I really shouldn't tell you, though," she said softly. "It's something no one but my dear Harry knew, God rest his soul."

"You can depend on me to keep quiet. And Jane. She would never betray a confidence." He realized that was true; despite all her spinsterish foibles, Jane was one of the few people he trusted.

"You have my word of honor, Lady Esler," Jane said earnestly.

Eleanor's white teeth sank into her lower lip. Slowly, as if it pained her, she said, "I'd give anything to have had a little baby to love. And I almost did." She sniffled once, then went on. "You see, shortly after my marriage twelve years ago, I gave the marquess the happiest of news, that he would be a father before the year was out. Oh, how

pleased we both were! The doctor warned me to take care
and rest, but . . .''

When Eleanor paused, Jane gently prodded, ''My lady,
what is it? What happened?''

''I was too rash and impetuous to lie abed all day. And
I refused to give up my riding. One morning, my horse
shied and I suffered a terrible fall. I . . . lost my baby.''

Reaching over to pat her hand, Jane clucked in sympathy.
Ethan felt inadequate to comfort Eleanor. Perhaps if he
hadn't dismissed her as a shallow coquette, he might have
prolonged their brief affair and learned her deepest secret.
''I'm very sorry,'' he said.

''That wasn't the whole of it.'' Tears seeped down
Eleanor's freckled cheeks, and she bent her coppery head,
her pale hand stroking the poodle. Her voice lowered to a
mournful whisper. ''The doctor said . . . he said I would
never bear another child.''

Clutching the note in her lap, Jane sat on the window seat
in her bedchamber. It had grown almost too dark to read
the disturbing message again, and she watched as two footmen lit the torches that lined the curved front drive. The
flickering yellow flames against the deep purple dusk made
the entry resemble the gateway to a fairyland. Tonight was
the betrothal ball, and she felt wrenched with indecision.

From the start, she had been determined not to attend.
She did not belong at the fancy gathering, no matter what
Lady Rosalind said to the contrary. She wouldn't know
how to act or what to say to these sophisticated Londoners.
Yet Jane couldn't deny that a part of her longed wistfully
for what could never be, and so she had let herself be carried along by the rush of preparations.

Over the past week Lady Rosalind had behaved like a
general preparing her troops for battle. A regiment of
housemaids had buffed and dusted and swept. An army of
manservants had polished and lifted and carried. Outdoors,

a battalion of gardeners had weeded and snipped and trimmed.

Jane had spent each morning closeted with a rather gloomy dancing master, who despaired of her two left feet. She had gone along with the lessons arranged by Lady Rosalind and hadn't told the countess that she meant to stay above stairs. Jane hoped that in the crush of guests, no one would notice her absence.

Then, only half an hour ago, a footman had delivered the note that lay clutched in her hand. A flowery fragrance clung to the paper.

Though the light was nearly gone, she unfolded the sheet and read it again:

> *My situation grows desperate, and I must speak to Chasebourne immediately. But he refuses to receive me into his house. Thusly, during her ladyship's ball, I shall endeavor to slip into the rear garden. At midnight, you must lure Chasebourne outside so that I may entreat him.*
>
> *Please, I beg of you, do not fail me. You are my baby's sole hope for the future, my one, my only true friend.*
> *Portia*

Jane knew she couldn't ignore the note. She had only to think of Portia, her belly gently swollen with child, and know that she would do all in her power to help. The problem was, Ethan despised his former wife and might well refuse to lend her aid. Somehow, Jane must convince him to find charity in his heart.

Now she fervently wished she had ordered the fancy ballgown that Lady Rosalind had selected. Then she could join the guests and not feel ashamed of her drab clothing. Instead, she would be forced to steal downstairs just before midnight. Jane assured herself it wouldn't matter what she wore. Her task would take only a few minutes, to call Ethan outside on a pretext. Then she would have done all she could.

For now, she would go upstairs and sit with Marianne. The baby would be settling down to sleep, but Jane could sit beside the cradle and read by the light of a candle. Then she would not feel so forlorn.

Like poor Lady Esler.

Jane's mind flashed to the widowed marchioness. For all her wealth and beauty, Lady Esler lacked a child to love. It was no wonder she doted on her pets. Was that how Jane would end up, alone, with no one who needed her?

No. Somehow, she must find a way to keep Marianne. She must convince Ethan not to give the infant back to the mother who didn't want her.

Jane hadn't expected to feel anything but disgust for Ethan's discarded lovers. But now she realized these women were not all heartless hedonists; they had suffered great tragedies, too. Lady Esler, miscarrying her unborn baby. Miss Aurora Darling, separated from her beloved daughter. Lady Portia, whose future had been ruined by a single indiscretion.

The only one who had disgusted Jane was Miss Diana Russell, whom Jane and Ethan had visited a few days earlier. A celebrated actress at a theatre in Haymarket, Miss Russell was a dainty woman with an overdeveloped bosom and an underdeveloped sense of propriety. Making dramatic gestures, she convinced them that it was ludicrous to think she could have grown large with child while acting onstage nightly, ridiculous to imagine she could have given birth without missing a performance, absurd to believe she wouldn't have gone to Ethan with her troubles. And then, despite Jane's presence, Miss Russell had seated herself on his lap and kissed him.

Kissed him on his *mouth*.

Jane had wanted to sink into the floorboards. Out of the corner of her eye, she saw the scandalous way Miss Russell squirmed against him, her hands sliding inside his coat, as if she couldn't get close enough to him. The kiss had lasted less than a minute, before Ethan had set her aside with a teasing reprimand, but by then Jane had felt flushed with mortification—

"Why are you sitting there?" Lady Rosalind said.

Jane spun around on the window seat. By the light of the candle on the bedside table, she saw the countess marching into the bedroom, trailed by several maids. Surreptitiously, Jane shoved the folded note under the cushion. "My lady! I didn't hear you knock."

"You must have been wool-gathering. It's no wonder, with you sitting here in the dark." Lady Rosalind swung toward the cortege of servants and clapped her hands. "Betty, light the candles. Alice, start a fire. It should have been done an hour ago."

Two mobcapped girls scrambled to do her bidding.

"It isn't their fault," Jane said. "When the maid came round earlier, I sent her away. I see no need to waste so many candles on one person."

"Pish-posh. I must see to do my work."

"Work?"

Smiling serenely, Lady Rosalind waved the line of servants toward the dressing room.

For the first time, Jane noticed they were carrying all manner of boxes, large and small. "What are they doing?"

"Yes, I should like to know that, too," Aunt Wilhelmina said from the doorway. Holding her purple dressing gown closed with one hand and her silver flask in the other, she minced into the bedroom. "I was resting before the ball, but the tramping of feet disturbed me."

"Excellent, for it is time to rise and ready yourself," Lady Rosalind said cheerfully. "We have but two hours before my guests arrive. And by lovely happenstance, here are Jane's new purchases from the modiste."

"New purchases—" Aunt Willy sputtered. "All *this*?"

"There must be some mistake," Jane said, though she felt a sinking suspicion. "I ordered but one gown."

"Shall we see what we have? Oh, I do adore opening packages." Lady Rosalind took Jane by the arm and guided her into the dressing room, where one maid was lighting the tapers of a candalabrum and the others were unpacking gowns and shoes and hats and undergarments, in quantities that left Jane reeling.

She sank down on the stool before the dressing table. "I told you," she said faintly, "I can ill afford so much."

"Do not dare 'speak of payment," Lady Rosalind said, bending down in a waft of violet perfume to give Jane a quick hug. "You mustn't spoil my pleasure in giving a gift to my dear godchild. I neglected you for too many years, and now I beg you to indulge me."

"But how can I?" Jane glanced at the bustling maids and lowered her voice. "How can I allow Ethan to pay for all this?"

"Ethan?" Aunt Willy screeched. She hobbled to a post beside the dressing-table mirror and took a sip from her flask. "No unmarried lady would accept such intimate articles from a *man*. And a scoundrel at that."

"Mind, you are speaking of my son," Lady Rosalind snapped.

Wilhelmina compressed her lips and lowered her gaze.

"And he has paid nothing," the countess continued. "I have funds of my own, an inheritance from my father." Her expression softened as she looked at Jane. "So do tell me you'll accept my gift. Please."

Jane glanced at the shimmering garments being deposited in the highboy and clothes press, and knew a flash of longing so fierce it stung her insides. Shameful or not, she harbored a secret wish for pretty, impractical garments. Besides, Lady Rosalind looked so woebegone that Jane lacked the heart to refuse. "You swear you didn't put it on Ethan's account?"

"Not a pence."

"Then I thank you, my lady." She grasped the countess's small, soft hands. "You are very kind."

Lady Rosalind smiled. "Kind, bah. You are Susan's daughter, and she would wish me to introduce you to society." She flitted behind Jane and began to unbutton her black dress. "And we should have just enough time in which to prepare you."

Jane sprang up from the stool. "I didn't intend to go to the ball."

"Not go? My dear, you *must* go. Tell me one good reason why you cannot."

"I don't belong there."

"Nonsense. You are as blue-blooded as any in the *ton*."

"I haven't mastered the dances."

"That is just as well," Aunt Willy said, "for you must keep me company. We shall find chairs in a quiet corner. My nerves cannot bear the loudness of music and the press of people."

"Jane has stronger nerves, I'm sure." The countess resumed her unbuttoning. "Besides, dancing is quite simple. Let your partner guide you."

"I have no skill for chitchat, either," Jane said.

"So much the better. Men love a mysterious woman."

Was it true? Jane wondered. Certainly not. There was nothing mysterious about Ethan's women; if anything, they were only too obvious in their assets.

"Jane is right to feel reluctant," Aunt Willy said. "People will gossip if a woman of her advanced age flirts with young gentlemen."

"Pish-posh," Lady Rosalind said. "People will gossip more if a lady of her youth and charm hides in a corner with the old maids."

"Well, I never—" Aunt Willy huffed.

"Thank you for agreeing. I know that *you* would never hear a harsh word said against our dear Jane." Lady Rosalind shooed Aunt Willy toward the door. "Run along now, Wilhelmina. It has been a delight to hear your advice, but I dare keep you no longer from your own preparations."

Once Aunt Willy had waddled out, the countess rolled

her eyes heavenward. "Oh, save us from middle-aged spinsters," she murmured. "If ever I become so annoying, you must promise to slap the sense back into me."

Jane repressed a bubble of hysterical laughter. "Perhaps she's right. Perhaps I shouldn't try to be someone I'm not."

"What balderdash. A ballroom is a woman's battlefield. It is where she uses her wit and wisdom to win a man's heart. And now you must don your weapons of war."

Clapping her hands, she directed the maids to carry away the last of the empty boxes and told one of them to fetch Gianetta immediately. With a brisk command, Lady Rosalind bade Jane to step out of her old clothes.

The dowdy black gown fell into a heap, and Lady Rosalind tossed it into the corner. When Jane would have retained her coarse linen underthings, the countess sent her behind a painted screen and handed her a cambric chemise. Jane stripped down to nothing, shivering from the cool air and a rush of excitement, and pulled the chemise over her head. The soft material felt heavenly against her skin, like wearing a cloud.

"My lady, I'm ready for my gown."

"Not quite," the countess said, laughing. "Come out here first."

Embarrassed, Jane crept out from behind the screen. She had never employed a personal maid and wasn't accustomed to anyone seeing her unclothed. As she caught sight of herself in the mirror over the dressing table, she gasped. The low-cut chemise barely covered her breasts and ended just above her knees. The garment was so sheer she could see the dusky points of her bosom and lower, a dark shadow where a lady oughtn't look at herself. She crossed her arms, but that only made the fabric pull tighter.

Her manner matter-of-fact, Lady Rosalind moved the stool and bade Jane sit, her back to the mirror. She produced a blue glass jar and a brush which she used to polish Jane's neck and shoulders with fragrant powder. Gianetta scurried in, her dark head crowned by a white cap, her pretty features soft with the beatific contentment Jane had observed while the maid was nursing the baby.

"Is Marianne asleep?" Jane asked.

Gianetta made a rocking motion with her arms. "Sleep, *si*, like *angela mio.*"

"I must go to check on her," Jane said, rising from the stool. "Sometimes she's fretful and awakens during the evening—"

"A nursemaid will watch over Marianne for the night," Lady Rosalind said, pushing Jane back down. "Which leaves you free to attend the ball and Gianetta time to practice her other skills."

The two set to work. While the countess blended coralline salve over Jane's lips and cheeks, Gianetta pulled out the pins holding Jane's tight bun and, with a heated wand, curled her long, straight locks. There was more brushing and pinning and primping; then they laced her into a long buckram corset until Jane felt breathless, as if her innards were being squeezed out the top. She tried to protest, but they were tying on petticoats and then instructing her to step into a fine gown, the very one she had seen sketched in *La Belle Assemblée*. She marveled at the delicacy of it, the luxurious richness. At last, Gianetta brought forth a pair of lace gloves while Lady Rosalind took one last critical look. Her brow furrowed, she touched the gold locket at Jane's throat.

"Why does this look familiar?" the countess asked.

"It was my mother's. The portraits of my parents are inside."

"May I see?" At Jane's nod, Lady Rosalind carefully opened the clasp. For a long moment she stared at the miniatures, the dark-haired lady and smiling gentleman. When she closed the locket and looked up, her eyes swam with unshed tears. "My dear Susan. How I do miss her. She would be so proud of you tonight."

Jane's throat felt thick as the countess enveloped her in

a brief hug, and then turned her toward the mirror. "*Voilà,*" she murmured. "A beauty is born."

The branch of candles on the dressing table cast a golden glow on the figure in the looking glass. Jane blinked, then blinked again, forgetting all about the locket. Was that really *her*? A tumble of copper-tinged curls softened her strong features. Tall and slender, she had a swanlike neck and pretty white shoulders in contrast to the dark green gown with its underskirt of pale sea-foam silk. The close-fitting bodice, cut low enough to make her blush, displayed decidedly feminine curves.

Jane forgot she could scarcely breathe. She forgot that she despised cosmetics and artificial enhancements. She felt imbued with amazement, filled with a glow of energy and excitement. Was she dreaming? If she was, then she wanted the dream to go on and on.

"I always admired your height," Lady Rosalind said, tapping her forefinger against her chin. "It is far easier to dance gracefully when your legs are long."

The countess was envying *Jane?* The world indeed had gone topsy-turvy. "Oh, but I'm not graceful," Jane protested. "I'll step on my partner's toes."

"You shan't do much damage in these." The countess motioned Gianetta forward, and the maid knelt to place a pair of embroidered green slippers onto Jane's feet. "But remember, no waltzing until I secure you a voucher to Almack's. A young lady is expected to waltz there first, only when approved by that tedious Lady Jersey."

"I'll remember."

"And keep in mind that elegance is all in how you regard yourself. If you wish to be graceful, then *believe* that you are." The countess stood on tiptoe to straighten the green ribbon woven into Jane's hair. "Besides, *you* have wit and wisdom, which is more than I can say for most young ladies."

"I'll do my best." Jane trembled to imagine the evening, which now sparkled with fairy-tale possibilities. On impulse, she kissed her benefactress on the cheek. "Thank you ever so much."

She had always felt secure in her intelligence, competent in her quiet life back in Wessex, able to accomplish any task set before her. Yet here in London, she had entered a whole new world. Ethan's world.

What would he think of her transformation?

She felt caught up in wild impatience. Tonight she would make her debut into glittering society. She would dance and mingle and converse with the highest members of the *ton*. Perhaps she would even dare to flirt. . . .

The countess pressed a feathered fan into Jane's hands. Regarding her protégée with approval, Lady Rosalind let her mouth curve into a wise smile. "Now, if there is one man in particular whom you favor, don't let him know it straightaway. Don't dance with him at first. Make him wait. Tease him, whet his appetite for you."

Ethan. Was it possible he would pay court to her?

Jane controlled a delicious shiver. "Oh, my lady. How will I not muddle things?"

"Follow your instincts," Lady Rosalind advised cryptically. "By the end of the night he'll be begging to kiss you."

"Kiss me? Am I to *let* him?"

"That, my dear, depends on how much you desire him." On that scandalous statement, she touched her fingers to her lips in farewell, then hastened away with Gianetta.

Jane could not sit still. She paced into her candlelit bedchamber and back again into the dressing room, startled anew each time she caught a glimpse of herself in the mirror. She liked to hear the swish of her skirts, to feel the silk caress her skin. She liked the faint fragrance that eddied from her. She felt as if she had not lived before this moment, that in all her six-and-twenty years she had been asleep, dreaming about this evening of enchantment.

Very soon, carriages would begin to arrive. She would glide down the grand staircase, as much a fashionable member of the aristocracy as any other guest. She practiced waving her fan, peering over it coquettishly, dipping it down over her breasts. She giggled aloud at her antics, feeling wonderfully alive, foolish and free.

Anything could happen tonight. Anything at all. . . .

Then she remembered.

Walking to the window seat, she retrieved the folded paper from beneath the cushion and stared down at the spidery handwriting. The reminder of Lady Portia's dire straits sobered Jane. Amid all her gaiety, she must not forget her mission.

She tossed the note onto the fire. The flames consumed the paper, the words glowing for a moment, then blackening to ash. But the message remained etched on her mind.

At midnight, you must lure him outside. . . .

~ *Chapter 9* ~

Greeting a few late arrivals, Ethan stood beside his mother in the entrance hall. He had to admit that Lady Rosalind had outdone herself in the preparations. Swaths of gilt cloth draped the tables. Masses of white lilies filled every corner, while statues of gods and goddesses created the aura of a Grecian temple. The silvery strains of harp and violin music drifted from the ballroom at the top of the grand staircase. Lady Rosalind wore white chiffon with lavish gold embroidery, managing to appear both innocent and worldly.

He bent down to mutter in her ear, "So, Mother, how much is your little party costing me?"

The countess playfully swatted his dark blue sleeve with her ivory fan. "Enjoy yourself and don't ask questions. Now do be a gentleman and walk me upstairs. Kellisham is waiting to squire me in the opening dance."

"I'm surprised he isn't ensconced in the library with his political cronies," Ethan said as they strolled up the broad, curving staircase. "Enjoying a glass of brandy and a cheroot, while solving the problems of the nation."

"Bah. It is our betrothal ball, and he has vowed to stay by my side the entire evening. He would have joined us in the receiving line had our nuptials already been announced."

Her serene smile grated on Ethan, stirring old resentments. He leaned closer so that no one else could hear. "It is not too late to change your mind. Kellisham is rather old, don't you think? I know you prefer younger blood."

At the doorway to the ballroom, she stopped and regarded him. "That is a cruel and unconscionable remark."

Pain shimmered in her blue eyes, a pain he denied. He had every right to condemn her past actions, he told himself. The previous year, she had carried on a wild, improbable affair with his best friend, Captain Lord John Randall. Their flirtation had begun in secret, while Ethan had been sowing his own wild seeds right after the divorce proceedings, and by the time he'd noticed the little looks they'd shared, their disappearances from *ton* events, it had been too late to prevent the liaison.

Even then, he'd been incredulous, unable to believe the truth. He could not imagine his mother—his *mother*—luring into her bed a man nearly twenty years her junior. A trusted friend whom Ethan had known since their schooldays at Eton. Randall had been his boon companion on drunken binges and rollicking adventures with women. They had been as close as brothers.

Ethan had been furious with his mother, and frustrated by her refusal to give up her lover. In a fit of rage he had challenged Randall. He had used his fists, and Randall, damn him, had not fought back.

Not a month later, Randall lay dead. Killed on the bloody fields of Waterloo after leading a daredevil cavalry charge.

Ethan realized that his mother stood gazing at him, distress on her fine-boned face. He loathed the shame that crawled from the dark place inside himself. Stiffly, he bowed to her. "I apologize for my bluntness."

"But not for your condemnation of me."

"Surely you cannot hope for my approval now. You didn't need it *then*."

"No, I didn't. It was my only liaison since your father's death nine years ago. Someday I hope *you* can bring yourself to love someone. And I pray you never know the pain of loss.''

''Thank you for the advice. But it still doesn't excuse the affair.''

''We were both adults, Ethan. Why is that so difficult for you to accept?''

He couldn't answer that without sounding like a prudish maiden aunt. Like *Jane*. He kept his voice cold. ''Ah, there is Kellisham. I don't suppose you ever told him about Randall, did you?''

Inside the crowded ballroom, the duke conversed with a group of stodgy aristocrats. He spied Lady Rosalind, and a smile gentled his stern features. Square shouldered and dignified, he made his way toward them.

''You mustn't say a word of this to him,'' Lady Rosalind whispered. Her eyes wide with worry, she pressed her white-gloved fingers into Ethan's sleeve. ''Promise me you won't.''

For the barest instant, he considered spilling the old scandal to the duke. He relished the notion of watching as Kellisham gazed in shock at Lady Rosalind, listening to her feeble attempts to make light of the truth.

But that would be petty revenge. Ethan wanted his friend back, that was all. He wanted to laugh and drink and trade stories. He wanted his life to be as carefree as it had once been.

''As you wish, Mother. Your little secret is safe with me.''

She relaxed, her fingers loosening their grip on him. He saw the effort it took for her to smile. By the time Kellisham approached and bowed over her hand, her mask of gaiety was firmly in place.

''Your Grace,'' she said in a warm, melodious voice. ''How handsome you look tonight.''

''I cannot begin to match your radiance.'' Hardly able to take his eyes from her, the duke nodded at Ethan. ''If you will excuse us, Chasebourne, the musicians are awaiting her ladyship's signal to begin the first set.''

"You would be advised to find yourself a dance partner,'' Lady Rosalind said to Ethan, before Kellisham could
lead her away. She pointed across the cavernous chamber.
"By the by, there is a beauty you haven't seen before. The
girl in dark green, over there by that large fern.''

He felt cynical amusement at the sparkle in his mother's
eyes, when she had appeared so disconsolate only moments
ago. As she and Kellisham disappeared into the throng,
Ethan looked in the direction she had indicated. Strange,
his mother had never been one to play matchmaker. She
had always been too involved in seeking her own pleasures.

Guests swarmed the area where the dancing would begin.
Here too were pillars and statuary and greenery to create
the impression of a Grecian temple. The mirrored walls
reflected the light from the chandeliers, and the long row
of glass doors had been opened to the balcony overlooking
the garden. People strolled from group to group, and for a
few moments his view was blocked.

Then he saw her.

She stood on the opposite side of the ballroom, a willowy
woman in dark green surrounded by a knot of gentlemen.
Not surprisingly, her admirers included Duxbury and Keeble, sharks drawn to fresh blood.

He didn't recognize her at first. She stood in profile, her
figure painted by the soft glow of candles. A charming
tangle of curls tumbled down to her white shoulders in a
style that invited a man to bury his face in her hair—and
other places. His gaze roamed down the expanse of bare
skin to a pair of small but shapely breasts. His interest
piqued, he scrutinized her features again, half-hidden by her
feathered fan. There was something naggingly familiar
about her, but he stood too far away to identify her.

His mother wanted him to meet this girl. That was
enough of an incentive to head in the opposite direction.
But she intrigued him, and he strolled toward her, not pausing to chat when acquaintances in the crowd nodded to him,

not stopping to flirt whenever a pretty woman smiled at him.

As he drew nearer, his sense of recognition grew stronger and yet more elusive. Copper highlights in dark hair. Eyes of indeterminate color. Dramatic features, not at all delicate, though she plied an opened fan that hid the lower portion of her face. There was no wedding band on her finger.

Perhaps he should mourn that. One couldn't seduce an untried girl.

Determined to solve the mystery, he approached her from the side. If they hadn't met, he would have to seek her chaperone to perform the introductions. Or perhaps he could bend convention and request that Duxbury present him.

She was listening politely as Keeble told one of his stupid jests. Taking refuge in the fronds of a huge fern, Ethan stood close enough to see the viscount lean forward confidingly and say, "The truth of the matter is, he keeps a harem at his country estate."

Guffaws and mutterings of disbelief came from the other gentlemen.

Keeble tugged self-consciously at the brown curls combed over his balding pate. "It's true. Chasebourne said so himself. Didn't he, Ducks?"

The Honorable James Duxbury vigorously nodded, his blue eyes avid in his baby face. "He is quite the irredeemable rogue. Not that we would ever speak ill of our host, of course."

"How wise of you," said the lady in green. "Especially since Chasebourne is standing right over there, eavesdropping." She snapped her fan shut and used it to point at him.

As one, her covey of admirers pivoted to stare at Ethan. But he took only peripheral notice of them. It was the woman who captivated him. She pinned him with her sharp blue-gray eyes.

Jane's eyes.

Impossible.

Stupefied, he posed like a statue amid the fern leaves. She couldn't be Jane. Where was the knot of scraped-back hair? The high, choking collar? The sallow skin and dreary black gown?

Where was his starched and disapproving spinster?

It was as if a sorcerer's spell veiled the two of them. He could hear the thrum of his pulsebeat, the muted murmurings beyond the bubble of silence enclosing him. In the candlelight, her mouth looked red and inviting. Her cheeks glowed and her hair curled attractively around her face. The expanse of creamy neck lured his gaze downward past her gold locket to her breasts. Her smooth and seductive breasts. He felt the urge to fondle them, to see if they were as soft as they appeared. To his horror, he felt the stirring of desire.

And he was lurking behind the fern, gaping at her like a besotted mooncalf.

He forced a casual grin, pushed aside the clinging leaves, and strolled toward the group. "Keeble. Duxbury. I see you are among the first to meet my houseguest."

"Miss Mayhew is the essence of innocence," gushed Keeble, clapping a beringed hand to his broad, brocaded waistcoat. "She is a true original."

"The paragon of perfection," added Duxbury, standing beside her and ogling her bosom.

Ethan fought the impulse to knock their fool heads together. Didn't they know this was only prim and proper Jane? "Well, Miss Mayhew," he said. "It seems you should be congratulated on *your* harem."

She made no reply. She merely spread her fan and peeked over the green-tinted feathers like a courtesan tempting him to come hither. The blue-gray of her eyes held mysterious depths, and Ethan had the mad urge to drag her into a deserted room and discover all her secrets.

Ridiculous. Jane had no secrets. His mother had created a masterful hoax, that was all.

Keeble cupped his hand to his ear. "Hark! I hear the musicians tuning their instruments for the first set. You promised me the opening dance, Miss Mayhew."

Ethan shouldered past the other men. "As her host, I'll do the honors."

Jane neatly sidestepped him and tucked her hand in the crook of Keeble's arm. As she did so, Ethan caught a whiff of her elusive fragrance. "I'm so sorry, Lord Chasebourne. I've promised every dance until nearly midnight, but I'll be happy to accommodate you then." She paused, studying him from behind the veil of her lashes. "In the meanwhile, I'm sure you'll have no trouble choosing a partner from *your* harem."

Chuckles swept the gathering. Ethan bared his teeth in a grin, but inside he seethed. He watched Jane and Keeble walk away, a preposterous pair if ever he saw one. She stood half a head taller than the viscount, despite his high-heeled shoes and fluffy curls. She was as slender as he was stout, as innocent as he was depraved.

The other men went in search of dance partners, leaving Ethan to his ill-humored thoughts. Jane had no inkling of what she was doing, encouraging that scoundrel. For all her intelligence, she had grown up in the country and didn't know the ways of men. Given half a chance, Keeble would lure her into a darkened room and plunge his hands up her skirts.

Ethan had envisioned performing that very action himself, but he discounted it. Certainly he'd felt an instinctual urge, the primitive response of male to female. However, he had the good sense not to act on his impulses—at least not all of them. He chose his women for their experience and worldliness. He had never preyed upon a maiden, even if she was six-and-twenty years old and in want of a thorough kissing.

He shut off another unbidden fantasy. Kissing, indeed. Jane would likely bite off his tongue.

"Ethan, darling. I've been searching all over for you."

A blond woman glided up to him, pressing her cushiony bosom to his arm.

He frowned blankly at her before memory oozed into him. The house party. The drinking. He had awakened with a throbbing headache to find her snuggled up to him the morning Jane had come storming into his bedchamber. "Ah, Claudette."

"Claudia," she corrected with a playful slap on his wrist. "Surely you haven't forgotten our night together." She pouted, tilting her head and thrusting out her lower lip. "*I* haven't forgotten how quickly you sent me packing. I am beginning to believe you didn't mean what you said before I left."

"Said?" He glanced at Jane and Keeble, making sure he could still see them among the dancers.

"About calling on me, you naughty boy." She wriggled closer to him, whispering, "My bed has been ever so cold lately."

Her antics left him cold, an odd circumstance considering he usually relished a woman of her frank sensuality. Tonight she was an annoying distraction from his duty to guard Jane.

Yes. He mustn't let Jane make a fool of herself.

He was about to make his excuses when he realized Claudia would enable him to keep a better watch. Carrying her dainty gloved hand to his lips, he kissed the back and then smiled his most charming smile. "Forgive me for neglecting you," he said. "Would you care to dance?"

He had lost no time in finding a partner.

From her position down the row of dancers, Jane surreptitiously eyed Ethan, his broad-shouldered form elegant in dark blue and silver. He squired a blond woman who looked familiar to Jane, but it took a moment to determine why. Then recognition slapped her so hard she felt the sting of heat in her cheeks.

Wessex. His bedchamber. The morning she had gone to challenge him about Marianne.

A hot resentment knotted Jane's belly. Now he was escorting his strumpet in full view of the *ton*. No wonder he had a rotten reputation.

". . . Miss Mayhew."

As the intricate pattern of the country dance brought her closer to Lord Keeble, she realized he was addressing her, a slight frown on his pasty face. "I beg your pardon, my lord," she said. "I was concentrating on the steps."

"I merely commented on how beautifully you dance. You move like an angel borne along by gently beating wings."

His gushing compliment was so ridiculous that she almost laughed in his face. He surely had noticed that she'd made a few missteps. "Thank you. But you would be advised to watch your toes."

He took several little mincing hops around her in accordance with the dance. "How droll you are. I vow, Chasebourne is a rogue for keeping you hidden in Wessex, away from the rest of us gentlemen."

"Hidden? What nonsense. You make me sound like one of his harem."

"Pray forgive me, I do not mean offense. I only wondered how long you have known him."

"We are neighbors, and our mothers were friends many years ago. That is our sole connection."

Keeble's thick lips turned down in disappointment. "I was so hoping you could tell me something delicious. Have you ever before been to one of Chasebourne's house parties?"

"Never."

"Tell me," he said, motioning her closer. "Did you ever meet his former wife? The Lady Portia—who is no lady, I hear."

"I . . ."

To Jane's relief, the dance pattern separated them for a

few moments. The last thing she wanted was to discuss. Lady Portia. It would be difficult enough to lure Ethan out into the garden.

And she could never share her private memories of Ethan and their awkward, exhilarating past. No one knew that as an adolescent, she had fallen madly in love with the boy who'd poked fun at her bookishness. Certainly not Ethan. She would hug that secret to her heart forever.

Pierced by poignant longing, she stole a glance down the line of dancers. Ethan was chatting with his partner, his face alive with a charm he hadn't shown to Jane. Then he looked in her direction and his smile vanished.

If anything, her transformation appeared to have annoyed him.

The knot inside her tightened. She had waited in the ballroom, impatient for his duty in the receiving line to be ended. Other gentlemen had obtained an introduction to her, and she had been pleasantly surprised by their regard. She had behaved as Lady Rosalind suggested, and let them do most of the talking, but for all Jane's enjoyment in the novelty of popularity, she longed for one man in particular to admire her.

Her hopes had soared when she'd spotted Ethan peering at her from across the ballroom, making his way toward her, listening to their conversation. There had been a gleam of appreciation in his dark gaze that she'd never before seen. Something hot and wicked, something that had set her heart to beating faster.

Then he'd recognized her. The light had vanished from his eyes, leaving them flat and stony. . . .

Lord Keeble bowed before her. She blinked at his balding pate, and realized the dance had ended. He kissed her hand a bit too fervently and said, "I am honored that you chose me for your first dance, Jane. *May* I call you Jane?"

She politely extracted her fingers and glanced over his shoulder, but Ethan was lost in the crowd. "If you like."

"I feel as if we've known each other forever. Perhaps

you won't think it too forward of me to ask if you would take a stroll? Chasebourne's house is magnificent. I should like to see more of it.''

His attention should be flattering. Yet there was something avid to his expression that made her skin crawl. ''Thank you, my lord, but I see the Honorable Mr. Duxbury approaching. I've promised the next dance to him.''

Lord Keeble grumbled, but he handed her over to his dandified friend, who turned out to be not quite so honorable as his appellation. Duxbury spent the first half of the dance trying to peer down her bodice. He spent the second half hobbling when Jane deliberately trod on his toes. Nonetheless, he too asked her to escort him on a private tour of the mansion.

The leer on his round baby face scandalized her. Did these gentlemen believe her immoral simply because she was a guest in Lord Chasebourne's house? Was everyone associated with Ethan tainted by his debauchery?

She hoped not, for Marianne's sake.

Jane's fears were allayed when she danced with a steady stream of gentlemen who treated her with respect. She marveled at their attentiveness, and began to believe she was more than just a curiosity, that they truly *did* find her pretty and charming. For the first time in her life, she felt the power of her own femininity. She relaxed enough to flirt a little, to ply her fan and trade witticisms.

Yet always she was aware of Ethan fending off a barrage of beautiful ladies. Several times she caught him glancing at her, but it must have been just a coincidence. He had no interest in her, none at all.

Well, she refused to let him spoil her magical evening. In between sets, she drank champagne, enjoying the burst of sparkling bubbles against her tongue. She seldom consumed wine, and it made her giddy and reckless, ready to practice her womanly wiles on a succession of suitors, gangly and short, stout and lean, gregarious and shy. She spied her aunt once, sitting in a corner with the other matrons and spinsters, and Jane felt a rush of unfettered joy to be out on the dance floor, moving to the music and in the company of an admirer.

As the night wore on, however, she discovered a drawback to the fine art of listening—more often than not, her partners were crashing bores. She had just rid herself of her latest, a paunchy baron who had droned on about his pack of hunting hounds, and lifted another glass of champagne to her lips, when someone plucked it out of her hand.

Heat prickled her skin. Even before she turned, she knew his identity. She caught his unique aroma, something dark, disturbing to the senses.

Ethan.

He glowered at her. "You've had quite enough to drink already."

"Give that back to me."

"No." He placed the glass on the silver tray of a passing footman. "I won't let you stumble around and make a fool of yourself."

Jane didn't tell him the ballroom was spinning already, forcing her to focus on his sinfully handsome face. Perhaps he was right about the champagne. That had to be why she felt so suddenly light-headed. Only a ninny would hope for his love; only a wanton would feel this flush of yearning.

"If you've come to scold me, then go away," she said. "I can find more pleasant company elsewhere."

"I'm sure you can," he said with a wry grimace. "But you promised me a dance."

She blinked, jolted by an unwelcome memory. She had made that promise so that she could fulfill her obligation to Lady Portia. Yet Jane felt an intense aversion to handing him over to another woman. Especially a woman he had once adored. . . . "Is it midnight already?"

"Nearly." He took a step closer, bending his head so that he could speak low into her ear. "Is that when the beautiful princess turns back into Cinderella?"

Beautiful. Was he saying . . . he found her *beautiful*?

Foolish longing spiraled in her breast. "That's how the story goes," she said, trying to read his obsidian eyes. "If one can believe in fairy tales."

. "Which you do not." He patted her gloved hand as he might stroke a favorite dog. "You're still my practical Jane. Not the sort of woman to let a few men turn your head." He looked at her questioningly, as if waiting for her to confirm his statement.

That hint of uncertainty in him exhilarated her. So he was not so sure of her, after all. Ever since childhood, he had always seemed confident, all-knowing, so much more sophisticated than she. Was it possible she held the upper hand over him tonight?

"The music is beginning," she said. "Shall we join the dancers?"

"Answer my question."

"Did you ask me something?"

"You've been flirting tonight. But these men don't really know you as I do. They don't know you're only playacting, behaving according to my mother's instructions."

"Oh?" she asked, giving him her most demure smile. "Perhaps this *is* the real me, sprung like a butterfly from my cocoon." She twirled in front of him, enjoying the flutter of silk against her skin, rejoicing in the way he glanced down the length of her. Did he appreciate what he saw?

He clenched his jaw. "Stop it, Jane. This isn't you."

"Others don't share your opinion. In fact, several of my admirers have requested permission to call on me. Now, we mustn't dally, or we'll miss this set." In a fit of daring, she started toward the dance floor, praying he would follow her. She would die if he did not. . . .

To her delight, Ethan stalked at her heels. His features looked grim and suspicious, as if he could not quite fathom the change in her.

She liked catching him off guard. It gave her a kind of power over him, a feminine allure that she was only just beginning to understand. So what if her behavior was merely a role? It would do him well to wonder.

As they reached the other dancers, she recognized the music and saw couples gathering. Disappointment pricked her high spirits. "It's a waltz. I'm afraid our dance will have to wait until later." Except there wouldn't be a *later.* In a few moments she would be obliged to lure him out to the garden. She would give him over to another woman.

"Devil take that silly rule," he said. "You're as old as I am, and you ought to be able to dance whenever you like."

"But Lady Rosalind said—"

"Live dangerously. Isn't that your motto tonight?"

With one hand, he caught hers; he clamped his other hand around her waist and propelled her into the throng of dancers. Surprised, she clutched at him. For a moment she could not think, could do nothing but let him guide her along, twirling around and around, her spirits soaring from an onslaught of pure joy.

She was dancing with Ethan. He held her in his arms, perhaps not as close as in her dreams, yet with a possessiveness that thrilled her. She liked the feel of his hand, big and strong, gripping hers. She liked the intimacy of his other hand resting at her waist. The heat of it spread a wonderful tingling through her breasts and down into her lower regions. Oh, she did feel wicked!

She caught flashes of the onlookers. People stared and whispered. Lady Rosalind smiled from the edge of the crowd while His Grace of Kellisham frowned at her side. A reckless pleasure filled Jane. She was waltzing with a renowned rogue. In full view of the *ton,* she was committing a scandal, and she didn't care what anyone thought.

Except Ethan. She cared intensely what *he* thought.

She focused her giddy attention on his face and saw his mouth quirked into that devilish grin. "Enjoying yourself, Miss Maypole?"

She threw back her head and laughed. "Yes, I am."

"No doubt the other guests are talking about us."

"Let them."

"My, you *are* daring tonight." He glanced moodily at her mouth. "Have a care. The wrong man might misconstrue your nature."

"How so?"

"He might think you willing to do his bidding."

His deep voice rasped across Jane's senses. Beneath her hand, his arm muscles shifted with the movements of the dance, and more than anything, she wanted to close the gap between them, to press herself to his hard body. "Fie, my lord. I do no man's bidding. I please only myself."

"And what pleases you, Jane?"

You. Only you. She caught herself in time, remembering to be mysterious. "Shame on you for asking such an impertinent question. But I'll answer it anyway. Moonlight on a lake. A roomful of exotic orchids. Silk against my skin."

He frowned as if displeased by her answer. "You've never been the frivolous sort. What do you hope to gain by this masquerade tonight?"

"Must I have a purpose? Other than pleasure, of course." She formed her mouth into a half-smile, the way she'd seen his women do. "Besides, *you* are the only one who thinks it a masquerade."

"I am also the only one who knows you'd rather read a book of sermons than snare a noble husband."

"Perhaps my tastes have changed."

"It's best they don't. Forgive me for being blunt, but you lack a dowry. The moment these vultures discover the truth, they'll fly off to a more lucrative prospect."

She didn't care. None of them mattered to her. Only this man. The one man who made her heart spin out of control.

The one man she could never have.

That was why she meant to savor this moment. She could remember it later, alone in her bed. She could treasure it, like a miser with his hoard of gold.

Her senses reeled from the constant twirling, from the nearness of him. *Ethan.* She closed her eyes and saw brilliant specks cavort against her lids. His tautly muscled arms flexed beneath her fingers. The world swam around and around and around. . . .

Cool air tickled her face. The music faded into the distance. The twirling slowed and ceased, though she could still feel his hands firmly holding her, spanning her waist.

Opening her eyes, Jane blinked. She stood with Ethan on the balcony outside the ballroom, close to the stone balustrade. The moon showered silvery light over his black hair, and shadows veiled his face.

"Are you all right?" he asked. "You looked as if you were about to swoon in there."

She felt like swooning now. His thighs pressed lightly against hers, and she longed to be one of those shallow women who inspired tenderness in a man, a seductress who knew how to entice him into a kiss. If only she dared tell him how much he meant to her, how much he'd always meant.

The effects of the champagne clouded her reason. Emboldened, she leaned into him, and his arm moved up to support her shoulders.

"Are you dizzy?" he asked. "Perhaps you should sit."

"Mmmm."

Her breasts brushed his chest. It was an incredibly carnal feeling, and like a cat, she wanted to rub herself against him. Her legs felt as limp as wilted flowers. She stood so close she could see his features in the darkness, the cheekbones she longed to trace with her fingertip, the eyes that watched her with hooded intensity, the mouth she longed to taste.

She sensed an awareness in him, a charge of energy as searing as a lightning bolt. "Jane?" He cupped her cheek in his big hand. His lips parted slightly, and he tilted his head at a watchful angle. Did he realize she was a woman now?

She ached to show him all the feelings kept locked too long inside herself. She wanted him to kiss her, wanted it with all her heart. And for a fleeting moment she thought that he might. The warmth of his breath mingled with hers, and the air seemed wrapped in magic. . . .

From somewhere inside the house a sound intruded from an opened window. The sonorous bongs of a clock.

The rhythmic noise shattered the trance surrounding Jane. With a gasp of dismay, she jerked herself backward, out of his arms.

Midnight.

The witching hour.

It was time for Cinderella to give away her prince.

Chapter 10

Ethan gulped in the chilly night air. Though she had moved away, he could still feel the heat of her body burning him. He could still feel the pressure of his own arousal. What madness had come over him?

This was *Jane*.

Jane Mayhew, repressed spinster.

Miss Maypole of the disapproving sneers and critical commentary.

It was insanity to desire her. Yes, she had thrown herself into his arms, but she had drunk too much champagne to realize what she was doing. That was why he'd brought her out here, half swooning, before anyone else noticed she was melting in his arms. He had never intended to take advantage of her inebriated state.

Yet if she hadn't pulled back, he would have kissed her. The realization galled him. He would have kissed Jane because she intrigued him, because he *wanted* her. Madness. He must be desperate; he hadn't bedded a woman in the fortnight since Jane had come marching into his chamber, on a mission to prove him a father.

Tonight, she didn't look at all like that prim old maid.

She stood at the stone railing, peering down into the darkened garden. Moonlight glowed on the curvy white expanse of her bosom, and he couldn't help staring again. He had always believed her flat-chested, sexless beneath the loose gowns she wore. But Jane had enough there to tempt a man. What other assets did she hide?

She leaned farther out, still gazing downward, like a moon maiden enthralled with the earth below. Spurred by fear, he caught her by the waist and hauled her back onto the balcony. "What the bloody hell are you doing?" he snapped. "You'll fall to your death."

"I was holding on to the railing." She giggled with un-Jane-like abandon. "Now I'm holding on to you."

She clutched at his coat, and again he was aware of her body, soft and pliant in his arms, ready and willing to be coaxed to his command. It was a novelty to hold a woman who was nearly as tall as he, his equal match. "We should go back inside," he said.

"Not yet." She groped for the fan dangling from her wrist, opened it, and peered at him over the feathers. "I'm really rather warm. And dizzy, too. Will you walk with me down in the garden?"

He shouldn't do it. He should escort Jane to her aunt. Wilhelmina would see to it that Jane behaved.

But another man might ask her to dance. Another man might lure her out to the garden and take advantage of her. A man of lesser willpower than Ethan.

"Come along, then." He guided her to the narrow stone staircase that led down to the ground floor. She clung to him, proving that her senses still reeled from the champagne. Afraid that she might tumble down the steps, he slid his arm around her waist as they descended to the garden. She had a strong, slim body that made him think of long, athletic sessions in bed.

Devil take it. He too must have drunk an inordinate amount of champagne, though a few glasses had never before troubled him.

Strings of lanterns lit the trees. Several other couples strolled the flagstone pathways, and the murmur of their voices blended with the distant music. He could smell the sweetness of roses carried by the breeze . . . or was it Jane's scent? He wanted to put his face to her bosom and breathe deeply.

Desperate for a diversion, he touched her locket, careful to avoid her warm skin. "This is a pretty piece."

"It was my mother's," Jane said, a melancholy note entering her voice. She reached up to clasp the locket, her fingers brushing his. "It's my most prized possession. I wear it all the time—though it was always hidden beneath my dress before tonight."

He wished to God she still had on that shapeless sack, buttoned to her chin. "You'll want to sit down," he repeated, steering her toward a bench in the shadows. "You must be weary from all the dancing."

"No!" she burst out. Then she whispered, "I mean, I would prefer to walk. In the country, I'm accustomed to walking for hours."

Her vehemence surprised him. Stranger still, she peered around the garden as if curious about the other couples. She wasn't a gossip, so why did she care who was out here? Did she worry about who saw her in the company of a seasoned rake? She ought to.

"As you wish," he said. "But we mustn't stay away for too long, lest people comment on our absence."

"I never knew you to fret over what others think."

"I'm not concerned about myself. It's you who need take care. Once a woman loses her good reputation, it can never be retrieved."

"While the man goes on his merry way."

"Precisely." Her words cheered him. This was his thorny Jane, the comfortable Jane he knew so well. "Let me give you a word of warning," he added. "You should stay away from men like me. Don't go walking in dark gardens with any of your dance partners. Especially not Keeble or Duxbury. They'll take advantage of you in a flash."

"But I'm perfectly safe with you." Sounding almost forlorn, Jane leaned closer to him, or perhaps he only grew more aware of her soft bosom pressing lightly against his arm. "*You* would never take unfair advantage of me."

"Of course not," he said, too quickly.

"Lower your voice," she murmured. She glanced around the garden, as if trying to make out the faces of the other strolling guests. "You don't want everyone to hear the truth."

"The truth?"

His fingers rested on the tender inner flesh of her arm, and she laid her gloved hand over his. She had a firm hand, well shaped and slender. "The truth, Ethan, is that you are not completely lacking in honor."

He stopped in the shadows, bringing her to a halt. She couldn't know how dishonorable his thoughts were right now. "Can I trust my ears?" he said. "Is that praise coming from Jane Mayhew?"

"Yes. I believe there is a core of goodness in you, a goodness you hide from the world. Remember all those days you sat and talked with old Yarborough, the gamekeeper, keeping him company after he'd been laid abed?"

"It was my duty. He'd been shot by a poacher on my father's estate. *My* estate."

"But Yarborough was only a servant, an employee." She nodded as if agreeing with herself. "Yes, the more I think on it, the more I believe you have a kind heart. Why else would you be standing here in the garden with me when you could be dancing with one of your women?"

With a shock, Ethan realized he would much rather be strolling these dark pathways with Jane, basking in her approval, than conducting yet another flirtation with a jaded coquette. Had his life grown so boring that he preferred the company of a nettlesome rustic? "Kindness has nothing to do with me bringing you out here," he denied. "You drank too much, and I won't see you make a goose of yourself in front of all my guests."

"Nevertheless, behind all your bluster and flirting,

you're a generous man. I believe you would always help a woman in need.''

He frowned, trying to make sense of her adulation. "Are you in need of funds, Jane? Is that what this is all about? Just say the word, and I would be happy to arrange a loan for you."

"No! I was merely making a general statement about your character." She sounded insulted, then went on in a rush, "You must try harder to demonstrate your goodness to people. You must take every opportunity to show that you have an unselfish, charitable side to your nature. Promise me that."

He found himself dangerously pleased by her favor. It had to be the champagne talking, he told himself. Either that, or . . .

He realized where they stood—in the same arbor where they had played with Marianne a week ago. Suspicious, he drew Jane deeper into the shadows and forcibly sat her down beside him on a stone bench.

"Marianne is the cause," he said. "This is another of your attempts to make me acknowledge her."

"No, you misunderstand. . . ." Jane blew out a breath and fell silent, staring intently into the garden. Most of the guests had returned to the ballroom for the supper dance. Ethan knew he would have to escort Jane back very soon. But not yet. Not until he had straightened out her tangled opinion of him.

"I don't misunderstand," he said, gathering her hands in his. "Jane, it's admirable of you to watch over Marianne's welfare. But I've already promised that I'll care for her. I'll do it even if we can never prove for certain that she is my daughter."

He surprised himself with the admission. Yet when he thought of the baby, smiling and gurgling, reaching for her rattle, he felt a clutch of tenderness in his chest, and he wondered if he might not enjoy having a family of his own, children who adored him, a wife to love him.

Addlepated nonsense. Wives were either frivolous like his mother or deceitful like Portia. All in all, they were manipulative creatures who seduced a man's heart, then squeezed him dry.

"You *are* Marianne's father," Jane asserted, her fingers pressing his. "We may very well prove that when we interview Lady Greeley."

"Perhaps." Clenching his jaw, he thought of Lady Serena Badrick. The dowager Viscountess Greeley had lived up—or rather *down*—to her reputation as a famous beauty and an infamous slut. She had been one of his few mistakes, a tigress both in bed and out. And far too possessive for his tastes. He had barely escaped with his manly parts intact. "It's strange that she hasn't come to town yet," he mused aloud. "If she delays much longer, I'll have to visit her in Hampshire."

"*We*'ll visit her," Jane stated. "You aren't going without me."

Her zeal nudged a smile from him. Perhaps *she* was the tigress, defending her cub. Would Jane be so passionate between the sheets?

Disturbed by the thought, he forced himself to concentrate on the distant strains of music. "The supper dance will be drawing to a close. In a short while, I must be present for the announcement of Mother's betrothal."

Ethan started to rise, to offer his assistance, but Jane grasped his arm and clung tightly, drawing him back down onto the bench. "Not yet," she said. "Please, I'm still feeling faint. I *can't* face all those people and that stuffy ballroom quite yet. Let's stay here for a little while longer."

She sounded so desperate that he frowned at her. "You aren't going to retch like you did that time on the lake, are you?"

"The lake?"

"On my estate." How could she not remember? "You rowed the dingy out to the island so that you could spy on me and—whoever I was with."

"Harriet Hulbert."

"Yes, her." He'd been fifteen, about to taste a bosom the size of a cow's udder, when Jane had come marching up to chastise him for luring the butcher's daughter into sin. Harriet had gone off squealing, rowing herself back to shore, leaving him to return in Jane's boat. During their quarrel, a storm had blown up, and they'd ended up navigating into a hard wind. Jane had turned pea-green, heaving her guts over the side of the dingy. "You're sure you won't be ill now."

"No. No, I'm just not . . . feeling quite myself."

"Then we'll sit here until you feel better."

She put her hand to her brow as if she were about to swoon. It seemed utterly right for him to place his arm around her back and offer his support. Utterly natural for Jane to cuddle closer and tilt her head against him. Her curls brushed the underside of his jaw. She smelled as fragrant as the roses twining the arbor that arched overhead. He felt a profound awareness of her that he told himself was concern for her well-being. The link between them had been forged in childhood, after all, and it alarmed him to see a weakness in Jane. But then, she'd shown him a lot of surprises tonight.

Her cheek cradled on his shoulder, she looked up at him. "This is something you've surely done many times before."

"What is?"

"Sitting in the moonlight, your arm around a woman." She lowered her voice so that he had to bend closer to hear. "But it's my very first time."

Her admission stunned him even as it filled him with a strangely tender exultation. He made a jest out of it. "What, no trysts in the hayrick with a stable lad?"

"Not a one. It's strange to realize that we grew up near the same village, yet you've had so many more experiences than me."

He shifted, uneasy with the wistful envy in her tone. If

only she knew all his regrets, the darkness that lurked inside him. "Believe me, you're better off keeping your innocence."

"Am I?" She lowered her lashes slightly, running her fingertip over one of the silver buttons on his coat. "There's something I never told you. Those times when I saw you kissing other girls, I thought . . ."

"You thought you had the right to be my conscience." He chuckled, determined to make light of her reminiscences. "No doubt you thought you were saving me from being damned to hell."

"No, that wasn't it. That wasn't it at *all*." Jane took a deep breath, her bosom brushing his chest. "I was jealous because . . . because *I* wanted to be kissed, too. I wanted to know what it felt like to be held and touched and loved."

He could not have been more shocked if she'd told him she'd lost her virginity in a flaming affair with the Prince Regent. "You can't mean that."

"I *do*. And even though I'm old enough now that it shouldn't matter anymore, it still does. Nothing has changed. I still feel that same ache inside myself. I still want to *know*."

Her voice rang with emotion, and she had a dreamy moonlit yearning on her face. An irresistible innocence that called to him. An innocence he should leave untouched.

Jane had felt physical lust. The knowledge quaked through him, realigning his opinions and completing her metamorphosis into flesh-and-blood woman. While he had mocked her for her bookishness, pitied her as a passionless virago, she had experienced the same bodily desires as any other young woman. She had kept those desires hidden within an unattractive façade—much as he had concealed his darkness behind a mask of charm. They were alike, both of them, reluctant to reveal themselves to the world.

But Jane had revealed herself to him now, and the insight into her vulnerability touched him deeply.

His gaze fell to her lips, lush and inviting in the darkness.

He could satisfy her curiosity. He could give her this one experience. Certainly it was better that he do so than allow her to seek out another man. God help her if she chose an unprincipled rogue like Keeble or Duxbury.

She sat up straight and turned her head downward, while her fingers plucked at the feathers of the fan in her lap. "I shouldn't have told you all that," she whispered. "I—I don't know what came over me."

He caught her cheeks in his hands and angled her face up to him. "Don't be ashamed of your honesty," he said roughly. "Don't apologize for feelings that are perfectly natural, either."

She shook her head, her eyes dark and troubled in the moonlight. "Please. I've said enough on the matter. I should like to stroll again—"

"Hush. First, let me see to your education." With that, he brought his mouth down on hers.

Her lips were soft, far softer than he had imagined. The rest of her body remained stiff, unyielding. She clutched awkwardly at his coat, and he feared for a moment she would push him away. His prickly Jane. With tender amusement, he brushed his mouth back and forth in a coaxing movement. His fingers stroked the curls of her hair in a beguiling pattern. All of a sudden, she uttered a sweet little moan and relaxed into him, her breasts pressing against his chest, her arms reaching up to encircle his neck.

He had meant to end it there, with one modest kiss, enough to satisfy her need for knowledge. But when she cuddled closer to him, he could not resist sliding his arms around her willowy form; he could not stop himself from tracing his tongue along the seam of her lips. She tasted of champagne. And she felt like a dream.

This could not be his Jane. And yet she *was* Jane. She showed a shy, untutored enthusiasm for his embrace, combing her fingers into his hair, moving her body against him. She felt slim and lithe to his touch, all warm, willing woman.

When he probed with his tongue, she let him into her mouth with a surprised gasp that he found both endearing and exhilarating. Her naïveté awakened a craving within him that burned harder and faster, a dark fire that knew no bounds. It was more than the simple lust he'd felt for other women, for his response to Jane was tangled with his memories of the girl he'd once known and the woman he had only just realized she had become.

She made small kittenish sounds in her throat, and he moved his mouth across the smooth skin of her cheek, relishing the softness of her, intrigued by her secrets. What had started out an act of benevolence had ripened into the richness of passion, a passion that delved far deeper than the needs of the flesh. Swept by hunger, he slid his hands over her body, seeking her sinuous curves. He touched her breasts, letting the back of his hand slide over soft hills and mysterious valley. But when he found himself reaching for the buttons at the back of her gown, sanity struck awareness into him.

The garden enclosed them in silence. The golden windows of the ballroom glowed through the darkness. The music had ceased, and his guests would be at supper by now. While their host seduced an innocent in full view of anyone who happened past.

Breathing hard, he gripped her shoulders and pushed her back. "Jane. We must stop."

"No," she murmured, her fingers caressing his face. "Not yet. *Please.*"

The way she was touching him, as if he were infinitely precious to her, made it difficult to speak. He wanted to press her down on the grass and introduce her to intimacy. The temptation of it shook him fully to his senses. "Listen to me. There are people about. Someone could see us."

As if to prove his words, the tap of approaching footsteps sounded on the stone pathway. Jane heard it, too; he could tell by the way she sat bolt upright, her head cocked to listen. "Dear heaven," she said in a strange, strangled tone. "I nearly forgot—"

Ethan put his forefinger over her mouth and shook his head warningly. The shadowy figure of a lone guest moved along the pathway. A woman. She was unaccompanied, perhaps desiring a moment away from the noise of the party. They would wait here in the gloom until she had gone past. Then he would escort Jane back to the ballroom, where she would be safe from him.

Safe from the lust that bedeviled his loins.

Her lips felt soft and damp to his touch, and he snatched back his hand, curling it into a fist. Incredible as it seemed, Jane had roused him to hard, raging need. His response to her must be an aberration, the shock of realizing she had depths he had never before imagined. Despite her transformation, Jane Mayhew was not his type of female. He preferred more worldly women, women who knew how to please a man, not an artless virgin from the country who had waited twenty-six years for her first kiss.

Jane shot to her feet. "Come along, Lord Chasebourne," she said in a clear, ringing voice that must have carried throughout the garden. "I vow I'm weary of sitting here any longer."

Her abrupt manner made him frown. As she sailed out of the arbor, he sprang to his feet and stalked after her. Damn the chit. Was she angry at him for kissing her? She had all but invited her own ravishment, and if she dared to accuse him of mistreating her, he would set her straight posthaste—

His angry thoughts ground to a halt. Jane had walked straight to the guest on the pathway, a foolish move, for it gave witness to the fact that Jane had been out here, unchaperoned, in the company of a rogue. Hadn't he already lectured her tonight on guarding her reputation?

Cursing her impulsiveness, he strode forward, searching for an excuse to explain their presence out here. He would say that she had felt indisposed, that he had merely been lending her aid.

Then the woman drew back the hood of her cloak. All other thoughts fled his mind as his gaze riveted to her moonlit blond hair and familiar features.

Portia.

Innocent, treacherous Jane had lured him out here to meet Portia.

Chapter 11

Clutched by cold misery, Jane stepped back so that Ethan could come face-to-face with his former wife. No longer did he look at Jane with tenderness; his attention was focused on Portia. Like a penitent Mary Magdalene, she stood with her head bowed slightly and her hands folded above her rounded belly, her exquisite features glossed by moonlight.

"How the devil did you get in here?" he said in a hard, icy tone. "Never mind answering that—you always did have a way with the menservants."

"Don't be angry, Ethan, please don't," Portia said in a soft, pleading voice. "You refused to see me, and this was the only way I could arrange a meeting."

"Ah. So this was *arranged*."

He flashed his coal-dark eyes at Jane, and she fought the urge to beg for his understanding. "I think you should listen to her ladyship," she said in an encouraging tone. "She asks only the courtesy of your audience."

"And I suppose this is where I show the unselfish, *charitable* side to my nature."

Jane winced to hear her own words hurled back at her. He knew now that she had been lecturing him, prodding him to help Portia, rather than giving him true praise. She wanted to say that she believed all those things, that hidden somewhere inside his wicked exterior was a worthy man, a man who really did possess a core of honor and goodness.

But was she right? She prayed so, for Portia's sake.

"Return to the ballroom," he said curtly. "Else you'll be missed."

Turning his broad back on Jane, he took Portia by the arm and guided her toward the house.

Jane stood watching as they entered a dimly lit room on the ground floor. They made a stunning couple, Ethan tall and manly beside dainty Portia. So much more glamorous a pair than he and Jane.

She had tricked him into meeting with his former wife. How he must depise her.

A lump formed in her throat, and she wished for all the world that they were back on that stone bench, and he was kissing her again as if she truly mattered to him. Their embrace had surpassed her most romantic dreams. She had not known that pleasure could feel so intense, that she could be so willing to let a man use her as he liked.

But she was fooling herself to think Ethan cared. Like any full-blooded rake, he had given her what she'd begged for. She had been dizzy with wine and moonlight, emboldened by her own alteration. She had felt like another woman, a beautiful woman, and so she had bared her soul to him, revealing her deepest longings. He couldn't be faulted for taking what she had offered to him. Nor could she blame herself. Her desire for him was more than a physical yearning; it had arisen from her unguarded heart.

The cool air chilled Jane to an awareness of her surroundings. Conversation and laughter drifted from the reception rooms above her. She could not brood out here all night. Rubbing her goosefleshed arms, she slowly ascended the stone steps to the balcony.

The evening had lost its enchantment. She no longer felt giddy and bold, only sober and dispirited. She wondered how Ethan would respond to Portia's request for money, and if Portia would throw herself on his mercy. At one

time, he must have felt an affection for her. Did love still
burn beneath his pain and anger?

I shall never make the mistake of marrying again.

He and Portia had shared a depth of experience that Jane
could never fathom. Perhaps he could never love another
woman because his heart still belonged to Portia.

No, Jane told herself. She mustn't speculate on something that was none of her concern. She must entomb her
newfound feelings. She wouldn't act as weak and silly as
other women, pursuing a disreputable rake.

She stepped into the ballroom. With everyone at supper,
the long chamber with its lighted chandeliers resembled a
deserted fairyland. Only a few guests lingered here and
there. Unwilling to attract attention, Jane kept her head
down as she went out the open double doors.

The buzz of convivial voices came from down the corridor. Turning away, she reached the grand staircase and
had mounted two steps when someone hailed her from behind.

"My dear girl! I've been waiting to speak to you."
Looking like a goddess in her gold-embroidered white
gown, Lady Rosalind hastened across the plush blue carpet.
"We're all at supper. Where are you going?"

Jane halted reluctantly. She had no wish to speak to anyone, not when her emotions felt so raw. It took an effort
to force a composed smile. "I need a moment in my chamber," she admitted.

"You do look a bit ruffled." Rather than glower disapprovingly, the countess's blue eyes sparkled as she drew
Jane into an alcove. "Didn't I see you go outside with my
son?"

Jane swallowed. "Yes. We . . . talked in the garden for
a time."

"And? Did he like the way you look tonight?"

"I . . . believe so. He really didn't say."

"Well, you've been missing for quite a long while.
Surely you must have talked about *something*." Lady Ros-

alind paused delicately. "But never mind, I shan't pry. Only tell me, where is he now?"

Jane's palms felt damp inside her gloves. How could she reveal that he had gone off with his former wife? She lowered her gaze. "I—I'm not sure."

"But I must find him," the countess said fretfully. "That's why I was looking for you—both of you. I did so want him to make the announcement about my betrothal. It's to be done at the close of supper, and Kellisham will be furious if Ethan isn't present. Those two don't get on very well."

"Why is that?" Jane asked, hoping to distract her ladyship. "Why does Ethan dislike the duke?"

Lady Rosalind looked away into the distance. "Well, I rather suppose it is because Kellisham is so like Ethan's father." She appeared troubled, as if she doubted her own explanation.

"How so?" Jane prompted.

"Chasebourne—my late husband, I mean—was a rather strict, moralistic man. He could not abide Ethan's high-spirited nature, and he tried to force our son into his own image. I felt it best to keep them apart, and that is why we so often left Ethan in Wessex while we stayed in London."

Jane remembered the old earl as a stodgy, nose-in-the-air aristocrat, the opposite of the blithe Lady Rosalind. "Forgive me for prying, but why *are* you marrying a man just like him, then?"

The countess returned her gaze to Jane and smiled. "Because I love Kellisham, of course." Reaching out, she took Jane's hands in hers. "I see the disbelief on your face, my dear. But we cannot always choose how our hearts are engaged, can we?"

That wise, all-knowing expression shook Jane. Was it possible that Lady Rosalind had guessed the attraction that ached in Jane's heart? Surely not. "I defer to your more experienced judgment, my lady."

The countess patted Jane's hand, then released her. "A

most sensible answer. If you continue to heed my counsel, all will be well, I promise you.'' On that cryptic statement, she added briskly, ''Now, my experienced judgment tells me that you do indeed know where my son is right now.''

''Oh.'' Jane bit her lip, wrestling with the dilemma of pretending ignorance. Then honesty won the battle. ''I suppose you'll find out. He's meeting with Lady Portia.''

Lady Rosalind's mouth dropped open. ''With *Portia*? In this *house*?''

''Yes, my lady.'' Feeling hollow inside, Jane didn't acknowledge her part in orchestrating the tryst. ''She came to beg a few minutes of his time, that's all.''

''What cheek, to invade my party and accost my son!''

The sharpness of Lady Rosalind's tone startled Jane. ''Oh, but she didn't accost him. She is in need of funds, and considering her delicate condition, I think he should help her—''

''My dear, you are very kind-hearted, but you cannot begin to understand how badly that little baggage has misused my son. Where are they?''

''Downstairs. They went in through the door beneath the ballroom.''

''I see. If you will excuse me.'' In an angry rustle of silk, Lady Rosalind marched down the grand staircase.

Leaving Jane to wonder if she had just given Ethan another reason to despise her.

In the library, Ethan settled on the edge of the desk and regarded the woman he had once thought his perfect mate.

The light of a branched candelabrum cast a glow over her delicate features as Portia seated herself in a leather chair and arranged her pale pink skirt, smoothing the silk over her pregnancy and leaning forward slightly to give him a better look at her voluptuous bosom. He was left cold. She had always been proficient at showing herself off to the greatest advantage.

The only daughter of an earl, Lady Portia Lovett had

been spoiled and fun-loving when they had met at a horserace during her first Season. He had been twenty-one, randy, and more keen on widows and whores than courting a milk-and-water miss with no knowledge of the world. That day, however, Lady Portia had lured him into a stable for a kiss. She might have just emerged from the schoolroom, but she already knew how to entice a man. She toyed with him for weeks, teasing him with promises, boldly touching him, brazenly granting him the liberty to caress her, though withholding the ultimate act until he was so out of his mind with lust that he fancied himself half in love. One fateful evening, they were found together by her irate father, and Ethan had not been altogether displeased to be forced into offering marriage.

Only later did he learn she had arranged the discovery. Only later had he had been disillusioned by his unchaste bride.

Now, with soulful blue eyes, she gazed up at him. "Ethan," she said in the melodious voice that meant she wanted something from him. "How forbidding you look tonight. I do apologize for taking you away from your guests. If my situation were not so desperate . . ." She paused, her hands resting on the gentle swell of her belly.

"What is it now? More gaming debts?" Ethan folded his arms and pinned her with a sharp stare. "In case you've forgotten, I am no longer responsible for your notes. You shall have to beg your father for the money."

"My family has forsaken me. Papa could not bear the stigma of a divorced daughter, and he's retired to the country. He hasn't your funds, anyway."

"I'm sorry. But I already granted you an amount that should have kept you in silks for the rest of your misbegotten life."

"You did, and I'm very grateful for that." In the candlelight, she managed to look as ethereal as a saint on her way to the lions. "But now a terrible event has left me penniless. You see, George Smollett has run off with all of my funds.''

Jane had told him so, but hearing it from Portia made Ethan suspect she was twisting the truth, that the money already had been frittered away at the dice table before Smollett had abandoned his plump pigeon for richer game. ''Contact the magistrate, then. Smollett will be apprehended and forced to return the money.''

''But he is gone! Fled to the Continent. He will never be found.''

''That is not my affair.''

''How can you be so unfeeling?'' she asked, her lower lip quivering. ''Please, Ethan, you would never miss five thousand pounds. You are my one, my only hope. I have nowhere else to turn.''

Without awaiting his reply, she rose from the chair and glided toward him, slipping her hands around his waist. Her flowery perfume eddied over him. She leaned closer and rubbed her breasts against his arm, while her fingers tracked down to his groin. Into his ear, she whispered, ''If you help me, darling, I could make it well worth your while.''

Revulsion churned in his stomach. He seized her wrist and pushed her away from him. ''Give up,'' he snapped. ''You can no longer cozen me.''

Her lips pouted in sulky displeasure while she stroked her distended abdomen. ''Does my pregnancy vex you? Do you find it provoking that *you* were never virile enough to get me with child in the four years of our marriage?''

''You never wanted my child. You said it would ruin your figure.'' Feeling more weary than angry, Ethan walked away from her, going to the window of the library, where he could see the garden. Lanterns glittered in the trees, and he found himself scanning the deserted walkways for Jane. *She* wanted his child. Jane would fight him to keep Marianne. She had an innate maternal instinct, and now he saw it as part of the mature woman she had become.

Had that kiss been merely a ruse to keep him outside

until Portia arrived? He had always believed Jane to be forthright and honest in her opinions. But tonight she had shown an utterly different side to her character, and he no longer knew what to think.

"It's Jane Mayhew, then, isn't it?" Portia's voice sounded calculating. "How delicious. You're planning to seduce that dry old spinster."

Her words shook him. He turned to find her standing directly behind him. "You don't know what you're talking about."

"Don't I? What *were* you doing with her in the shadows when I walked up?"

"I was warning her about treacherous women."

Portia laughed knowingly. "Keep your little secret, then. It matters naught to me. However, I would not care to see you use her ill."

"Why? Do you reserve that right for yourself?"

Portia shook her head, all humor vanishing from her face. "She alone has been kind enough to befriend me in my hour of need."

Befriend. Portia had manipulated Jane, played upon her sympathies and told her lies. No doubt Portia had made herself out to be the tragic heroine in a melodrama. Of course, Jane lacked the experience to spot a skilled actress. She possessed a compassionate heart and a willingness to help those whom she perceived to be less fortunate than herself. She had been charmingly earnest in her attempt to make Ethan into a better man than they both knew he was.

I believe you would always help a woman in need . . . you have an unselfish, charitable side to your nature.

"All right, then," he said abruptly. "I will purchase a cottage for you in the country. There, you shall have a safe place to raise your child. That is all I am willing to do for you."

Portia's eyes rounded. "But it is *money* I need. I won't have you dictating where I live."

"If I give you coin, you'll squander it at cards. Take the cottage or nothing."

"I won't be banished to the country. My life is here in London."

"Then so be it. Live on the streets, if you prefer."

She released a huff of fury. Her cloak swirling, she seized a book from a table and hurled it at him. He caught the volume deftly before it could slam into his chest.

"You are a vile man," she said between gritted teeth. "Perhaps I will make certain your Jane knows that."

The cold sword of fear sliced him, and he flung down the book. "You'll leave her out of this, by God—"

Someone rapped on the door. Before he could order the intruder away, the door opened and his mother walked into the library.

Lady Rosalind flashed a glare from him to Portia. "You are not welcome in this house. Leave here at once."

"With pleasure," Portia said. "Believe me, I haven't missed either you or your charming son." Her head held high, she stormed out of the library and slammed the door shut behind her.

"She still thinks she's the queen," Lady Rosalind said, scowling. "The wisest act you ever did was to rid yourself of that harlot."

Ethan was in no humor to discuss his life with his mother. "I'll thank you for not interfering. Now, we should return to the party."

She glided into his path when he would have walked out of the room. "Wait. I saw her condition. She's *enceinte*."

"Don't worry. I'm not the father."

"I didn't suggest you were. But after she denied you an heir for so long, you must be angry—"

"Who told you she denied me anything?" he asked coldly.

"I guessed, that's all. It was obvious you weren't happy, that she had kept you at a distance." Lady Rosalind shook her head, the candlelight playing on her fair hair. "Please don't look so annoyed. I'm concerned about you, that's all. I'm concerned that you'll let your experience with Portia sour you toward marriage.''

He hid his moodiness behind a forced laugh. ''It's a few years too late to prevent that, Mother.''

''Yet you should marry again,'' she persisted. ''All women are not like Portia.''

''Ah, but why should I buy the cow when I can get the milk for free?''

Try as he might, he could not shock his mother—or distract her from her meddling. She merely pursed her lips. ''You have Marianne to consider now, that's why. She needs a mother.''

''Let Jane do the honors, then. She seems to relish the role.''

Lady Rosalind took a step toward him. A determined light shone in her eyes. ''Oh, Ethan. What an excellent notion. Why did I not think of it before?''

''Think of what?''

Smiling, she reached out to grip his arm. ''Why, my dear. Jane would make you the perfect bride.''

⌒ *Chapter 12* ⌒

Jane gazed out the carriage window at a pair of hawks wheeling against the charcoal clouds. Beneath a sky that portended rain, the rolling countryside of Hampshire showed the vivid green of springtime. A pink-blossomed apple tree swayed in the wind, and a clump of buttercups flashed yellow beside a thatched cottage. The rural scene made Jane lonesome for the wild Wessex downs.

She felt even more lonesome for companionship.

In the opposite seat, Aunt Wilhelmina dozed over her knitting. Her white spinster's cap hung askew, and her bosom lifted and fell in rhythm with her light snoring. On the valise beside her lay the ubiquitous silver flask. What did she dream of? Was there a shattered love, a broken heart in her past? She had never spoken of any particular man.

Fingering her locket, Jane saw herself in twoscore years, set in her ways and soured on life, dependent on medicine to quiet her creaky bones. An old maid who looked back nostalgically on the night when she'd been kissed by a dashing rogue.

No. She wouldn't waste her time mooning over Ethan. He wasn't worth the trouble. He had ignored her these past three days, not having the courtesy to respond to her repeated messages.

Yet she found herself watching for his roan gelding along the road. He had ridden ahead, disdaining to travel in the carriage with the women. He had insisted on bringing Aunt Willy on their visit to Lady Greeley. Jane suspected he wanted a buffer so that he would be spared the trouble of talking to her.

Ever since the betrothal ball, when she had maneuvered that meeting with Portia, he had acted cold and distant. Jane felt faintly ashamed of her collusion with his former wife, justified though it was. She felt duty-bound to apologize. But he had spent most of his time closeted in the tower room.

What was he doing up there?

She pictured him entertaining one of his mistresses, perhaps that odious blonde he had danced with at the ball. She had not seen anyone coming or going, but on one of her outings with Marianne in the garden, Jane had noticed a nondescript back door in the ivy-covered wall. A gardener told her it led to the earl's private chambers. Ethan could have any number of women traipsing in and out at all hours of the night.

She had questioned his mother, but Lady Rosalind professed not to know what he had told Portia. The countess had oozed disapproval toward her former daughter-in-law and gushed compliments about her son's heroic qualities. She was understandably loyal, unwilling to acknowledge his faults or to show sympathy toward the woman who had betrayed him.

Yet whatever sins Portia had committed, she deserved a second chance for her baby's sake. Jane's heart clenched at the thought of a helpless infant like Marianne suffering because of her mother's mistake.

A gust of wind spattered raindrops against the window of the carriage. Lightning flickered, followed by the vibrant roll of thunder. As if the heavens had been split open, rain coursed down in a deluge, drumming on the roof.

She heard a muffled shout; then the carriage slowed and

stopped. Aunt Willy muttered restlessly in her sleep while Jane peered out into the gray downpour. Why had they halted? Were the wheels stuck in the mud? Where was Ethan?

She didn't have long to wonder. After a moment, the door swung open and the earl ducked inside.

He brought with him the cold scent of rain and horses. His wet black hair brushed his collar. Water trickled down his face. Before he could wrest the door shut, the wind blew a shower of droplets into the carriage and Wilhelmina awakened with a snort.

"What now?" she sputtered. "Have we arrived at last?"

He peeled off his leather riding gloves and ran his hand through his rain-slick hair. "We've at least an hour's drive ahead of us yet."

"This is the most interminable journey," she said. "And chasing all over the countryside for Marianne's mother. Why, it's scandalous, that's what."

Removing his dripping greatcoat, he scowled at the valise filling the space beside Aunt Willy and then settled himself beside Jane. "Ah, but you make a perfectly respectable chaperone," he said. "And do pardon me for disturbing your nap."

"I wasn't napping. I was knitting a scarf for Jane." Aunt Willy rummaged through the tangle of black yarn in her lap, found the wooden needles, and resumed working, the long sticks clacking rhymically. "Our Wessex winters can be cold and damp. Mark my words, she'll catch a chill and end up with rheumatism like me."

"I don't mind the cold, Aunt," Jane protested, rebelling against elderly complaints. "I'm quite warm-blooded, really I am."

Ethan's gaze flashed over her, swift and hostile as the lightning that seared the dark sky. She realized belatedly that he might put another interpretation on her words.

Instead of a chill, she felt hot all over. Her body burned

with the memory of their fervent embrace. She shouldn't care what he thought of her. But she did.

She was glad she'd worn one of her new frocks, a deep copper silk topped by a fine gold pelisse. It still felt strange and wonderful to be garbed as fashionably as one of his London ladies. Lady Rosalind had disposed of all Jane's old clothing. The dowdy dresses had been taken away by the ragman, and in her heart, Jane didn't mourn the loss. She liked her new appearance, the gowns that swished as she walked, the silk stockings held up by a scrap of lacy garter, the low-cut bodice that made her feel naughty, as if she were flaunting her femininity. Whenever she saw her reflection in the mirror, she had to look twice, unable to believe that polished lady was really her.

Unfortunately, Ethan seemed unaffected by her new image.

"There's an inn a few miles ahead," he said in an abrupt change of subject. "If the storm doesn't abate, we'll stop there for shelter." He turned to stare outside as raindrops sluiced down the window glass.

Lightning lit the unnatural darkness. Jane tried to concentrate on her book of poetry, though she was vividly aware of the man who sat beside her. She could smell his dampness, the leather of his boots, the musk of his cologne. He sat mere inches from her, and she felt the heat radiating from him. She wanted to smooth back the wet locks of hair that curled around his ear. She wanted him to caress her again; she wanted to open her mouth beneath his and let him taste her deeply. . . .

The rain beat down like a voice scolding Jane for her foolishness. It was best to face the truth. Their kiss had meant nothing to him. He was a scoundrel who had seduced scores—nay, *hundreds*—of women. Quite likely, he'd already forgotten his passionate encounter in the garden with a lovelorn spinster.

Gradually, the clacking of needles slowed and ceased. Once again, soft snores emanated from her aunt. This was her chance, Jane thought. Her chance to ask him the questions that had nagged at her.

"What is that you aren't reading?" Ethan drawled.

Startled, she clenched her fingers around the book. "This?" she said, murmuring so that she wouldn't awaken her aunt. "It's a collection of poems by William Blake."

" 'Tyger! Tyger! burning bright.' His verse charms ladies with words so trite."

His irreverent rephrasing almost made her smile. "It isn't hackneyed. Blake writes beautiful verse."

"Then why were you staring everywhere but at the book? Come, admit the truth, it's sentimental pap."

"It's *not*." Jane found herself bristling and took a deep breath. "Ethan, I don't wish to quarrel. There's something more important I have to say."

His gaze did another sweep of her bosom. "If it concerns the night of the ball, I don't want to hear it."

Did he mean Portia? Or the kiss?

Surely Portia.

"I know you're angry that I arranged the meeting with Lady Portia, and I've been wanting to apologize for tricking you."

He flashed her an enigmatic look. "If there's one thing I dislike, it is a meddlesome woman."

She met his gaze squarely. "My cause was just. And I must know. Will you help her?"

"She has refused my offer of aid." He glanced out at the storm. "So there, your conscience may be at ease. You did all you could."

"Refused?" Jane blinked in bewilderment. "I don't understand. Did you offer too paltry a sum?"

"I offered her a cottage in the country. But she wanted five thousand pounds. To pay off her gaming debts."

Jane was shocked into momentary silence. Five *thousand*? She'd had no idea Portia would ask for so staggering an amount. And for gaming debts?

Judging by the way he drummed his fingers on his buckskin breeches, he wasn't telling her everything. "Surely you mean George Smollett's debts. Gambling is a man's sport."

Ethan lifted one eyebrow in cynical amusement. "I see you have not lost your skill at making assumptions."

"Then tell me the whole truth so that I won't have to guess."

"The truth is that some people find betting irresistible, men and women alike. The lure of winning is so strong, they will wager funds they don't possess, the deed to their house, even the food from the mouths of their children."

Jane shuddered to imagine such an obsession. Was that what Lady Portia had done? Had she been too mortified to admit her weakness to Jane? "You gamble, don't you? Yet you don't seem wanting for funds."

"I know when to stop. Self-control is a gambler's greatest asset."

"I've always thought you a man who indulged his urges to excess."

"Indeed so. Though my favorite vice has to do with more fleshly pleasures." His lips cocked in a half-smile as he scanned her again without interest. "And more . . . experienced women."

Sharp as thorns, his ridicule pricked her. Despite Jane's improved appearance, he viewed her as undesirable, a rustic without appeal. "About Lady Portia—"

"You seem fascinated by my former wife."

"I'm worried about her child. Portia cannot have but three months left until her confinement. She will need funds to care for the infant."

He shrugged. "I'll send her enough to get by, then. And not a penny more."

Even as Jane felt thankful for his aid, he reached across the carriage and picked up Aunt Willy's silver flask. He uncorked it and sniffed. Then he tilted his head back and took a deep swallow while Jane stared in surprise at his audacity.

He grimaced, wiping his mouth on the back of his hand. "How can your aunt drink this disgusting stuff?"

"Put that down," Jane said in a biting whisper. "It's her medicine."

"It's brandy mixed with molasses. Along with a dose of opium, I'd hazard." He glanced at her aunt, snoring in the corner, her fingers tangled in her knitting. With a hint of his familiar deviltry, he leaned closer to Jane and whispered, "I fear your aunt is a drunkard."

That suspicion had crossed Jane's mind a time or two, but she wasn't about to admit it. "And you're a rake. We all have our faults."

"Except you, Miss Maypole. How did Duxbury put it? Ah, yes. You are a paragon of perfection."

She ached to see more than humor glinting in his dark eyes; she wished he would pull her into his lap and kiss her giddy. "No one is perfect, Ethan. I've certainly made my share of mistakes."

"Perhaps you have at that."

His gaze flicked over her mouth. Did he regret their kiss in the garden? *She* didn't. Not one glorious moment of it. But better she remember her true purpose, to protect Marianne. "Tell me about Lady Greeley," she said.

Ethan shifted on his seat, stretching out his long legs so that he did not disturb her slumbering aunt. "The rain would have been preferable to this inquisition," he drawled.

"Pardon me for persecuting you. But if Lady Greeley is Marianne's mother, then I ought to learn everything about her."

"So. What gems of insight do you wish to know?"

"How long did your affair with her last?"

"Less than a week."

"Is she the sort of woman who could leave her baby on a stranger's doorstep?"

"Yes."

His unhesitating reply irritated Jane. "Why would you

consort with a lady of such callous, unconscionable nature?''

''Must you ask? Physical attributes mean more to me than moral character.''

He was teasing her, she thought, giving her the answer she expected. Was it only wishful thinking that made her want to see the good in him? ''Why would Lady Greeley not have contacted you directly? Why would she feel that she couldn't turn to you for help?''

''Devil if I know.''

''She left Marianne on *my* doorstep. And with your signet ring. Don't you find that peculiar?''

''Everything about this situation is peculiar.'' He stared down at the embossed ring on his finger, the gold glinting dully in the gray light. ''To be honest, I don't know when she would have taken the ring. I wasn't in the habit of wearing it back then.''

''Where was it kept?''

''In a jewel case in my dressing room. It took a while for me to notice it was missing.''

''Well, then. Lady Greeley must have slipped downstairs to your bedchamber while she was visiting you in the tower room.''

All warmth vanished from his face, leaving his eyes cold and black. ''What do you know about the tower room?''

Her mouth went dry. She riffled the pages of the book in her lap. ''Just that Mrs. Crenshaw said I was not to disturb you there. It's obvious that's where you entertain your women.''

He stared at her for another minute, and Jane had the impression of secrets lurking behind his expressionless features. She waited for him to say that she was mistaken, that he used the room for some innocuous purpose, perhaps as an office for his business affairs.

Turning away, he peered out the window. ''The rain is slowing. If you will excuse me.''

He rapped on the roof to signal the coachman to stop,

then scooped up his greatcoat and gloves and went out the door. Through the rain-streaked window, Jane watched his broad-shouldered form disappear around the rear of the carriage where his horse was tethered.

Aunt Willy awoke again. "Have we arrived, then?" she asked, focusing her bleary eyes outside.

"No, Aunt. Not yet."

"Merciful heaven." Wilhelmina fumbled with her knitting again. "My nerves are quite worn out. If only we could tell the coachman to return us to Wessex, where we belong. How pleasant it would be to settle back into our own cottage."

Jane was used to her aunt's prattling, even welcomed it when they were alone in their cottage with no one else around for miles. But now, she wished for quiet, a chance to think.

The carriage resumed its gently rocking pace. The interior seemed curiously empty without Ethan. Surreptitiously, she slid her hand across the leather cushion, still warm from his body heat. His male scent lingered in the rain-swept air. She felt an aching awareness inside herself, an awareness that was heightened by the memory of their kiss. Despite all her doubts about his character, one truth remained certain.

The rakish Lord Chasebourne fascinated her more than ever.

Badrick Hall looked more like a prison than a mansion. Built of gray stone, the grim façade featured rows of mullioned windows and a turreted roof. With monotonous regularity, rainwater dripped from the downspouts. Smoke drifting from one of the tall chimneys gave the only sign of life.

Ethan was aware of Jane picking a path through the puddles on the graveled drive. He wished to hell she would have stayed at the inn with her grumbling aunt. But Jane never behaved as he bid. She wore an impractical copper silk gown and gold pelisse that brushed her willowy curves—curves that still had the power to astonish him. Her skirt dragged in the mud, and the dampness would have soaked her dainty slippers by now. She ought never to have given up her sturdy half-boots. But he gritted his teeth and kept his opinions to himself.

The problem was, he couldn't look at her without hearing his mother's demented declaration: *Jane would make you the perfect bride.*

Jane, his wife. He would sooner wed an inmate from Newgate Prison.

The mere suggestion of marriage made him want to run in the opposite direction. He couldn't possibly live up to Jane's high expectations—not that he wished to, either. He was a man, not a god. And never again would he make the mistake of devoting himself to one woman.

He mounted the granite steps to the tall front doors, made of thick, studded oak like the portcullis of a castle. His knock caused deep, booming echoes inside the house.

Touching the pitted, discolored stone of a pillar, Jane gave him that determined look that warned him to prepare for another prying question. "Is Lady Greeley married?" she asked.

So, she thought him so vile he would carry on with another man's wife. "Serena is widowed. She lives here with the present viscount, her brother-in-law."

He had time to say no more. The door swung open on creaky hinges, propelled by a white-wigged Adonis in crimson and gold livery.

The footman stood gaping, as if visitors were a rare event. "M'lord?"

"We've come to see her ladyship," Ethan said.

"Lady G-Greeley?" His voice squeaked and he cleared his throat. "You can't . . . that is . . . she isn't . . . er . . ."

"She isn't in London, so she must be here," Ethan said impatiently. Quite likely, Serena was entertaining in her bedchamber, and the footman had orders not to interrupt.

"Tell her Lord Chasebourne requests her presence in the drawing room." He thrust back the door and strode into the entry hall, his footfalls sharp and echoing.

Jane followed him, and he saw her expression of awe as she glanced around at the medieval shields and weaponry decorating the timbered walls. On this cloudy day, with no candles lit, the atmosphere was gloomy. But she didn't seem to notice. With a soft exclamation, she went straight to a broadsword and caressed the engraved hilt. "This must date back to the time of the Conqueror."

She had touched him with the same loving tenderness. To his consternation, he found himself growing jealous of a damned sword.

"We aren't here to do scholarly research." Even as she frowned at him, he turned his back on her and addressed the footman. "Off with you now. Tell your mistress I must see her immediately."

"But . . . but I cannot," the servant said, wringing his white-gloved hands. "What I mean is, m'lord . . . well . . . she isn't here. I shall fetch Lord Greeley, though. Perhaps he'll speak to you." He slid a nervous glance up the broad staircase, and Ethan knew the man was protecting his employer.

He curbed his annoyance. Certainly he could order Adonis to deliver the message, but why give Serena the chance to play cat-and-mouse?

"Never mind," he said. "I know where to find her."

"But m'lord, you can't—"

Ignoring the footman's squawk of protest, Ethan strode up the polished oak staircase, past the first-floor landing with its suit of armor, and then ascended to the floor of bedrooms. The scuffle of Jane's hurrying feet came from behind as she caught up to him. Her scent eddied its freshness through the musty air. Not for the first time, he wondered if her skin smelled so sweet all over.

"That footman was behaving rather strangely, don't you

think?'' she whispered. ''I doubt Lady Greeley is at home.''

''She's here.''

He found the right door at the end of a dimly lit corridor and knocked. There was no answer, so he put his hand on the knob. Jane grabbed his wrist before he could open the door, her strong, gloved fingers curling around his.

''You can't walk in on her,'' she murmured. ''What if she's dressing?''

He thought it far more likely they would find Serena stark naked and cavorting with her latest lover. Not a sight he wanted Jane to witness. ''You're right,'' he said. ''It's best that you wait outside here.''

''And allow you to conduct the questioning?'' She shook her head. ''Absolutely not.''

''Show a little common sense for once. In all likelihood, she's in there with a man.''

''It can't be any worse than finding you in bed with that blond female.''

He shot Jane a withering look, but she didn't wither. With forthright challenge, she held his gaze. Again he felt that peculiar shifting inside himself, the shock of seeing her arrayed so attractively, her hair soft and curling around features that were familiar . . . yet different. But her formidable stare remained that of his childhood nemesis.

She was still prickly Jane beneath her rose-pretty trappings. He must never forget that.

''Have it your way, then,'' he muttered.

He opened the door and entered the darkened boudoir. The curtains were drawn in the bedroom beyond, and it took a moment for his eyes to adjust to the gloomy interior. A familiar heavy aroma of musk pervaded the air, tinged by another, sharper smell. Tobacco smoke?

He was right. She had a man trapped in her lair.

''Serena,'' Ethan called out. ''It's Chasebourne. I need a word with you.''

The darkness swallowed his voice and answered with

silence. Was she asleep? It was late afternoon, but she was known to stay up all night.

Carefully picking his way past shadowy lumps of furniture, Ethan walked through the boudoir and into her bedchamber. Memories crowded him—loathful longings, evil excesses, dark depravities. It made his flesh crawl. He must have been mad to bring Jane in here.

Thrusting his arm out, he pushed her behind him and shielded her with his body. He could see the shape of the massive four-poster in the shadows, but the bed was empty. The coverlet was drawn up to a mound of pillows. Where was Serena?

In the corner of the room, a tiny orange circle glowed like the single eye of a Cyclops. He had an eerie sense of being watched, which he shook off impatiently.

"Who's there?" he snapped. "I won't tolerate any of your games, Serena."

A chair creaked. The pinprick of light moved, and a candle flared to life at the end of a cheroot. The flame illuminated the gaunt, unshaven features of Viscount Greeley.

A powerfully built man, he wore no coat or cravat. His fair hair looked like a rat's nest, and he reeked of whisky. On the table beside him sat a decanter with an inch of dark liquor remaining. A china saucer overflowed with ashes.

Ethan had never liked Edgar Badrick. He was a bully who hit below the belt, a greedy younger son who had coveted his elder brother's possessions, even his widow. He had gained the title upon his brother's death in a hunting accident some five years ago. People had whispered of foul play, but nothing had ever been proven.

"Greeley," Ethan said, acknowledging him with a curt nod. "Where the devil is Serena? I want to ask her a few questions."

Lord Greeley made a harsh sound in his throat. Lounging in a flowered wing chair, he took a deep drag on his cheroot, blowing smoke into the foul air. His eyes glittered like blue diamonds, and one corner of his mouth lifted in a sneer.

"You're a month too late," he said in a gravelly voice, his words a trifle slurred. "Serena is dead."

⌦ *Chapter 13* ⌦

Shocked, Jane stepped out from behind Ethan. There had been no funeral wreath on the door, no crepe bunting on the windows to indicate a house in mourning. Now she understood why the footman had acted so flustered. It was not his place to impart such momentous news.

Ethan stood very still, his keen dark eyes pinned to the other man. "I'm sorry. I read no announcement in the London papers."

Lord Greeley stared back. "I never sent one."

Jane wasn't fooled by Greeley's nonchalance. Instinct told her that a man didn't sit in the dark in his sister-in-law's bedchamber, rumpled and intoxicated, unless he was grieving.

She took a cautious step toward him. "My lord, I realize we're strangers, but you must allow me to express my deepest condolences on your loss."

"Thank you." Lord Greeley's eyes skimmed up and down the length of her. "You look too decent for Chasebourne. Has he stooped to seducing virgins these days?"

"Leave Miss Mayhew out of this," Ethan snapped. "So, how did Serena die? Was it another *accident*?"

Lord Greeley flung his cheroot into the empty grate and rose unsteadily to his feet. "Swine. I ought to call you out for that."

"If you were a decent shot, I'd be tempted to accept. But I prefer a challenge."

"Bloody braggart. Did you think you'd come here and entice Serena with a new game?" Resentment twisting his dissipated features, he glanced cryptically at Jane, then back at Ethan. "Well, she's dead now. Not that you would care. You only wanted her because Randall had her first. Captain Lord John Randall in his fancy red cavalry uniform."

Ethan balled his fingers into fists. A dark and dangerous harshness descended over his face. "You are not fit to utter his name—"

"Stop it!" Jane thrust herself between the two men before they could come to blows. Why was Ethan acting so hostile? And had he really shared mistresses with his friend? The thought of it sickened her. She met his glower with a scowl of her own. "For pity's sake, we aren't here to quarrel." She spun toward their host. "Please, Lord Greeley, don't be offended. Ethan is dismayed by the news, that's all. Do sit down."

Greeley stood, swaying. Then he sank back into the chair and buried his face in his hands, his fingers further tousling his fair hair.

He was the picture of misery, and Jane's heart went out to him. "We don't mean to pry," she said gently. "But could you please bring yourself to tell us about Lady Greeley's death?"

" 'Twas a fever," he mumbled. "She died of a damned fever. A month ago, it was."

Jane bit her lip, striving for a delicate way to phrase the next question. Ethan apparently had no such scruples.

"Was it a lingering childbed fever?" he asked bluntly. "Had she given birth recently?"

Lord Greeley jerked as if he'd been struck. His head shot up to reveal haunted eyes and a stark expression. His reaction pointed at an affirmative response, and Jane held her breath, waiting for him to admit that Lady Serena Badrick had mothered Marianne and left her on a stranger's doorstep.

In a blur of motion, Greeley seized the decanter and smashed it against the table.

Jane flinched as the table toppled under the force of the blow. Shards of glass flew over the carpet. The stench of liquor filled the air.

Leaning forward, his teeth bared in a grimace, Greeley brandished the jagged end of the decanter. "Get out," he snarled. "Get out before I murder the two of you."

Horror clutched at Jane. The wildness in his eyes made her shudder. He meant it. He really meant to kill them.

Her heart beating madly, she tugged at Ethan. She felt resistance in him, the bunching of his muscles, a man's arrogant need to fight back with his fists. "Come," she whispered. "We have to leave."

"Not until that bastard tells me the truth."

"But he won't. You saw to that." As she spoke, she pulled him toward the door. It was like towing an iron statue. Into his ear, she whispered, "There's a better way, I promise you. Just come with me."

He cast her a suspicious glance, then went grudgingly with her out into the corridor. She caught one last glimpse of Lord Greeley staring like a malevolent demon. An instant after she shut the door, there came a thump against the wooden panel and the muffled sound of glass shattering.

Jane recoiled. Greeley must have thrown the remains of the decanter.

"So," Ethan said, hands on his hips in a belligerent stance. "What is this *better way* to determine if Serena is Marianne's mother?"

Jane cast about for an idea. "We'll ask one of the servants. Someone here will know."

She marched down the passageway, and Ethan stalked beside her. "Unless Greeley has sworn his staff to secrecy," he said. "Having your sister-in-law give birth to a bastard isn't something one trumpets in the newspapers."

"Do you have a better plan? Perhaps you think you can pummel the truth out of a grieving man."

"Greeley? Grieving?" He loosed a harsh laugh. "The only thing he mourns is the loss of his whore."

Jane frowned. "His whore?" Then his meaning staggered her, and she stopped to stare at him in the gloomy corridor. "Are you saying . . . he and Lady Greeley . . . ?"

"Yes."

"But . . . you must be mistaken. She was his brother's widow. That would have made them like brother and sister."

"Common decency meant little to Serena. She was worse than any strumpet who walks the streets."

Jane didn't like hearing him denigrate the woman who might have been Marianne's mother. "For shame. You shouldn't speak ill of the dead."

"And you shouldn't leap to the defense of a stranger."

"I'm not defending her actions. But neither will I defame her. After all, you were the one who had an affair with your best friend's mistress—"

He turned suddenly and crowded her against the wall. His body blocked her escape, his arms forming a prison around her, his palms flattened to the wall. "Why is it that you always cast doubt on *my* character? That you always believe *I* must be the villain in the piece?"

She could have escaped had she wanted to do so. He wasn't touching her, only surrounding her with his addictive male presence. With every breath she took in his thrilling scent. She had to concentrate to answer him, and even then, her voice came out sounding appallingly weak. "You must be a villain. You seduce women."

"And women seduce me. It's a mutual process. Even you begged for a kiss from me."

He was a scoundrel for reminding her of that, for what living female could resist that sulky mouth, looming mere inches from hers? "You tempt decent women."

"Not by design." His dark brows lowering, he looked

her up and down. "You see, decent women don't tempt *me*. I prefer the Lady Greeleys of the world."

"Why?" Jane couldn't stop the question that burned inside herself. The question that reared like an insurmountable wall between them. "If you disparage her so much, why do you continue to seek women like her?"

"For pleasure. Pleasure that no *decent* woman can give to me."

"How can you be so sure?" she whispered. "Perhaps you'd be happy if you settled with a good woman."

In the gloom, his eyes took on a predatory glitter. "And perhaps you'll understand better if I tell you about one of Serena's favorite sports. She would pretend to be my captive, hands and feet tied to the bedposts. Like this." Shackling Jane by the wrists, he stretched out her arms against the wall. He leaned closer, his chest lightly pressing hers, making her keenly aware of his hard muscles and heated body. "She liked a man to touch her while she lay helpless to stop him. She liked to feel ravished. What do you say to that, Miss Maypole? Do I shock you?"

Jane couldn't speak; she could only shakily nod her head. She had never dreamed that people engaged in such wickedness. The very notion made her breathless, riveted by the image of lying helpless and spread-eagled while Ethan towered over her, caressing her as he willed. He would lift her nightdress, perhaps touch her bare legs. . . .

With an appalling fierceness, she wanted to allow him that liberty—and more. She wanted to know where he would put his hands and how they would feel moving over her skin. She wanted to know all the details she couldn't begin to imagine.

What other lewd games had he played with Lady Greeley? What carnal pleasures had they shared? Jane gave herself a mental shake. How depraved of her, to envy a dead woman.

Releasing Jane, he stepped back and combed his fingers

through his rain-dampened hair. "I shouldn't have spoken of such private matters."

A wistful yearning flooded her. Slowly she lowered her hands to her sides. "Don't apologize. Perhaps . . . since Captain Randall is gone, *I* could be your friend in his stead."

Ethan stared at her, his gaze a dark blank. Then he let out a humorless laugh. "Hardly. You aren't the type to go drinking and gaming and whoring."

"I only meant that if you needed someone to talk to—"

"I don't. So do us both a favor and cease pestering me." Turning from her, he stalked toward the grand staircase.

His rejection hurt, especially since his touch lingered on her skin, a tingling warmth, a memory to be treasured. Yet it wouldn't do to harbor illusions. He had made it very clear that his tastes ran to strumpets.

Women more experienced than a scholar's daughter who had spent the past six-and-twenty years with her nose in a book.

In her heart, she knew it wasn't too late for her to embrace life. And she *would* change, with or without his approval. If nothing else, she would be a mother to his child.

Clinging to that purpose, Jane followed him down the stairs. The same footman who had opened the front door still lurked in the entrance hall. His white-wigged head peered around the corner of the staircase. The moment he spied them, he drew back, slinking away down a corridor.

Ethan strode after him. "You there. I'll have a word with you."

The footman hunched his shoulders and turned slowly, casting his gaze downward. "I'm sorry, m'lord. I meant no trickery about her ladyship."

"Never mind that. I need some information. I wish to know if Lady Greeley gave birth in the weeks before she died."

The footman shook his head so violently a fine powder

from his wig dusted his crimson coat. "I—I wouldn't know."

"Come now. You must have heard talk in the servants' hall. It would be nigh impossible to hide the pregnancy of the mistress of the house."

" 'Tisn't my place to say, m'lord."

But he knew something; Jane saw it in the guilty shifting of his eyes. "Please help us," she said. "It's vitally important that we learn the truth. We won't tell anyone where we heard it."

He gulped. "But Lord Greeley don't allow us to gossip."

"Perhaps this will help you to overcome your scruples." Ethan reached into his pocket and flipped a gold sovereign at the footman.

Catching the coin in midair, he hesitated another moment, looked furtively around the empty hall, and nodded. " 'Tis as you say, m'lord," he whispered. " 'Twas I who was sent to fetch the midwife."

Jane's heart squeezed taut. "Was the baby a girl?"

He nodded again. "So I heard."

"Where is she now?" Ethan snapped. "Is the infant here? Or did Lady Greeley send her away for fostering?"

Jane leaned closer, her muscles tensed, her mind preparing for the confirmation she dreaded to hear. A part of her resisted finding out for certain that Ethan had fathered Marianne. Because that would make it all the more difficult for Jane to keep the baby herself.

The footman stared in obvious consternation, his Adam's apple bobbing in his throat. Then he made a quick sign of the cross. "Talk is, the baby died, m'lord. The poor mite be buried in the same coffin with her ladyship."

Ethan ran his finger over the inscription on the marble sepulcher. *Lady Serena Badrick, Viscountess Greeley, beloved wife.*

The oblong tomb rested in the shadows alongside the grave of her husband. It made no mention of her being a mother. But then, Ethan hadn't expected as much. Unable to summon any grief, he felt empty inside, and it struck him that he'd never formed an emotional attachment to any of his women.

Nevertheless, he closed his eyes and said a brief prayer for the repose of her soul. If Serena was indeed Marianne's mother, he owed her a debt of gratitude for having the sense to send the baby to him. Even if her method of doing so left much to be desired.

Accompanied by Jane, he had questioned the village midwife, a brisk, middle-aged woman who lived in a cottage surrounded by an herb garden. After some monetary persuasion, she confirmed that Lady Greeley had been delivered secretly of a sickly infant, but she knew nothing more except what the villagers whispered, that the child had vanished around the time of her mother's death and was presumed dead.

Next, they had gone to the vicar of this small church, only to encounter evidence to the contrary. The elderly cleric had expressed astonishment at the idea that an illegitimate infant had been buried with her ladyship. The tale could only be false, he insisted, for *he* knew nothing of any child.

Who was telling the truth?

An intense frustration knotted Ethan. It was just like Lord Greeley to play games with the whereabouts of a child.

A small sound echoed through the church. He felt a presence near him, a presence that disturbed him far more than it should. *Jane.*

Opening his eyes, he saw her watching him from the entrance to the crypt. The dimness of dusk trickled through a stained-glass window and submerged her in murky jeweled light, as if she were a mermaid glimpsed underwater. She glided toward him, and he hated the weakness in himself, the aching need to take her into his arms and absorb her warmth. Her naïveté drew him, along with her fierce devotion to Marianne. For all her transformation, Jane was vastly different from his other women.

What had possessed him to push her up against a wall and spill out his depravities? When she had stared at him with those eloquent gray-blue eyes, he had wanted to kiss her again. To lose himself in her goodness. To draw her into an empty bedchamber and end her innocence.

"You've had enough time alone," she said. "What have you concluded?"

" 'The grave's a fine and private place, / But none, I think, do there embrace.' "

"Andrew Marvell, *To His Coy Mistress.*" A faint blush colored her cheeks. "You memorized that indecent poem?"

"In school, when I was supposed to be doing my sums. It's a fitting eulogy for Marianne's mother."

Jane shook her head. "Nothing has been proven."

"On the contrary, I am convinced of one fact." He propped his elbow on the marble railing. "There is no baby buried in this tomb. She was left on your doorstep."

His voice echoed off the stone walls. He surprised himself with his vehemence, and he surprised Jane, too, because she frowned in that spinsterish way of hers, eyebrows lowering, lips compressing.

"I disagree," she said. "I believe Lady Greeley's baby did indeed perish, just as the footman and the midwife said."

"They were voicing hearsay, that's all. The vicar confirmed that."

"Lord Greeley hid the truth from the vicar in order to protect his sister-in-law's reputation."

"Or he paid his servants to lie for him. Then he smuggled the baby out of the house."

"But why to *my* doorstep?" Jane asked. "Why not yours?"

"Whoever delivered the infant simply made a mistake. Took a wrong turning, perhaps. Or lost his bearings and left Marianne at the nearest house."

Stubborn to the core, Jane shook her head again. "I don't believe in mistakes. You can't be sure that Marianne is yours, anyway. You said that Lady Greeley had had an affair with her brother-in-law."

He watched her lips curl in distaste, and he whipped his gaze back to hers. "There was my signet ring."

"So? Greeley clearly resents you. Perhaps he wanted to trick you into taking a baby that isn't yours."

"Stealth is a woman's game, not a man's. It would have been far simpler for him to ship off an unwanted child to a workhouse or an orphanage." Impatient with her unyielding nature, he drummed his fingers on the marble tomb. "I do realize, however, that my theory cannot be proven, short of exhuming the grave. Which I very much doubt Greeley will allow."

As expected, Jane jumped on his concession. "Well, then. We've questioned every woman on your list. Aurora Darling. Lady Esler. Miss Diana Russell. Unless you can think of another possibility, I can only conclude you're not Marianne's father, after all."

"Or so you would like to think." Scourged by the double-pronged whip of resentment and fascination, Ethan strolled toward her. She looked like a model of morality with her hands folded primly at her waist. "The truth is that you want to keep Marianne for yourself. So you'll grasp at any tale that suggests she isn't mine."

Jane's eyes widened. He stopped close enough to caress her, though he kept his hands locked to his hips. He wouldn't make the mistake of touching her again. Nor would he make the mistake of softening to the wounded vulnerability on her bold features.

She whirled away and paced the small mausoleum, her footsteps echoing off the stone walls. "I *do* want to be her mother. I've never denied that. But we mustn't fool ourselves, either. The weight of evidence proves that Lady Greeley's child is dead."

"I disagree. It's too much of a coincidence that she had a baby about the same age as Marianne."

"Hundreds of babies are born every day. That doesn't mean anything." She firmed her chin and gave him that typically Jane look. "Why are you arguing, anyway? I should think you'd be thrilled to waive the responsibility of a child."

Ethan told himself she was right. He ought to rejoice, to snatch the easy escape she offered. All along he had known he would hand over Marianne the moment he proved he was not her father.

But when he thought of Marianne, so small and trusting in the crook of his arm, he could not deny a fierce desire to be her father, to watch her grow, to earn her smiles and to protect her from harm. She brought hope into his life, turned him from aimless pleasures onto a path of purpose. The truth of it seized him. If there was any chance she was his, any chance at all, then he could not relinquish her. Not ever.

He looked at Jane, who stood watchful and waiting against the stained glass of the window, and felt a twinge of regret. She'd had so little joy in her sheltered life. And now he meant to take away one vital happiness.

"You're right about one point," he said, steeling himself. "There is no reason for us to quarrel anymore. At the end of the Season, you shall return to Wessex. And Marianne shall remain with me."

⇜ *Chapter 14* ⇝

Jane's first act upon returning to London the next day was to visit the nursery.

In contrast to the rain the previous afternoon, the sun shone brightly in a cloudless sky. Ethan had ridden the roan gelding, while Jane and her aunt shared the carriage. He had been gentleman enough to escort them back to his house; then he had shut himself in the downstairs library.

Jane resisted the childish impulse to make a face at the closed doors as she walked past. She thrust her pelisse at a footman, ignored Aunt Willy's plaintive whining, and ran up the staircase to the top floor, heedless of how hoydenish she might look, her heels kicking up the back of her skirt. She didn't care about acting the lady. Not any more.

When she opened the nursery door, she came upon two surprises. First, Marianne was splashing happily in her bath, a round tin tub set atop a table in the schoolroom. Second, Lady Rosalind was doing the bathing.

A frilly apron protecting her rose-pink gown, the countess held the baby under the arms and spoke in a soft, high-pitched tone. "There now, my little angel. You like the warm water, don't you? Look at you splash! Aren't you a clever girl?"

Marianne cooed back, her arms waving, sending droplets flying.

Jane's heart expanded until her chest ached. A prickly heat stung her eyes, but she blinked away the incipient tears. She wouldn't weep; she hadn't lost Marianne yet.

She walked slowly toward the pair. Sunlight shone on the baby's sprinkling of dark hair, on her plump cheeks and ivory skin. Reluctantly, Jane found herself comparing Marianne's delicate features to Ethan's mother. *Was* there a family resemblance in the dainty nose and fine bone structure, the smiling mouth?

No. Surely it was only fear that made her see similarities. If she had a painting of Serena Badrick, she might well imagine a likeness there, too.

Lady Rosalind looked up, the vivacity on her face altering to something oddly akin to guilt. "Why, Jane. I didn't expect you back until teatime." She laughed a trifle self-consciously. "You've caught me playing *grand-mère*."

She didn't look like a grandmother. Slim as a girl, she had but a few fine lines at her eyes and mouth to betray her age. If strands of gray threaded her hair, the tawny-gold hue concealed them. "I'm glad," Jane said sincerely. "Marianne enjoys your company."

"So she does." The countess smiled proudly at the splashing baby. "Are you ready to come out, my little mermaid?"

The baby displayed a toothless grin.

Lady Rosalind lifted her from the water and laid her on a linen towel beside the tub. The happy smile vanished. Marianne screwed up her face and howled a protest. Making matters worse, the countess attempted to wrap the infant, but her chubby legs kicked off the towel.

"Oh, dear," Lady Rosalind fretted. "I never could get this part right."

"Allow me." Jane stepped forward and handed a silver rattle to the baby, then deftly folded the linen towel like a swaddling blanket around those flailing legs. She picked up Marianne and cuddled the infant to her bosom, welcoming the warm weight, the clean, soapy scent of her. The baby quieted and looked up at Jane, blessing her with a smile of pure, joyous recognition.

Jane smiled back. A bond of infinite strength stretched between them, tempered by heartfelt anguish. Again, she felt the burn of tears, a weakness she hid by leaning over the baby and smoothing her soft, damp hair. How could she return to Wessex and leave Marianne behind? How could she fill the void in her heart by copying academic manuscripts? From the first moment she'd held Marianne, that morning at the cottage, she had felt as if she'd finally found what was missing in her life, a baby to love and nurture.

And now she realized something else, something deeper. To know that Marianne might be Ethan's child gave her an undeniable thrill. In Marianne, she would have a part of him, for always. . . .

"Look how well she's taken to you," Lady Rosalind said, wistfulness in her smile as she gazed at them. "You are the perfect mother for her. She's never as happy as when she's with you."

Jane swallowed past the lump in her throat. She wanted to act nonchalant, as if motherhood didn't matter. But the wretched torment pushed past her defenses, and hot tears spilled down her cheeks. Cradling her precious bundle, she turned away, though not quickly enough.

"Why, Jane! You're weeping. Whatever is the matter?" The countess stepped in front of her and put a hand on Jane's arm, preventing her from hiding again. "Please, my dear, you must tell me what's wrong."

"I can't be Marianne's mother. Not ever."

Lady Rosalind frowned. Then suspicion tightened her mouth. "Is that what my son told you?"

"Yes."

"Devil take him." The curse sounded absurd coming from a lady who barely reached Jane's chin. The countess whirled around and called out, "Gianetta."

The Italian maid appeared in the doorway to the nurse's

bedchamber. A tiny, dark-haired girl clung to Gianetta's skirt, her child whom she had weaned in order to provide sufficient milk for Marianne.

Gianetta swooped forward and took the baby from Jane. "*Angela mio*," she crooned, and Marianne immediately turned her head and fussed for her dinner. Jane felt a pang of longing as the wet nurse bore the infant into the next room and closed the door. Then Lady Rosalind put her arm around Jane and guided her to a bench beneath the sunny window.

"Now," the countess said, pressing a handkerchief into Jane's hand. "Tell me everything Ethan said to you."

Jane took a deep breath. Using the lacy scrap of fabric, she wiped her cheeks. "You know that we went to Hampshire to interview the last woman on his list."

"Yes. That odious Serena Badrick." Lady Rosalind's mouth curled in distaste. "I'm sorry you were forced to meet such a despicable creature."

"But we never did meet her." Jane spilled out the miserable tale, that Lady Greeley had died a month ago, and her bastard infant was rumored to share her tomb, though Ethan believed that before her death, she had made arrangements for the baby to be delivered to him, and somehow, Marianne had been left on Jane's doorstep by mistake. Jane kept silent about the fact that she had accused him of being an unfit father.

"*I'll change,*" *he'd said glibly, as if gaining scruples were as easy as switching his frock coat. "I'll become the model of propriety.*"

"*You can't change. You're a rake, a divorced man. You can't properly raise a little girl. She needs a mother.*"

He gave her a look that chilled her with its intensity. "Marianne is mine," he'd said. "And what belongs to me, I shall never forsake."

"He wants to keep Marianne," Jane said, her fingers taut around the handkerchief. "He won't listen to reason. But it's only conjecture that Marianne is his child by Lady Serena. We have no real proof.''

''And it seems you're not likely to get any.'' Lady Rosalind reached out and patted Jane's hand, stopping her from twisting the handkerchief into knots. ''My dear. Marianne *must* be Ethan's child—the signet ring proves that. And she looks just like he did as a baby. Did you know his eyes were blue until he was six months old?''

Jane's heart sank a little lower. ''You mentioned that once before. Even so, we can't be *sure*.''

''Then we must accept the fact that we may never know the identity of her mother. Perhaps because it's fated to be you. Sometimes women who were never meant to be mothers do give birth.'' Lady Rosalind pursed her lips. ''Oh, I'm sorry this is so upsetting to you, Jane. I know you wish to raise Marianne yourself. But Ethan must be commended for wanting to keep his daughter. Could you respect him if he gave her away?''

Her throat tight, Jane whispered, ''No . . . but I don't wish to lose her, either.''

''Perhaps you won't.'' Arching a slim eyebrow, the countess studied her with a faint, calculating smile. ''I wonder if you've considered every possible solution to your dilemma.''

''What do you mean?''

''Well. Ethan is determined to be a father to Marianne. And you are equally determined to be her mother. It seems to me you both share a common goal.''

''But if I return to Wessex at the end of the Season, I'll never see her again, never hold her, never watch her grow up.''

''Then you must arrange for her to have you both.'' Lady Rosalind lifted her hand, her gold betrothal ring glinting in the sunlight. ''If you play your cards well in the next few weeks, you can entice my son into marriage.''

Jane's heart slammed against her breastbone. She fought against the longings inside herself, longings that had been born many years ago and renewed a thousand times by his kiss. "Oh, my lady," she breathed in anguished denial. "He would never, ever marry *me*."

"Why not? You are pretty and witty and practical, too. And you understand him, I think." The countess tapped her chin. "Yes, the more I consider the matter, the more I believe you *are* the perfect match for him."

"No." Jane shook her head vehemently. The thought of marriage to him was so appealing it mortified her. To share his bed, to know his touch on her naked skin . . . She remembered that charged moment when he had imprisoned her against the wall, taunting her with his intimate secrets, and she had nearly swooned from wanting him. "He prefers women like Lady Greeley. He told me so himself."

"Bah. Like any man, he thinks with his . . ."—Lady Rosalind paused—"that is, he *thinks* he knows his own mind. But in truth, Ethan can never find happiness dallying with such women. Because he is an honorable man at heart."

Honorable? Jane wanted to believe so, but she'd seen too much evidence to the contrary. Betraying his marriage vows led the list. Desperate to deny her foolish hopes, she blurted, "No man of honor would do the things he has done. He even shared mistresses with Captain Randall."

Lady Rosalind's smile died. In an odd, subdued tone, she repeated, "Captain Randall?"

"Yes." Seeing pain in the countess's blue gaze, Jane felt abashed to have blurted out the sordid truth. "Oh, my lady, forgive me for repeating gossip. You knew him, too, of course. He and Ethan were good friends. I should never have said anything to demean a man who died a hero."

Lady Rosalind focused her gaze out the window. A ray of sunlight picked out the delicate lines on her face, and for a moment she looked weary and sad, as old as a grandmother. But when she turned back, a smile elevated the corners of her mouth, and the illusion vanished.

She patted Jane's hand again. "That is all the more reason for you to wed Ethan. You see, ever since he lost his best friend, he's needed the love of a good woman. He was hurt and humiliated by Portia, and it drove him to take too many mistresses. But none of them made him happy.''

"He could never be happy with *me*. We quarrel too much.'' It was more than that, far more. They were opposites, he with his devil-may-care attitude and she with her strict views on propriety. She was a prim sparrow wishing she could fly with a magnificent hawk.

"You quarrel because you are both strong-minded,'' Lady Rosalind said with an airy wave of her hand. "But he needs a bold, resourceful woman to help him be a good father.''

"My lady, you flatter me, but the truth is, he and I don't suit.'' She bit her lip. "Perhaps I should not have gone to his house when I found Marianne on my doorstep. Perhaps I ought not have told him about her.''

Lady Rosalind leaned forward, her expression fervent. "Never say that, my dear. Never. You would have denied him the chance to be a father, the chance to better himself by loving his own child.''

Jane hoped the countess was right, for Marianne's sake. "If he really cared about Marianne, he would see that she needs a mother.''

"So make him want *you*. Flirt with him, entice him the way you did on the night of the ball. Is he not a handsome man, a man you find exciting?''

The question flustered Jane. Half of her wanted to deny it; the other half ached to pour out the longings that flowed like a deep, unending river inside her. Stiffly, she said, "Handsome is not one of the qualities of a good husband.''

"But it can make up for quite a lot of faults.'' Smiling, the countess rose from the bench. "Think on it, my dear. Most of all, do what is best for Marianne.''

As Lady Rosalind strolled out of the nursery, Jane indulged the temptation to dream. *Could* she somehow lure Ethan into offering for her? Could she guard her sharp tongue as other ladies did? Could she make him notice her, make him desire her? It was a heady notion to imagine herself flirting with him, attracting his attention.

If she wed him, she could be Marianne's mother forever.

Foolish hope. He would never choose an inexperienced woman like her. He had made his preferences quite clear. Ever since that night in the garden, when he'd kissed her senseless, he had acted cool and distant, indifferent to her, as if she were unworthy even of his dislike. She might have changed her feathers, but Ethan still viewed her as that plain sparrow. No doubt he hadn't forgiven her for tricking him about Lady Portia. It would be difficult for Jane to win his trust back.

But if she wed him, she could always be with Marianne. She could see her take her first steps and hear her speak her first words.

Ethan would hardly make the ideal husband. He had proven himself a philanderer. He had broken his marriage vows and then punished his wife with the scandal of a divorcement. He'd known so many women, he couldn't even be sure which one had borne his child. He had no interest in finding another wife. She remembered him standing in the cold mist outside Portia's town house.

I shall never make the mistake of marrying again.

Could she convince him to change his mind? If they wed, she and Marianne could retire to Ethan's estate in Wessex. Jane could read books to her, share her confidences, teach her good morals, and prepare her for womanhood.

Jane glanced around the sunny schoolroom, at the round tub sitting on the table, the primers and slates stacked on the shelves, the freestanding globe that Ethan must have twirled as a little boy. He thought this was enough for Marianne, to provide her with shelter and a staff of nursemaids. But Jane knew better. Without a mother's protection, Marianne would be scorned as she grew to womanhood. As the natural daughter of a notorious rake, she could never take her rightful place in the *ton* like all the other young ladies.

She would be ostracized, unhappy and lonesome.

But if Jane wed him, they could formally adopt the baby. Marianne would grow up with all the privileges of a lady. She would be respectable, accepted by society.

Marianne needed a mother who would spend time with her, not a father who brought strange women into his chambers at all hours of the night. Jane didn't believe he had changed, not really. After all, *he* hadn't come straight to the nursery. *She* had.

He didn't love Marianne to distraction. *He* didn't worry about whether she'd kicked off her blankets at night or if the nursemaid had remembered to check her nappy. *He* was not the one who took Marianne on outings and played with her each day. Oh, perhaps he would visit her from time to time, but not with any regularity. Jane knew what it was like to grow up lonely, with no mother to shepherd her, and a father who was focused on his own selfish pursuits.

And she couldn't depend on Lady Rosalind to watch over Marianne. In a matter of weeks, her ladyship would marry the Duke of Kellisham and move into his house. She would be too busy in her new role of wife and duchess to give her granddaughter all the love and attention she needed.

But Jane could provide that affection. She could devote herself to being a mother. *If* she wed Ethan.

Taking a deep breath, she tried to contain the giddy excitement that broke free inside her. It didn't matter that he was the most notorious rake in London, that she had once loved him in secret with all the dreamy hope of her girlish heart. Let him dally with his wicked women. She didn't require fidelity from him. She wanted only the protection of his name for Marianne's sake.

Yes. She could do it. She *must* do it. She must marry him.

Ethan made his way through the darkened nursery. It was so quiet he could hear the pad of his bare feet on the cold floor and the nursemaid's rhythmic snoring from the open door beyond the wooden rocking horse.

His candlestick cast a feeble light onto the dwarf-sized chairs and table he had used as a child on his rare visits to London. He remembered the time he'd been so excited to visit his parents that he'd made himself ill on the trip. Upon his arrival, he'd been put straight to bed, and although his mother paid a brief visit to lay her cool hand on his brow, it had been his father's presence he had craved. But the fifth Earl of Chasebourne did not wish to be bothered with a sick child. He could not abide weakness, especially in his son and heir.

Ethan grimaced at the bitter memory. He had never been able to please his father, and after one shattering humiliation in early adolescence, he had stopped trying. Instead, he had molded himself into the sort of man his father despised most: a dissolute rake who wasted his life on wine, wagering, and women.

The trouble was, he had fallen so deeply into debauchery he was not certain he could change his ways now. And he must change. The reason lay sleeping in the gilt cradle near the hearth.

He stepped closer and raised his candle so that golden light haloed her.

Marianne rested on her stomach, her head turned to the side and her knees tucked up, her bottom thrust into the air. Dark lashes fringed her closed eyes, and her tiny fist lay curled beside her mouth. As he watched, she pursed her lips and sucked, as if she were dreaming of sweet milk.

His chest tightened with an emotion so fierce it hurt. He'd never imagined a man could feel so attached to a child. She was only a baby, after all. She couldn't walk or talk yet. She spent most of her time sleeping or eating or crying. There were scores like her born every day.

But Marianne was *his* baby, his to protect and his to guide.

His to love.

The thought shook him. It no longer mattered that he had proven nothing about her parentage, that the woman who had given birth to her had vanished without so much as a note of explanation. It didn't matter if that woman were Serena Badrick or some other unnamed, forgotten woman whom he'd used in a drunken stupor. It didn't matter that Marianne complicated his reckless life. He intended to raise her well.

Would she someday come to love him? Or would he fail her, too, as he had failed to earn his father's love?

Panic surged in him, and he wanted to flee—to run as far and as fast as he could. But as he stared down at the infant in the cradle, something magical happened. His fear dissipated and a sense of peace stole over him.

She had kicked off her blanket, and he drew the covering over her tiny pink nightdress. He would take care of her. He would see that she wanted for nothing. That her every need was met.

She needs a mother.

The thought made him step back as if Jane were there to scold him. With uneasy clarity, he pictured her stricken face when he had informed her of his decision. She had argued with him, laying out all the reasons why he could not raise Marianne. But he discounted her self-serving logic. She only wanted a child as a salve for her spinsterhood. He wouldn't give away his child and go on his merry way. Nor would he follow his mother's ridiculous advice. He would have to be mad to shackle himself to an outspoken faultfinder who would make his life a living hell.

His mind conjured up the image of Jane in the garden, soft and willing, sweet-tongued for once. He had reacted like a randy adolescent with his first girl.

I wanted to know what it felt like to be held and touched and loved.

Something burned his hand, snapping him out of the vivid fantasy. He peeled a soft blob of candlewax off his skin and rolled it between his fingers. What the hell was wrong with him? Jane wasn't any goddess of passion; she was a pathetic spinster who had been drunk on champagne.

He flung the bit of wax into the banked coals on the hearth. His response to her disturbed him. At least she would soon be gone, and good riddance. She was a constant reminder of his flaws and failings.

He reached down and touched Marianne's cheek, pale as pearls, soft as swansdown. She sighed without awakening. The strength of his attachment to her tightened within him. She was the only person who mattered to him.

He certainly didn't need Jane.

"Have I told you about my hounds?" asked the earnest young gentleman sitting beside Jane in the drawing room.

Three times already. "I believe you mentioned them," she said politely.

"They are the finest pack to grace the county of Leicestershire. Never once have they let the fox escape."

His freckled face aglow with enthusiasm, he launched into another monologue on the joys of riding pell-mell after his beloved dogs, his horse leaping ditches and galloping over fields on bitter-cold winter mornings.

Jane listened with only half an ear. Her mouth ached from smiling. She sat with her hands folded in her lap, her mind aware of the conversations around her, Lady Rosalind chatting with a group of noblemen and Aunt Willy trading gossip with a stoop-shouldered old matron.

The drawing room was filled with afternoon callers, several of them gentlemen who had danced with Jane at the ball. Lord Avery, her fox-hunting companion, was one of those who had a fortune of his own and no need to marry for money. With his thatch of reddish hair and his friendly features, he would make a fine husband for some hunt-mad lady.

But not Jane.

She stole a glance through the open doors at the corridor beyond. A tall man walked into view. She sat up straighter, then relaxed back against the chaise. It was only a footman.

For the past three days, she had seen little of Ethan. Each morning, he went for an early ride in Hyde Park. She had never learned equestrian skills, as her father hadn't had the means to keep a horse, so she could not invite herself along. Each afternoon, Ethan had gone out to heaven knew where. Each evening, he had declined his mother's invitations to escort her and Jane to soirées and balls, the theater and the opera. Instead, he'd shut himself in his chambers.

So much for enticing him. Yet she remained firmly committed to this course of action. Especially since he never visited Marianne at all.

"Would you like that?" Lord Avery said.

Jane blinked at his hopeful expression and had no notion what he had asked her. "Forgive me. I must have been wool-gathering."

He blushed. "Mama always scolds me for rattling on so. But I asked if you and your aunt might care to visit us in the country. I walk my hounds four times each day, and thought it might be pleasant to have your company."

"Thank you for the kind offer," Jane said gently, "but I fear my aunt travels little these days."

"I see. Ah, well, I shall just have to describe my estate to you, then. We have the finest woods and fields for hunting . . ."

Jane heard no more. Every muscle in her body tensed as she spied the broad-shouldered man who entered the doorway.

Ethan wasn't dressed for company. He wore polished black boots and buckskin riding breeches, a plain white shirt and gray waistcoat beneath a dark blue frock coat. In his gloved hand, he held a riding crop. Without noticing Jane, he strolled toward his mother.

Jane rose from the chaise. "If you'll excuse me, I need a word with Lord Chasebourne."

Lord Avery looked crestfallen to lose his audience, and Jane disliked being rude, so she smiled to soften the blow

of her departure. Then she headed across the Aubusson rug
to join Ethan and his mother. The soft cinnamon silk of her
gown swished around her ankles. She knew she looked
fetching in the low-cut bodice, her mother's locket nestled
between her breasts. The small gold ear bobs added a feminine touch to her upswept hair.

Her pulse fluttered when she neared him. But Ethan
barely glanced at her.

"Jane." He acknowledged her with a nod, then turned
with a sardonic bow to his mother. "You sent an urgent
message, Mother. What is this pressing emergency?"

"Pish-posh, how else was I to get you here? We've seen
so little of you these past few days." Lady Rosalind waved
her hand at the unoccupied chaise across from her. "Come,
sit with me, you and Jane. Tell me why you've been too
busy for us."

He looked amused at her maneuverings. "Much as I
would enjoy the company, I must decline. I was on my way
out."

His mother pursed her lips in a pout. "Again? But we
have guests. Where are you going?"

"To nowhere of interest to you ladies."

Jane saw her chance slipping away. "It's a fine, sunny
day," she said, touching his sleeve and leaning closer, the
way she'd seen other women do. "If you're going for a
pleasure drive, might I accompany you?"

"What a capital idea," Lady Rosalind said, smiling in
approval. "You two run along together."

One black eyebrow arched, Ethan slapped the riding crop
across his gloved palm. "I wouldn't dream of taking Jane
from her suitors. If you ladies will excuse me." Without a
backward glance, he strode out of the room.

Jane bit her lip in frustration. When was she to flirt with
him if he refused to cooperate? Perhaps it was a foolish
plan, anyway, thinking she could attract such a jaded man.
But she had to do *something*.

A familiar ache tightened inside her. In another month,

the Season would end and she would return to Wessex. Without Marianne.

"Did you say you wished to take a drive?" said a voice behind her.

She turned to see the round form and grinning face of Lord Keeble. Beside him towered the not-so-Honorable Mr. Duxbury. They wore identical smiles, polite yet with a hint of something else. Something improper.

An idea sparked in her mind. These two gentlemen might just be the answer to her dilemma. "A drive would be lovely," she said.

She announced her intentions to Aunt Willy, who gave her grudging approval so long as they went nowhere but the park. Within minutes, Jane had collected her bonnet and pelisse and settled herself in Keeble's open landau.

Her spirits rose at the warmth of sunlight on her face. A light breeze blew wisps of hair against her cheeks. The gently rocking pace of the carriage lent the illusion of setting out on an adventure.

Perhaps she was.

She focused her attention on the two men who sat opposite her, their backs to the coachman on his high perch. "Gentlemen," she began. "You both seem most knowledgeable about the comings and goings of people in society."

"There's nary a secret we can't ferret out," Keeble said. "Ain't that so, Ducks?"

Duxbury nodded. "Not that we're gossips, mind."

"Of course not," Jane said. "I know I can trust you both to be discreet."

"Discretion is my middle name," Keeble said.

Duxbury shot him a puzzled look. "I thought your middle name was Henry."

"It's a saying, you dolt. The point being that if Miss Mayhew has a secret to tell us, I can keep quiet about it."

"So can I." Duxbury locked his lips with an imaginary key, which he pretended to toss out of the carriage.

Jane refrained from rolling her eyes. "It's not precisely *my* secret. I'm hoping you can give me some information. I am curious to learn where Lord Chasebourne goes each afternoon. Would you happen to know?"

The two men glanced at each other. Duxbury let out a snigger. Keeble elbowed him in the ribs. "Don't laugh. 'Tis rude."

Duxbury clapped his hand over his mouth, though his baby-blue eyes danced with mirth.

"I presume you do know, then," Jane prompted.

"Perhaps so." Keeble winked at her. "But Chase won't like us to reveal his secrets."

"As a guest in his house, I am not precisely a stranger," Jane said with forced patience. "I have a matter of importance I wish to discuss with him. Will you take me to him?"

"Now?" Keeble asked, a pout denting his plump cheeks. "But what about our drive in the park?"

"It ain't fair," Duxbury whined. "Chase gets all the women."

"I am hardly his property," Jane said, caught by a curious thrill at the thought that she *would* belong to him if they married. "Please, it is vital that I speak with him today. He departed so quickly from the house that I didn't have an opportunity."

The two men exchanged another covert glance. Duxbury said, "Might prove amusing, old chap."

"Might, indeed." Looking at Jane, Keeble added, "Though it ain't a place for ladies, I warn you."

"I quite understand," Jane said, and hoped she wasn't getting in over her head. But what other choice did she have? If Ethan kept eluding her, then she was forced to seek him out.

Keeble relayed an address to the coachman, and the landau made a wide circle past the gated entrance to Hyde Park with its green trees and winding pathways. Jane clasped her gloved hands tightly in her lap. A sense of excitement leapt inside her, the feeling that at last she was doing something to snare Ethan's attention.

The drive carried them eastward, past the fine houses of Mayfair and into crowded neighborhoods of Covent Garden. The streets narrowed, and the landau squeezed past a cart piled high with cabbages and drawn by a bony nag. Along the foot pavement, housewives hustled by on errands, a pieman shouted his wares, and several urchins played a game of tag.

At last the carriage stopped before a building of soot-stained brick. An iron railing marked the small yard and prevented passersby from venturing too close. It was not a residence, that much Jane surmised from the undraped windows. If the place was a business establishment, no sign indicated its purpose. What purpose had Ethan here?

"If you gentlemen would rather wait . . ." Jane began, stepping out as the footman opened the door.

"Wouldn't miss this for the world," Keeble said.

He and Duxbury scrambled down from the carriage and followed her to the front steps. Another visitor preceded them into the brick building. He was not a gentleman, but a ham-fisted brute with a misshapen nose and the plain garb of a commoner.

Jane's curiosity heightened. "Is this a gaming hell?"

Keeble and Duxbury looked at each other and sniggered. "You'll see soon enough," Duxbury said.

Jane gritted her teeth at their mirth, but said nothing. If it meant having time with Ethan, she'd go along with their silly game. Perhaps he might even be jealous to see her in the company of two other men. It was worth a try.

Climbing the steps, she scrutinized the building again. The ground-floor windowsills were too high even for a woman of her height to peer over. A magpie pecked at the dirt yard, then flew off in a flutter of black wings. The place looked austere with no flowers or shrubbery to soften the grimy woodwork. If houses had a gender, Jane thought in a flash of whimsy, this one was definitely male.

Keeble turned the knob. "No need to knock," he said.

Puzzled and wary, Jane walked into a small, bare foyer paneled in oak. A narrow staircase hugged one wall. The place had an aura of utilitarian starkness with no furnishings to relieve the monotony. The muffled rise and fall of male voices came from beyond another closed door.

She went to the base of the stairs and peered up into the dimness. This couldn't be a brothel; the house belonging to Miss Aurora Darling had been decorated with lush sensuality. The air had smelled of rich perfume, not . . . what *was* that scent? Something musky and male.

"Are you certain he's here?" she asked.

"Every afternoon," Duxbury assured her.

"This way, Miss Mayhew." With a flourish, Lord Keeble threw open the door.

Instead of a smoky den filled with card tables and disreputable gamesters, she found herself viewing an airy chamber that extended the width of the house. Sunlight poured through the tall windows and onto . . . several half-naked men.

One lay on the floor and lifted what looked like iron weights attached to either end of a pole. His arm muscles bulged from the effort. Other men stood hitting long leather bags, but Jane spared them only a cursory glance.

Her attention fixed on a throng of fashionably dressed gentlemen gathered around a ringed arena where two fighters sparred, circling each other and ducking punches. Some of the spectators shouted in savage excitement. A fist connected with a dull thud that made Jane wince. The air smelled of sweat and leather and sawdust.

Dear heaven. A prizefight. Was Ethan among those bloodthirsty bystanders? He had to be.

The gentlemen stood two and three deep, their backs to her. Craning her neck, she looked for his tall form, his black hair and sinful profile.

Keeble stepped past her and gawked. "By Jove, that's Savage Saxton sparring with Terrible Tom Headly," he exclaimed. "Why didn't I hear about this fight?"

"Dash it all," Duxbury said, his eyes avid. " 'Tis too late to place a wager."

"But we can still watch the action."

Abandoning Jane, they trotted off toward the arena.

She hurried after them. "Gentlemen," she said in exasperation. "It would be polite to wait for me."

"Do fighting men interest you?" Keeble asked, slowing down to her pace. "The truth now, Miss Mayhew. 'Tis no shame to admit you admire them half-naked bucks."

"Most ladies squeal at the sight. Don't know why." Duxbury's face lit with enthusiasm. " 'Tis jolly fun to see men smashed to the floor, the breath beaten out of their bodies, their eyes blackened and their lips split open."

"Oh, that does sound marvelous," Jane muttered.

"Make haste, then," Keeble said. "Else we'll miss the gory finale."

He and Duxbury propelled her through the large gymnasium, heading toward the arena in the far corner where Ethan surely stood in the throng of spectators. Male voices shouted encouragement to the two boxers. Several onlookers shook their fists and shouted obscenities. The grunts of the combatants mingled with the thud of flesh on flesh.

Why couldn't she see Ethan?

Halfway across the room, she found out why. A familiar deep voice startled her.

"Jane?"

Keeble and Duxbury dropped her arms posthaste. She spun around toward the voice.

To her left, poised beside a long leather punching bag, stood Ethan. His fists were raised as if he'd been interrupted in mid-exercise. A lock of black hair adhered to his brow. Stripped to the waist, he wore only his buckskin breeches. Sweat sheened his muscled chest, and as she watched, a tiny bead rolled downward and disappeared into his waistband.

Jane could only gape at him as a giddy warmth unnerved

her. A tingling awareness swept downward from breast to stomach to legs. She felt boneless, in need of support. How ridiculous, she chided herself. Certainly she had seen him unclothed before.

But this time, his expression was as hard as frost and he looked furious. Not at all in a mood to be enticed.

He took a step toward her. ''What the deuce are you doing here?''

~ *Chapter 15* ~

"She begged us to bring her," Keeble said hastily, eyeing Ethan's fists. "Told us she likes this sort of event."

"Bloodthirsty," Duxbury agreed, edging away. "Never would have guessed it of her."

"Come now, you wouldn't desert a lady, would you?" Jane chided. She looped arms with her companions and glanced coyly from one to the other. "The fact of the matter is, these gentlemen were kind enough to escort me to the prizefight."

"The fight." Ethan frowned at the crowd, the air vibrating with their wild cheers. It was so unlike Jane to make such a declaration, she might as well have said she liked baiting the mad folk at Bedlam Hospital. "Since when do you enjoy fistfights?"

"Since now." She purred a throaty laugh. "It's a new experience, and I find it rather stimulating."

He wanted to jeer, but no sound came out. He was distracted by the way she looked at him, her gaze flitting to his chest. An involuntary response tightened his groin. Aware of his state of undress, he snatched his shirt from a hook on the wall and thrust his arms through the sleeves.

He had always been able to count on Jane to speak her mind. But he didn't know this new Jane, this flirty, full-breasted Jane, and that fact infuriated him as much as her unexpected presence. "You're leaving," he said flatly. "You don't belong here."

"I'm staying," she said with a toss of her copper-hued curls. "You just go on hitting that sack over there. Shall we proceed, gentlemen?"

She flashed a brilliant smile at her companions and leaned toward them. Duxbury's gaze fixed on the bodice that displayed inviting swells of flesh. Keeble almost drooled down his fat chin.

Ethan wanted to knock their fool heads together. Buttoning his shirt, he stepped in front of Jane before she could take more than two steps toward the ring. "I want a word with you."

"You'll have to wait your turn," she said breezily. "It would be rude of me to desert my escorts."

"We're more than escorts," Keeble said, sliding his arm around her slim waist. "We are your most ardent admirers, Miss Mayhew."

He was half a head shorter than she, the top of his balding head no higher than her nose, and she gazed at him as if he were Romeo prattling a romantic soliloquy.

Ethan flexed his fists. "Release her," he stated in a hard voice. "Now."

For once, Keeble didn't act with all the sense of a peahen. He withdrew his arm and curled his lips in a sickly grin. "No need to get angry, Chasebourne. We were only having a bit of fun. If you want her back, she's all yours."

"But she said she ain't your property," Duxbury protested. "And you already have a harem in the country—"

"Never mind that, you sapskull. Come along or we'll miss the fight." Keeble yanked the taller man away. Looking like a pair of mismatched bookends, they trotted to the arena, where a boy rang the bell to signal the next round.

"Well," Jane said brightly, looking around. "So this is where you spend your afternoons."

"And it's not where you spend yours." Ethan took hold

of her arm and propelled her toward the exit. "You belong at my house, taking tea with my mother."

"But I must wait for Keeble and Duxbury. I came in their carriage."

"The coachman can drive you home and return for them later. What are you doing alone with them, anyway? Those two would ruin your reputation if you give them half a chance."

"They behaved like perfect gentlemen. Unlike you." She gazed pointedly at his hand on her arm.

Her flippant manner irked him. "On the contrary. I seem to be the only person capable of keeping you out of trouble."

"Then let me stay here with you. You could show me around. I've never been to a place like this before."

"With good reason. Ladies aren't allowed."

"Oh, don't be a prig." At the door to the foyer, she came to a halt. She tucked her chin down and looked up at him, her dark lashes thick over clear gray-blue eyes. "Please, Ethan, don't send me away just yet. Mayn't I stay for a little while longer?"

This impudent behavior was so unlike Jane. She nibbled on her lower lip, making him aware of how kissable it was. He wanted to haul her into a corner and test the softness of that mouth. He wanted to cup her breasts and see if all that flesh was real. It was probably padding, though he supposed she could have hidden quite spectacular assets under those shapeless gowns she used to wear.

And why the hell was he even wondering?

He marched her into the deserted foyer and closed the door, shutting out the noise and distractions. She was distraction enough. He couldn't accustom himself to how she had changed, his frumpy childhood nemesis who had watched disapprovingly while he sneaked a hand up Harriet Hulbert's skirt behind the butcher's shop or let loose a mouse in church to make all the girls squeal. Now that he thought on it, Jane had told on him only once, when she feared he'd endangered himself in a mine. Perhaps that was the reason why he felt this bond between them.

A bond betrayed by the change in her.

"You can stay long enough to tell me why you came here." His demand echoed off the bare walls like the voice of an irate father. But he couldn't help the suspicion that nagged at him. "And don't give me that nonsense about the fight."

Her gaze faltered; then she looked him square in the eyes. "How can you be sure it's nonsense? Do you know anything about my preferences, my interests? Anything at all?"

"Of course I do. We grew up together."

"But we aren't friends. We're merely acquaintances. Friends know each other's thoughts and feelings."

"I know you. Your mother died when you were born. Your aunt raised you. And your father made you spend hours indoors, studying dusty old books."

"Those are facts any stranger could find out." She tilted her head to the side and regarded him thoughtfully. "But you don't know what I'm really thinking. You don't know *me*."

That annoyed him. He didn't want to believe there were depths to her he had not fathomed. It was too disturbing. Did she still yearn to be held and touched and loved? And why the devil did he feel this dark compulsion to find out?

"Very well," he growled. "I can't read your mind. But I still know when you're lying."

She let out a little huff of breath. "All right, then. It isn't a coincidence that I'm here. I asked Keeble and Duxbury to show me where you go each day." She took a step closer, gazing at him with a wide-eyed innocence. "I came because . . . well, I want us to be civil, for Marianne's sake. We need to get along better."

He saw a dark humor in that. "Oh? Why do I suspect this sudden friendliness is a ploy to take her away from me?"

"I don't want to take her from you. I promise you that."

"Then what's brought about this change of heart?" Disturbed by her nearness, he went to the sunny window and leaned against the sill. "It can't be that you think I'd make a more suitable parent. I've never known you to speak well of me."

"You said you've reformed."

"But you don't believe me. That's why you don't think I can raise a little girl. Do you." He made it a statement, not a question.

"Well. You *are* a rake, a divorced man, a gambler. It will be difficult to live down your reputation." She added quickly, "Even if you *have* changed."

Ethan was still skeptical about her motives. Why did he have the feeling she was up to a secret purpose?

She walked back and forth, betraying a veiled nervousness, the gown skimming her willowy curves. He doubted she would meekly return to Wessex next month, leaving Marianne behind. She was devoted to the baby, that much he knew from questioning the nursemaids. Jane spent part of each day in the nursery, without fail. He couldn't help admiring her devotion, and yet he felt a nagging suspicion that she sought to get past his guard, to charm him into keeping the baby for herself.

To see if he was right, he deliberately goaded Jane. "I'd sooner take my chances raising Marianne myself than send her off to live with two crotchety old maids."

Jane's eyes flashed. "I give her love and attention. How can she get that from a father who disappears all day?"

"Seems to me you've deserted her today, too, Miss Maypole."

He knew she hated that name. Predictably, she bristled, planting her hands on her hips. "I would make her a good mother. You know that."

"I do, indeed. However, *I* can give her all the advantages of wealth and status. What have you to offer her but a drunken aunt and a rundown cottage?"

"You leave my aunt Willy out of this," she flared. "She is an ailing old woman who deserves your respect. She has nothing to do with Marianne."

"Forgive me for saying so, but she would set a poor example. Look at how her influence turned you into a shrew."

He could see Jane struggle with her temper. She pursed her lips and clenched her fists. Then she blinked several times, and the next thing he knew she'd walked closer to him, pressing her hand to his arm and looking at him earnestly. Awareness of her enveloped Ethan, the desire to pull her close and breathe in her rainwater scent. A feral cheer resounded from the gymnasium, but he barely heard it. Did she know he had a view down her bodice?

With Jane, he was never sure of anything anymore.

"Ethan, I don't want to quarrel with you," she murmured. "Truly I don't. Let's try to forget our differences."

The differences he was thinking about right now had little to do with words. He despised himself for wanting to thrust her against the wall and test the softness of her body against his. Long ago, he'd learned a harsh lesson about dallying with virgins.

He pushed away from the windowsill and yanked open the front door. "There's only one way to forget our differences. You go back to Wessex. I'm done trading insults with a sour old spinster."

"There is no excuse for his rudeness," the Duke of Kellisham intoned from the head of the long table. "None at all."

Lady Rosalind leaned over to pat his hand on the snowy white tablecloth. Candlelight flickered on her fine features. "Darling, please forget about him. Ethan is a grown man. We can no longer command him."

"Nevertheless, he should have joined us. It is most impolite of him to scorn the company of his family. And after the spectacle he made of himself this evening."

"I must concur with His Grace," said Aunt Wilhelmina, sitting across from the countess and fanning herself with a linen serviette. "His behavior at the poetry reading was quite shocking. My nerves cannot bear all this strife."

Jane bit her tongue to keep from making an acid comment regarding Ethan's disappearance. She would not sound like a sour old spinster. If the unconscionable rogue chose to boycott their little dinner party, let him.

They had attended a soirée that evening, she and Ethan along with Lady Rosalind, the duke, and Aunt Willy. According to the invitation, it was to be a musical evening with violins, flute, and harp. But their hostess, the snobbish Lady Jersey, had announced a special presentation, a reading from a selection of Wordsworth's latest poems.

"Good God," Ethan had proclaimed to all around them. "That isn't entertainment. It's torture."

A smattering of uneasy laughter had greeted his words. No one else dared make fun of her ladyship's choice.

While a violinist played softly in the background and an actress from a theater in Haymarket read the poems, Ethan had sat at the rear of the crowd and flirted outrageously with Lady Big Bosom, or so Jane had dubbed the raven-haired widow. She could hear their whisperings behind her, their stifled mirth, as they behaved like a pair of rowdy schoolchildren. She didn't know how he could bear that twittering laugh or the girlish posturing. More to the point, she didn't know how he could admire a woman like that.

Not that she cared, really. So long as he married *her*.

Surprisingly, he had returned to Chasebourne House with them instead of going off with Lady Big Bosom for a tryst. But he had declined to join the small party for a light supper and had gone straight upstairs.

A footman set a bowl of consommé in front of Jane. She picked up her spoon and took a sip of the clear golden soup. It was difficult to swallow past the knot in her throat. After today, she felt farther from her goal than ever. It was partly her own fault. She had let him goad her into that quarrel.

But how was she to lure him into wedlock if he taunted her at every turn?

Go back to Wessex.

His edict loomed in her mind like a threat. He saw no future for them, nothing but more bickering. He would not seek out her company, and that made her task all the more desperate. She couldn't lose Marianne. But the possibility haunted Jane.

She brooded through the courses of poached sole and tiny green peas, *filet de boeuf* and potatoes *au gratin*, champagne sorbet and sugared apricots. When at last Lady Rosalind stood up at the end of the meal, Jane felt as taut as an overwound clock. "I must excuse myself," she said. "I'm rather weary."

"But we're about to have Cook's famous raspberry cake in the drawing room," Lady Rosalind said. Her expression soft, she looped her arm through the duke's. "Kellisham will be joining us. There is no sense in him taking his brandy by himself."

"Nor to miss the company of three such fine ladies." He directed a smile at his fiancée.

Their devotion made Jane's heart ache. "Thank you. But I fear I should be dull company, indeed."

Casting a thoughtful glance at Jane, Lady Rosalind escorted Kellisham to Aunt Willy. "Why don't you two go on and I'll join you in a moment? I need a word with Jane before she retires."

"As you wish, my dear." The duke gallantly escorted Aunt Willy out of the dining room.

Lady Rosalind drew Jane into the dimly lit morning room next door, away from the footmen who were clearing the table, china and cutlery clinking. "You seem preoccupied this evening. I trust my son hasn't upset you in any way."

"Upset me?" Jane said quickly. "Why would you think that?"

" 'Tis only a suspicion. You two seemed to be avoiding each other lately." The countess leaned forward, her tawny gold hair shining in the light from the crystal chandeliers, her expression avid. In a whisper, she asked, "Are you having any success in your campaign to win him?"

Jane felt reluctant to confide in his mother. So she hedged. "Ethan has made it clear he has no interest in taking another wife. He told me he shall never remarry."

To Jane's surprise, the countess laughed. "Well, at least you two are talking about marriage. That is a step in the right direction."

"It is a step in *no* direction. He has *no* interest in me."

"Then why does his gaze follow you so much? Why does he stare at you when he thinks no one is watching?"

Did he? Hope fluttered in her breast, but Jane resolutely crushed it. "He dislikes me, that's why. He is wishing me back to Wessex."

"On the contrary. I believe he is fascinated by you—and by the fact that you are so different from his usual brand of female." In a motherly gesture, Lady Rosalind rubbed Jane's hand. "You mustn't think anything of his behavior tonight with that woman. You see, deep down, he is a confused man in need of subtle guidance. Your guidance."

"My lady, obviously that sort of woman has something to attract him, something I lack—"

"Yes. Loose morals." A disdainful grimace flitted over her ladyship's face. "But we might turn that into your advantage. I would venture to guess you don't realize how attractive and persuasive a woman you can be."

"I . . . thank you." Jane self-consciously smoothed her shimmery turquoise skirt. The dress did make her feel elegant and strong somehow, as if she were clad in a woman's soft armor. "But really, he and I aren't suited in temperament. To him, I'm just . . ." *A sour old spinster.*

"You're a friend to him, that's what. He knew you in childhood, and he can't bring himself to accept that you're all grown up." Lady Rosalind tilted her head at a thoughtful angle. "Now, if you two have quarreled, I would advise you to go and speak to him at once. It isn't good for the constitution to sleep on anger. And don't think it improper to go to his chambers. You will be perfectly safe with him, considering the lesson he learned from Portia.''

''Lesson?''

''Why, he was forced to marry her after they were caught together. I thought you knew.''

''No.'' The revelation startled Jane. She remembered seeing him and Lady Portia on their wedding trip. From her hiding place in the hedgerow, Jane had watched them laughing and talking as their carriage passed by. ''I believed it a love match.''

Lady Rosalind wrinkled her small nose. ''He was taken in by her artfulness, that's all.''

''Do you mean . . . Lady Portia tricked him? On purpose?''

''Precisely. You see, despite his reputation, my son is an honorable man. If he were to seduce a virgin, he would do right by her.''

Was Lady Rosalind only reassuring her? Or was she suggesting something shocking, something outrageous?

No, Jane told herself, it was her own wayward intellect that leapt ahead to a possibility she had never before considered. She should not—*would not*—even let herself form the thought.

Lady Rosalind guided Jane toward the door of the dining chamber. ''Go to him, my dear. And remember, men like to be flattered. They also like to believe they are in charge, though of course, we women know better. We must use our wits to coax them to behave as they ought.''

''I can't coax Ethan. He won't let me.''

Lady Rosalind laughed. ''Nonsense. He is not so indifferent to you as he would seem. I would venture to guess he is up there brooding about you right now.''

Jane wanted to deny his interest in her. She wanted to say they were enemies, not friends. But when she opened her mouth, she said, ''He doesn't brood. He sulks.''

Lady Rosalind laughed again. "There, you see? You understand him better than anyone. So please, for the sake of peace in this house, don't let him sulk any longer."

A short while later, Jane stood in the shadows of the garden. The smell of rain hung in the night air, and thunder rolled in the distance. She paid little heed as she gazed up at the tower. The crenellated black teeth of the roof bit into the scudding clouds. The faint yellowish eye of a candle glowed in the single window.

Ethan was up there. And she intended to seduce him.

Her palms felt damp and her heart raced. She had arrived at the scandalous decision after leaving Lady Rosalind. If indeed he was honorable enough to wed the woman whose innocence he took, then Jane would offer herself to him. It was an act of desperation.

Go back to Wessex.

Time was growing short. She had to act fast. Besides, the countess's revelation also made Jane see his rejection of her in a new light. If he disdained marriage, of course he would avoid all virgins. He would avoid *her.* It was a startling explanation for why he'd goaded her, why he kept her at arm's length.

The question was, how could she break through the wall of his scorn?

She stood near the very bench where, a week ago, he had kissed her. He had taken her in his arms and made her feel wanted . . . loved. If she closed her eyes, she could still feel that rush of excitement, the swooning heat and dreamlike pleasure. If Portia hadn't come along just then, perhaps their embrace might have grown more intimate.

Jane had attracted him then. She could do so again.

Shivering in the damp, chilly breeze, she rubbed her arms. Her eyes strained through the darkness to pick out the door half-hidden in the ivy-covered wall. She hadn't gone to his bedroom because that odious little valet would bar her entry. She had deemed it prudent to enter the tower

room by way of the garden. *If* she could find the courage.
Go back to Wessex.

She couldn't go back. Not without Marianne. And there
was only one way to ensure no one could ever take the
baby from her.

Drawing a deep breath, Jane marched through the darkened garden to the tower door. She tried the knob. Locked.
But she had come prepared.

She drew out the ring of keys she'd borrowed from the
pantry while the butler was in the dining room. Metal jan-
gled musically; she made an effort to be quiet. There had
to be at least twenty keys, and she tried them methodically
until she found the one that fit the slot.

The tumbler clicked. To her relief, the door opened with
only a minimal squeaking of iron hinges. She stepped into
blackness. The air smelled as musty as ancient leaves. In
the dim flash of lightning, she could discern a stone staircase that spiraled upward into inky oblivion.

She propped the door open with a rock from the garden.
Not because she was frightened of the dark, but because
she hated to lose her only source of light, faint though it
was. Then she mounted the stairs.

Jane had to hug the wall to keep herself oriented in the
darkness. She fought against giddiness and the irrational
fear that her next step would send her plunging down into
a black void. The stones felt cold and damp against her
hand, and she swallowed a yelp when something sticky
adhered to her cheek.

A spiderweb, she realized, brushing it away. She only
hoped its creator had long since moved on.

Was this how Ethan spirited his lovers to the tower
room? Did he meet them at a prescribed time in the garden
and guide them upstairs to his cozy love nest?

A thought jolted Jane. What if he had a woman with him
right now?

The stairs ended at a narrow landing. She inched forward, sliding one slipper, then the next. Feeling cautiously

with her hands, she located the square outline of a door. A feeble light leaked from the bottom.

She put her ear to the heavy wood panel. No sound came from within, not even a murmur of voices. Did people talk while they engaged in bedsport? Or did they just hug and kiss and touch?

She felt flushed just wondering about it. Her legs wobbled, and she braced herself against the jamb. She would be mortified to find Ethan with a woman—again. But she had come this far. She couldn't turn back now.

She would do it for Marianne's sake. An innocent little girl needed a mother to watch over her, to love her. To shelter her from a father who would leave her to the care of nursemaids.

Jane took a breath of stale air, gritted her teeth, and quietly turned the knob.

⌒ *Chapter 16* ⌒

Peering through the narrow opening, she saw a shadowy chamber decorated in masculine hues of green and brown. She could see part of a medieval tapestry covering the curved stone wall. Beneath a massive chimneypiece, a coal fire glowed on the grate.

Ever so slowly, she eased the door back a few more inches. A well-worn wing chair came into view. Beside it stood a table piled haphazardly with books. A volume had been left open on the chair with a glass paperweight to mark the spot.

There lay Ethan's coat, draped over the footstool. One of his shoes sat near the hearth and the other rested by the table as if he'd kicked them off in haste. She listened again for voices, but could hear only the faint hissing of the coals.

Mentally counting to three, she pushed the door all the way back. Her gaze swept the circular chamber. Empty. To her surprised relief, there was no bed draped in silks and covered in pillows. There was no bank of burning candles, no paramours entwined in sin.

Bookshelves fitted the curve of the wall. A massive knee-hole desk with many compartments occupied the space to her left. An oil lamp illuminated a blizzard of papers. As if waiting for its owner's return, a wooden armchair upholstered in dark green velvet sat at an angle.

This was Ethan's tower room? The place where he engaged in secret acts of corruption? The private territory he had forbidden to one and all? It looked no more sinister than a study.

Then she spied another door in the wall. Perhaps behind that half-open panel stood the wide feather bed, the braziers holding exotic incense, the perfumed trysting place where he practiced the art of seduction. A thrill eddied through her, raising a fine dew on her skin. With every breath, she could smell a trace of his male scent, the dark mystery of man.

She tiptoed across the plush oriental rug and pushed the door open. To her disappointment, she found herself gazing down another narrow stone staircase lit by a single candle flickering in a wall sconce. The winding steps curved around so that she could not see the bottom.

This could only be the passage down to Ethan's bedchamber.

She hesitated to venture there just yet. Not because of any cowardly misgivings, but because she was curious. If he didn't entertain women in this tower room, what did he do here that was so secretive? Her gaze flitted to the desk with all its papers. Did he transact business? Manage estate matters? Pay gambling markers?

She shouldn't peek at his private papers. They had nothing to do with her purpose tonight. Yet it wouldn't hurt to take a quick look. She wanted to know everything about him, to understand him better.

She veered toward the desk. Built of mahogany, it had numerous niches stuffed with documents. Crumpled paper littered the floor around a small rubbish bin. More foolscap scattered the flat surface of the desk, along with several quills, a sharpener, and an uncapped inkwell. Then something else captured her attention. A pair of gold-rimmed spectacles lay atop the clutter.

She gingerly picked up the eyeglasses, bringing them to her face to peer through the glass ovals. She turned her gaze downward to the papers, and the handwriting looked blurred.

Ethan wore *spectacles*?

The notion struck Jane as so startling, she laughed aloud, covering her mouth and glancing toward the door down to his bedchamber. It was not that she thought the less of him for a physical imperfection. But picturing him in spectacles jarred with his image of devil-may-care rake.

She put the eyeglasses in a cubbyhole and examined the papers strewn across his desk. Rather than being bills or dun notices, they bore his handwriting.

Her first impression was that his penmanship had taken a turn for the worse. He wrote untidily with numerous ink blots and crossed-out words. At times the nib of the quill had torn a hole in the paper, as if he were writing fast, driven by the force of emotion. The words were difficult to decipher. More like a list than a personal letter, there were many short lines. She plucked another paper out of the mess, and her gaze riveted to the name at the top of the page.

Marianne.

Jane sank into the chair, tilted the sheet to the lamp, and scanned the rough writing.

In moonlight glow she slumbers,
Little angel, one of numbers
Born in shame with hearts so pure,
And anguish destined to endure.
In this world where rules reign,
She rests in beauty unprofaned . . .

In a disbelieving daze, Jane deciphered several more stanzas of scribbled lines and scratched-out words until she reached the bottom of the page. A poem. This was a poem. A poem written by . . . *Ethan*?

Impossible.

Shaken, she read on, and the words exuded tender emotion, deep-felt and sincere. Dear God. If Ethan had penned these words—and he must have done so—then he truly did love Marianne. The revelation stabbed like a hot sword into Jane; she wanted to weep and exult at the same time.

Ethan had composed these exquisite words brimming with feeling and eloquence. Poetry so lovely it brought tears to her eyes.

This was his secret vice? This penchant for writing?

Glancing over the desk, she saw more poems in various stages of completion. In a delirium of discovery, she found sonnets and odes carelessly stashed in cubbyholes. None had been copied over to a neat, finished work of art. It was as if once he poured his thoughts onto paper, he never wanted to see them again.

A poet.

The notion astonished her. She had always thought him an intelligent man but an indifferent scholar, someone who preferred vice to visionary thinking, someone who fell shamefully short of his potential.

Now she remembered the ink stains she'd often seen on his middle finger. She thought about the long, late hours he'd spent up here. And there was the time she'd gone to his bedchamber to ask him about Marianne's mother. She had glimpsed a paper with his handwriting and had assumed it was a list of potential mothers before he'd snatched it away.

She was wrong. It had been one of his poems.

Her hands trembling, she riffled through the papers, reading random passages, picking out perceptive phrases. She marveled at his command of lyrical language. This, from a man who professed to despise all verse as pap for milksops. The man who had scorned to listen to the readings this evening. He had lounged at the back of the chamber, whispering and laughing with Lady Big Bosom, behaving like the conscienceless rake he was.

The conscienceless rake everyone believed him to be.

Was he truly that man? Jane didn't know what to believe

anymore. It was as if the Earl of Chasebourne had turned into two different characters. She knew the outrageous charmer who loved women. Now she wanted to know the man who had written these poems. His thoughts and feelings called to her heart.

Thunder rumbled in the distance. Then another sound came from the inner door. The unmistakable thud of footsteps.

Jane sprang to her feet, Marianne's poem clutched to her bosom just as Ethan came through the doorway.

He didn't notice her at first. His dark head was bent as he leafed through the book in his hand. He wore black breeches and a white shirt with no cravat. His feet were bare. He looked wickedly handsome, yet it was more than his demon-dark attractiveness that fascinated her. Now she could discern a sensitivity to his mouth and eyes, the hint of emotional depths.

He looked up and his gaze clashed with hers. His eyes widened, and for one instant, she felt as if she could see straight into his soul, into the unguarded man who had penned profound verse, the father who had poured out his love into a poem.

He glanced at the paper in her hands. His black eyebrows lowered and his face hardened into a grimace of fury.

"I know I shouldn't be here." Her voice trembled, still shaken from the revelation of reading his poems. "But I was lonely, and I thought—"

"Damn you," he said through clenched teeth. *"Damn you."*

Flinging aside his book, he sprang at Jane.

Her first impulse was to step back, out of his path. But she stood wedged between the desk and the chair. She didn't wish to run, anyway. She felt no fear of him, only a compelling need to learn why he'd concealed his talents.

He snatched the poem out of her hand. "Who gave you leave to come in here? Who?"

Your mother. "No one. I was curious to find out what

you did up here, that's all. And now that I *do* know—''

He hurled the paper onto the desk. ''My mother told you to invade my privacy. She told you to wait for me. Didn't she? This has the mark of her scheming.''

''Her scheming—'' Jane paused, feeling sick inside. *If you two have quarreled, I would advise you to speak to him at once.* Had Lady Rosalind put the idea in Jane's head? Yes, but it didn't matter. They both wanted the best for Marianne. ''Ethan, don't blame your mother. I came here of my own free will. No one forced me.''

''Quite so. You are both determined to make hell of my life.'' His eyes shone like dark mirrors, reflecting nothing. ''So tell me. What are you supposed to do next? Offer yourself to me?''

Despite his anger, she felt a thrill of longing. She could smell his scent, dark and feral, enticing. They were alone here. He could do whatever he liked to her. And in the morning, he would feel obliged to wed her.

She stepped toward him, stopping so close she could feel his heat. ''Is that so impossible?'' she whispered. ''For you to desire me?''

With a snakelike hiss, the coals settled in the grate. Another roll of thunder sounded closer. The lamplight flickered on his hard expression, bad-tempered and suspicious. There was nothing of the vulnerable man visible; he might have been Lucifer himself.

''Get out,'' he said.

Her heart sank. Yet she couldn't give up. She had to think of a way to distract him. ''No. Not yet. First, we must talk about your work. Why did you never tell me you wrote poetry?''

He walked away, pacing the circular chamber. ''It's scribbling, that's all. Forget you ever saw it.''

''I can't forget. It's too beautiful. Especially the poem about Marianne.'' Emotion tangled her throat and made her voice hoarse. ''You really do love her, don't you?''

"She is my daughter. I told you, I shall never forsake her."

"I know." His vehemence made Jane more determined than ever to stand at his side as Marianne's mother. If only she had the chance, she could teach him to be a good father. "I could see your feelings for her in your poem. You have a way with words—"

"If you like trite nonsense."

He swung around and swept his arm across the desk. While Jane stared in frozen shock, he shoveled the papers off the surface. They snowed down into the waste bin and onto the carpet.

Aghast, Jane hastened to his side. "Stop! Have you gone mad? You must have worked hours on these poems."

"Whether I did or not is no concern of yours. You're meddling."

"Yes, I am." She snatched a wrinkled paper out of his hand and smoothed it out against her skirt. "These are your thoughts, your feelings. They should be treasured, recopied and properly preserved."

"They should be kept away from busybodies like you. Now, get out of here." He clamped his hand around her upper arm and gave her a push toward the door.

She stepped in front of him and seized his muscled arms. "Stop it, Ethan. I'm not leaving. And I bloody well won't let you destroy a part of yourself."

Against her bosom she could feel the rise and fall of his chest. He glared fiercely, and in the silence, lightning crackled. Slowly the wildness fled his eyes, and the rigid set of his mouth eased a little. "You swore, Miss Maypole."

Oddly, she felt a little twist of pleasure at hearing him use that pet name. "Only in the interest of making my point—that your poems are precious. They express your unique vision of the world."

Turning abruptly, he walked away. She tensed, prepared to stop him from scattering more sheets, but he merely combed his fingers through his hair and prowled the circular room. "*My* vision," he muttered. "You had no right to snoop through my private papers."

"I apologize for intruding. I thought I knew you—but I didn't even know you wore spectacles for reading."

"Why should you? As you said, we're merely acquaintances."

"But why did you never tell me you're a poet? Why did you behave so badly at the poetry reading this evening? Verse is nothing to be ridiculed. Do you not realize how gifted you are?"

"Keep your false praise. I don't need anyone's approval, least of all yours."

Though he spoke harshly, Jane felt a flash of tenderness. He paced like a caged wolf. It surprised her that a confident man like him could be so defensive about his writing. Poets held an honored status in society—even those tainted by controversy like Lord Byron and Mr. Shelley. Yet Ethan didn't seem to realize just how wonderful he was, or that his writings added a deeper, richer dimension to his character.

Kneeling by the rubbish bin, she gathered a handful of papers, carefully smoothing the crumpled ones and making a tidy pile. "Gaining approval isn't the point. I've studied enough poetry to know the good from the bad. I helped my father with translations of old English epics. I believe you ought to have your work published so that people can share your thought-provoking insights. I could help with the re-copying—"

"*Don't.*" He spun on his heel and scowled at her. "Don't you dare even suggest it. My private life will not become fodder for the amusement of the masses."

Jane pursed her lips. "If you think your work has no merit, then why do you continue to write?"

A dull red flush crept up his cheeks. He stood with his arms crossed, his jaw raised. "It's a bad habit, that's all."

Jane gathered more papers and added them to her stack.

"Rather like biting one's nails? Or taking too many mistresses?"

"Precisely."

"I disagree. I think you are a creative genius who has an obligation to share his God-given talents."

He snorted. "I have an obligation to no one, and that is the way matters shall remain. Now go back to your room and stay out of my life."

"Not yet." She held up a paper to the lamplight and read through the maze of crossed-out words. " 'Beneath these vast and silent fields / Lie the bones of those unyield / Whose blood sustained the living men / And nourish now the victory coffin—' "

He snatched the paper out of her hand and crushed it. "Jane, I'm warning you for the last time. Get out. Or I'll throw you out."

"No you won't," she said. "Oh, Ethan, you have such a faculty for language. How can you belittle it? How can you let people go on thinking you're worthless?"

"It's my true nature," he snarled. "You've said so yourself."

Furious that she had made him voice his deepest fear, Ethan teetered on the verge of violence. He hurled the ball of paper into the waste bin, but he couldn't stem the black tide inside himself. He hated her in that moment. He hated her for probing, for stripping away his defenses.

An oasis of calm, Jane knelt in the pool of her turquoise skirt. She had made tidy piles of the poems—*his* poems—and now gazed expectantly at him as if she had the right to pry into his secrets. He felt compelled to wipe that sympathy off her face, to make her see him as he really was—moody, broody, and beyond redemption.

He resumed walking, determined to burn off the dark fire inside himself. "Tell me I ought to be proud of myself," he said. "While Napoleon marched his army into Belgium, I cast wagers on his success. While men like John Randall gave their lives for their country, I stayed at home to drink and whore. I didn't even realize the battle had taken place until five days later. You see, I'd spent that time in bed with Serena Badrick.''

He could still remember surfacing from the hellhole of her bedroom, drained, dogged by self-disgust. And the shock of reading the news reports, the papers from London that had piled up during his sordid affair. He had ridden straight for home, ill to his soul, unable to flee the knowledge that at last he had fulfilled his father's most dire prophesy.

Jane sat on her heels, watching him with unruffled acceptance. ''You wrote a moving tribute to the captain and the other men who died,'' she said. ''Surely that counts for something—''

He cut her off with a slash of his hand. ''It's meaningless. A few words on paper signify nothing to the men who bled on the battlefield.''

''But you aren't a soldier. You're a writer. And if you share your poetry with others, you've fulfilled a purpose in making people aware of the horrors of war.''

He was drawn to her wise, innocent features, to the glimmering of light there. Turning away, he braced his hands on the carved mantelpiece and stared down into the dying fire. ''No. You're mistaken. There is no purpose to poetry other than vain self-indulgence. Words mean nothing. Only actions matter.''

''Who told you that?''

He clenched his jaw. But for once he could not stop the dark memories inside him from pouring forth. ''My father.''

''Then he was wrong.'' She scrambled to her feet and hurried to his side, a long-legged filly with more eagerness than grace. ''Just because he didn't appreciate poetry doesn't mean your writing lacks value. He wasn't capable of understanding your aesthetic thinking. It's a matter of taste and preference.''

She didn't understand. Or wouldn't. In her own way, she

was as stubborn and unrelenting as his sire. "It's more than that," Ethan said. "You're simplifying the matter."

"Did he ever read any of your work?"

"Yes."

"And?"

Ethan snatched up the poker and stirred the coals, adding a few more lumps from the scuttle. Keeping his voice flat, he said, "When I was eleven, I wrote a poem for him on his birthday. I spent hours composing it, finding just the right words, recopying it. I made him out to be a god among fathers. And when I presented it to him, he ripped up the paper and threw the pieces into the fire." Watching the flames leap up, he could see the parchment blackening, turning to ash. He could taste the sickness in his throat and feel the churning in his belly. Angry that the past still affected him, he jammed the iron poker back into its stand.

Jane touched his arm. "How cruel of him. If I had known . . ."

"If you had known, it wouldn't have made a bloody bit of difference." Ethan told himself to step away from her; the warm pressure of her hand felt dangerously comforting. Yet he didn't move. "He wanted me to spend my time preparing to run the estate and to take my seat in Parliament someday. He sent me to read the law, but I failed in my studies. My sole interest lay in literature, a fact that enraged him. He told me . . ."

"Told you what?"

His throat taut, Ethan forced himself to go on. "He told me I would end up in the gutter if I didn't do as he said. I'd be worse than the lowest gin-sotted derelict—because I'd had all the advantages and wasted them." He pulled his gaze away from her. "And that's precisely what's happened."

"So he is the reason you've denied your brilliant writing all these years." Her eyes flashed with ire. "Well, I wouldn't give a copper farthing for his narrow-minded opinion."

"He wanted me to accomplish something with my life, the way he did."

"Balderdash. He wanted to remake you in his own image—instead of allowing you to follow your own interests."

Ethan resisted her logic. It was easier to taunt her. "Is this really Miss Maypole, commending me for ignoring duty and responsibility?"

"Yes," she said, moving in front of him, her skirt rustling. She grasped his arms like a governess intending to drill a fact into an obstinate pupil. "You've closed yourself away here, scorned your talents, all because your father was too dull and dictatorial to understand your abilities. Can't you see that you must be true to yourself, not become what someone else decides you should be? Your talent isn't a vice. It's a blessing."

Her intensity drew him. The last thing he'd expected was for Jane to champion him. He'd only told her the truth in an attempt to disgust her, to make her see the mistake in exposing his secret to the world. And still she didn't understand the tempest of emotions that compelled him to write. She didn't grasp how personal those feelings were, how raw and exposed he felt from just one person reading his work, let alone hundreds—even thousands. The very prospect repelled him.

Judging by her fervent expression, Jane would not easily give up her new crusade. She stood before him, clutching his arms as if she could impose her will on him, a meddlesome woman telling him how to think and feel. And when she looked at him, her eyes shone as if she could see good inside the fallen archangel.

Damn her. Damn her for trying to change him into some idealistic vision of a hero. And damn himself for wanting to believe her.

"To hell with poetry," he muttered, crowding her against the stone wall. "I'll show you who I really am."

His mouth caught hers, pressing hard. He slid his hands

over her breasts and hips and bottom, making no conces-
sions to her innocence. She was tall and willowy, almost
his equal in height, yet soft and curved in all the right
places. She wasn't drunk on champagne this time, and so
much the better. Jane would see that he truly was the dis-
graced man the world saw.

He cupped her breasts, massaging her through the rigid
corset, expecting her at any moment to slap his hands away
and accuse him of being a wicked rake. He wanted her to
do just that, to run away in disgust and leave him the hell
alone.

Instead, she uttered a small sound in her throat. Her arms
looped around his neck and her fingers tangled in his hair.
"Ethan." Breathing his name, she parted her lips and
pressed her body to his.

Heat flashed to his loins. It was intense, mindless, intox-
icating, and he reacted without thinking, tasting her more
deeply, fitting himself into the cradle of her hips. He felt
the powerful urge to join with her, to make the bond between them physical as well as cerebral. He knew passion,
how to control it, how to shape a woman to his will. And
he would do just that to Jane; he would make himself the
center of her universe. He would dominate her, give her
pleasure, until she forgot all else. Reaching for the back of
her dress, he had the buttons undone to her waist when
sanity broke through his madness.

Jane. He intended to make love to Jane Mayhew. Miss
Maypole.

He jerked himself back, bracing his shaking hands on the
stone wall. His head bent, he fought for breath. "We can't
do this."

"Why not?" Her voice sounded husky, and her fingers
moved back and forth over his collarbone. "Don't you like
kissing me?"

He lifted his head. Gray-blue eyes studied him with open
yearning. Her lips looked damp and reddened, inviting as
heaven. Damning as hell. "Kissing is for virgins," he said

bluntly. "Go back to your room. Lest you find yourself ruined."

He stepped back, allowing her space to leave. But she didn't move. The short sleeves of her gown sagged halfway down her shoulders, giving her a vulnerable, waiflike appearance.

"Perhaps I want you to ruin me," she said. With a sinuous shrug of her shoulders, she let the dress slip down. It clung stubbornly to her bosom for a moment before pooling at her waist. "I'd like it very much, please."

She might have been requesting a teacake. Her gaze fixed on him, she plucked at the front laces of her corset.

He stared at the pink-ribboned undergarment that defined her slender form and pushed up her breasts, tantalizing him with a glimpse of what lay beneath. She must have drunk too much wine at dinner. That was the only explanation for her astonishing behavior.

"The devil you say." Before she could do more than loosen the corset, he yanked up her bodice, his fingertips brushing her flesh. The fabric clung there, revealing a tantalizing swath of ivory skin. She felt soft and warm, and he wanted only to strip away that last defense and take her in his hands. He wanted to press her down to the floor and introduce her to mindless lust. Harshly he said, "Cover yourself."

Making no move to obey, she lowered her chin and regarded him through her lashes. It was an incredibly erotic look coming from an untried maiden. "Oh, Ethan, you make me feel so warm and shivery inside. If you don't make love to me now, I'll never know what it's like. Please, let me show you I'm not a sour old spinster."

If she had punched him, she could have not have shocked him more. He couldn't think, he could scarcely breathe. His body was on fire.

For her. For Jane.

Unable to stop himself, he settled his shaking hands on her bare shoulders. "My God, you deserve better than a sordid affair.'' He lowered his voice to a gruff murmur. ''I'm not good enough for you.''

''Perhaps not.'' She graced him with a rueful little smile. ''But I don't want any other man. I want *you*.''

A gust of wind rattled the windowpanes and lightning flashed, closer now. Desire gripped his loins. He could scarcely believe this was Jane, prim and prudish Jane, declaring her passion for him. He knew he should send her away, push her out of the tower room and bar the door. He could offer her only a fleeting ecstasy.

Yet he couldn't walk away.

She stood in the flickering light of the lamp, gazing at him with those clear gray-blue eyes, her expression radiating a richness of emotion that called to a yearning buried deep inside himself, something both tender and terrifying, something that overruled the few scruples he had left.

And he knew in that moment that he was lost.

⌒ *Chapter 17* ⌒

His sudden move caught Jane by surprise.

Seizing her in his arms, he swept her up and half carried her to the rug before the hearth. Startled hope stole her breath. Even as her toes met the floor, his mouth came down on hers with stunning ferocity.

She had no time to think, no chance to revel in the knowledge that her plan had worked. With one hand he cradled her head so that he could taste her, with the other he explored her form. He tugged down her bodice, yanked at the ribbons, parted her corset. And then he thrust his hand inside her shift and cupped her breast in his palm.

She had dreamed of a man's touch, *his* touch, but the reality was so much finer. He moved his thumb across the crest, and the sensation sparkled downward, causing a place deep inside her to contract. By instinct, she arched against him, obeying the need to be closer, to feel the pressure of her body against his.

His mouth left hers and she mourned the loss, but only for a moment. He kissed a path across her cheek, licked her inner ear and made her shiver, moved down to her throat and lower still. Even as his hands pushed off her bodice and corset, he put his lips to her breast, not bothering to move her shift aside, suckling her like a babe.

She gasped, unprepared for the shock of it, the tugging

sensation that spiraled down to her belly in a warm wave. As he bent to her bosom, she threaded unsteady fingers into his thick hair. She tipped her head back and closed her eyes, the better to feel the magic of his mouth.

"Oh, Ethan."

Her legs went weak and she must have swayed, for he guided her down to her knees and knelt before her, peeling away the cambric shift until she was bare to her waist. Looping one arm around her waist, he touched her breasts with his fingertips, tracing the contours of hills and valley.

"No padding," he said with intensely male satisfaction. "How did you hide these for so long?"

She ducked her head, absurdly pleased by his approval. "How did you hide your writing?"

His mouth quirked into a wry grimace. "We've both had our secrets. But I confess, I like yours better."

He replaced his hand with his mouth, applying himself to her bosom again in that uncommonly delicious kiss. She felt the rasp of his tongue first on one side, and then the other, filling her with wanton warmth and sending liquid shivers over her skin. The feeling expanded throughout her body and pooled deep in her belly.

With unsteady hands, she cupped his neck inside his collar, absorbing the heat of his flesh, caressing his jaw and feeling his movements as he suckled her. *Sweet heaven.* How had she lived for so long without knowing this pleasure? No wonder women flocked to him.

She swallowed against the furious ache in her throat. She didn't want to think about all his lovers, not tonight. It was futile to wish for fidelity from him. That had nothing to do with her purpose. For now he was hers and nothing else mattered.

He plucked the pins from her hair, letting the rich brown mass flow down to her waist. "God, how I've wanted to do this," he muttered, bending his head and nuzzling her neck. "To strip away your starch. To know how you taste and feel."

He was touching her as he spoke. One hand kneaded her breast, the other slipped inside her gown to cup her bottom. His big palm felt solid and possessive over the thin barrier of her petticoat. Her breath quickened, as much in response to his words as his caress. "Did you, truly?" she asked, gripping his shoulders, not caring if she let her wistfulness show. "Did you really imagine doing this with *me*?"

The sound he made in his throat was part groan, part laugh. "Jane, ever since you stormed into my bedchamber in Wessex, I've thought about nothing else. Nothing but you."

Her insides curled sweetly. She didn't want to think he might be embellishing the truth. Tonight she would believe whatever he told her. She would revel in his charm and learn all he was willing to teach her. And perhaps if—*when*—he married her, they could do this every night. Perhaps he wouldn't be so angry when he realized she'd come here to trick him. . . .

She lifted her face to him, and he plunged her into another deep, drowning kiss. Her senses swam giddily, leaving her gasping and limp, clay in his capable hands.

The next thing she knew, he had her falling backward, onto the carpet in front of the fireplace. But it wasn't the heat from those flames that warmed her. It was Ethan kneeling over her, Ethan unknotting the ties of her petticoats with expert ease, Ethan peeling off her gown and undergarments in one smooth pull. Only her gauzy silk stockings and lacy white garters kept her from utter nakedness. Through the mist of her desire, she felt a certain shyness as he gazed upon what no man had seen before. Instinctively, she brought her hands low to shield her most vulnerable place.

He took hold of her wrists and gently moved her arms. "Don't," he said. "Don't ever be ashamed. You're beautiful. The perfect woman."

For several heartbeats he gazed at her, and she wanted to weep at the appreciation on his face. Then his hand met her thigh. His fingers feathered up and down, until her embarrassment melted into a different sort of tension, an impatience to move beneath him. No longer could she lie still and watchful. She ached for something she could not name, something that made her twist her hips toward his hand in unabashed eagerness.

"Ethan?"

"Don't be afraid," he murmured. "Let yourself feel it."

"Feel what?"

"This."

He cupped her between the legs, the heel of his palm pressing lightly, insistently. Even as she gasped in startled wonder, he lay down beside her, his leg anchoring hers with a gratifying weight. He still wore his shirt and breeches, and it seemed utterly decadent for him to be clothed while she sprawled like an offering for his pleasure.

He nuzzled her hair, his breath warm against her ear. He kept his hand in place, circling slowly against her. Then, in a move that stunned her, he stroked her inner folds. "So soft you are," he whispered. "If I'd known how willing you'd be, I'd not have waited so long."

His touch was so intimate, so extraordinary, she turned her face into his shirt and moaned. She forgot all else as he worked his sorcery, caressing her with a familiarity she had never dreamed possible. She arched against him, the need inside her sharpening, intensifying until she quivered in his arms and clutched handfuls of his shirt, her legs opening fully to him. She felt dizzy and aching as if she hovered on the brink of a world too marvelous to behold.

"Let go," he murmured, kissing her hair. "I'll catch you when you fall."

"Fall?" she asked, mystified, yet trusting him utterly, ready to do whatever he willed. In the next moment, all her questions were answered as she tumbled into paradise, her body pulsing with rapture.

Wonderfully sated, she drifted back to awareness to see him sitting up, shucking his shirt and breeches. There was a wildness in his dark eyes, a heaviness to his breathing.

The firelight made his skin glow like bronze, and her mouth went dry at the magnificence of him. She had not known the male member could be so . . . impressive.

She shivered as he settled down onto her, solid and real and warm. How amazing to be here with him like this, both of them naked. She had begged to be seduced by a scoundrel, the most notorious rake in society. But it didn't feel like a sin. It felt gloriously right, a blessing from heaven.

She kissed his smooth-shaven cheek. "I love what you did to me."

"That was only the beginning."

"What more—"

Before she could finish, he brought his mouth down onto hers. The kiss went on and on, and she grew aware of his maleness, burning into her thigh. Intensely curious about their physical differences, she wondered how he would reach his pleasure. Was she supposed to touch him . . . *there*?

The moment she thought it, she wanted to do so. The need throbbed inside her, a reprise of the sensations he had aroused in her already. Her skin felt dewy and warm. Succumbing to wicked impulse, she slid her hands down his tautly muscled body. But their hips were tightly locked. She was wondering how to get him to give her access when he shifted position, kissing her throat and breasts.

Her heart racing, she closed her fingers around him. How hot he was, thick and hard and velvety. As she explored him, he sucked in a hissing breath.

She snatched back her hand. "Am I hurting you?"

His tortured laugh rumbled against her breasts. "Only if you stop."

He took her hand and cupped it around him again, guiding her up and down. Then he dipped his finger inside her. She gasped as he circled and skirmished, then slipped in deeper, his strokes slow and sure, driving her mad. She knew now the ecstasy that awaited her, and she strained toward it. But just as she reached the precipice, he withdrew his hand.

"Please . . ." she moaned.

Breathing unevenly, he nipped her ear. "Tell me what you want."

"You know what."

"I wonder," he muttered, sounding smug and secretive, "if you do."

In lieu of explanation, he settled himself between her thighs, large and heavy, a welcome weight. She felt a touch at her most private place, mistook it for his hand and eagerly pressed toward it. In that instant, she realized how the act was accomplished. The knowledge seized her in a thrill of awe and fierce longing, and she wriggled against him.

His dark eyes gleamed down at her. "Patience. There's no need to rush."

He resumed his dallying, fondling her breasts, smoothing his hands along her body, kissing her all over. Except for a sheen of sweat on his chest and the tension she felt in his muscles, he looked in control, focused on her pleasure before his.

How could he torture her like this? She wanted to hurry. His slow hands stirred her anticipation to an agonizing pitch. She tried to press down on him again, but he shifted himself lower, out of her reach. She was about to protest when his lips kissed the place his hand had just been.

The heat of his breath startled a gasp from her. *"Ohh."* She could utter no more as the wicked work of his mouth sent fire over her skin and through her body. Closing her eyes, she fell straight into bliss.

As she lay relaxed and dazed, he brought himself over her again. This time, he entered her in a smooth thrust. There was a flash of pain, enough to make her stiffen, her nails raking down his back. He held himself still, his arms trembling ever so slightly around her.

"Forgive me," he murmured. Then he gave a shaky

laugh. "Hell no, don't forgive me. You feel too damned good."

He filled her, hard and deep, linking them in a way she had never imagined possible in all her dreams of making love with him. The pain melted into a feeling of utter completeness as if she had lived all her life for this one precious moment. They were one, truly one. Tears of joy stung her eyes, and she arched up and kissed his throat.

"Ethan . . . oh, Ethan, I love you."

He went still and searched her face. "Don't delude yourself," he said in a rough undertone. "This is what you love. *This.*"

He moved inside her, slow and deliberate, arousing her to panting heights. She absorbed the pounding of his heart against her breasts. Need washed through her, tantalizing and wanton, urging her to join his rhythm. But tender understanding held her back, and she seized hold of his shoulders. "No . . . I won't let you deny it. I love *you,* Ethan. *You.*"

His eyes darkened with an unguarded yearning. Then his gaze went unfocused, feral in its intensity. He pressed harder inside her, frantically, as if he could no longer contain himself. His breath came fast and furious; his movements became jerky and agitated. But she wasn't afraid. Locking her ankles around his calves, she embraced his wildness with a vigor of her own. Each thrust brought them closer to the light, higher and brighter, until she lost herself in the radiance, aware only of him burying his face in her hair, his body shuddering.

"Jane. My God . . . *Jane.*"

Consciousness returned to Ethan by degrees, the whispering of the fire, the fragrance of her skin, a sense of well-being. Rain drummed on the roof, and lightning flashed in the window. How fitting that the storm had broken, he mused. Jane lay relaxed beneath him, her arms around him, and tender torment tightened his chest.

He had ruined her. Yet no woman had ever felt so good.

No woman had ever sounded so sincere in her declaration of love.

She was deluding herself, of course. Having been brought up with strict morals, Jane wouldn't have given away her virginity without convincing herself she was in love. He must not allow her to deceive herself.

Reluctantly, he started to lift himself from her. And then a second shock wave resonated through him.

He had not withdrawn.

Closing his eyes, he groaned in disbelief and horror. He rolled onto his back and plunged his fingers through his hair. He had spilled his seed inside her. God help him, he had not been so reckless since his first time, when a randy widow had taught him that trick of contraception.

"Ethan? Is something the matter?"

He opened his eyes to see her lying on her side gazing at him, an earnest little pucker on her brow. She was the picture of sensual perfection. Tendrils of dark hair, tinted with copper highlights, curled down around her breasts. One nipple peeked out, and he felt the untimely urge to kiss it.

She had caused him to lose control. Why Jane, of all women? He'd kept his head with more experienced, more inventive partners. Had it been his irrational reaction to her misguided words of love? Or the fact that she knew his secret?

"Get dressed," he muttered, sitting up and tossing the chemise at her.

The scrap of linen landed across her hips, and she clutched at it, bunching it in her fingers. Fingers that had caressed him only moments ago. She scooted into a sitting position. "Get dressed?" she asked in a voice so low he had to strain to hear over the beating rain. "Is that how this ends?"

He stepped into his breeches. "It's time you returned to your bedchamber."

"Are you always so cold . . . to your other women?"

The bewildered pain in her voice pulled at him. She stared up, her chin raised, both fists clenching the chemise to her bosom. The knowledge that he had wronged her struck him anew.

Hunkering down, he brushed a lock of hair from her brow. "Forgive me. I should never have made love to you. Pray God nothing comes of it."

"What do you mean?"

"Jane. I could have made you pregnant."

Her hand stole over her belly. A faraway look entered her eyes, as if she were imagining herself fertile with his baby. He had the sudden fantasy of her smiling at him, her hands on her rounded abdomen.

He shouldn't want that. One natural child was enough to complicate his life.

"Merciful God," she whispered. "But you've done this many times before and there is only Marianne. I assumed you knew . . . some way to prevent conception."

It galled him to admit that he had lost control. "I do. But I erred just now. I released my seed inside you."

"You don't always do so?"

He shook his head. "Never—almost never. Though admittedly, the method is not foolproof."

"Then why with me?"

"It was . . . just a mistake." When Jane frowned and opened her mouth to question him further, he caught her by the bare shoulders. "Should you discover you're pregnant, I wish to know immediately. Do you understand me?"

Her eyes were large and luminous, the eyes of a woman well pleasured. "Do you mean . . . you would marry me?"

A cold sweat chilled his body. His throat closed tightly, and he looked away from her, no longer able to meet her gaze. "Let's not worry about that yet. We'll deal with the situation if it arises."

"Not worry?" She scrambled to her feet, arms crossed over her bosom, the chemise tucked to her chin. "Ethan, we have to talk about this. I don't even know how to tell if I'm . . . pregnant.''

"You would cease your monthly flow. When did you last bleed?''

A blush tinted her cheeks, but her gaze remained steady. "A few days ago.''

He breathed a sigh of heartfelt relief. "Good,'' he said, pulling on his shirt. "We're likely safe, then.''

"How can you be sure? I won't know for weeks if you're right. And in the meantime . . .''

"In the meantime, you're returning to your chamber. God forbid someone should discover you here. Your reputation would be ruined.''

"Not if we were to wed.''

His blood ran cold. "That happened to me once. Believe me, I don't intend for it to happen ever again.''

"Then you'd let me be ruined.''

He didn't know what the hell he'd do. His palms damp, all he could think of was to get her away safely and forget his mistake. "It won't happen,'' he repeated. "With luck, no one will ever know I seduced you.''

She stared at him another moment; then she frowned down at the rug. Her lips were pressed tightly together, lips that had been soft and moist, whispering her love for him. . . . He wished to God he knew what she was thinking now. Was she sorry she'd given herself to him?

Abruptly she rose to her feet. She slipped the chemise over her head and the fabric slithered downward to her knees. Her movements graceful, she reached for her corset. "Now that we have that settled, I must leave,'' she said, her voice cool and composed, Jane-like again.

So why did he sense that nothing was settled? That he had destroyed their friendship and deepened the chasm between them?

He donned his shirt, watching as she bent her head to retie the ribbons of her corset and then step into her gown. The turquoise silk grazed her slender form, and when he noticed her struggling to button the back, he stepped behind her to help. As his fingers brushed the creamy skin of her upper back, she stiffened ever so slightly.

It was happening already, so soon. She despised him. He couldn't blame her, only himself. She had not considered the aftermath, when she faced the realization that she'd given her purity to a cad. But he had known from the start that lovemaking would change their relationship forever. He had known that once her passions cooled, she would no longer view him in a romantic haze. He had known, and yet he had been unable to resist what she offered to him.

He slipped another dainty gold button through its loop. He had performed this service a hundred times for women, acting the abigail after a satisfying frolic. But never before had he felt so full of regrets.

Or so ready to do it all again.

"Jane," he murmured.

When he bent his head to kiss the tender nape of her neck, she spun away, crouching to gather the tortoiseshell pins that had fallen from her hair. "There," she said. "I've found all of them. I'm ready to go."

She didn't look ready. Her hair drooped over her shoulders and down to her bodice. Her lips were reddened from his kisses. But she marched briskly past the cluttered desk to the garden door.

He went after her and caught her arm, smooth and warm to his touch. Like the rest of her. "You'll have to leave by the other stairs. It's raining."

"So it is."

Surprise made her voice breathy, as if she hadn't noticed until now the lashing of raindrops against the window or the rumbling of thunder. It would have been less risky to leave by way of the garden, but it was so late, he doubted anyone was still awake, anyway.

He was tempted to linger with her, to somehow bridge the rift between them, but she veered away from him, heading toward the staircase that led down to his chambers. Her willowy form disappeared through the opposite doorway, and he hastened in her wake.

A candle in a wall sconce cast a flickering light over the narrow, curving stairs. The tower room had been used for storage in his father's day, crammed with chairs and trunks and miscellaneous castoffs. One of Ethan's first acts as the new earl had been to order the door unsealed and the junk banished to the attic. Since then, he had gone up and down these steps a thousand times, taking refuge to write.

Jane knew his secret now.

The thought disturbed him in an elemental way. Although he trusted her not to betray him, he still felt uneasy that she had seen into his soul. He preferred to keep his relations with women light and amusing, inconsequential.

Instead, he had lost his head over a virgin. And not just any virgin. Jane Mayhew, his prickly nemesis. His not-so-sour spinster.

She hesitated in the doorway and looked at him questioningly. "Your valet?"

"He's retired for the night."

She nodded and went into the bedchamber, hurrying as if she feared he might entice her into the four-poster and have his way with her again. He burned to do just that, though he'd never brought a woman here. He always met his lovers elsewhere, at their homes or at a discreet town house he owned in Haymarket.

But Jane deserved better than a clandestine affair. Tonight had been an aberration, a terrible lapse in judgment. He should not wish to repeat it. He should not remember how perfect she had felt beneath him.

Or that he didn't want her to walk out and never return.

His chest tight, he stopped her just as she opened the door to the outer corridor. He placed his hands around her slim waist and spoke without thinking. "Jane, don't go."

The flickering candlelight from a wall sconce played on her strong, feminine features as she met his gaze squarely. "I've stayed too long already. You said so yourself."

"I know, but—" He bit off his words, frustrated by his powerful need to keep her close, to know that she did not despise him. He swore under his breath, pulled her to him, and kissed her.

She stiffened, but only for a moment. Then she put her arms around him and kissed him back, her body arching against him, a moan vibrating in her throat. The knowledge that she still desired him filled Ethan with immense gratification and reckless lust. Intending to draw her back into his bedchamber, he broke the kiss and lifted his head.

And then the worst possible event happened.

He looked over her shoulder to see three people walking down the shadowed passageway. Two women and a man.

His mother. Aunt Wilhelmina. And the furious Duke of Kellisham.

ᐃ *Chapter 18* ᐃ

The tension in Ethan penetrated the haze of desire sur-rounding Jane. Weak-kneed, she clung to him, not ready to let go. She caressed his cheek, but he caught her wrist and pushed it down. Confused and hurt, she turned her head to see what had distracted him.

And gasped. "Aunt Willy!"

A cold knot tightening inside her, Jane jerked her arms to her sides and watched the trio approach. How much of that steamy kiss had they witnessed? And why did she feel so mortified? Being discovered together would suit her plan. Or at least it would have before Ethan had made it clear he would never marry her.

The Duke of Kellisham stopped in front of them, his gaze flicking over her in a way that made Jane aware of her dishabille, the loose hair that hung down to her waist. In her hand, she clutched the pins that she had gathered from the rug in the tower room. The pins that had fallen free while Ethan had made love to her.

"What is the meaning of this, Chasebourne?" the duke demanded.

Ethan kept his hand lightly at the back of her waist. With a level gaze, he met the duke's rage. "The meaning? I'm sure my mother can tell you all about it. After all, she had the foresight to bring you here."

He glowered at Lady Rosalind. She stared regally back, one fair eyebrow arched.

"I was showing His Grace and Wilhelmina the family portraits along this passageway," the countess said. "I never dreamed I would reveal a family scandal."

"And I presume next you would have knocked on my door on the pretext of showing them the paintings in my chambers."

"Do not chide me, Ethan. *You* are at fault here, not I."

Aunt Willy wept into her handkerchief. "How could you have done this?" she wailed at Jane. "How could you have shamed me? Where did I go wrong in raising you? Oh, I do need a draught of my restorative."

Ridden with guilt, Jane rushed to put her arm around her aunt's pillowy waist. Wilhelmina sagged against her, and Ethan strode forward to grasp the woman's arm. "You should lie down, madam. I'll ring for a footman to take you to your room. Jane can go with you."

"Yes, perhaps that would be best," Lady Rosalind said. "His Grace and I can settle matters with Ethan."

"I'm not leaving." Jane had no intention of letting others decide her fate. They would attempt to force Ethan to marry her. And when he refused, they would feel obliged to send her back to Wessex in disgrace. "I am a grown woman and able to speak for myself."

"I must stay, too," said Aunt Willy, leaning heavily on Jane. "She is my dear niece, after all. It is my duty to guard her interests, especially in such terrible circumstances."

"Very well, then." Lady Rosalind lifted her hand in a majestic wave. "Shall we all step into the earl's chambers? We can talk privately there."

A few moments later, Jane sat on a stool beside the chaise where Aunt Willy lounged, sniffling and muttering. Jane bit her lip and tried not to feel as low as a worm. She regretted nothing. She had devised her plan for a pure and righteous reason, so that Marianne would have a mother.

Ethan took up a stance by the fireplace and faced his mother and the duke. His expression was etched in stone, utterly opposite from the warm, irresistible lover of the tower room.

Kellisham clasped his hands behind his back. His nostrils flared as he looked down his long nose at Ethan. "Well, Chasebourne. You have despoiled a young lady living under your protection. And do not think to make excuses."

"I have no intention of denying anything," Ethan said.

"Then I wish to assure myself that you intend to make an honorable offer to Miss Mayhew."

His harsh words fell into silence. No one spoke, though Aunt Willy snuffled into her handkerchief. Jane sat tensely, waiting for the explosion when Ethan refused.

Without taking his eyes from the duke, Ethan inclined his head in a sharp nod. "Indeed so, Your Grace. I am aware of my duty toward her."

Unable to believe her ears, Jane gaped at him. The hairpins pressed into her palm, but the pain barely registered. He would change his mind just like that? He would marry her?

Even as her heart soared, she felt sick inside. He was acting against his will. That fact was evident in his rigid stance, in his thinned mouth and grim expression. She had been a convenient affair to him, nothing more, and now he felt forced to pay the consequences.

"Oh, praise God!" Aunt Willy exclaimed. "Her reputation is saved! Though I would never have thought my Jane would succumb to the wiles of a wicked rake, a divorced man living on the very fringes of society—"

"That is quite enough, Wilhelmina," Lady Rosalind broke in. "Let us rejoice in the alliance of our families rather than dwell upon the past." As she turned to Jane, a smile gentled her lips. "I, for one, am delighted to welcome Jane as my daughter."

Jane told herself to be happy. Her plan had succeeded.

As Ethan's wife, she would have an unshakable claim to Marianne.

Yet she realized bleakly that she wanted him to be willing. She wanted him to love her. And now he never would.

His eyes black as midnight, Ethan stared from his mother to Jane. "I should like a word with my bride. In private."

"I hardly think that is appropriate," Lady Rosalind said, frowning.

"My dear," the duke said, "we can allow them a few moments alone. A man deserves the chance to properly propose to his future wife."

Lady Rosalind glanced worriedly at her son, but she made no further protest as the duke helped Aunt Willy to her feet and escorted both women out of the bedchamber. The door shut with a decisive click.

They were alone.

Jane rose shakily from the stool. She folded her hands at her waist and hoped Ethan couldn't tell how hard her heart was pounding. Before he could make her an insincere offer, she blurted, "I know you don't wish to wed, and if you will give Marianne to me, I'll tell the duke that I refused you."

He walked toward her, his face cold in the candlelight. "It's true, then. This was a plot to take Marianne from me. And now you would use my child as your bargaining chip."

He made it sound so sordid. She couldn't bear the disgust darkening his eyes. Swallowing painfully, she said, "I have her best interests at heart, that's all."

"That's all? You came to the tower room to seduce me. You read my private papers. You pretended an interest in my verse to get past my guard."

"That's not why I praised your work. I truly believe you are gifted—"

His hand slashed through the air to cut her off. "Don't cozen me again. You've duped me twice now, first with

Portia and again tonight. You conspired with my mother to catch us in the act.''

"Don't blame Lady Rosalind. I acted on my own.''

"Then how did my mother know to visit my chambers? Answer me that. How did she know she would find us together?''

I advise you to go speak to him at once. How had the countess known for certain he would make love to Jane?

"Perhaps it was feminine intuition. It doesn't matter. What does matter is that I am at fault, and no one else.'' Her voice went husky with the need to feel his arms around her again. Unable to stop herself, she placed her hands on his shirt, absorbing his heat and strength, willing him to listen. "Yes, I deceived you. I was desperate. I love Marianne, and I was afraid to lose her. I would beg you to understand that.''

With a grimace of distaste, he caught her arms and shoved her away. "So you sold your virginity to a man you despise.''

"I don't despise you, Ethan. I meant it when I said . . . I love you. I've always loved you, even when we were children.''

He gave a harsh laugh. "How inconvenient for you, then. To be shackled to a man who despises *you*.''

His cruelty flayed her. She wanted to protest further, but knew from his stony expression that he would never believe her. If not for the incident with Portia . . . But it was too late. In his eyes, she had proven herself a liar, a conniver who would say or do anything to achieve her objective. Even so, she would not—could not—give up the baby.

Doggedly, she forced herself to go on. "It is not too late to tell the duke that I refused your offer. Please, Ethan. If we can reach an agreement about Marianne, if you will allow her to live with me in Wessex—''

"No. She stays with me. That is final.''

Jane clenched her trembling fingers into fists. She turned away and walked to the night-darkened window. The storm had died to a drizzle, the lightning only a flicker in the distance. The garden below lay shrouded by a blackness as thick and suffocating as the pall around her heart. Sensing his presence behind her, she stiffened, though he did not touch her.

"You will marry me, Jane," he said in a flat voice. "As soon as I can obtain a special license from the archbishop. Tomorrow evening, if possible."

His edict died into silence. A burst of raindrops struck the window. She could see his reflection in the glass, the set features, the dark eyes revealing no warmth of emotion, only an icy determination. Why was he allowing himself to be trapped into this marriage?

Because he had a sense of duty. Honor. Decency. All those virtues she had doubted he possessed. She had thought the worst of him. Yet she was the one without principles, the one who would stop at nothing to gain her will.

A hard core of regret throbbed beneath her breastbone. She should do the noble act. She should reject his proposal. But there was Marianne to consider. The baby needed a mother, a constant presence in her life, someone to give her love and guidance.

And Jane saw herself returning to her solitary cottage in the country with only Aunt Willy and her books to keep her company. She envisioned the years ahead, long and lonely years, empty of the joy she had found for a brief interlude tonight. Would Ethan make love to her again? Or had she destroyed his desire for her? Somehow, she had to believe there was hope for them, that a caring man dwelled underneath his anger, the man who had written poetry to his infant daughter.

And so for the second time that night, she let her heart speak.

"All right, then. I'll marry you."

*   *   *

"Seldom have I seen a lovelier bride," Lady Rosalind said, unclasping the heavy heirloom necklace from Jane's neck. "You looked like a princess dressed in gold silk and diamonds." She handed the necklace to a maid, who bore it away to a velvet-lined jewel case in the wall safe.

" 'Twas a fine wedding," Aunt Willy agreed. "Even if 'twas done in haste. Mercy me, we must prepare for gossip when the announcement appears in the papers tomorrow."

"Pish-posh," the dowager said. "Any scandal will be outweighed by the fact that it is the match of the Season. More so even than my marriage to Kellisham."

Their chatter swirled around Jane. She felt numb, her limbs as wooden as a dressmaker's mannequin. She let them remove her corset and chemise. Dutifully, she raised her arms to receive a nightdress over her head, the sheer white fabric slithering over her cold body.

Seating herself at the fancy gilt dressing table, she removed the circlet of rosebuds crowning her head. She plucked the pins from her hair, letting them plink one by one into a blue porcelain dish. Then she picked up the ivory-backed brush and dragged it through her unruly hair. The oval mirror reflected her pale face and haunted eyes, the features too strong and stubborn to be considered beautiful.

She was a wife now. Ethan's wife.

In spite of everything, the thought gave her a delicious shiver. As she brushed her hair, the narrow gold band on her finger flashed in the candlelight. Earlier in the evening, she had wed Ethan in a private ceremony with only a few close friends and relatives present.

She had entered the drawing room to see him waiting for her by the marble fireplace. How handsome he had looked in blue and silver, how coldly he had behaved toward her. His aloof expression held no warmth. He had spoken his vows in an indifferent tone and then kissed her cheek as if she were his cousin or perhaps a maiden aunt. With all the yearning of a bride, Jane had wanted him to gaze at her with love in his eyes. It was the dream that had lain dormant since she was a girl, longing for the boy who took no notice of her. And now that she belonged to him, the charming rogue had become a passionless stranger.

A stranger who hated her for trapping him into wedlock. *How inconvenient for you . . . to be shackled to a man who despises you.*

"There, you're ready now," Lady Rosalind said, bending down to straighten Jane's delicate lace sleeve. In Jane's ear, she whispered, "Never fear. The moment Ethan sees you tonight, he will forget his anger. Men are like that." She beckoned to the maids. "Give your curtsy to her ladyship, quickly now."

The two young servants bobbed up and down before Jane, casting awed glances at her before trailing the dowager out of the dressing room.

How strange to be the Countess of Chasebourne, Jane thought. By virtue of her new rank, she had become an object of obeisance, mistress of this mansion, a respected member of the *ton.*

And she would trade it all for Ethan's love.

Jane set down the brush and turned the ring on her finger around and around. *Would* he forget his anger so easily? She doubted so. Lady Rosalind didn't fathom the depths to which he blamed his bride.

Aunt Wilhelmina lingered by the dressing table, a wistful smile on her jowly face. "Pray forgive me for disapproving of his lordship, Jane. Though his reputation is tarnished, he did wed you, and that means he is not lacking in honor."

"Better I should forgive myself," Jane murmured. "I've believed ill of him, too."

Her aunt gave her a motherly pat on the shoulder. "Don't fret, my dear. You, at least, have a chance for happiness. I only wish I'd had the courage to do as you did."

Startled, Jane met Wilhelmina's pale blue eyes in the mirror. "To force a man into marriage?"

"To accept an honest proposal." The older woman

sighed, her plump fingers twisting the linen handkerchief into a knot. "Oh mercy, I've never told anyone this."

"Please. What is it?"

"In my youth, I became enamored of a local gentleman, the eldest son of a prosperous farmer. But I thought myself too good for a man who earned his living by tilling the soil, and so I refused his offer of marriage." Aunt Willy's gaze went unfocused as if she were looking into the past. "Oftimes I've wondered if I made the right choice."

A lump crowded Jane's throat. No wonder her aunt relied upon her bottle of restorative; she had never forgotten her heartache.

Rising from the stool, she enveloped Wilhelmina in a hug, breathing in her faintly medicinal scent, feeling the familar pillowy softness of her form. "I'm so sorry. I never knew."

Aunt Willy returned the embrace. "I am glad, truly glad you did not become like me, old and alone, with no one to love."

"You are not alone," Jane said fiercely. "And you may stay here for as long as you like. You shall always have a home with me."

"Bless you, Jane. You always were a good child." The older woman gave Jane a dry peck on the cheek and shuffled out of the dressing room.

Jane heard the outer door close; then silence whispered around her. She felt ashamed for all the times she had resented her aunt's complaining and made uncharitable judgments about her. She hadn't understood that Wilhelmina had once been young and hopeful, pretty enough to catch the eye of a man. How sad to look back on one's life and feel regrets. How dreadful to pine for a love that couldn't be returned.

As she pined for Ethan.

Staring at her pale reflection in the mirror, she braided her hair as she always did. Tonight her fingers were clumsy and the task took twice as long. She tied the end with a ribbon, then tossed the plait over her shoulder so that it lay heavy against her back. She imagined Ethan untying the ribbon, running his fingers through her hair. . . .

A faint scent lingered in the air, a hint of old perfume. Jane uncorked several pots and jars on the dressing table until she found the source of the smell in an elegant cut-glass bottle. She held it up to her nose and sniffed. The flowery aroma brought a memory into sharp focus.

Lady Portia had worn this cologne. She had once occupied these rooms. She too had tricked Ethan into marriage.

Jane hastily capped the bottle and pushed it away. She was not like his first wife. She would never betray her marriage vows, no matter if Ethan was unfaithful. And she did not require fidelity from him. So why did the thought of him with another woman rouse a fierce wrath inside her?

She padded into the bedchamber, the rug soft beneath her bare feet. Her belongings had been moved from the guest room to this sumptuous suite adjoining Ethan's in the east wing. The huge chamber with its gilt cornices had been furnished with exquisite taste. The primrose velvet draperies on the tall windows had been drawn against the night. A silver branch of candles glowed on the white marble chimneypiece, and a fire burned cheerily in the hearth. The canopied four-poster bed stood on a dais, the covers folded back to pristine linen sheets and a bank of fluffy pillows.

Jane's gaze went to the door that connected her room to Ethan's. The white-painted panel seemed to mock her. Was he in his chamber? Or was he upstairs in the tower room, writing poetry? Perhaps he was composing an ode to deceitful wives.

In a rush of a dismal certainty, she knew Ethan would not open that door. He would not come to her tonight.

How inconvenient for you . . . to be shackled to a man who despises you.

An ache assailed Jane, the feeling so brutal she closed her eyes and pressed her fists to her bosom. Despite all her excuses to the contrary, she needed Ethan. She needed to feel his arms around her, his lips against her hair. She needed him to touch her, to kiss her, to put himself inside her and make them one body, one soul.

By her own deception, she had destroyed his trust. She had gained Marianne, only to lose Ethan.

A wild grief tore at her, and she took several shuddery breaths to calm herself. She must not succumb to regrets. She must remind herself of the true purpose for this marriage.

She snatched up an ivory silk robe, thrust her arms into the sleeves, and knotted the sash. Taking a candle, she hastened out of the bedchamber.

The brandy had failed to do its work.

Ethan sat in his bedchamber, his bare feet propped on the fireplace fender. The fire had died to glowing coals. His moody gaze flitted to the crystal decanter on the table beside the leather wing chair. Over the course of several hours, the dark liquid inside the container had dipped steadily lower as he refilled his glass. Even so, he felt clearheaded and awake, denied the relief of oblivion.

He couldn't purge Jane from his thoughts. Nor could he forget she was his wife.

Angry denial burned in his chest, and he took another long drink to cool the heat of his resentment. She had known his opinion of marriage, yet she had lured him nonetheless. She had invaded his privacy, pretended enthusiasm for his writings, and maneuvered him into lowering his guard. Like a besotted fool, he had believed her lies.

Or were they all lies?

Now that he'd had time to reflect, he remembered that Jane had wanted to leave the tower by the garden door. Because of the rainstorm, he had brought her down to his bedchamber to exit through the other door. Which meant she hadn't planned for his mother to entrap them. He could absolve Jane of that deed at least.

But he could not forgive her for taking his freedom.

Tonight when she had walked toward him in the drawing room, wearing a slim gold gown and the Chasebourne diamonds, a halo of white rosebuds in her hair, she'd looked as innocent as an angel. Showing no shame, she had spoken her vows in a clear, ringing tone. As if she really meant to honor and obey him, in sickness and in health, for so long as they both should live. He knew as well as she did that she only wanted his child.

I meant it when I said I love you.

In spite of everything, the memory of her soft voice worked like a powerful aphrodisiac. Heat pooled in his groin, a heat fueled by the fantasies that plagued him without mercy. He imagined Jane warm and wanton in his arms, her hips lifting to meet his, her arms clasping him close. She couldn't have faked her physical response to him; that made another point in her favor. He had coaxed her to climax thrice, the last time while he had been sheathed deep inside the tight velvet glove of her body.

He wanted to be there again.

Uttering a vicious curse, Ethan slammed his glass onto the table. He leaned forward and plowed his fingers through his hair. To Jane, he was only a means to an end. He must never forget that. Never.

Especially now, when his unwanted bride occupied the adjoining chamber.

Lifting his head, he scowled at the connecting door. A hundred times, he'd been tempted to open the white-painted panel and seek her out. A hundred times he'd reminded himself what a mistake that would be. Yet he knew if he stayed here, he would go to Jane.

He would claim his rights as her husband.

Ethan pushed up from the chair. He swayed a little; perhaps the spirits had had some effect, after all. Ignoring the ache in his loins, he strode out the door, past the place where he'd been caught with Jane only twenty-four hours ago. With no particular destination in mind, he walked down the corridor. He had to put distance between himself and temptation.

The house was silent, dark except for a candle in a glass sconce at the end of the passageway. He picked up the lamp and used it to light his way. His steps led him up a back staircase to the nursery, his bare feet silent on the wood floor. He walked through the gloomy schoolroom and headed for Marianne's bedchamber.

Rhythmic snoring came from the nursemaid's room next door. As always, he moved carefully to avoid awakening the servant. He preferred that no one know of his nightly visits. It was a time when he could be alone with Marianne without prying eyes to observe him. He liked the peace of watching her sleep, the satisfaction of knowing he had done at least one good deed in his life.

Tonight, a faint glow came from his daughter's bedchamber. Had the nursemaid left a candle burning? He would have to chastise her. To prevent a fire, he had given strict orders to extinguish all flames at bedtime.

He hastened through the doorway and stopped dead.

A lone taper shone on a table that held an assortment of baby-care items, a washbasin and pitcher, a dish of pins, a pile of neatly folded nappies. In the shadows beyond the small circle of light stood a rocking chair. In it sat Jane, cuddling the swaddled baby.

Both were asleep.

A storm of emotions battered Ethan: anger that she had usurped his child, bitterness over her trickery, resentment that she had stolen even this private moment from him. Yet beneath those volatile feelings flowed a traitorous softness, an undeniable tenderness. Marianne rested a tiny fist on Jane's bosom. Jane's head was tilted onto the thick plait of hair that draped her shoulder. Her arms clasped the baby if she were more precious than gold. They looked like mother and daughter.

I love Marianne, and I was afraid to lose her.

In all his angry brooding, he had lost sight of that truth.

He had made it brutally clear that he meant to separate her from the baby. Rather than return to Wessex alone, she had found a means to keep Marianne. Whatever her other faults, Jane would make a devoted mother. Didn't her willingness to marry him prove that? She had acted out of love for his daughter. It was a devilish draught for his pride to swallow, to concede that she might have had cause to gull him.

Yet that didn't absolve her of the deception.

He told himself it was concern for Marianne that drew him closer. If he didn't restore the baby to her cradle, Jane might accidentally drop her.

The rug muffled his footfalls. He placed his lamp beside the candle, the added light illuminating the slumbering pair. Jane looked vulnerable in sleep, her lips soft and her lashes dark against her cheeks. The pale robe gaped in front, revealing a sheer white nightdress. He wanted to untie the ribbon at the bodice and slip his hand inside; he wanted to cup her unbound breasts and kiss her awake.

He cursed his foolishness. She couldn't be trusted. She had robbed him of choices, forced him into making vows he did not believe in.

Slowly he slid his hands beneath the baby's small form. He couldn't avoid touching Jane's robe, warm and silken as the flesh beneath it. Annoyed with the direction of his thoughts, he lifted his daughter from her.

Something nudged Jane from a dreamlike doze. Her arms clutched for the baby and met emptiness. A cry of alarm burst from her throat. "Marianne!"

Horror jerked her upright. Her eyes snapped open to see a dark shape looming over her.

"It's all right," a deep voice murmured. "She's safe with me."

Ethan.

The awful panic ebbed. "Thank heaven," Jane breathed.

Limp and shaken, she watched him carry the slumbering baby to the lavish gilt cradle and deposit her carefully inside. She hadn't meant to fall asleep. She had only wanted to rock Marianne for a few minutes, to hold her close and know she was loved. The last thing she remembered was the quiet tranquility that had washed through her, a sense of peace and rightness.

The candlelight touched Ethan's white shirt and dark trousers as he bent down to tuck the blanket around the baby. For the space of a heartbeat, gentleness softened his hard features.

She knew in that moment why he had come here. He loved Marianne, too.

Anguish twisted inside Jane. If only they could be a family. If only he could forgive her. If only he would turn to her, take her into his strong arms, hold her close and never let go. . . .

He picked up the lamp and walked to the door. She called out softly, thoughtlessly. "Ethan. Wait!"

Over his shoulder he said gruffly, "Go to bed." Then he vanished into the darkened schoolroom.

Jane lurched up, the rocking chair swaying, her tangled skirt catching her legs. She darted after him, but he was already striding out into the corridor. Clearly, he wanted nothing to do with her.

She sagged against the door frame. The wood felt cold to her sleep-warmed skin. She could not forget that brief moment of tenderness. He loved his daughter. That was the one bond they shared.

No, there was more. She knew from his poetry that he had hidden depths, that he was not the shallow scoundrel the world considered him to be. She wanted desperately to believe that in time he would understand her motive, that his fury at her would cool.

Lady Rosalind had said he'd been coerced to marry Portia, too. Yet Jane had seen them on their honeymoon, and he had looked happy, carefree, his attention wholly focused on his bride. If he'd been angry with Portia over the forced nuptials, he'd certainly overcome his rancor.

Was it possible he could be coaxed into forgiving his second wife?

A shiver of longing sent goose bumps over her skin. Wide awake now, Jane tiptoed back to the rocking chair and sat there for a long time thinking, pondering the problem from all angles.

Could she persuade him to relent and make their marriage real? Or would he reject her with cruel words? Would he disdain her in the years to come?

The candle had guttered and nearly gone out when she made her decision. Somehow, she would win him back.

⸺ *Chapter 19* ⸺

"If you won't share my bed," Jane said, "at least we could pretend to be madly in love to stop all the gossip."

Scorched by her statement, Ethan jerked his gaze to Jane, sitting on the bench beneath the sunny window in the nursery. Her deep blue gown skimmed the lithe body he had denied himself for the past week. She had tricked him, and now she wanted him to behave like a smitten lover?

Angry, he calmed himself by looking down at Marianne, who lay in the secure perch formed by one of his legs propped on the other. His silver pocket watch dangled from his fingers, and the baby reached out to grasp the new toy. "What the devil do I care about gossip?" he said on a laugh.

"Why, you *should* care, for Marianne's sake. Our behavior reflects upon her."

"She's an infant. By the time she grows up, people will have forgotten about our hasty wedding."

"Perhaps. But I wonder if you know all they're saying." Jane shook her head. "Of course, you wouldn't know. You've been hiding in the tower room for the past week."

"Hiding? I haven't been *hiding*." He objected strenuously to the implication that he was craven, and catching his strident tone, Marianne whimpered. He stroked her soft cheek in a soothing caress. Moderating his voice, he stated,

"I've been working." At least he'd been trying to concentrate. But he couldn't seem to write two lines that satisfied him. He had squandered far too much time brooding about his wife.

"Oh, well, if you say so," Jane said breezily. She leaned forward so that he had a view of the lush terrain of her bosom, and his body reacted with annoying swiftness. "But *I've* been out in society," she added. "I've noticed the looks, the stares. People believe I was seduced by the wicked earl."

He refused to feel sympathy when it was a situation of her own making. "So let them. They'll move on to another scandal soon enough."

"That's not all. Just yesterday at tea, Lord Keeble and Mr. Duxbury were kind enough to inform me about something else people are whispering."

"Don't believe those two buffoons. They start half the rumors that circulate."

"I fear they're right about this one. The entire *ton* is speculating that Marianne is not a foundling, but your child—"

"That's nothing new."

"—and mine. They're saying *I* am her birth mother."

He should have thought of that, and he covered his shock with a jest. "Then we should remind them that at the time of Marianne's conception, you wore shapeless black gowns buttoned to your chin. And you were peevish enough to wither a man."

Instead of gasping in outrage, Jane smiled and rose from the bench, strolling to his chair. She bent down to stroke the baby's hair, and he caught a whiff of Jane's feminine scent, a scent that made him hunger to press his face to her skin. "Is that so impossible to believe?" she murmured. "That you might have been mad with passion for the dowdy Miss Maypole?"

He was mad with passion now. Seven nights had passed since they'd lain together, seven days in which she had controlled his thoughts. It didn't help that her breasts loomed just inches from his mouth, an offering for his pleasure. His wife. He wanted to drag her back to his chamber, strip her naked, and lose himself in her heat.

Gruffly, he said, "People here didn't know you back then, so the point is moot."

She arched an eyebrow, but didn't argue. "Lord Keeble and Mr. Duxbury also said—"

"Said what? If they insulted you . . ."

"They merely brought to my attention that there's more talk. People suspect that I'm increasing—again. Hence, our hurried wedding."

That shouldn't surprise him. Nor should he feel seized by the notion of making that particular bit of gossip come true. He already had a daughter to love. She lay warm and contented in his lap, gumming his pocket watch with single-minded determination.

No, he shouldn't want another child, a child by Jane. He was angry with her for beguiling him into wedlock. For pushing her way into his life and robbing him of freedom. For discovering his secret penchant for writing poetry.

He was angry with himself, too, for being duped. Again.

"Time will prove that rumor false," he said. "Nine months, to be precise."

"Will it?" she said in a suggestive voice. "We don't know that yet."

Her warm smile lured him though he kept his expression bland. "I suppose not," he conceded. "It's a few weeks too soon to tell."

Jane nodded, her eyes flashing silvery blue in the sunlight. "And what of the talk that you seduced me? I won't have anyone telling Marianne someday that her papa is a scoundrel who took advantage of her mama. That is why we must convince people we married for love."

A jolt of denial burned him. "Don't be absurd. Everyone will have forgotten by then."

"Not if we still behave coldly toward one another."

Quite unexpectedly, she slipped her fingers inside the back collar of his shirt and stroked the nape of his neck. That one touch sent heat flashing to his groin, and he curbed the inappropriate reaction. Couldn't she see he held a baby in his lap? He twisted his neck away. "For God's sake, stop that."

"Why? Ethan, I've waited a week for you to come to my bed. I've lain there all alone, thinking about you, remembering our night together. I want to experience that again. I want you to teach me all you know."

Sweat broke out over his skin. Where had her bold eroticism come from? Much as his body liked it, he was suspicious of Jane the seductress. Their old acquaintance had felt comfortable, like a well-worn riding boot. He wanted her to behave again like Jane, the prickly spinster.

"Ours is hardly a normal marriage," he said sharply. "So you can't expect me to treat you with all the attentiveness of a husband."

She threw back her head and laughed, not daintily as young ladies were taught, but with full-throated vigor. The same vigor she had showed him that night in the tower room. "Oh, don't be a prude," she said. "Scruples have never stopped you in the past."

"A prude?" he choked out. *"Me?"*

"Why, yes. People will think that if you ignore your bride. They expect newlyweds to be enthralled with each other." Her voice grew husky, her gaze seductive. "And I am enthralled by you, Ethan. Very much so."

Her suggestion shouldn't tempt him; he despised the restrictions of marriage, being shackled to one woman for the rest of his life. The woman who had betrayed his trust in her. "Enough," he said through gritted teeth. "I have no interest in playing out another of your lies."

Rather than look offended, she smiled at Marianne. "Isn't your papa grumpy this afternoon?" she crooned. "Perhaps he needs a moment alone."

The baby cooed and smiled.

Jane gathered Marianne in her arms and dangled the pocket watch by its fob in front of Ethan. When he caught it, the silver was wet from Marianne's mouth and it almost slipped from his grasp. He yanked out his handkerchief and polished the scrolled cover.

All the while he moodily watched Jane, eyeing her willowy grace when she carried the baby to the window, noticing the curve of her bottom as she leaned forward and pointed to a swift building its nest in the oak tree, listening to the charming lilt of her voice as she spoke to Marianne. The late afternoon sunlight bathed them in brilliance, picking out the coppery strands in Jane's dark hair, reminding him of the fire hidden in her.

He ought to leave. Now, while she was preoccupied with the baby. He had come here to spend a few minutes alone with his daughter; instead he'd found Jane already in the nursery, and she had persuaded him to stay. Now he knew why. She'd wanted to put another scheme before him, to twist him into knots. When had she changed into a creature of passion?

She had seduced him once already, and look at where his self-indulgence had landed him. Locked in a marriage he did not want, bound to a wife who had proven herself a liar, tortured by memories of the sweetest pleasure he'd ever found. The last time he had been set so off balance by a woman he had been made a fool, a cuckold, an object of censure. Yet Jane was not Portia. He could never imagine Jane lowering herself to that level.

And she *was* his wife. He had every right to use her body.

As he watched her play with Marianne, love softening her face, he could grudgingly understand how wrenching it would have been for Jane to have lost the baby. She was right; it was best for Marianne to have two parents. For that reason alone, he must accept their marriage.

It was a disturbing truth to face. He must do his best to forget Jane's deception; he must try to get along with her.

It would serve Marianne ill to have parents who behaved like cold strangers. They could be civil, partake of meals together, discuss the trivialities of their daily lives.

And he could make love to Jane. He could slake his passion until he purged himself of this obsession for her. Why practice celibacy when she was there for his pleasure? His wife, his lover.

Even as the prospect excited him, he resolved to keep her from probing his private thoughts. She knew too much about him already. What would she do with that knowledge?

Very soon, Gianetta came to feed the baby and it was time to dress for dinner, so they went downstairs. Seeming to have forgotten their quarrel, Jane chattered on about Marianne's future, how she needed a governess who would train her in the same subjects a boy would learn. He liked the way Jane gripped his arm firmly, without false girlish delicacy, and he didn't object when she followed him into his bedchamber.

"I've been thinking, Ethan. We cannot allow Marianne to remain illegitimate. We must adopt her so that she has all the privileges of being your daughter."

"My solicitor is already seeing to the matter. She'll be legally ours before the month is out."

Jane threw her arms around his neck. "Oh, I'm so glad."

He caught her close, relishing her slim form, strong and yet womanly, fitting him to perfection. Her breasts felt soft against his chest. Her fresh rainwater scent made him long to take down her hair, to unbutton her gown and kiss every inch of her fragrant flesh. He fought the urge to rub himself against her.

She was his wife, he reminded himself. His to use as he willed.

But the sound of drawers opening and closing in the dressing room stopped him. Wilson was in there, readying the earl's clothes for dinner. Ethan swore under his breath. He must wait for nightfall and go to her then.

Reluctantly, he released Jane and walked her to the connecting door. She didn't yet know of the change in his thinking, and somehow he wasn't quite ready to enlighten her. In a formal tone, he said, "Run along now. I'll see you downstairs shortly."

She didn't obey, but when had Jane ever obeyed him? She fingered the ivory buttons on his shirt and murmured in his ear, "Send Wilson away. Let me act as your valet."

Fire flashed to his loins in a searing bolt. God, it was tempting. *She* was tempting with her enticing eyes and come-hither smile. To hell with restraint. He wanted her. *Now.*

He strode to his dressing room. Wilson stood brushing a dark blue coat, whisking the fabric with meticulous care. A pair of highly polished black shoes sat on the carpet. Fawn breeches lay on the clothes press, along with a pristine pair of stockings.

"Ah, m'lord," the valet said. "I've prepared your garments, though if you prefer different apparel from what I've chosen, I would be happy to—"

"This is fine. You may go."

Wilson's narrow face twitched with dismay. "Go? But you'll require help with your coat and cravat—"

"I'm sure I'll manage."

"Well, then." The officious little man started for the door, then paused. "A message arrived for you just now, my lord. I left it on the desk. The footman said it was urgent."

Urgent. Ethan had an urgent need right now. He burned from it.

He followed the valet into the bedchamber and saw Jane waiting where he'd left her by the connecting door. Her hand rested on the lever, and she gazed at him with wide-eyed caution, her head tilted to the side, her lips parted. He knew she wasn't certain of him. She didn't know about his decision. But she would soon.

Very soon.

He started toward her. He could see the fervor in her eyes, the longing. She wanted this as much as he did. His sensuous Miss Maypole. Why had he denied himself for so many nights? His anger at her seemed unimportant now. There was no reason to refuse her favors. He would enjoy her as he willed, rid himself of this preoccupation so that he could concentrate on his writing again.

He had almost reached her when the valet thrust a sealed missive at him, along with his spectacles. "My lord, here is the letter. A messenger is waiting downstairs for your reply."

Curse it. Ethan wanted to drop the letter into the rubbish bin. But rationality broke through his fevered senses. If there was a crisis at his estate or some other pressing business, he should at least know about it. Was he so obsessed with Jane that he could not stop to scribble a swift reply?

No woman should command him so.

Ethan donned the gold-rimmed eyeglasses, broke the wax seal, and unfolded the paper. The flowery scent triggered an unpleasant knowledge in him even before he saw the familiar feminine handwriting.

He scanned the brief note, grimaced, and then read it again.

Jane walked to him, her dark brows drawn in curiosity. "What is it, Ethan?"

He made an impatient motion at the valet. Wilson bowed and left the chamber.

Only then did Ethan reluctantly reveal the contents of the message. "It's from Portia," he said tersely. "She's suffered a miscarriage and begs me to allow you to come to her."

⌒ *Chapter 20* ⌒

In the unforgiving light of the setting sun, the red brick town house had an aura of neglect, more so than the night Jane had last visited here. The white paint on the door was peeling. The porch roof listed slightly, one of the columns rotting. The brass ram's-head knocker, which Ethan had just used to rap on the door, had gone dark and dull for want of polishing.

Jane had been surprised when he'd offered to accompany her to the residence of his former wife. Despite the gravity of their visit, his presence thrilled her. Back in his bed-chamber, something had been about to happen, she was sure of it. She had felt the spark leap between them, sensed a change in his manner.

He had left her standing by the connecting door while he'd gone into the dressing room. She had heard only a murmur of voices; then his valet had hastened out with Ethan strolling after him. Ethan's gaze had burned into her. His intensely sexual look made her heart race, a dark promise that roused a slow pounding deep in her belly. Then the wretched valet had given him the letter, and the moment had vanished.

Now, Ethan stood beside her on the porch, a silent stranger, his thoughts focused inward to places she could never fathom. Had she mistaken his intent? Had he meant to banish her to her lonely bedchamber? Or had she truly succeeded in enticing him?

The door swung open on a squealing of rusty hinges. The same timid maidservant let them in, scampering up the narrow steps as if anxious to discharge her duty and be done. Jane followed her to a musty, dimly lit bedchamber.

Despite the derelict state of the house, this room held a suite of fine mahogany furnishings, highboy and dressing table, chaise longue and chairs. Lady Portia occupied a magnificent four-poster bed. Her blond hair loose around her fragile features, she reclined against the pillows, her eyes closed and her hands folded as if in prayer. She looked as pale as a corpse.

Alarmed, Jane rushed to her side. "My lady! Are you all right?"

Lady Portia opened her beautiful violet eyes. A weak smile touched her dainty lips. "Jane. My dear friend. I knew you would come." Her gaze shifted to the man standing at the foot of the bed. "And Ethan. How pleased I am that you would visit me in my hour of need."

"I wouldn't dream of letting Jane come here alone."

Was that guarded hostility in his voice? Jane hastened to ask, "How are you feeling, my lady?"

"Somewhat better. Please, if you will sit down." Portia patted the place beside her, waiting until Jane gingerly seated herself on the bed. "Oh, if only I might relate what happened without offending your sensibilities."

"You may speak at will," Jane said. "I am happy to listen."

"It is horrid to remember, yet I can think of naught else." Portia took a shaky breath. "Yesterday morning I fell ill, with small cramping pains at first and then a terrible agony. My maid ran for the physician, but by the time he arrived, it was too late. I had lost my baby." Tears seeped down her cheeks, and she groped for a handkerchief on the bedside table.

Jane felt helpless, inadequate to give comfort for the vast

loss. She could only imagine how dreadful it would be to lose the child she'd carried for months—or to lose Marianne. "Oh, my lady. I'm so sorry. I wish I had known. I would have come sooner."

Portia lifted her head, her eyes like moist pansies against her wan features. "There was nothing to be done. Nothing." Reaching out, she took Jane's hand in her cool, dry fingers. "You are so fortunate to have your little baby, your Marianne. You cannot guess how empty I feel right now."

"How do you know my daughter's name?" Ethan said sharply. "I'm certain I never mentioned it."

"Jane must have, then." Portia stared regally at him. "After you left that night, she and I had a cozy talk."

Jane couldn't remember speaking of Marianne, but that seemed trivial now. "Where is . . . George Smollett? Has he returned?"

"I told you, the cad has vanished to the Continent. He took the last of my funds and left me. Alone to suffer the loss of his son."

"It was a boy, then," Jane whispered.

"Yes. The physician has seen to the burial."

"Whatever the expense," Jane said, "Ethan and I shall see to it. Send any bills to his steward."

She looked at him, lifting her chin, half expecting him to challenge her.

He stood with one hand braced on the bedpost. To her surprise, he inclined his head to her. "It shall be as you say."

"How sweetly you defer to your new wife," Portia said. "I'd heard you two wed in haste. Jane, so you are Lady Chasebourne now. I must say, you are looking very pretty these days. Pretty enough to tempt the Earl of Sin."

Jane detected a note of bitterness. Something in Portia's manner disturbed her, a narrowing of the violet eyes, a hardening of her facial features. But how could she feel anything but sympathy for the poor woman who had lost so much?

"We've overstayed our welcome," Ethan said, walking around the bed to Jane. "My wife and I must leave you to rest."

"No, wait," Portia said in an urgent tone. She clung to Jane's hand, her fingernails biting like claws. "I need more than a few bills paid. George's creditors have been hounding me for weeks. I need ten thousand pounds."

Jane's mouth went dry. It boggled her mind to wonder how anyone could run up such high debts. Certainly there was nothing in this house to show for it beyond this one roomful of expensive furniture. And hadn't Ethan said that she needed money to pay off her own debts? Jane struggled with the notion that Portia was milking him for her own greedy purposes.

"Ten thousand, is it?" Ethan drawled. "Last time we met, it was a mere five."

"Other men have come forward to threaten me. You see, George left unpaid gambling markers, too." Releasing Jane, Portia wept brokenly into her handkerchief. "Oh, please, do not forsake me. I'm all alone and without protection. Those men would think nothing of ill-using me."

In spite of her doubts, Jane cast a horrified glance up at Ethan. "We must do something. We must help her."

Hard and assessing, his gaze was fixed on Portia. "You and Smollett never married. You have no obligation to pay off *his* debts."

"Tell that to the men who badger me unmercifully."

"I'll make arrangements for you to move out of the city immediately, then. One of my men will aid you, so that no one can trace where you've gone. That should take care of the problem."

"No! I like living in London. I told you before, I won't be banished to the country."

"I'm sorry. That is my final offer."

A breath hissed from Portia, and she clenched her fists. "Beast! You're the same tightfisted miser you've always been. I pity you, Jane, for marrying such an unfeeling monster. He will treat you ill, too. He will seek out other women and ignore you.''

Startled by the furious outburst, Jane leaned over to place her hand on Portia's dainty shoulder. ''Please, my lady. Calm yourself. The strain cannot be good for you in your weakened state.''

Portia glowered at Jane. ''If you wish to help me, then convince him. Ten thousand is nothing to him. He has more wealth than he could spend in a hundred lifetimes.''

Jane felt caught in a quandary. She could understand why Ethan would not wish to lay out such a vast sum for gaming debts incurred by a knave. The knave who'd cuckolded him. And what was to stop Portia from gambling again and expecting Ethan to foot the bill? ''My lady, will you not consider the fair offer he has made to you? You could move far away from here, begin anew in a place where you will be safe. Really, it is for your own good.''

Portia took several deep breaths. Then her shoulders slumped as if the rage had drained out of her, and she lowered her gaze to her hands. ''Yes,'' she said in a quavering voice, ''you're quite right, of course. I must leave London. I have no choice but to accept the offer of a house.''

She looked so dispirited that Jane gave her a brief hug. ''You won't regret it,'' she said. ''Country living is peaceful and pleasant. In truth, you'll grow to love it once you're able to take long walks in the fresh air.''

''You are too kind.'' The handkerchief clutched to her throat, Portia turned to Ethan. ''But where will you send me?''

''To a land agent I know in Cornwall,'' Ethan said. ''Be ready tomorrow at dawn. Pack only a valise. Everything else will be provided for you.''

With a nod, Portia sank wearily against the pillows. ''You must leave me now,'' she said. ''I am most weary.''

Jane murmured a farewell, and Ethan's arm encircled her, strong around her waist as he drew her toward the door.

She had one last glimpse of Portia staring pensively after them. Jane couldn't help remembering Portia's furious outburst. Did that brief display give her a glimpse into his first marriage? How often had Ethan faced such petulant anger?

He will seek out other women and ignore you.

Anxious to depart the house, Jane emerged onto the porch and took a grateful breath of cool evening air. Coal smoke had never smelled so good. The barouche with its pair of matched grays waited at the curbstone, the coachman and footman standing at attention. Ethan kept his arm secure around her, helping her into the closed carriage, then seating himself beside her. With a slight jolt, the vehicle started down the street.

"A pity you had to witness that scene," Ethan said.

"It wasn't *your* fault." She looked at him through the shifting shadows. "Oh, Ethan, I do hope Portia will find happiness."

Warm and firm, his hand came down on hers. "I'll send my man round tomorrow to move her out of the city and far, far away. Aside from that, I cannot force her to behave reasonably."

His closeness stirred a sweet softness in her. When he took his hand back, Jane missed the security of it. She sensed him withdrawing, saw him turn his head to stare out the window, and said quickly, "Portia tried to manipulate you while you were married to her, did she not?"

He flashed her a grimace. "Quite so."

A hollow regret throbbed inside Jane, and she turned the gold band on her finger around and around. "No wonder you despise me for duping you. I've behaved just like her."

"You aren't like her." He spoke quickly, then paused as if groping for an explanation. "She was deceitful in other ways."

"What ways?"

"Jane, it doesn't matter. I don't wish to discuss her with you."

Jane felt compelled to sort fact from fiction, to understand what had really happened. "It *does* matter. I think . . . I suspect she lied to me." She laid her hand on his sleeve, aware of his heat, the hardness of his flesh. "I want the truth. Please, it's important to me."

"Miss Maypole of the impertinent questions. You never give up, do you."

She heard no hostility in his voice, only exasperation, and that encouraged her. "Portia told me she made only a single misstep. Because she was lonely after enduring years of your affairs."

He laughed, the sound more mockery than amusement. "I don't suppose she would mention the gaming debts, the costly jewels, the constant flirtations."

"Flirtations? Then George Smollet wasn't her only lover?"

"He was the only one I discovered her with. They took to my bed while I was up in the tower room." His tone bored, he glanced out the window at the gathering darkness. "She admitted later she'd known I was there, that she wanted me to catch her in the act. As revenge for my ignoring her."

No wonder Jane had felt uneasy with Portia's confidences. Perhaps in some deep part of her, she had sensed a web of untruths. "She did say that you . . . no longer came to her bed. That you refused to give her a child."

His quiet chuckle filled the carriage. "Bearing a baby would have ruined her figure. She couldn't tolerate that. Smollett's child can only have been a miscalculation."

Portia had refused to conceive Ethan's child? Jane was shocked that any woman could be so vain and selfish. She herself yearned to have his baby growing within her. The wish wrapped around her heart, and she forced her mind back to the one question she had delayed asking. "And what of *your* affairs?"

He sat silent, uncommunicative. She heard the hollow clopping of hooves, the clatter of wheels on cobblestones. His reticence intensified her need to *know*. "Ethan, did you drive her away by seeking out other women?''

"I've always enjoyed women. Ask anyone.''

His flippant answer frustrated her. "A simple yes or no will suffice. Did you betray your marriage vows?''

He thinned his lips, his gaze hard on her through the gloom. His fingers tapped restlessly on his thigh. He glanced out the window, then back at her. "No.''

"Never?''

"You heard me. Now cease your questions.''

Jane sank back against the velvet cushions. His brusque tone could not diminish the jumble of emotions inside her, shock and amazement and a strange elation. He had kept his vows. Through four years of marriage to a faithless wife.

His affair with Marianne's mother must have occurred after he'd obtained the bill of divorcement. Assuredly he'd been no saint then. He had made love to many women. Nevertheless, he was an honorable man, a man who kept his promises.

And Jane had believed the worst of him. But what else was she to think? He'd hidden his honor behind the rakish mask he showed the world.

The barouche drew up in front of Chasebourne House, and he lent her his hand to help her down. Night had fallen, and torches flickered at either side of the entryway. Even when his assistance was no longer necessary, his fingers gripped hers, drawing her inexorably into the house.

Inside the vast foyer, his footsteps were sharp on the black-and-white marble floor. "Come upstairs,'' he said.

It was an order, not an invitation, delivered without a smile or his customary jest, though his gaze made a leisurely sweep of her body. What did he intend? More recriminations? Or something else?

Something intimate.

Her heartbeat surged, but a glance at his bland expression gave her little clue to his thoughts. He took hold of her arm, guiding her up the grand staircase. She fancied his touch possessive, more than a gentleman's courtesy to a lady, and she reveled in his closeness.

Ethan would respect their marriage vows. He would not seek out other women. And she *did* want him to be faithful. Oh, how she did. She wanted him to love her. Only her.

He escorted her into her chambers. Several candles were lit, giving the large room a cozy, intimate aura. She was keenly aware of Ethan, the masculine power in him, the dark sensuality that made her skin tingle. He couldn't mean what she hoped, could he? He had spurned her all week. Was it possible he had reconsidered her overture that afternoon?

He left her standing in the middle of the carpet while he strode to the dressing room to peer inside. It was the dinner hour, and her maid would be downstairs in the servants' hall. Then he returned to the door and twisted the key.

The click of the tumbler set off a slow pounding deep inside her. She stood very still, watching him approach her, his gaze intent, his mouth tempting. His fingers worked at his neckcloth, undoing the knot and dropping the length of white linen to the floor.

Yes. Oh, yes. A thrill that was pure arousal shot through Jane. Her legs felt weak, her mind dizzy. She wanted him to make love to her. So much.

"Ethan." Her voice sounded breathy, uneven. "You really are an honorable man."

"Fine. Now let's move on to more important matters." He cupped the back of her neck in his big palm, his fingers slowly kneading the taut cords, the pressure bringing her forward until her aching bosom met his waistcoat. In a gravelly tone, he muttered, "I believe this is where we left off."

Then he brought his mouth down on hers.

His kiss was deep and slow, stirring a wild yearning in her. She slid her hands into his hair and held him for fear he might end this delight too soon. No wonder women adored him, for he was a master at kissing, plying his lips and tongue in ways that fed the riotous passion in her, the need for him that transcended all thought, all rationality.

His fingers plucked at the buttons of her gown, his mouth moving over her face, descending to her throat. She moaned, pushing off his coat as frantic desire surged in her. The gown melted away and then her undergarments. When she stood naked before him, he undid the clasp of her locket and caught the trinket as it fell against her breasts, the warm gold chain trailing against her skin. He dropped the locket on a table, lowered his head, and suckled her until she swayed on her feet and clutched at him, too weak with need to stand alone.

Then he carried her to the canopied bed and laid her down on the cool counterpane. He stood watching her while he undressed, dropping waistcoat and shirt and breeches without taking his dark eyes from her. His gaze roved over her nudity, so that her breasts tightened and her skin flushed with heat. A place deep inside her ached at the magnificence of him, his maleness standing thick and erect.

He came down on her, his large form blocking out the shadowed room. A candle on the bedside table cast a faint flickering light over his sinfully handsome features. Wanting him, Jane opened her legs, but he rolled onto his back, bringing her over to straddle him. She gasped at the unfamiliar wonder of it, her hands braced on his shoulders, her breasts hanging unfettered, her loins touching his hardness.

"Take me inside you," he said roughly.

His command inflamed her. She took him into her hand, lifted her hips, and guided him to her soft folds. His penetration was gradual, and she whimpered with impatience, pushing downward until he filled her completely. The feel of him inside her caused her to tremble, her breath shuddering out in a moan. Dear God, she had forgotten how beautiful their joining could be, though she had relived it a thousand times in memory since that night in the tower.

"Ethan. How I've missed you."

"You've missed this."

She meant to correct him, but he reached up to caress her breasts, bringing her down so he could take one peak into his mouth and then the other. The need in her became frantic, unrelenting, and she thrust her hips in an effort to ride the flood of sensual tension. He held her bottom, forcing her to go slow, denying her the release that lay just beyond her grasp.

His control frustrated her. In a frenzy, she strained against him, undulating her hips, instinctively tightening her inner muscles until he hissed out a groan, his breath hot against her bosom. With a swift upward thrust, he seized dominion, and it took only a few deep strokes to shatter her. Lost in ripples of rapture, she heard his hoarse cry against her throat.

Utterly replete, she lay limp and spent, draped over him. She was aware of the heat of his body and the coolness of air against her back. Agaisnt her cheek, she could feel the raspy hairs on his chest and the slowing thrum of his heartbeat. The musk of his skin filled her senses. He was still inside her, not as large as before, but his very presence there was enough to cause a gentle echo of pleasure to unfurl through her belly. She would be content to stay here forever.

His hand drifted up and down her back in a comforting sensation. They lay together for timeless moments until he spoke in a low tone. "I've a proposal for you, Jane."

Curious, she raised her head, a curl of hair trailing down her shoulder. He tucked his arm behind his head, and he looked every inch the sinful rake. *Her* sinful rake. "I accept."

He chuckled, a sound ripe with male satisfaction, his teeth flashing white in the candleglow. "Just like that?"

"Yes."

He lightly slapped her bottom. "Does this mean I've finally tamed you, Miss Maypole?"

"The real question is, have I tamed *you,* my lord?"

His smile abated to a faintly wolfish slant. His eyes were

inscrutable, dark as a midnight shadow. "That, Lady Chasebourne, remains to be seen."

She adored the way he spoke her title, as if he were pleased she belonged to him—though his words were evasive. "So what, pray, is your proposal?"

"We both find pleasure in bed. And I should like to sire an heir. So I propose that from this night onward, we indulge our desire for each other."

And what about love?

Her small stab of dismay was assuaged by a fierce longing. This was her chance to win his heart, and the challenge excited Jane. She cupped his cheek in her hand, loving the bristly male texture of his skin. In a tender flash of understanding, she realized she could give him what he had been denied by his first wife. "Oh, Ethan. I want to bear your child . . . your children. I want that with all my heart."

His dark gaze went soft, unfocused, while another part of him grew harder. Closing his fingers around her waist, he turned her over onto the pillows and lay flush against her, his heavy leg anchoring her thighs, his hand stroking her sensitized breasts. "I'm pleased we're in agreement, then."

His calm response made it sound like a business arrangement. But there was nothing businesslike about the way he touched her, nothing indifferent in his skilled seduction. Surely they could build a marriage on their attraction for each other. Surely in time he would grow to love her. The longing burned as intensely as the carnal cravings he aroused in her.

She caressed his broad shoulders, the column of his neck, the crisply curling hairs that roughened his skin. And she kissed him, tasting the saltiness of his throat and the wild wonder of his mouth, gasping when he reached between her legs to circle her tender flesh. The delight of it spread through her like heated honey, and within moments she reached the shuddering peak of pleasure.

He hadn't come with her; he lay iron-hard against her

thigh. She was gripped by the hunger to make him lose control. Curling her fingers around him, she explored him intuitively, letting her forefinger swirl around the tip, taking the tiny drop of moisture there and spreading it over him. A harsh groan rumbled from him; emboldened by her success, she let her fingers trail downward until she held his soft sacks and squeezed lightly.

The breath hissed out of him. "Blast you," he muttered. "Who taught you that trick?"

A keen sense of feminine power made her smile. "You," she whispered. "You inspire me."

With a feral growl, he mounted her, a wolf taming his mate. She loved the weight of him, the scent of his skin, the feel of his coarse hair rasping against her flesh. His chest was solid, his arms muscular from hard exercise at the gymnasium. He took her mouth in a drowning kiss that left her breathless, and without further ado, he joined their bodies. She cried out from the joy of it, tilting her hips and locking her legs around his waist so that he could penetrate deeper. She needed this closeness, this physical bond. She needed *him*.

Her hands threaded into his hair, and she pressed her lips to his jaw, helpless to stop the feelings that poured from her. "I love you, Ethan. I love you."

His arms tensed around her as he thrust hard and fast, heat radiating from him in waves. This time, he reached his climax first, and the quivering of his powerful body sent her over the edge with him. She drowsed in the aftermath, and she must have fallen asleep, for she had a sudden, hazy awareness of his weight lifting from her. The feather mattress dipped and swayed as he rose from the bed. She murmured a groggy protest, but he drew the coverlet over her, nestling her in a cocoon of warmth.

At the click of the door closing, Jane came fully awake. She pushed up on her elbow and blinked at her shadowed chamber with its gilt furnishings and primrose draperies.

Ethan was gone. She felt bereft without him, empty, though her loins felt heavy with sated pleasure.

How inconvenient for you . . . to be shackled to a man who despises you.

The warm sheets carried his scent, and she breathed deeply, hugging her pillow and fighting off a wave of despondency. She should have expected him to leave her. It was customary for aristocratic couples to keep separate rooms so they could lead separate lives.

Nevertheless, she wanted to be with him, to share every aspect of his life. He was her husband. She wanted to snuggle in his arms all night, to wake up in the morning and see him lying beside her.

The truth struck her like a blow. They were lovers . . . and strangers. And that was exactly the way Ethan preferred it.

⌐ *Chapter 21* ⌐

"What do you think of this one?" Lady Rosalind asked. She studied herself in the pier glass at the milliner's shop, turning her head back and forth as she examined her extravagant hat.

Jane looked askance at the tall blue bonnet with its huge cluster of curly foxtail feathers. "I think it's a bit too . . ."

"Gaudy," the dowager pronounced, and lifted her gloved hand in an imperious motion.

The prissy proprietor had been waiting anxiously by a table filled with trays of trimmings. He scurried forward to remove the bonnet, bearing it back to the window.

While Lady Rosalind conferred with the shopkeeper, Jane strolled past the colorful display of hats along the wall, stopping now and again to touch a silk flower or to stroke a ribbon. Lady Rosalind had asked Jane to help her choose the last few items for her trousseau. Jane didn't dare plead weariness for fear she might blush and the dowager would guess the truth, that Jane had forsaken several hours of sleep the previous night for a long bout of lovemaking.

A fortnight had passed since she and Ethan had reconciled. Two weeks of unbridled passion. He had tutored her in the ways to please him, and in turn, he lingered over her, curbing his own release until she had succumbed to his patient ministrations. Sometimes he visited her chamber in the dark of night, and she would awaken to find him already inside her, an erotic dream come true.

And always, he returned to his own bed. She scarcely saw him during the day, and he never invited her up to the tower room. On several occasions, she had asked him to accompany her to the lending library or to the park with Marianne, but he had refused politely but firmly. When they were together in the evenings, he kept their conversations light and amusing, devoid of deep emotion, and she had gone along with his wishes, biding her time and hoping that eventually he might grow to love her.

"Does m'lady wish to try that one?"

Jane blinked. The proprietor gazed politely at the turban of striped blue silk in her hands. "Oh, heavens no." Quickly she extended the hat to the dowager. "This is for you."

"Ah! That is the very thing. I knew I was right to bring you along, Jane." Smiling in delight, Lady Rosalind nestled the turban over her tawny gold curls, adjusting the plume of white ostrich feathers and preening at her reflection. "This will make a cunning addition to my trousseau. Did I tell you His Grace is taking me to the Continent for an extended wedding trip?"

"No, you did not." Jane frowned in alarm. "Is Gianetta attending you? You said you can't manage without her. Who will feed Marianne?"

Lady Rosalind laughed gaily, walking over to pat Jane's hand. "Spoken like a true mother. Never fear, I'm leaving Gianetta behind. I wouldn't dream of denying my granddaughter her source of sustenance."

Jane's tension eased. "I'm so glad, my lady."

"Oh, do call me Rosalind. *My lady* is too formal, and *mama-in-law* makes me feel horribly old." She sighed. "It is hard to believe I have a son who is about to reach twenty-seven years. You did remember his birthday is next week, did you not?"

"No, my—Rosalind." Jane searched her brain for the date. "It is June the fifth, is it not?"

"The eighth. Two days before my wedding to Kellisham." Her pastel blue skirts swirling, she turned to regard her hat in the mirror again. In a distracted tone, she added, "Do not purchase a cravat pin for him, though. I give him a new one every year."

Jane had no intention of buying jewelry for him. She wouldn't begin to know what to select, nor did she have the funds to pay for an expensive piece. Though Ethan had granted her a generous allowance, she wouldn't use his money to buy him a gift. So what could she give to the man who had everything? A book? But somehow, that didn't seem enough. . . .

Then she had an idea so perfect, so wonderful, she was stunned by its brilliance.

That afternoon, Jane waited until Ethan had left for the gymnasium before she slipped into his bedchamber. His valet was gone; she had overheard him say he was to supervise the earl's laundry in the basement. Lifting her skirts, she hastened up the winding steps to the tower room.

Though sunlight streamed through the window slits, the stone walls kept the circular room cool. The grate was swept clean of ashes. As she glanced at the hearth rug where Ethan had introduced her to ecstasy, warmth filled her. She didn't regret deceiving him. No, she did not.

She had come here that first time to trap him into marriage. Now she intended to prepare a gift for him.

Buoyed by anticipation, she hurried across the chamber. The big mahogany desk with its many cubbyholes looked as untidy as ever. Surveying the clutter, she shook her head and wondered how Ethan ever found anything. Perhaps the lack of order would work in her favor. He would never miss the few pages she borrowed.

For a moment, her hands hesitated over the papers. He had been so furious that night she had read his poems. He

had despised her invasion of his privacy. This was his secret, the depth of thought he hid from the world behind a
mask of charm and wit. The part he shut off from *her*.

She subdued the hollow ache inside herself. Things
would be different once he realized she could be his helpmate. And the surprise she had planned would be for his
eyes only. He surely would appreciate her thoughtfulness.

She began a methodical search of the papers, being careful
to replace them exactly, in case he knew some mysterious
order in the scattered piles. Of course, her absent-minded father had never possessed that skill. Hector Mayhew had de-
pended on Jane to rummage through the clutter on his desk
and extract the papers he needed.

It was logical to assume that Ethan was working on the
top-most poems, and those she left alone. She explored
swiftly, systematically, stopping only to scan the ink-
spotted, crossed-out lines. She probed in compartments and
poked through niches, seeking the poems he would be least
likely to miss. Parchment rustled; the familiar smells of ink
and paper brought a wave of nostalgia. How she welcomed
the opportunity to work again. Much as she loved spending
time with Marianne, Jane looked forward to this new un-
dertaking.

At last she had gathered a slim sheaf of verse, which she
tucked into the crook of her arm. She took one last survey
of the desk. All looked as Ethan had left it, from the silver-
capped ink pot and array of fine quills to the unlit lamp
and jumbled papers.

She descended the stairs, peeked out to make sure his
chambers were empty, and then slipped back into her own
bedchamber to begin her task.

The sound of gentle splashing came from within Jane's
dressing room.

Ethan put his forefinger to his lips and motioned to the
young maid who appeared, toting an empty coal scuttle.
Her dark eyes rounded. She bobbed a curtsy, stifled a gig-

gle, and went scurrying out of the bedchamber.

He walked quietly into the dressing room. A gown of deep amber gauze hung from a wall hook. On the carpet rested a pair of dainty tan leather slippers. Frilly undergarments draped a chair. The air held the scent of powders and perfumes and the indefinable essence of Jane.

His gaze focused on the black-and-gold japanned screen that had been moved in front of the dressing room fireplace. From behind the screen came the sound of more splashing. Denied the pleasure of seeing Jane at her bath, he cursed under his breath. In the next moment, he realized that the dressing table mirror reflected a clear view of his wife.

Her back was turned, so she could not know he was watching. He settled his shoulder against the wall and enjoyed the sight. Immersed in the gleaming copper tub, she caught the cake of soap that bobbed in the water. She lathered her hands, then lifted her arm to wash it, her skin rosy and glowing from the heat of the water and the fire on the hearth.

A few dark curls had tumbled down her back. He could hear the contented sound of her humming. She looked slim yet sturdy, and he knew well that blend of softness and strength, the feel of her long limbs wrapped around him in bed.

His body tightened with need, and the force of his desire disturbed him. Other women never held his interest for more than a fortnight, yet his passion for Jane showed no sign of burning out. He found himself thinking about her at odd hours, wanting to be with her, as much to talk as to make love. She distracted him from his writing and tempted him to visit her. This morning, the impulse had proved impossible to resist.

His steps silent, he walked toward her, and when he rounded the screen, she gasped, her arms lifting to shield her bosom in an age-old feminine action. Droplets of water rolled like dewdrops down skin flushed from the water.

Then a smile tilted her mouth, and she lowered her arms. "Ethan. Good morning."

Her voice held a velvety hint of the pleasures they'd shared the previous evening. The water lapped at the undersides of her breasts.

"You're an early riser today," he said.

For a moment she looked flustered; then she glanced at his breeches. "So are you, my lord."

He chuckled. "How observant of you to notice."

"I don't suppose you've come to say you've finished reading my father's translation of *Topographia Hiberniae*."

"It's a bit early to discuss the travels of a priest through twelfth-century Ireland." He let his gaze roam over her. "However, I'd be happy to assist you with your bath."

A faint smile lingered on her mouth. "My back, please."

He rolled up his sleeves and soaped his palms. She bent forward, holding the sides of the tub as he glided his hands over her glossy skin, following the sweep of her shoulders, pushing aside the tendrils at the base of her neck and working his way down the nubs of her spine. Her head drooping, she sighed, that soft little sound more erotic than any made by a seasoned courtesan. Her relaxed state encouraged him to slide his hands around her rib cage and fill his palms with her breasts. The peaks were taut, and against the heel of his left hand, he could feel the quickened beat of her heart.

He reached lower to legs already parted for his touch. His fingers found a slickness there that had nothing to do with soap or water, and he caressed her slowly until her head fell back against his arm and her breath came in panting gasps and the arching of her body caused gentle ripples in the water as she climaxed.

Breathing hard, he cupped her mound and struggled to contain his own raging need. Opening her eyes, she graced him with a dreamy, trusting smile. "Ethan." Then she delved into the water and brought his wet hand to her mouth, placing a soft, loving kiss in his palm, kissing each finger in turn.

A wild surge of passion shattered his restraint.

He lifted Jane out of the tub. Water coursed down her in rivulets. He crowded her against the wall and wrested open his breeches. With a low cry, she put her arms around his neck and locked her legs around his waist. In the next instant he drove inside her, into her snug velvet heaven.

She clung tightly to him as he rode her, fast and furious. Her frantic breaths, her straining movements, tore a groan from him. Then with fierce exultation, he felt her shudder again, her inner folds clenching around him, and he convulsed with the violence of his own release.

The intense pleasure slowly abated to the glow of satisfaction. He held her close, her legs still wrapped around him, her head lying on the hard pillow of his shoulder. There was a quiet joy in the aftermath, a tender contentment he had never experienced with any other woman.

Jane. His wife. How well matched they were.

The thought shook him, and reluctantly he drew back, holding her waist until she lowered her legs. She looked sweetly tousled, her skin moist and glowing, her hair half-fallen from its pins. "Well," she said on a breathy laugh. "I'd wondered if it could be done while standing."

He was intrigued to think Jane speculated about carnal acts. "What other fantasies have you had?"

She blushed and glanced away. "Nothing of consequence."

He slid his hands up her rib cage, his thumbs lightly brushing her breasts. "Tell me anyway."

She drew in a breath, ducking her chin to gaze at him through the screen of her lashes. "I once read about an Eastern seraglio . . . with braziers burning . . . incense in the air . . . a bed draped in silk. I've wondered what it would be like . . . to be a slave in a harem . . . to be seduced by the pasha."

"A slave girl."

"Never mind," she said, shaking her head. "It's silly, really."

"Not at all." Her fantasy became his. He could imagine her draped in gauzy silk, gliding toward him, defiance flashing in her eyes. He would command her to undress, make her lie on the bed while he used all his skills to coax a response from her. . . .

"Look at you," Jane said suddenly. "Wilson will suffer an apoplexy when he sees the state of your clothing."

Her silvery blue eyes danced with amusement, and Ethan glanced down at himself. His damp, wrinkled shirt adhered to his chest, and there was a button missing from his breeches. Grinning, he reached for a towel. "The least I can do is to finish drying you."

She made a purring sound in her throat as he passed the linen over her shoulders, taking one smooth arm and working his way down to her dainty wrist, turning her pliant hand over to dry her palm and then each finger. He paused over her middle finger, rubbing at the dark smudge beside her nail. "Ink," he said. "You've been writing."

She curled her fingers into a fist, hiding the stain. "Letters. And replies to invitations."

"Refuse them all. We'll find a better way to fill our time."

He meant it. He would like nothing more than to spend his days and nights pleasuring Jane. Despite their frantic coupling, obsession still burned inside him. He knelt before her, gliding the linen over her breasts, along the indentation of her waist and down her long legs, blotting the moisture between each curling toe before moving upward again to gently wipe away the traces of his seed. Her breath came faster, and she held his shoulders to steady herself.

"Ethan," she said on a low, pleading gasp.

"Is something the matter?" he teased.

"I do have a perfectly fine bed in there."

"Is that an invitation?"

She blinked down at him, then tilted her head back and

laughed. "No. No, you debaucher, it was *not*. You've made me late already."

Stepping away from him, she walked to the chair and collected her shift. He admired her tall, willowy form, the sway of her hips, the curve of her behind. Then she pulled the garment over her head, and to his disappointment, the cloth fluttered down to her knees.

Reluctantly buttoning his breeches, he strolled to her. "Late?" he asked. "Where are you off to so early in the morning?"

She glanced at him, then turned away to pick up her corset. "First, I must check on Marianne. She was fretful yesterday, remember? Gianetta says it was nothing, but I wish to reassure myself she is feeling better."

"And then?"

"Then I must go out in the barouche."

"For what purpose?"

"Oh, to visit the shops," she said with an airy wave of her hand.

He caught her by the waist and kissed the tender nape of her neck, breathing in her fresh fragrance. Spurred by impulse, he said, "I'll accompany you."

"But you can't!"

Her vehemence surprised him. It was the first time he'd offered to spend the day with her, and he was annoyed by her refusal. "I can, indeed. I had intended to go over the accounts, but that can wait for another day."

"You detest shopping. It will be horribly tedious, for I must hunt down the perfect pair of shoes to wear at your mother's wedding."

"Forget the shoes, then." He pulled her back against him so that her bottom cradled him. "Stay home with me."

She deftly slipped away and donned the stiff corset. "Oh, Ethan, I cannot, not today. In addition to my many other errands, Lady Rosalind asked me to fetch a hat from the milliner's. It's the least I can do with her wedding less than a week away."

He clenched his jaw. She didn't want his company, and so much the better. It wouldn't do to let himself get too involved with her daily activities—she might start wanting him to reciprocate. She might insist on reading his poems, probing his innermost thoughts, forcing him to spill out his unmanly emotions. . . .

He broke out in a cold sweat. Thankfully, she presented her back to him while she fastened her locket around her neck, and he busied himself tying her corset strings. When his fingers brushed her warm skin, he welcomed the stirring in his groin. It reminded him that his principal interest in her was for physical pleasure.

His anger at her deception had faded to a dark cloud on the horizon of his consciousness. Somehow, he could no longer resent Jane for robbing him of his freedom. He could even admit to finding satisfaction in their marriage. It was convenient to have a lover right next door, where he could avail himself of her body at any time. All in all, Jane was pleasant company and a fine mother for Marianne.

That was all he required from a wife.

The printer's shop was quieter than Jane expected. Lanterns were lit to augment the watery daylight. The pungent smell of ink and paper filled the air, along with the remains of someone's meat pie tossed in the rubbish bin. Along the back wall, several men were bent over trays of type on slanted tables. All around the room, newly printed broadsides hung from drying rods.

She had chosen this shop because it was unlikely she would encounter any member of the *ton*. Standing by the press, a tall wooden affair that smelled of varnish and lampblack, she regarded the barrel-chested master printer in his ink-stained apron.

Extending her hand, she showed him her mother's locket. "Sir, I am offering you a superb piece of jewelry. Solid gold, the finest workmanship."

Staring greedily at the piece, he poked it with a dirty

fingertip. "How do I know ye ain't cheatin' me?"

"Take it to any jeweler's shop. You've two days until I return to examine the proofs. Please, the locket will more than meet your price."

"Eh? Mayhap 'twill do, then."

With fingers deft from setting type, he plucked the piece out of her hand. The gold gleamed in the dim sunlight. A pang of regret clutched at her breast as her treasured locket disappeared into the pocket of his grubby apron.

It pained her to give up her most prized possession, though she had removed the miniature paintings of her parents. But she owned nothing else of value, nothing that belonged to her alone. She could not use Ethan's money to purchase his birthday gift. She wanted it to be an offering from her heart.

The poems lay in a tidy pile, tied with a pink ribbon Jane had found in her drawer. She had copied them in her finest penmanship and returned the originals to the tower room. Yet still she hadn't been satisfied with the result. To hand Ethan a sheaf of loose papers, however prettily done, simply wasn't good enough. So she had made discreet inquiries and, on this back street of the Strand, found a printer who was willing to set the type and bind the poems into a book with a fine cover of tooled morocco leather.

"You will have it finished by Thursday?" she asked. "It is a gift for my husband, and imperative that it be ready on time."

"Aye, but that'll cost ye extra."

"I quite understand. And you will print one copy—and only one. You are to show no one these papers."

"Aye." He ducked his head in the crude imitation of a bow. " 'Twill be done as ye instructed, Mrs. Mayhew."

She nodded, satisfied that he would comply with her insistence on secrecy. To further safeguard her mission, she had given him her maiden name. He didn't even know her husband and the poet were one and the same. The frontispiece listed the author as simply *Ethan Sinclair*.

She took her leave and wound a path through the print shop with its stacks of paper and boxes. Excitement fluttered in her stomach. In just a few days, on Ethan's birthday, she would present the bound volume to him. He would be surprised—and pleased by her unique gift. Any writer would delight in seeing his work printed. Even her unpretentious father had proudly displayed his published treatises on the mantelpiece.

She wanted to see that same glow of satisfaction on Ethan's face. She wanted to deepen their union, to make him realize how much she loved him and how well they suited each other. She wanted him to see that she could be his helpmate, his assistant, his friend. In addition to his lover.

She blushed to remember their wild coupling that morning, the passion he aroused in her. More than their intimacy, though, his attentiveness gave her hope that he felt an affection for her. He had wanted to accompany her on her shopping expedition, and it had frustrated her to refuse him. Of all days for him to show an interest in her company!

She pushed open the door of the print shop and went outside to find the hackney waiting at the curbstone, the driver dozing, the sway-backed nag nibbling the straggly blades of grass between the cobbles. The shops and houses were crammed close together, the scent of soot and horse droppings heavy in the air. Down the street, two workmen were unloading furniture from a dray and carrying it into a building.

Jane gathered up her skirts and hastened to the hired hackney. She had been careful not to take the Chasebourne barouche on this errand. The coachman had left her at the fashionable shops on Bond Street, and she had given him instructions to return later. He had wanted to leave a footman to carry her parcels, but she refused firmly.

Sometimes it helped to be the Countess of Chasebourne.

Intent on that pleasant thought, she didn't notice the open carriage parked beyond the dray. Or the eyes that avidly watched her.

~ *Chapter 22* ~

"You're smiling a lot this afternoon," Ethan murmured.

Jane felt a bubble of happiness as they walked up the grand staircase at the Duke of Kellisham's mansion. The muted echo of conversations swirled through the domed foyer. Along with a bevy of aristocrats, they were attending a formal tea in honor of the duke's wedding to Lady Rosalind.

This morning Jane had fetched the book of poems from the printer. She had felt a thrill of pride to hold the slender volume with its soft calfskin binding, to leaf through the vellum pages and know that Ethan had written such beautiful words. She could scarcely wait to present the book to him this evening, when they were alone.

"Was I smiling?" Jane said, attempting a sober expression. "I must have been reflecting on the fact that today is your birthday."

"Ah." Ethan gave her a penetrating look. "I have the distinct feeling you've planned something."

"It's a surprise. But I'm certain you'll love it."

He leaned closer, his breath warm against her ear. "If it involves you removing your clothing, I'm all in favor of it."

She swatted his coat sleeve with her closed fan. "*That* would hardly be a surprise, my lord," she whispered.

"Quite so. But I would appreciate it nonetheless."

As much as she enjoyed their banter, Jane was aware of another ache within herself, a yearning for something more. Their repartee was like all their conversations: light . . . amusing . . . never delving beneath the surface. She hungered to know his deepest thoughts, to share in his confidences. But he used his charm like a shield between them. Never once had he said he loved her. And her longing to hear those words gnawed at her heart.

She bolstered her smile as they neared the grand saloon. Lady Rosalind and the duke stood in the doorway, greeting a steady stream of guests. They made a striking pair, the dowager with her tawny gold hair and delicate features, the duke square-shouldered and dignified.

"My dear Ethan and Jane," Lady Rosalind said, her blue eyes sparkling, her hands clasping theirs. "How splendid to see you both."

"You just saw us at luncheon, Mother," Ethan said dryly. "Remember? You presented me with your annual gift of a cravat pin."

"Oh, fie. I will not hear your criticism. You must allow me my high spirits. I am to be a bride in two days' time."

She glanced adoringly at her betrothed, and the duke smiled at her with such love, Jane again felt the tug of longing.

After tonight, when she gave Ethan the book of poetry, perhaps he would love her. Yes. Even if he were a little angry at first, he would get over it quickly. He would realize how helpful she could be to him in his work. She looked forward to sharing a true intimacy of mind as well as body.

Smiling, she strolled with him into the stately saloon decorated in blue and gold with elaborate gilt cornices and two massive fireplaces. Jane looked around with interest. This world was so far from her humble cottage in the country, where teatime meant sitting by the parlor fire with her aunt, sipping tea from a cracked china cup and nibbling a thin slice of buttered bread. Here, liveried footmen stood at attention behind huge silver trays of delicacies, sandwiches and sugared confections and a fine array of pastries. She liked both worlds, this one because Ethan was here to share it with her, and the country for its quiet peace.

Aunt Willy had already seated herself with a group of older ladies. Jane saw many familiar faces, and she was soon separated from Ethan. She was happily discussing books with several elderly gentlemen when someone spoke behind her.

"Lady Chasebourne. You look as though you're hiding a secret."

Her heart lurched. She spun around to see Lord Keeble standing behind her, Mr. Duxbury grinning at his side. They were like a pair of mismatched jesters, one short and stout, the other tall and thin. She scolded herself for letting them fool her. "If I am," she teased, "I certainly shan't tell either of you."

"You wound me." Clapping his hand to his peacock-blue coat, Keeble studied her with keen eyes. "But never mind, you needn't say a word. We always ferret out the truth. 'Tis our talent, ain't it, Ducks?"

"Yes, indeed. Ferrets, that's us."

Duxbury twitched his nose in a weaselly manner, and both men glanced at each other and chortled. Jane almost laughed, too. Really, they were too silly for words.

"Well, Lord Ferret, Mr. Ferret, I see my husband is approaching with two cups of tea. If you will excuse me."

She made her escape, and Ethan met her beside a potted fern. He wore that faint glower she had noticed on his face whenever she flirted with other men. Rather than vex her, his jealousy gave Jane a warm glow.

He handed a cup of tea to her. "If those two were bothering you—"

"They weren't." She placed her hand on his arm, his muscles solid and warm. "You must admit, they're rather amusing in a witless sort of way."

The rigid set of his mouth eased. "So long as they aren't spreading gossip about you or Marianne."

"Of course not. I'm afraid we've become yesterday's scandal."

He leaned closer. "Shall we create a new scandal, my lady?"

A wolfish grin lit his darkly handsome features. He stood so near she could feel his heat, and it sparked a slow burn inside herself. He could kiss her right here in this company, and she would not resist. He knew it, too; she could see the confidence in his dark eyes. She ought to reject him, the swaggering rogue.

But his brash masculinity appealed to her too much, and in the dangling fronds of the fern, her hand found his. She stroked her thumb over his big palm, loving the way his eyelids lowered slightly, his gaze intensifying. She could almost fancy he felt more for her than lust. . . .

His gaze drifted over her bosom. Then he frowned slightly. "You aren't wearing your locket."

"Oh, I . . ." She paused, disliking the need to fib. "I misplaced it, but I'm certain it will turn up eventually."

"Be sure to ask the maid." He gently squeezed her fingers. "I know how much that locket means to you."

Genuine concern shone in his eyes, and something very sweet took wing inside her, that he remembered how much she valued the sentimental keepsake. He mustn't learn she had bartered it in order to give him a gift from her heart.

A clapping of hands shattered the moment. She stepped back, almost spilling her tea. A voice called out over the hum of conversation, "If I may have the attention of everyone here."

By one of the fireplaces, Lord Keeble clambered onto a footstool. The added height made him as tall as Duxbury, who grinned at his side. Keeble's portly chest was puffed out in an air of self-importance, and Jane cringed to think that he might offer an idiotic toast.

To Ethan, she whispered, "I do hope he doesn't spoil the party for Lady Rosalind."

"She'll give him a proper set-down if he does. My mother is quite good at looking after her own interests."

His fingers stroked the back of her waist, a gesture both soothing and energizing. She was impatient to return home, to give him her gift. Instead, she had to sit here and listen to Keeble's ridiculous posturing.

"Ladies and gentlemen, I have a special surprise for all of you today. We have in our midst a rare talent, a man of mystery who is a member of the *ton*. A man who has hidden his genius from us until today." Keeble paused, and Duxbury bobbed his head as if to confirm Keeble's pronouncement.

A buzz of interest filled the chamber. People turned to one another in curiosity to see if someone could identify the subject of Keeble's eulogy.

"What a pretty speech," Ethan murmured to Jane. "He should play ringmaster for Astley's Circus."

Her throat dry, Jane couldn't answer. She took a sip of tea and tried to subdue a sudden twinge of uneasiness. There was something about Keeble's manner that disturbed her. He kept glancing at her and Ethan.

The duke's voice rang out. "Keeble, if you intend to repeat hearsay or innuendo, I must ask you to step down."

" 'Tis no rumor, Your Grace, but a fact I am prepared to prove right here and now." Like an excited child, Keeble bounced up and down on his toes. "This man of secrets is a poet whose work surpasses that of Lord Byron and Mr. Shelley. And it is my great pleasure to be the very first to read a short selection from his new book."

A dizzying shock swept over Jane. Her cup rattled down into its saucer. She gripped the porcelain as Keeble surveyed the throng, then stared with undisguised glee at Ethan.

No. Impossible. The viscount couldn't know about the

book. She had made certain no one followed her to the printer's shop.

Frowning, Ethan placed his untouched cup on a side table.

Keeble reached into an inner pocket of his peacock-blue frock coat and extracted a slim volume. A second jolt shook Jane, and a rising panic pressed on her lungs. The binding looked identical to Ethan's book.

But she had locked the gift in her desk in her bedchamber. How could Keeble have obtained it?

She must be mistaken. There must be another gentleman who penned poetry in secret. It could only be a horrid coincidence.

Keeble riffled through the pages, cleared his throat theatrically, and began to read with melodramatic flair.

To One Who Sleeps at Waterloo

In valor he did ride to war,
One of many called to more
Righteous cause than those who wait
By hearthside comfort for his fate ...

As the familiar words resonated in her ears, Jane stood paralyzed. A sense of unreality made her sway. This could not be happening. It could not be true.

She jerked her head toward Ethan. His gaze focused on Keeble, he gripped his fingers into fists, his knuckles white. An expression of panicked fury tautened his profile. Then he turned his head and looked straight at her.

She felt pinned by that dark, penetrating stare. There was a stark question in his eyes, a mirror of her own disbelief. And a raw agony she had glimpsed in him only once before, in the tower room the evening he had caught her reading his poems. Aghast that she was the inadvertent cause of his pain, she lowered her head and squeezed her eyes shut.

Her action had answered his question. She knew that, yet she could not disavow the truth. She had taken the poems to the printer. And somehow, Keeble had put his hands on a copy.

She was aware that he had ceased reading. A hush blanketed the saloon. Then a woman sniffled loudly, and a whispering of voices gathered force like wildfire, sweeping through the chamber.

"By Jove, that's demned good!" a gentleman exclaimed.

"My dear James gave his life for his country, too," a lady said brokenly.

"Where might I purchase this book?" someone else asked.

"Who is he?" several people clamored. "Tell us the name of the poet!"

Keeble preened with self-importance. "I am pleased to be the first to reveal his identity—"

Ethan uttered a low growl.

Jane jerked her chin up, opened her eyes, and saw him striding toward Keeble and Duxbury.

The sly triumph vanished from Keeble's round face. He backed to the edge of the footstool. His voice changed to a sputtering falsetto. "I say . . . ah . . . perhaps he does not wish his name unveiled just yet . . . perhaps he would rather his wife do the honors."

Ethan snatched the volume out of Keeble's clutches. He paged through the book, his scowl deepening. Then his gaze shot to Keeble. "Perhaps he despises snoops."

His fist flashed out and met Keeble's jaw. The short man tumbled backward, straight into Duxbury. Both men landed in a tangled heap on the carpet.

Several ladies screamed. The clamor of voices rose to a fever pitch. Mouths agape, everyone stared at Ethan.

Jane dropped her teacup. Heedless of the liquid that splashed her lavender gown, she hastened toward him. She had to get him out of here. She had to make amends for her role in this scandal.

The duke strode forward. "What is the meaning of this outrage?"

"You should thank me," Ethan drawled, flexing his fingers. "I was clearing the rabble from your home."

Keeble groaned and rubbed his reddened jaw. "I ain't rabble," he protested. "All I did was read a poem."

Duxbury sat up, his cravat crooked. "A pack of fancy words, that's all."

Lady Rosalind appeared beside the duke. Her eyes glistened with unshed tears as she gazed at Ethan. "You wrote that poem?" she whispered. "*You?*"

A dull flush crept up his throat and cheeks. He said nothing.

"You wrote it for John—for Captain Randall, your friend," she said softly. "Oh, Ethan, it is a wonderful tribute—"

"It is a private matter," he said grimly, shoving the book inside his coat. "I will thank you not to mention it again."

The murmurings took on an excited edge. Jane could see that people were amazed to discover the most notorious rogue in society could have such perception. And in spite of her distress, she was glad. Fiercely proud of him.

She slipped her arm through his. "Forgive us, Your Grace, my lady. I'm afraid we must take our leave. My husband and I have a pressing engagement."

His dark glance seared her. "We do, indeed."

With a tug imperceptible to anyone but her, he urged Jane toward the open doors.

"Wait!" someone called. "Do tell us where we might purchase a copy."

Several people murmured and nodded.

"I fear," he said with a hard-edged smile, "that you shall have to content yourselves with Lord Byron and Mr. Shelley. Good day."

His arm rigid, he marched Jane out of the saloon and down the grand staircase. Their footsteps echoed in the vast foyer with its pale marble floor and crystal chandelier. One footman fetched their wraps while another held open the front door and scurried to fetch their carriage. They waited on the long portico, the sky gray and a chilly breeze blowing.

Ethan paced back and forth, as if unable to contain his agitation.

Jane could bear his silence no longer. Swallowing past the tightness in her throat, she said, "Ethan, please understand, I did not mean for anyone else—"

"Enough," he snapped. "We will have our words in private."

Her spirits descended even lower. She knew how highly he valued his privacy. And she had had a hand in destroying his peace. But surely . . . surely he would listen to reason, at least once his anger burned out. In the meantime, she would do everything in her power to make him comprehend that her intentions had been pure.

The sleek black barouche drew up in front of the mansion. Ethan ushered her down the broad marble steps and into the vehicle, taking the seat opposite her, his back to the horses. The closed carriage seemed to throb with tension, and she felt as if she were riding with a stranger.

"Now," he said, "you will explain what happened in there."

She forced herself to face his piercing glare. "I copied some of your poems. I took them to a printer and had them bound into a book." Her voice wobbled and her eyes stung. "It was to be my birthday surprise to you."

"Is it Keeble's birthday, too?"

"No! I did *not* give him that book." She leaned forward, desperate to erase the mistrust from his face. "I told the printer to make one book, and *only* one. He was not to allow *anyone* to read the poems. But . . . Keeble and Duxbury must have seen me enter or leave the shop. And somehow they convinced the printing master to disregard my instructions."

"Money is a powerful persuader."

He was right. It all made a sickening sense. "Then you do understand. You know that I meant the book for no one's eyes but yours. Yours alone."

His expression remained stony. "I know that you took my papers without permission. That you read what I wished no one to read. That by your actions, my ramblings have been exposed to the world."

"That poem was more than ramblings. You touched the heart of every person present."

"And wreaked hell on my reputation as a heartbreaker."

"Don't make a jest of it." She lifted her chin and stared unflinchingly at him. "To be truthful, Ethan, I'm not sorry for what's happened. People *should* know that you are more than a shallow rake."

The hollow clopping of hooves filled the silence. The carriage swayed as it turned into the drive in front of Chasebourne House.

Ethan said nothing, his glower set in granite. There was no time to plead further with him as the barouche came to a stop and an impassive footman opened the door.

Feeling ill from the quarrel, Jane stepped down onto the paving bricks. The breeze tugged at her bonnet and sent a smattering of cold raindrops at her face. Not wanting anyone to witness her misery, she walked a few steps toward the grand mansion with its soaring columns and many tall windows. How magnificent was her new home. And she would trade every last stone for Ethan's love.

Only then did she realize he hadn't followed her.

She turned to see him standing by the front wheel, speaking to the coachman. Was he leaving? Before she could convince him to forgive her? Struck by panic, she hastened back just as Ethan was stepping into the carriage.

"Where are you going?" she murmured.

"To a place that caters to shallow rakes." His gaze flashed over her in a dark, moody sweep. "You needn't wait up."

He shut the door and she stepped back automatically as the carriage rattled off down the drive.

The finality of his action struck her in full force. Her knees shook, and with effort, she mastered her trembling and walked slowly toward the house. Ethan didn't care to hear her explanations. He didn't care that she had printed his poems with the best of intentions. He could see only that she had provided the means for him to be unmasked before the world.

To him, her gift of love was another betrayal.

Ethan returned home very late and very drunk.

Stepping down from the carriage, he staggered. The footman grasped his elbow to discreetly steady him, but Ethan waved him away. "Thass won't be neshessary." He was faintly surprised to hear the slurring of his words.

The house seemed to sway in the darkness, and four torches flanked the doors where he could have sworn there were only two. Dimly he heard the clatter of the carriage as it set off to the mews. He took a deep breath, and the chilly air revived him enough to walk.

Right foot, left foot. He made his way toward the broad steps and had a flash of memory, of running up these very steps only to trip on the last one and fall flat at his father's feet. Though a knot swelled on Ethan's forehead, the fifth Earl of Chasebourne had reprimanded him for behaving like a common urchin. For crying, he had been banished to the nursery.

He felt the heat of moisture in his eyes now. He blinked it away in denial of a more piercing memory. Jane. The poems. The raw torment that burned despite the brandy.

He reached the portico and somehow his shoulder sank against the massive stone column. A second footman rushed to help him, a second time Ethan motioned him away. Reluctant to go inside just yet, he turned from the bright light of the torches—there really were just two—and gazed past the iron-fenced drive to the darkened square.

The book lay in his coat pocket. He could feel it pressing into his rib cage. In the carriage after he'd left Jane, he had been unable to resist examining the slender volume. He had donned his eyeglasses and viewed the pages in crisp clarity. Reading his own words, he had felt . . . a lifting inside himself . . . a feeling curiously like elation. . . .

Something moved in the darkness of the square. A tall man, watching from the shadows.

Ethan blinked his bleary eyes, and the image melted into nothingness. He stared into the depthless gloom beneath the trees. The clouds hid the moon, and the gaslights at either corner were too distant to penetrate the blackness. This prickling of unease he felt was another illusion.

An illusion like his trust in Jane.

She would be in her bed now. Asleep at this late hour. He wanted to go to her, to touch her, to feel her move against him with sleepy sensuality. He wanted to hear her cry out with love for him.

No. He wished her gone. She knew him too well. As he knew her. A cold shudder gripped him. She would poke and pry until she had opened his soul for all the world to see.

Muttering a curse, he pushed away from the pillar and managed to walk without stumbling to the front door. The brightness of the torches hurt his eyes. He'd be damned lucky to make it upstairs to his bed.

He would deal with his wife in the morning.

Jane awakened to the muffled sound of raised voices.

Pushing up on her elbow, she squinted at the pale light streaming through a crack in the draperies. It could not be far past dawn. Her mind felt drugged, her limbs heavy. She had not fallen asleep until the wee hours.

Yesterday's events came rushing back at her. The poems. The ruined birthday gift. Ethan's fury.

The voices came from his bedchamber. She had not been dreaming his deep, angry tone. A quieter male voice answered him. Wilson? And a woman. There was a weeping woman. Jane could hear her broken sobs.

For one wild moment, she feared he'd brought home a whore. Cold sickness clutched at her belly. Then reason asserted itself. He must be berating a servant, that was all. She would not allow him to take out his wrath on a helpless employee.

Throwing back the coverlet, Jane scooted out of bed. She stepped through the semidarkness to pick up her silk robe from a chair. As she headed to the connecting door, she thrust her arms through the sleeves and tied the sash.

She didn't bother to knock. She turned the handle and marched inside.

The draperies had been drawn to let in the meager light. Clad in a dressing gown, Ethan paced a path from the fireplace to the rumpled bed. Wilson clutched a white shirt and trailed after him, beseeching him to get dressed.

Her dark hair straggling from a white nightcap, Gianetta knelt wailing on the carpet.

Foreboding seized Jane by the throat. "What is going on here? Has something happened to Marianne?"

Ethan swung toward her. His eyes were dark and hollow, his face haggard and unshaven. He strode toward Jane and took her by the arm, guiding her toward a chair. "Sit down."

His heavy voice chilled her. Fighting a wild alarm, she wrenched free and rounded on him. "Just answer my question. Is Marianne ill? Have you sent for a physician? I must go to her—"

"Jane. She isn't ill." He paused, a muscle working in his jaw as he raked his fingers through his hair. "She's been abducted."

Chapter 23

Ethan saw disbelief darken Jane's face, followed by horror. The same horror that gripped his chest. He had been awakened only a few minutes ago, groggy from the brandy he'd drunk. The news had hit him like a fist to his gut. He still could not fully grasp the truth of it.

Jane shook her head, her thick braid swinging. "How can you be sure?"

Gianetta sobbed, "Baby ees gone from her cradle. Someone steal her while I sleep." She lapsed into a babble of Italian.

Wilson's thin face had a gray pallor. "I checked the nursery myself," he said, sounding uncharacteristically rattled. "The child is missing."

"There must be an explanation," Jane said wildly. "Perhaps one of the nursemaids took Marianne for an early walk. We must look for them."

"No." Ethan put his shaking hand on her shoulder. "Jane, there was a note left in the cradle."

"From whom? Let me read it!"

He wished to God he could shield her from this. But he could not. Grimly he handed over the paper he held crushed in his palm. She snatched it away, smoothing the wrinkles and hastening to the window to read by the light. For a moment, the only sounds were the whistling of a passerby on the street and the sniffling of the wet nurse. Then Jane dropped the note to the floor and swayed. A keening moan broke from her.

Ethan sprang to her side and caught her against him. He felt her pain as sharply as his own, a knife blade to his heart. Trembling from shock, she buried her face in his neck, and he held her tightly, giving her what little comfort he could.

Over her head, he snapped to Gianetta, "Fetch tea for my lady immediately. And summon her maid."

The distraught woman scrambled to her feet and fled the room. Wilson discreetly melted into the dressing room.

Jane lifted her head. Tears glossed her eyes and seeped down her cheeks. Looking dazed, she clutched at his dressing gown. "Lady Portia. It was Lady Portia who took Marianne."

"She must have slipped inside the house during the night."

"But she was gone . . . settled in Cornwall."

"Yes. My man of affairs attested to that fact." Ethan cursed himself for not anticipating this treachery. "But it seems she tricked all of us."

"How could she do such an evil act? How could she take my baby?"

Her desperate eyes looked to him for answers, and he had only one. "For money," he bit out. "The note says she wants fifty thousand pounds by tonight."

"Can you procure so large an amount in a day? Isn't your wealth invested? In land, paintings, jewels?"

"There's sufficient cash available." Or so he hoped. But he wouldn't alarm her further. He massaged his aching brow and tried to think. "I'll go to several banks. Loans can be arranged."

"But will it be enough?" Jane asked fervently. "If Portia refuses to return Marianne until we have the money . . ." Her voice faltered. "Who will care for Marianne? Who will feed her?"

"Don't worry. I'll get the ransom. Today."

He despised giving in to Portia's démands. But he would sign away his soul to get his daughter back. He was tortured by the thought of never seeing her toothless smile again, never touching her silken skin, never holding his little angel.

Fury and panic battered his control. And down deeper, a dark guilt clawed him. *He could have prevented this from happening.*

He could no longer stand still. Putting Jane aside, he hastened into the dressing room, where he tore off his dressing gown and snatched his breeches from Wilson.

Jane rushed to his side. "We must gather what we have here. Empty the strongboxes, collect the jewels."

"Wilson can manage that."

"Yes, my lord," the valet said, taking a shirt from the clothes press. "I shall do whatever I can to assist you."

"And you will instruct the staff to keep quiet about this," Ethan added. "I want no gossip to leave this house."

"It shall be as you say."

Ethan had fastened his breeches and yanked on his shirt just as the outer door opened and rapid footsteps approached. Lady Rosalind burst into the dressing room and stopped, her eyes large and blue against her pale features. Her upswept hair straggled in wisps around her face, and she wore a pink silk robe tied crookedly at the waist.

"Is it true?" she gasped out. "Someone has taken Marianne?"

"Yes." Ethan motioned Wilson out of the room, and then told her about the note.

Her mouth quivering, she sagged against the door frame, and Jane hurried to her side, guiding her to a chair. As if boneless, his mother sank onto the seat and bowed her head, digging her fingers into her skirt.

"Portia," she whispered. "Dear God. That female has Marianne."

"She cannot mean to harm her," Jane said. "She needs

the money too badly. She'll find a wet nurse for the baby.
She *will*.''

Jane glanced at Ethan as if seeking reassurance, and he
gave a jerky nod of agreement. Then he turned away, hiding his dread from her, fumbling blindly with his cravat.
Jane couldn't know just how unscrupulous Portia was. To
sustain her gambling habit, she would lie, cheat, steal.

But would she murder? He prayed he was wrong to fear
so.

''How did that woman get into this house?'' Lady Rosalind cried out. ''Was a door left unlocked?''

''She may have kept a key,'' Ethan said. ''Or enlisted
the aid of a skilled housebreaker.''

The dowager sprang up and paced toward him, her robe
swishing. ''You cannot let her get away with this! You
must find her. Call in the Bow Street Runners!''

''The note warned there is to be no interference from the
law.'' He spoke sharply, forcing himself to voice his
darkest fear. ''Lest we never see Marianne again.''

Lady Rosalind faltered to a stop and braced her hand on
the mahogany clothes press. ''Oh, dear God. What shall we
do?'' Her voice rose to an hysterical pitch. ''Whatever shall
we *do*?''

Ethan paused in the act of drawing on his waistcoat and
frowned at his mother. Never had he known her to shatter
emotionally. She was always calm and collected, seldom
worrying about anyone but herself. He felt a bond with her,
a shared anxiety and heartache, a love for his child.

Jane slid her arm around the dowager's waist. ''Please,
Rosalind. There *is* a way for you to help. You must return
to your room and gather up your jewels. We shall need to
pawn them for the ransom.''

''You're quite right.'' The dowager took several deep
breaths. ''And I must appeal to His Grace, too. He will
help us to obtain the money.''

''An excellent notion,'' Jane said, walking her to the
door. ''We mustn't panic. We must all work together. I am

sure by this evening, Marianne will be back here with us, safe and sound.''

''Yes. Yes, we must believe that.''

Lady Rosalind enveloped Jane in a brief hug. Then quite unexpectedly, she ran to Ethan and put her arms around him.

Returning the embrace, he inhaled her familiar scent of expensive perfume. His mother was slender and dainty as a girl half her age, and a powerful affection washed over him. He couldn't remember the last time she had held him with unguarded love.

Without saying another word, she let go and hurried out of the room. He swung back to the mirror and straightened his cravat, his emotions too raw to share.

Jane stepped to his side. ''It's too early to visit the bank. Where are you going?''

''To seek information.''

''Where? How?''

''I'll go to Portia's old neighborhood. There's a chance someone might have seen her. You will wait here.''

''No! I'm going with you.''

Turning, he put his hands on her shoulders and looked into her stormy eyes. ''You must stay, Jane. In case Portia sends a message telling us where to leave the ransom.''

Jane shook her head. ''She won't. Not so early in the day.''

''It may be dangerous. She must have an accomplice. God only knows what manner of ruffian she hired.''

''Then that's all the more reason for me to go. Please, Ethan. Don't ask me not to help save our daughter.''

His head throbbing, he rubbed his temples. He could well understand her stubborn insistence. She loved Marianne as much as he did.

He pulled Jane into his arms and held her fast. He kissed her hair, needing her warmth and support with a despera- tion that went far beyond the physical. Their estrangement seemed insignificant now. He could think of nothing but getting their daughter safely back home.

"All right, then," he said heavily. "You'll go with me."

Jane stood at the front window in the library and peered out into the street. The last rays of sunlight bathed the square in golden splendor. People strolled beneath the trees, and an elderly gentleman sat reading on an iron bench. Seeing a nursemaid pushing her charge in a pram, Jane felt agony clutch her breast anew. The pain caused her heartbeat to quicken, and she took several deep breaths to calm the panic that had lurked in her all day.

She would hold Marianne in her arms again. Soon. Very soon. She had to believe that. Portia needed the money Ethan was still out collecting. Even so, it frightened Jane to think that Marianne might be hungry or neglected.

Their visit to Portia's neighborhood had been fruitless. As expected, the shabby rooms had been empty, the furniture long since carted away. Though Ethan had offered a reward, no one on the street had seen Portia since she had moved to Cornwall.

Behind her, Jane heard the rhythmic clacking of Aunt Willy's knitting needles, and the murmur of voices as the Duke of Kellisham soothed Lady Rosalind on the chaise. He was trying to convince her to put off the wedding, but the dowager kept insisting that would bring bad luck for rescuing Marianne. Their conversation struck Jane with a pang. In all the tumult, she had forgotten the ceremony was scheduled for tomorrow. Then she saw the barouche coming up the drive.

She spun around. "Ethan is back."

Lifting her skirts, she ran for the front door. A footman opened the door, and she emerged onto the portico in time to see Ethan striding grimly up the marble steps, a leather satchel in his hand.

He looked weary, his brow furrowed and his hair mussed, as though he'd run his fingers through it countless times. His eyes were dark and hollow, but he smiled briefly at her, enough to reassure her that his mission had met with success.

"Any word yet?" he asked.

Biting her lip, Jane shook her head.

She wanted to put her arms around him, to feel his heart beating against hers. There was so little she could do to banish the starkness from his face. As they entered the house, she saw Mrs. Crenshaw walking in the corridor and asked her to send a tray of tea and sandwiches to the library.

Concern etched the housekeeper's severe features. "Yes, m'lady. And if I might be permitted to say so, all of us downstairs are praying for the young one's safe return."

"Thank you," Jane whispered, blinking away tears. Only with effort did she subdue the constant worry. She hurried into the library, closing the double doors behind her.

Lady Rosalind had risen from the chaise and clutched her son's sleeve. "You obtained the money?" she asked anxiously.

Ethan placed the satchel on a mahogany table. He opened the latch and displayed the bundles of bank notes. "It's all here. Fifty thousand."

"My word!" Aunt Willy exclaimed from her chair by the fireplace, her knitting lying forgotten in her broad lap. "Why, it boggles my mind that a criminal could place any price on a baby."

"I trust my man of affairs was of assistance," the duke said gruffly.

"Very much so," Ethan said, snapping the case shut. "I owe you a debt of gratitude, Your Grace. I would have been hard-pressed to gather the amount so swiftly."

The two men solemnly shook hands. Their accord gave a moment of gladness to Jane. At last they had ended their hostility.

"Thank your mother," the duke said. "She sets great store by her granddaughter."

He smiled at Rosalind, but she didn't smile back. Her fists clenched, she burst out, "I deplore this waiting. Oh, why doesn't that woman send the message?"

"She'll wait until dark," Ethan predicted. "She won't want to be seen."

"Surely you don't think she'll come herself, do you?" Jane asked.

He shook his head. "But we'll be prepared, nonetheless."

He stalked to the front window and parted the green brocaded curtains to peer out into the gathering dusk. Burdened by tension, Jane walked to his side. "I regret trusting Portia," she said in a low voice. "I know I've told you so before, but I must say it again. I should never have believed any of her lies."

Letting go of the drapery, he turned to Jane. "I am to blame, not you," he said. "If only I had paid off her debts, it would never have come to this."

The haunted quality to his eyes reached her heart. She brought his hand to her mouth and kissed it, briefly laying her cheek against his strong, warm fingers. "Oh, Ethan, you did as you thought best. You couldn't have known what would happen. Besides, Portia would have gambled the money away and then wanted more."

If anything, his expression grew harder, so that he looked every inch the powerful lord. "I will get Marianne back safely. I promise you that."

"I know." But she didn't know. A voice of doubt whispered in her mind, and she wrapped her arms around his waist, hiding her face in his coat and fighting off despair. Gloomy thoughts would solve nothing. She needed to think clearly, to keep up her spirits, to be ready when the message came.

He held her for a long moment until the library doors opened and she quickly turned her head. Her rise of hope died a swift death. It was only a maid to light the candles, followed by a footman bearing the tea tray, which he set on a table.

Sitting beside the duke, Lady Rosalind leaned forward. "Has a letter arrived yet, Tucker?"

"Only those her ladyship opened earlier."

The dowager sank back on the chaise. "Thank you."

Troubled, Jane glanced at Ethan. The letters. She had forgotten about them. She would as soon he didn't hear about them just yet.

As the servants went out, she pulled him to the tea tray and poured a cup for him, adding the dash of cream he liked. It was a breach of etiquette to serve him before the duke, but she didn't care and she didn't suppose His Grace would, either. Ethan took the cup and drank automatically, his brooding gaze focused on the wall of books.

"Well, Chasebourne, you've been quite the popular fellow today," the duke said with forced cheer. "All those congratulatory notes."

Jane froze in the act of filling another cup. Her gaze went to Ethan, but he shot a perplexed frown at Kellisham.

"Congratulatory?"

"About your poem," Lady Rosalind said distractedly. "We had an unusual number of visitors, too. But of course, the footman turned them all away."

"I see."

Ethan glanced at Jane, and in his dark gaze flickered a weary awareness, as if he were sorely disappointed in her for her part in exposing his secret. Then he turned to contemplate the shelves of books again.

He couldn't have slept more than a few hours the previous night. She had waited up until the wee hours, hoping to hear him return home, but finally she had succumbed to exhaustion. Then this morning, she had smelled brandy on him, and she knew he'd been out drinking to escape his pain. The abduction of Marianne had brought them back together. But Jane couldn't help wondering how much damage she'd done to his trust in her.

With mechanical movements, she delivered tea to Lady Rosalind, the duke, and Aunt Willy, who added a dollop of her restorative to it. Jane was relieved that no one seemed inclined to pursue the topic of his poetry. She would think about it later, make it up to Ethan somehow. Only Marianne mattered now. How desperately she wanted to hold her small form, to see her lift her head, her eyes bright with curiosity about the world. . . .

Jane wrapped her fingers around her cup, needing the warmth more than sustenance. The ormolu clock on the mantelpiece ticked away the agonizing seconds. It was the only sound save for the clacking of Aunt Willy's knitting needles and the quiet voice of the duke talking to Lady Rosalind. Outside, the darkness deepened to night.

Then the noise of scuffling footsteps came from the foyer, the library door opened, and two footmen dragged in a squirming, filthy urchin.

"Caught this one trying to run away," Tucker said, his white wig askew. "Sneaked right up to the house and left this on the porch, he did." In his gloved hand, he held out a sealed note.

Ethan strode forward and took the missive. "Thank you," he said. "Leave the boy here."

The two footmen bowed out. The urchin made a dash to follow them, but Ethan seized him by his ragged collar and marched him to a footstool.

"Lemme go," he cried, wriggling and fighting. "I done nuthin' wrong, guv'nor. Just brung the letter."

"You aren't in trouble," Ethan said calmly. "Now sit. There's a guinea for you if you cooperate."

The boy's eyes grew big and blue against his small, dirty face. "Cor," he said, and promptly plopped down on the footstool.

"Read the note," Lady Rosalind urged. "What does Portia tell us to do?"

"One moment," Ethan said. He hunkered down in front of the urchin. "Who gave you this letter?"

The boy shrugged warily. " 'Twas a gent. 'E told me ta leave it an' run."

"A gentleman. Not a man of the streets?"

"Nay, 'e wore fancy stuff . . . like ye."

"Was he tall or short, dark or fair?"

The urchin scratched his spiky brown hair. " 'E were tall, but 'twas too dark ta see naught else."

"Did you note the color of his eyes? Any scars or markings? Anything about his voice?"

" 'E spoke like a gent. Dunno more, m'lord."

With a grimace of frustration, Ethan stood up. He took a coin from his pocket and tossed it to the lad, who caught it in his grubby fist. Then Ethan escorted him to the door and called to a footman. "Take the boy to the kitchen for a meal."

"What was that all about?" Jane asked as he closed the door. "Do you know who the man is?"

Giving a distracted shake of his head, Ethan paced the chamber. "Last night, I saw a tall man watching from the square. I thought my eyes were deceiving me. I wish to God I'd had the wits to be more suspicious."

"You couldn't have known," Jane said. "Please, read the letter and tell us where we can find Marianne."

They all crowded around him as he broke the seal. Jane looked over his shoulder and glimpsed Portia's familiar, flowery penmanship, but she wasn't close enough to discern the words.

Ethan looked up, his mouth thinned as he glanced at all of them. "Portia requests the money be brought at midnight to a house in the Devil's Acre."

Lady Rosalind moaned. "She has Marianne in that hellhole?"

"Where is it?" Jane asked in anxious bewilderment.

"The Devil's Acre is a slum near Westminster," the

duke said grimly. "The area is notorious for harboring all manner of criminals."

"Good gracious!" Aunt Willy exclaimed. "You must get the child from there, and quickly."

"That is not the worst of it." Ethan's stark gaze focused on Jane, and a quiver of tension ran through her at his intense look.

"Portia," he said, "insists that Jane bring the money. Alone."

⌐ *Chapter 24* ⌐

Despite her warm cloak, Jane shivered in the open phaeton. The clopping of the horse's hooves echoed in the narrow lane. On either side, squalid tenements loomed against the moonlit sky, and the stench of poverty permeated the chilly air. Here and there, a pinprick of candlelight shone in a window. She saw someone's wash strung out, pale against the darkened buildings. Black shapes moved through the shadows, slinking down the byways and alleys. Swindlers and coiners lived here, Ethan had said, along with thieves and whores who roamed the streets at night.

The note had stipulated she arrive in an open carriage with only a driver in attendance. It had taken much persuasion by Jane and Lady Rosalind to convince Ethan to agree, and in the end he had complied only because the alternative meant endangering Marianne.

So they had come up with a plan to protect both Jane and the baby. Since Portia would recognize Ethan, the coachman was none other than His Grace, the Duke of Kellisham.

He sat beside her, broad and sturdy, a welcome presence. Lady Rosalind had insisted on waiting in the barouche farther down the street, guarded by a trio of footmen. Ethan had accompanied his mother. He would slip behind the house and stand watch in case something went awry. Jane shuddered to think of the possibility.

The phaeton slowed as the duke searched for the address, the carriage lamps flickering over the dingy façades of buildings. At last they came to a house with the front window boarded up and a faded sign that read, Peebles Gin Shop.

The duke stopped the vehicle, clambered down from the high perch, and lent a hand to Jane, helping her down to the dirt street. He reached up and fetched the leather satchel. In his other hand he took the lamp. Then he inclined his head in a deferential bow. "After you, my lady."

"Thank you."

It felt odd to treat a duke of the realm as her minion, but she walked ahead of him to the door. Portia had instructed Jane to come straight inside and go to the rear chamber. Portia and her accomplice would not object to the presence of a lowly servant. Not when he was holding the money. If all went well, they would be in and out in a matter of minutes.

Rubble lay thick against the front of the building, accumulated dirt, old bricks, several broken bottles. A foul stench came from a nearby alley. Her palm felt damp inside her glove as she gripped the knob. Hope and fear raised goose bumps on her skin. Marianne was inside. In a few moments, she would hold her baby in her arms. Pray God someone had taken care of her.

"Have courage," the duke whispered.

His fatherly advice bolstered her; she opened the door and stepped into pitch darkness. Her footsteps echoed as the duke held up the lamp to illuminate the squalid room. Other than a broken chair and a few old newsheets lying on the floor, the place was empty. Something small and dark scuttled along the wall and vanished into the shadows.

She shuddered to think of her precious little girl in this rat-infested tenement. Quickening her pace, Jane hurried to another doorway that led into a back room.

At one side of the room, a shuttered lamp sat on a table, illuminating the boarded windows along the back wall. Portia stood behind the table, the eerie light shining on her dainty, cloaked form. Jane glanced swiftly around, but the shadows were dense, and she could see no sign of Marianne.

Dear God. Was she even here?

Portia snatched up the lamp and marched forward. "Stop right there," she snapped. "I told you to come alone."

"It's only my coachman," Jane said, glancing back at the duke, who stood impassively in the doorway. "The money weighs a lot."

Portia glared suspiciously, holding up the lamp so she could see his ruddy face. Jane prayed she wouldn't recognize Kellisham. He'd attested that they had never been introduced, though they'd attended some of the same parties. Garbed in the blue and silver Chasebourne livery, a coachman's tall hat on his graying hair, he looked nothing like the esteemed duke.

"He isn't one of the regular coachmen," Portia said.

"He's been there longer than I have," Jane said, pretending bafflement. "I'm sure that servants come and go—"

"Ethan wouldn't have sent a man too new to trust." Cautiously, Portia advanced on the duke, letting the lamp shine brighter on him. "What is your name?"

Before he could reply, a voice drawled from the shadows. "Never mind him. He's just an old geezer."

Jane spun around to see a tall, handsome man saunter into the light. Fair-headed, he wore the dark suit of a gentleman, and a diamond pin glinted in his snowy cravat. But his sudden appearance was not what made her skin clammy. Her gaze riveted to the pistol in his hand.

"You there," he said, negligently waving the gun at the duke. "Put the money on the table. I'd advise you move slowly lest I mistake your intentions."

Smiling as if he'd delight in doing just that, he stepped

back to allow Kellisham to pass. The duke walked to the table and set down the satchel. Keeping his manner deferential, he stepped quietly back and resumed his square-shouldered stance by the doorway.

Portia ran to the case and opened it. With a chortle of glee, she snatched up a packet of bank notes and clutched it to her bosom. "Look, George. We're rich! We can play for high stakes now."

George? Jane's gaze riveted to him. George *Smollett?*

It must be. This was Ethan's former valet, the man who had slept with his master's wife.

Shaken, she watched as he took the lamp from Portia and let it shine on the money inside. Smollett had not fled to the Continent to escape his gaming debts. That had been another of Portia's lies.

Portia glowered at Jane. "The money had better all be here."

"There's fifty thousand, just as you asked," Jane said, trying to keep her voice steady. "I would like my child back now."

"All in good time," Smollett said.

Holding the lantern, he walked around her, his pale blue eyes raking her, increasing her uneasiness. His footsteps echoed like gunshots. "Well, well. So you're the new Lady Chasebourne." He spoke over his shoulder to Portia. "You told me she was plain, a right ugly female. But I'd say she's a rather tasty-looking morsel."

"Never mind her," Portia said, closing the case. "Let's take the money and go."

Smollett laughed, waving the gun at Portia, his gaze on Jane. "You'd think she was the one in charge here, wouldn't you? The arrogant bitch still thinks she's a lady."

"I'm more a lady than you are a gentleman," Portia retorted.

Her throat dry, Jane repeated, "Where is Marianne? We've fulfilled our part of the bargain."

Smollett ignored her and strolled to Portia. "Not a gentleman, am I? But that is what you like best about me.''

"And what *you* like best about *me* is my blue blood. You would never have obtained this money without my connections.''

"So you've reminded me more than once.''

While they quarreled, Jane peered into the dense shadows. She could discern a closed door near the back corner. Was that where they were hiding Marianne?

Keeping an eye on Portia and Smollett, she inched toward the door.

Portia seized the heavy satchel and dragged it off the table. "I don't care to stand here discussing your lack of breeding.''

He narrowed his eyes. "The trouble with us vulgar men,'' he said, "is that sometimes you get more than you bargained for.''

Her attention was focused on hefting the satchel. "Oh, do shut up, and come here. This money is damned heavy.''

"Then let me help you as I did with that brat in your belly.''

He had caused Portia's miscarriage?

Before Jane could absorb the horrifying realization, he lunged forward. Metal flashed as he lifted the pistol and struck Portia across her face.

The blow resounded through the room. She cried out, staggering sideways, dropping the satchel. Falling against the boarded window, she slid to the floor and lay there unmoving, her eyes closed. In that same moment, a baby whimpered in the next room, then quieted.

Marianne.

Spurred by desperation, Jane sprang for the closed door.

Darkness shrouded the narrow alleyway. Gripping a dueling pistol, Ethan felt his way through the rubbish that strewed the ground. Intent on his purpose, he barely noticed the stench. He couldn't shake off the claws of fear. Jane. Marianne. If anything happened to either of them . . .

His boot heel slid in something wet and slimy, and he thrust out his hand to catch his balance. The bricks scraped his sweating palm.

Without pause, he hastened onward, making his way to the back of the building. The hardest moment of his life had been letting Jane set off in the phaeton without him. Just seconds ago, he had seen her enter the building, followed by the duke.

He had to trust in Kellisham to guard his family. The exchange would go smoothly, he told himself. Portia wouldn't jeopardize her chance to take the money. But Ethan intended to be nearby to ensure that nothing went wrong. And he had another purpose in mind, a burning resolve he had kept from Jane.

He did not intend for Portia and her accomplice to get away with their crime. Because this could happen again. When they gambled away their funds, they might kidnap someone else's child.

At the rear of the tenement, he found a door with a cracked stoop. The windows were boarded, though a small glow of light seeped out. He put his eye to one of the cracks and bit back a curse. He could see nothing but a slice of blank wall.

But he could hear muffled voices. Quarreling voices. Portia. Then Jane's level tone. And a man's deeper timbre. There was something naggingly familiar about the man's voice, something that fed the suspicion inside him. *'Twas a gent. . . .'E were tall.*

Ethan's fingers tightened around the pearl grip of the pistol. He had a damned good guess as to the man's identity.

He inched along the back of the shop, seeking a chink in the boards. Whoever had barred the windows had been overly diligent about keeping out prowlers. Then the man's voice took on a sharp edge.

A blow sounded, then a woman's scream. Something thumped against the boards directly in front of Ethan.

He reacted on gut instinct, leaping to the door. Locked. He kicked it open and surged inside. Pistol brandished, he took in the scene in one sweep.

The satchel lay on the floor. Portia was sprawled by the window, a nasty cut marring her cheek. In the middle of the room, Kellisham stood frozen, his hands held high.

But that was not what made Ethan's blood run cold.

In the far corner, in a shadowed doorway, two figures struggled. One was George Smollett. He had a grip on Jane, her face pale against the gloom.

And he lifted his pistol to her neck.

The cold metal circle of the gun pressed into her skin.

Jane went still, gazing in terror at Ethan. Garbed in black, a comma of hair dipping onto his brow, he looked as fierce as a pirate. In his hand he held a long-barreled pistol.

"Take care," she said urgently. "Marianne is in the next room."

Smollett's grip tightened, painfully twisting her arm behind her back. His breath hissed against her ear. "Well, if it ain't Lord Chasebourne," he said, his voice taking on a cockney inflection. "What a pity you should find me 'olding your second wife. Brings back old times, don't it?"

"Release her," Ethan said in a steely tone.

"I'm in charge 'ere. Put your gun down on the floor."

A muscle tightened in Ethan's jaw. But he complied, slowly lowering the weapon to the rough boards.

"Now kick it into the corner," Smollett instructed.

Ethan did so, and the gun went clattering into the shadows.

"Can't say I'm sorry you showed up, m'lord. 'Ow's it feel, taking orders from me for a change?"

"Let Jane go. If you want a hostage, take me instead."

Smollett loosed a nasty chuckle. "I'll make you a trade all right," he said. "The new wife for the old one."

Jane clenched her teeth to keep them from chattering. She must think. Think of a way to escape.

"Be reasonable, man," the duke said in a level tone. "If you take her, you'll have every magistrate in the land after you."

"Shut up, you old codger. You talk mighty fine for a servant."

"All you really want is the money," Ethan said. "I'll put it on the table for you."

He reached slowly for the satchel, but Smollett cocked the gun with a loud click. "One more step and I'll kill 'er."

Ethan went still.

"'Ow do I know you don't 'ave rozzers swarmin' outside, waitin' to cart me off to Newgate?" Smollet shook his head. "Nay, you broke the bargain. And now you'll pay for it."

He jammed the gun against Jane's neck. "Walk, m'lady. *You* pick up the case."

Jane willed strength into her wobbly knees. She must stay calm. Ethan stood unmoving, but she could tell by the murderous gleam in his eyes that he would snatch at any opportunity to save her.

It was up to her to give him that opportunity.

She went forward carefully, aware of the gun pressing into her flesh. Her heart thundered against her rib cage. Out of the corner of her eye, she saw Portia, lying as still as death, blood trickling from a swollen gash on her cheek. *Dear God. Oh, dear God.*

Jane forced herself to take even breaths. When she reached the valise, she lowered herself into a crouch. Smollett was forced to release her arm so that she could grasp the leather handle. He bent down with her, enough to keep the pistol at her neck.

A sudden cry came from the doorway. Lady Rosalind rushed into the room. "George Smollett! How dare you take Marianne's mother. Release her at once!"

"Rosalind, stay back!" Kellisham barked.

Feeling Smollett's hold loosen slightly, Jane twisted around and heaved the heavy satchel upward. She caught him under the chin and his teeth snapped together. The force of the blow sent her tumbling sideways, crashing into the table.

Ethan lunged forward and thrust Smollett's arm upward. The pistol fired harmlessly into the ceiling, dust and debris raining downward. Ethan wrestled him down onto the floor and yanked both arms behind his back. Smollett let out a string of curses.

It was over in a matter of seconds. Jane sat up, aching from the fall, trembling from the release of tension.

Lady Rosalind marched forward, ignoring Kellisham's attempt to keep her back. Her lip curled, she stood over Smollett. "Riffraff," she said scathingly. "Now where is Marianne?"

"I'll show you," Jane said, struggling to rise.

Three footmen surged into the room. "Her ladyship slipped away from the carriage," one of them said.

"Fie," said the dowager, lending a pristine gloved hand to Jane. "As you can see, I am perfectly safe."

"See to the lady lying there," Ethan growled. "Tucker, fetch me a length of rope."

A footman rushed off as the other two stayed to guard the prisoners, one of them bending to check Portia. "She's alive, m'lord. Just knocked out."

Kellisham held the lamp as Lady Rosalind hurried into the next room, Jane at her heels. By the wavering light, they found an ill-clad woman lying on a pallet, her hands tied behind her back, her dark frightened eyes peering over the gag in her mouth. Marianne was nestled against the wet nurse's ample bosom.

While the duke bent down to untie the woman, Lady Rosalind sank to her knees, seemingly oblivious to the filthy floor. She reached for Marianne, then drew her arms back and smiled rather wistfully at Jane. "Grandmothers come second, I suppose."

Jane scooped up the baby and cuddled her close, reveling in her precious form. Checking her over quickly, Jane assured herself that the infant was well and unharmed. Marianne blinked her blue eyes and yawned as if being the center of a momentous event was nothing unusual. Then she gazed up at Jane and her little mouth curved into a toothless smile.

Awash with love, Jane felt tears sting her eyes. She smoothed the baby's downy dark hair, running her fingertips over plump cheeks, the tiny shell of an ear, marveling in her softness and warmth. "Marianne," she whispered. "You're safe now with Mama."

"Is she unharmed?" Lady Rosalind asked, hovering anxiously.

"She seems perfectly well." Jane laughed with boundless joy. "Though her bottom feels rather damp."

"Oh, Grandmama doesn't mind. May I?" Lady Rosalind efficiently gathered the baby to her cloak. She crooned to the baby, her face alight with the glow of tenderness.

Jane noticed Ethan standing in the doorway. A curious look on his face, he intently watched his mother and the baby for a moment. Then he strode forward to gently rest his hand on Marianne's head. "Praise God," he murmured. "Praise God."

His voice shook, and Jane saw him clench his jaw as if to control his emotions. She slipped her arm through his and together they gazed at their daughter.

"How is Portia?" Jane asked, shuddering to recall that horrible blow.

"She'll recover," Ethan said grimly. "In prison, where she'll never again steal a child."

Kellisham cleared his throat. "You'll wish to be with your family, Chasebourne. Three footmen and one old codger should be sufficient to escort two prisoners to the magistrate at Queen Square station."

"Who is calling you old?" Lady Rosalind demanded, looking up from her contemplation of the baby.

A grin creased his ruddy features. "Never mind, my dear." Walking forward, he caressed her cheek. "You must promise to rest now. It is our wedding day tomorrow.''

Her blue eyes soft on him, she said, ''So it is, my darling. So it is.''

Back home, Jane couldn't bear to be parted from Marianne, and Ethan seemed to share her sentiment. So after being fed and fussed over by a tearful Gianetta, then outfitted in a fresh nappy and pink nightdress, Marianne promptly fell asleep in Jane's bed. She had her thumb in her mouth, and the candlelight flickered on her tiny, slumbering form. Lady Rosalind smiled fondly from the foot of the bed.

''Well,'' she whispered. ''Now that all has been settled quite nicely, I shall be off to my own bed.''

''One moment,'' Ethan commanded in a low voice. ''I want a word with you first. With Jane present.''

Taking his mother by the arm, he walked her across the vast bedchamber to the hearth with its quietly snapping fire. Jane followed, curiosity about his serious manner outweighing her weariness.

''Can this not wait until another time?'' Lady Rosalind asked. ''We must be at the church by eleven o'clock in the forenoon.''

''Then let us settle this quickly,'' he stated. ''I noticed today your inordinate distress over Marianne. Is there something you wish to tell me?''

Her gaze locked with his, then flitted to the fireplace, before returning to him. ''Tell you? I can't imagine what you mean. I was concerned about my granddaughter.''

He paced slowly before the hearth, his hands behind his back. ''Your granddaughter,'' he said in a strange, soft tone. ''You're more affectionate with this child than you were with me. Of course, you were very young when I was born—eighteen years old, I believe.''

''That is so. And perhaps I *was* rather flighty back then.'' She eyed him cautiously. ''If you're troubled by that, I can only beg your apology.''

''That isn't necessary.'' A distracted look on his face,

Ethan shook his head. "Just now, I was remembering how you breezed into my house in Wessex on the day Jane found Marianne on her doorstep."

"Why, yes. I'd just returned from my winter's sojourn in Italy."

"Where you had conveniently employed a maidservant who could nurse the baby."

"Gianetta was nursing her own child. Do you think me so cruel as to force the poor woman to leave behind her young daughter?"

Ethan didn't reply, but went on. "Then you arranged for Jane to come to London, where you orchestrated my marriage to her. So that Marianne would have two parents."

Lady Rosalind waved her fine-boned hand. "Oh, la, the child needed a mother, and when I realized Jane's interest in you, naturally I encouraged it. There is nothing wrong with a little matchmaking on behalf of my son and my goddaughter. And Jane did come to you of her own free will. Isn't that so, Jane?"

Jane sank slowly down onto a chair. She remembered how skillfully Lady Rosalind had convinced her to go to the tower room, ostensibly to talk to Ethan. But why was he now dredging up the past?

"Yes . . ." Unable to sort out his meaning, she asked, "Ethan, what are you saying?"

He fixed his intent stare on the dowager. Lady Rosalind twisted her gold betrothal ring and gazed at him. Though she stood regally straight, there was a wariness to her blue eyes, a vulnerability to her fine mouth. The fire bathed her in golden light, and the amber gown shimmered around her slender form.

"I am saying what I should have guessed from the start," he uttered in a quiet tone. "Marianne is my half-sister."

⌒ *Chapter 25* ⌒

Ethan prepared himself to counter another pretty denial. Instead, his mother's mouth quivered, and her queenly expression crumpled. She wilted onto a footstool and buried her face in her hands.

"Yes," she said in a broken voice quite unlike her usual breezy tone. "Yes, it's true. I gave birth to Marianne."

A gasp of disbelief came from Jane. "Oh, my lady!" she whispered, her mouth agape. "*You?* How can that be?"

"I left Marianne on your doorstep, Jane. How I wanted to tell you, both of you. Marianne is ... John Randall's child."

Though he had suspected as much, her words knifed into Ethan. He turned away, bracing both hands on a chair and staring at the baby on the bed. The old pain tasted bitter in his throat. God! Randall's child.

Marianne was John Randall's daughter.

He couldn't fathom the wonder of it. Instead, he recalled his fury at discovering his mother was having an affair with his best friend. It had happened the previous spring, right after his divorce from Portia. At first he had been incredulous, unable to believe his mother had the audacity to carry on with a man nearly twenty years her junior. Then when the truth had sunk in, Ethan had reacted in rage, challenging Randall to a bout of fisticuffs. He had fought his own friend, and Randall had not returned the blows. Shortly afterward, Randall had left with his regiment. Within the space of a month, he had fallen on the bloody fields of Waterloo.

Leaving behind his seed, his child.

Ethan felt a treacherous softening inside himself. He clenched his jaw lest anyone see how moved he felt.

"Captain John Randall?" Jane said, her voice lifting in amazement. You and he . . . ?"

"Yes," Rosalind murmured. "For a brief time last year, we were lovers. Does that shock you so much?"

Ethan turned to see Jane kneel beside the stool and place an arm around her mother-in-law. "I'm very surprised, that's all," Jane said. "I never once suspected Marianne's mother could be *you*. It must have been a terrible secret to bear." She gently pressed a folded handkerchief into the dowager's fingers.

Rosalind lifted her tearstained face and dabbed at her eyes. "I thought myself too old to conceive. I was forty-four years of age, after all. Even when I had the signs, I thought . . . I thought I was experiencing the change of life. And when I did realize the truth, it was too late." Her voice lowered to an anguished whisper. "John was already dead."

"How dreadful for you," Jane said with compassion. "It is never easy to lose someone you love. And to be left alone in such circumstances."

"I know we were far apart in age, but I did love him. So very, very much."

She raised her tear-wet gaze to Ethan, and as he took in her torment, his chest constricted and he swung away in a panic. He didn't want to feel this bond with her. But it was there nonetheless, a shared grief for his friend. Her lover. Marianne's father.

"I must beg you to understand my reason for the deception," Lady Rosalind went on, weaving the handkerchief between her fingers. "I could not bear an illegitimate child.

I would have been scorned, ostracized. I had renewed my acquaintance with the duke, you see, and I knew—''

Ethan pivoted back around. ''You knew he would not wed you.''

Her lips formed a wobbly smile. ''On the contrary, I am afraid he *would* have. And I did not wish my disgrace to taint him. So I went off to Italy for my confinement.''

''Already planning to dupe me into believing the child was mine,'' Ethan said. ''Which is why my signet ring turned missing months ago.''

''Yes, that is so.''

''And the notecard left with Marianne,'' he said, ''I suppose you had someone else write it?''

''A passenger onboard the ship back to England.'' She drew a tenuous breath. ''Think ill of me if you must, Ethan. But things have worked out for the best, have they not? You have Jane and Marianne now.''

He should resist that pleading look from his mother. He should not be swayed by the yearning in Jane's eyes. Yet in the midst of his confusion and pain, he could not deny the strength of his attachment to Jane and Marianne. It was both tender and fierce, something deep and rich, so personal and private he felt panicked at the thought of voicing it to anyone.

''Certainly I'm not displeased with my wife and daughter,'' he hedged. ''But you ought to have told us the truth sooner.''

Jane appeared disappointed by his words. She lowered her eyes and looked at Lady Rosalind. ''And I believe,'' she said firmly, ''that when he has time to reflect on it, Ethan will be glad to know that Marianne is the child of his friend. And yours, too.''

''Thank you,'' Rosalind whispered. ''Please, I must beg one favor from you both. That you will mention none of this to the duke.''

''Of course not,'' Jane vowed. ''There is no need for anyone else to know.''

She shot a glower at Ethan, her expression typically zeal-ous, and in the midst of his raw emotions, he felt a tug of gentle amusement.

Biting back a smile, he inclined his head in a nod. "Jane and I shall raise Marianne as our own. Far be it from me to betray a lady's secret."

On the front drive, Jane stood with Ethan and said their good-byes to the Duke and Duchess of Kellisham. Ethan held Marianne for Rosalind's kiss; then he caught his mother in a swift embrace, pressing his lips to her brow. The newlyweds climbed into the open landau. Rosalind touched her gloved fingers to her mouth and blew a kiss before bending her head to her husband. The white feathers on her modish turban fluttered in the evening breeze as the carriage started down the curved drive.

Awash in wistfulness, Jane turned with Ethan and walked back up the marble steps and into the house, where Gianetta stood waiting. Jane's heart melted as he kissed the baby, then handed her to the dark-haired nursemaid. Gianetta cud-dled Marianne to her ample bosom and crooned softly in Italian, heading for the staircase.

Jane and Ethan followed more slowly. The past two eventful days had taken a toll on her, and Jane felt a need to be alone with him, to settle her place in his affections once and for all. Last night, after the startling revelation from his mother, he had held Jane for too brief a moment. Then he had muttered an excuse about both of them need-ing rest, and he had vanished into his own chambers.

It was plain he didn't wish to talk about Captain Randall and his mother. Why could he pour out his emotions on paper but not share them with her?

"It was a beautiful wedding, was it not?" she said as they walked up the grand staircase. "I'm so glad your mother is happy at last."

"She will adore being a duchess. For one thing, it sounds much younger than *dowager*."

His cutting quip disturbed Jane. "But that isn't why she married the duke. They truly love each other. Really, Ethan, you don't credit your mother with any goodness at all."

"She does have a way of turning events to her own advantage," he said lightly. "You cannot deny that."

"Perhaps so, yet she means well. She brought us together. And she gave us Marianne. Were it not for her, I would still be living in a cottage in Wessex."

"A sour old spinster." As they started down the deserted passageway to their chambers, Ethan slid his arm around her waist and nuzzled her hair. "Instead of a lusty young wife."

In spite of her troubled spirit, Jane felt a thrill of desire, along with a giddy realization. She truly *had* blossomed into a confident, beautiful woman, the woman she had always dreamed of becoming. She was Ethan's wife now, and awareness of him coursed through her, his masculine scent, the firm pressure of his muscled arm, the heat of his breath against her temple. But she fought to master the passion inside herself, wanting some answers from him first.

His bedchamber was quiet and empty, the draperies already drawn against the night and a fire burning low on the grate. Now that the guests were gone, the servants would be at their celebration downstairs. Ethan lit a candle at the hearth and carried it to the bedside table. The golden light created an intimate bower, a scene made for seduction. Though her body yearned for his touch, her mind and her heart craved to know his thoughts, his feelings.

When he reached for her, she put her hands against his chest to stop him. She could feel his heart beating against her palm. "Ethan, you knew about your mother's affair with Captain Randall, didn't you? Did you quarrel with him?"

He gave her a moody look, then shrugged. "What matter is it now? It's over with and done." Bending his head, he brushed his lips over hers.

She controlled a delicious shiver. "Please . . . I want to understand what happened back then. You were grieving when you wrote that poem, and I think . . . I think you were angry at yourself. Is that true?"

A muscle worked in his jaw. "Leave it alone, Jane."

"I can't. Captain Randall fathered Marianne. I want to know more about him. You knew him best."

"We drank and gambled and chased women. Two shallow rakes out for a fine time."

His flippancy hid his true feelings, she was sure of it. She shook her head in frustration. "There is no shame in admitting you cared deeply for his friendship. Nor in being glad that Marianne is a part of him."

"Quite so. Now, come to bed."

Ethan pulled Jane to him and brought his lips down on hers. She knew he was placating her, intent on distracting her, but for a moment his expert kiss proved too tempting to resist. She looped her arms around his neck and gave herself up to the physical, to the taste and scent and touch that stirred her, to the feelings that arose from her unguarded depths.

She arched her body, wanting to be one with him. "I love you, Ethan. I love you so."

He said nothing, only continued his tender assault, moving his warm lips to her throat, his hands reaching for the buttons at the back of her gown. His silence broke through the sensual haze surrounding her. She took a shaky breath, fighting the uncertainty that ached within her.

She willed herself to voice the most important question of all. Taking his face in her palms, she made him look at her. "Ethan . . . do you love me?"

His gaze was dark, unfathomable. Making an impatient sound in his throat, he glanced away, then returned his eyes to her. His hands moved up and down her sides, brushing her breasts with rousing urgency. "I love what you do to me. I love to make love with you."

At one time, his answer would have exhilarated her. But

not tonight. Heartsore, she pulled out of his arms and stepped back. "I need more than charm and wit from you. Don't you see, Ethan? I need to know I'm loved in return."

"Jane," he said in a gently indulgent tone. "We get along better than most married couples. We enjoy each other's company. That is all that matters."

"Not to me," she whispered. "I want us to share what's in our hearts. I want you to talk to me as you did that night in the tower, when you told me about your father."

He stared at her, then swung away and thrust his hand through his hair. "You ask a lot, Jane. You expect me to change who I am."

"No. I just want you to show me who you are."

He didn't answer, and his silence *was* an answer. He would not allow her to breach the wall around him, not even now, after all the anguish they'd endured over Marianne.

Jane closed her eyes and tried to think beyond her pain. She needed to get away, to be alone, to return to the place that felt safe and familiar. "The country," she murmured. "Tomorrow I shall take Marianne to Wessex."

He turned on his heel and gazed sharply at her. "You're leaving me?"

For a moment she thought panic flashed in his eyes. Was it she that he would miss . . . or the baby? "I wish to go home for a while. To think about us . . . and our marriage."

Then before she could give in to her weakness for him, she turned her back on him and fled into her chamber.

⌒ *Chapter 26* ⌒

Pausing before the whitewashed door, Jane contemplated the stone cottage that had been her home for twenty-six years.

Marianne lay snugly in a sling secured at Jane's neck and waist, in the manner the local women sometimes carried their babies as they went about their work. But Jane rather doubted those infants had been nestled in a fancy blue shawl from one of London's finest shops.

She looked down at Marianne and smiled. "Do you remember this doorstep, little angel?"

Her daughter looked around with bright, curious eyes. Then she thrust out a chubby hand to bat at the fringe on the scarf.

Jane laughed. "Silly girl. This is very special place. It's where you first came into my life."

Now that she was here, she was glad she'd walked the three miles across the downs. The breeze had invigorated her, blowing away the cobwebs of sadness. In the past fortnight, she had spent all her time at Ethan's house—her home now. Initially, she had thought to stay at the cottage, but the moment she had stepped into his large foyer with its graceful staircase and spacious rooms, she had felt an urgency to settle there, to fit into her new life as Countess of Chasebourne.

So she had explored every nook and cranny from the attic to the stables, from the ballroom to the kitchen. And in the process, she had gleaned more about Ethan, the books he liked to read, the places where the housekeeper said he liked to sit, even learning how to make his favorite cherry pudding. She had spent a long time contemplating the portrait of his father in the picture gallery, wondering how a man could have tossed his son's poem into a fire. And reflecting on how that cruelty had shaped Ethan.

But now she felt a lightness inside herself, a sense of homecoming. She was glad Aunt Willy had shooed her out the door, asking her to fetch a favorite sewing thimble the older woman had forgotten on her dressing table. Wilhelmina had been unusually vehement that she required the thimble as soon as possible. And so Jane had set off.

Had she been afraid to come here before now? Afraid she might be tempted to return to her former life?

Jane unlatched the door and entered the dim interior. The place looked small, yet so familiar, the air musty from being shut up for so many weeks. There was the narrow staircase straight ahead, and on one side, her father's tiny office, crammed to the ceiling with books and papers.

She walked into the opposite room, the parlor with its shabby wing chairs set on either side of the tiny hearth, where her father and aunt used to sit of an evening, Jane on the cushioned window seat. Nostalgia glowed in her, as warm as the sunshine that glinted on the clock that had stopped in their absence. She wound it with the key and listened to its friendly ticking.

Then she strolled around the room. "Look," she told the baby. "There's the window seat where I liked to curl up and read."

Marianne gurgled and cooed.

"Properly awed, are you?" Jane said. "Let's go find Auntie's thimble."

As always, the steps creaked and she had to duck her head a little beneath the eaves. In her aunt's room, she found the thimble tucked behind a collection of long-empty bottles of medicine. Jane slipped it into her pocket, then peeked into her own bedchamber.

The row of empty hooks had held her three gowns. A straight-backed chair sat before a tiny desk with its quills and ink pot, the well-worn blotter. And there was the single bed where she had slept alone.

How long ago that seemed, the years before she had known the joys of a man's embrace. Though she felt a sentimental attachment to this chamber, she had no wish to remain here. Her hopes and dreams centered on the new life she had built with Ethan.

All the confusion and grief of the past weeks vanished like smoke, leaving her spirit light and free. She knew what she wanted now. Her gaze wandered out the window, following the familiar view across the wild downs, the hills and valleys. Now that rocky pathway had a special meaning.

It led home.

She looked down at the baby. "I must write a letter to your papa. I'll ask him to join us in the country. What do you think of that?"

Marianne smiled a toothless grin.

"I'm pleased we're in agreement," Jane said. "Come, darling. There's little to keep us here."

Heading downstairs and out of the cottage, she turned for one last survey of the stone walls and thatched roof, the garden that had gone to seed, the thicket of trees where Ethan had once fallen into a bramble bush. She smiled and then started down the pathway.

She composed her letter as she walked briskly, enjoying the sun on her face, one arm braced around Marianne's compact form. She would tell Ethan of her decision and list all the reasons why she wanted their marriage, that he could keep his secrets and she would love him anyway. A tremulous smile rose from deep within her. She had a secret of her own now, one she longed to share with him. But it was too precious to put in a letter. She would tell him about it in person.

And if he didn't come?

Pushing away the dark uncertainty, she took a deep breath. Well, then. She would go to London and fetch him.

By the time she reached the wrought-iron gates that marked the drive, Marianne had been lulled to sleep and Jane had every word clear in her mind. She could scarcely wait to put it all down on paper. How foolish she had been to think she could live without Ethan. The truth was, she didn't know how she could wait even a few days to see him again.

As she walked up to the house, she recalled marching here one fateful morning on a crusade to make Ethan Sinclair face up to his responsibilities. The memory brought a smile to her lips. Never had she imagined then that she would live here someday, in this glorious, ivy-covered mansion with its long rows of windows and the broad steps leading up to a columned portico.

A single white orchid lay before the threshhold.

Frowning, she picked up the exotic flower and twirled it between her fingers. Were there orchids growing in the conservatory? Apparently so, and the gardener must have dropped this one. Or perhaps Mrs. Wiggins, the housekeeper, had been busy making a flower arrangement.

Jane pushed open the door. The foyer was cool and quiet, the crystal chandelier glinting in the sunlight. Unlike their London house, the reception rooms were comfortably situated on the ground floor. There were no servants about, as on that morning in April. She had been so determined, so distraught over Marianne, she had stormed past the footmen and gone straight upstairs to Ethan's bedchamber.

She stopped at the grand staircase. More orchids scattered the pale marble steps, the blooms a mixture of pink and lavender and white.

Aunt Willy hurried out of the drawing room. "Ah, Jane.

Did you fetch my thimble so quickly? What a dear you
are."

"It was no trouble." Anxious to write her letter, Jane
handed over the thimble. "Why are there flowers all over
the stairway?"

"Why, mercy me. I can't imagine." Wilhelmina barely
glanced at the stairway. "You must be weary from your
long walk. Do let me take Marianne to the nursery for
you."

Jane blinked in surprise. Though her aunt had warmed
to the baby, cooing at her from time to time, she had never
offered to hold her. "If you're quite sure."

She unknotted the sling and carefully handed the slumbering baby to her aunt.

Wilhelmina awkwardly cuddled the baby to her maidenly
bosom. Her faded eyes sparkled with an odd wistfulness.
"Why don't you go on upstairs, my dear? Perhaps you can
solve the mystery of all these flowers."

Her aunt headed up the staircase, careful not to tread on
the orchids. Jane stared after her until she and the baby
disappeared around the corner, on their way up to the
second-floor nursery. There was no doubt about it. Wilhelmina was maneuvering her. But to what purpose?

Ethan?

Her heart leapt in wild, improbable hope. Jane closed her
eyes for a moment, clutching the single white orchid to her
breast and breathing a fervent prayer. *Please, God, let him
be here.*

Lifting her skirts, she dashed up the stairs. The trail of
blooms led down the corridor and to the master's suite. She
paused there, her pulse thrumming. A faint scent drifted to
her. Something dark and rich, exotic. Memory flashed to
her of the day she had burst into his chamber and found
him naked in bed.

She would love to discover him there again. Alone. Waiting for her.

Awash in anticipation, she opened the door and stepped

inside. And stopped in surprise. The large chamber was dim, the draperies drawn against the late afternoon light. An extravagance of candles flickered everywhere, on tables, the desk, the mantelpiece. The smell of incense was stronger here, enticing and erotic. And there were more orchids scattered across the carpet and over the bed.

The empty bed.

Candlelight illuminated the bank of tasseled pillows, the embroidered coverlet folded back invitingly. Where was Ethan?

Trembling with eagerness, Jane closed the door and hastened in search of him. The flower slipped from her fingers when she saw him.

One entire end of the room had been transformed into a tent with swaths of white silk. More candles glowed inside, illuminating the vases of orchids. Like a prince of depravity, Ethan lounged in a thronelike chair. He wore a dressing gown open to the waist, his nakedness visible between the lapels of the ruby silk. His fist rested on his lap.

With an imperious flick of his hand, he beckoned to her. "Come, slave girl."

This was her fantasy. He had created this romantic scene for *her*. She wanted to weep. She wanted to be in his arms.

Wild for his seduction, she hurried toward him. "Ethan! When did you arrive? I was just intending to write to you—"

"Silence," he said in a deep, compelling voice. "You will sit." He pointed to the fringed hassock at his feet.

"But I want to tell you what I've decided—"

"Do not disobey the pasha. Defiance will be punished."

"Oh." Bemused, she sank down onto the hassock. His bare leg brushed her skirt, and a flutter of excitement took wing inside her. She pressed her palms together in a deferential pose. "What is your command, O Great Master?"

He quirked an eyebrow. "I would grant you three gifts."

"But I don't need gifts," she said softly. "I'm your slave. Yours to take as you will." She wanted him to do

just that, to draw her onto his lap and have his wicked way
with her.

"Hush," he said. "You will listen while I speak."

She closed her mouth, happy just to be with him.

"Now there's an obedient slave girl," he said with an
approving nod. "My first gift to you is this."

He opened his fingers and held out his hand. In his big
palm gleamed a bit of gold jewelry, a delicate chain and . . .

"Mama's locket!" Feeling tears heat her eyes, Jane
picked it up and smoothed a trembling finger over the scrolled oval surface. The gold held a trace of Ethan's warmth.
She fervently clutched the locket to her breast. "How did
you find it?"

"Never question the ways of the pasha," he said in a
mysterious tone. "You will sit quietly now for my second
gift."

He reached inside his robe and drew forth a folded new-
sheet, which he passed to her. Mystified, she opened the
paper, scanning stories and headlines until her gaze riveted
to the neat type enclosed in a fancy border. A poem, unfamiliar to her. Had he allowed it to be printed?

She glanced at him questioningly, but he motioned to her
to read the poem, and so she did just that.

She Holds My Heart
by Ethan Sinclair, Lord Chasebourne

She holds my heart in bright of day,
In cloudy climes and moon-dark night.
Her smiles enchant, her kisses play
Tender music for my soul's delight . . .

In a soft haze of wonder, Jane read every word and then
slowly raised her head. She could scarcely believe the richness of emotion expressed by his words. "You wrote
this . . . for me?"

"Yes." No longer the arrogant pasha, he looked vulnerable, his gaze dark and solemn as if he feared her rejection. "I arranged for the poem to be published in the newspaper so that you would know . . . how very much you mean to me."

"Ethan," she whispered, her voice shaky.

"Shhh." Leaning forward, he placed his forefinger lightly over her mouth. "And now, let me give you my third gift."

She waited, afraid to hope, afraid even to breathe.

He cleared his throat. "Jane. These past weeks have been hell without you. I couldn't bear it any longer. I want you with me, for always." He paused, his face intense. "I love you."

Brimful of exultation, she sprang up from the hassock and threw her arms around him, dropping the locket in her eagerness to hold him. She felt the strong beating of his heart against her breasts. "Oh, Ethan, I love you, too. So much."

Their lips met in a frantic kiss, rich with promise and alive with need. Reveling in the knowledge that he was hers, truly hers, she moved her hands through his hair, down his neck and shoulders and chest, relearning his heat and strength. When she wrestled with his knotted sash, he chuckled at her eagerness and caught her hands. "The pasha does the seducing, slave girl."

"It's my fantasy," Jane objected. "I can amend it however I like."

"Ah, but I'm sharing your fantasy. And I will have you in bed where I can properly love you."

Lifting her from his lap, he stood up and turned her around so that he could unfasten her gown. As each button was freed, he bent to nuzzle her upper back, his lips raising delicious goosebumps over her skin. The gown slithered to the floor. By the time she stood clad in only her shift, she needed him too desperately to remain docile. She whirled toward him and slid her hands inside his robe, caressing him. He sucked in a breath and laughingly groaned.

"You enslave me," he murmured. "You and no other."

"Oh, you do know my fantasies, don't you?"

Leaving a trail of clothing among the flowers, they kissed their way to the bed. There, he knelt over her, his body bronzed by the light of the candles. She gazed dry-mouthed at the sheer male perfection of him, the brawny muscles of his chest and thighs and arms, the black hair that dusted his skin, the heavy thrust of his manhood. Heat pooled within her, a need so powerful she felt dazed by the force of it.

Parting her legs, she drew him down to cover her. She loved the weight of him, the rasp of his body sliding against hers. And oh, his touch, his lips on her breasts and his hands, caressing her inner folds until her desire reached a fever pitch. On a moan, she reached between them and guided him home. He took control then, making them one body, one soul. He cradled her face in his hands and said huskily, "I love you, Jane. For now and for always."

She could only sigh, too aroused for speech. When he moved, she shattered at once, the pleasure explosive in its intensity. Caught up in sensual fury, she was only dimly aware of him thrusting into her, shuddering from the force of his release. She returned to awareness in leisurely degrees, replete with happiness.

His satisfied chuckle rumbled against her breasts. "I really had intended to take my time with you."

"Mmmm. We have the rest of our lives to perfect this."

"Jane, listen." He shifted so that he could look at her, his fingertips touching her hair, as if she were infinitely precious to him. "I do wish to talk to you. To tell you all my secrets."

"Oh, Ethan." With a glad cry, she remembered the knowledge she hugged to her heart. "I have a little secret, too."

"You?"

"Yes." Taking his hand, she settled his palm over her belly. "It's right here."

His brows drew together; then as awareness dawned, his eyes went velvety soft, dark as midnight. "A baby?"

She nodded, smiling at his dazed look. "By next spring, Marianne will have a brother or sister."

"My God." Taking great care, he rolled onto his back, carefully bringing her on top of him. She could feel his hands tremble as he touched her cheek. "Have you been ill? Tired? And here I took you straight to bed."

She laughed from sheer pleasure. "I'm perfectly fine. A bit of queasiness in the mornings, that's all."

He smiled, tears sheening his eyes. And this time, he made no attempt to hide his emotion. "My darling Miss Maypole. You've brought such joy to my life."

"As you have to mine," she said softly. "And to think I once considered you too wicked to love."

Survey

TELL US WHAT YOU THINK AND YOU COULD WIN

A YEAR OF ROMANCE!
(That's 12 books!)

Fill out the survey below, send it back to us, and you'll be eligible to win a year's worth of romance novels. That's one book a month for a year—from St. Martin's Paperbacks.

Name _____

Street Address _____

City, State, Zip Code _____

Email address _____

1. How many romance books have you bought in the last year?
   (Check one.)
   __0-3
   __4-7
   __8-12
   __13-20
   __20 or more

2. Where do you MOST often buy books? *(limit to two choices)*
   __Independent bookstore
   __Chain stores *(Please specify)*
       __Barnes and Noble
       __B. Dalton
       __Books-a-Million
       __Borders
       __Crown
       __Lauriat's
       • __Media Play
       __Waldenbooks
   __Supermarket
   __Department store *(Please specify)*
       __Caldor
       __Target
       __Kmart
       __Walmart
   __Pharmacy/Drug store
   __Warehouse Club
   __Airport

3. Which of the following promotions would MOST influence your decision to purchase a ROMANCE paperback? *(Check one.)*
       __Discount coupon

    __Free preview of the first chapter
    __Second book at half price
    __Contribution to charity
    __Sweepstakes or contest

4. Which promotions would LEAST influence your decision to purchase a ROMANCE book? (Check one.)
    __Discount coupon
    __Free preview of the first chapter
    __Second book at half price
    __Contribution to charity
    __Sweepstakes or contest

5. When a new ROMANCE paperback is released, what is MOST influential in your finding out about the book and in helping you to decide to buy the book? (Check one.)
    __TV advertisement
    __Radio advertisement
    __Print advertising in newspaper or magazine
    __Book review in newspaper or magazine
    __Author interview in newspaper or magazine
    __Author interview on radio
    __Author appearance on TV
    __Personal appearance by author at bookstore
    __In-store publicity (poster, flyer, floor display, etc.)
    __Online promotion (author feature, banner advertising, giveaway)
    __Word of Mouth
    __Other (please specify)_____

6. Have you ever purchased a book online?
    __Yes
    __No

7. Have you visited our website?
    __Yes
    __No

8. Would you visit our website in the future to find out about new releases or author interviews?
    __Yes
    __No

9. What publication do you read most?
    __Newspapers *(check one)*
      __*USA Today*
      __*New York Times*
      __Your local newspaper
    __Magazines *(check one)*

    __*People*
    __*Entertainment Weekly*
    __Women's magazine *(Please specify:_____)*
    __*Romantic Times*
    __Romance newsletters

10. What type of TV program do you watch most? *(Check one.)*
    __Morning News Programs (ie. "Today Show")
     (Please specify:_____)
    __Afternoon Talk Shows (ie. "Oprah")
     (Please specify: _____)
    __All news (such as CNN)
    __Soap operas *(Please specify: _____)*
    __Lifetime cable station
    __E! cable station
    __Evening magazine programs (ie. "Entertainment Tonight")
     (Please specify: _____)
    __Your local news

11. What radio stations do you listen to most? *(Check one.)*
    __Talk Radio
    __Easy Listening/Classical
    __Top 40
    __Country
    __Rock
    __Lite rock/Adult contemporary
    __CBS radio network
    __National Public Radio
    __WESTWOOD ONE radio network

12. What time of day do you listen to the radio MOST?
    __6am-10am
    __10am-noon
    __Noon-4pm
    __4pm-7pm
    __7pm-10pm
    __10pm-midnight
    __Midnight-6am

13. Would you like to receive email announcing new releases and special promotions?
    __Yes
    __No

14. Would you like to receive postcards announcing new releases and special promotions?
    __Yes
    __No

15. Who is your favorite romance author? _____

WIN A YEAR OF ROMANCE FROM SMP
(That's 12 Books!)
No Purchase Necessary

OFFICIAL RULES

1. To Enter: Complete the Official Entry Form and Survey and mail it to: Win a Year of Romance from SMP Sweepstakes, c/o St. Martin's Paperbacks, 175 Fifth Avenue, Suite 1615, New York, NY 10010-7848, Attention JP. For a copy of the Official Entry Form and Survey, send a self-addressed, stamped envelope to: Entry Form/Survey, c/o St. Martin's Paperbacks at the address stated above. Entries with the completed surveys must be received by February 1, 2000 (February 22, 2000 for entry forms requested by mail). Limit one entry per person. No mechanically reproduced or illegible entries accepted. Not responsible for lost, misdirected, mutilated or late entries.

2. Random Drawing. Winner will be determined in a random drawing to be held on or about March 1, 2000 from all eligible entries received. Odds of winning depend on the number of eligible entries received. Potential winner will be notified by mail on or about March 22, 2000 and will be asked to execute and return an Affidavit of Eligibility/Release/Prize Acceptance Form within fourteen (14) days of attempted notification. Non-compliance within this time may result in disqualification and the selection of an alternate winner. Return of any prize/prize notification as undeliverable will result in disqualification and an alternate winner will be selected.

3. Prize and approximate Retail Value: Winner will receive a copy of a different romance novel each month from April 2000 through March 2001. Approximate retail value $84.00 (U.S. dollars).

4. Eligibility. Open to U.S. and Canadian residents (excluding residents of the province of Quebec) who are 18 at the time of entry. Employees of St. Martin's and its parent, affiliates and subsidiaries, its and their directors, officers and agents, and their immediate families or those living in the same household, are ineligible to enter. Potential Canadian winners will be required to correctly answer a time-limited arithmetic skill question by mail. Void in Puerto Rico and wherever else prohibited by law.

5. General Conditions: Winner is responsible for all federal, state and local taxes. No substitution or cash redemption of prize permitted by winner. Prize is not transferable. Acceptance of prize constitutes permission to use the winner's name, photograph and likeness for purposes of advertising and promotion without additional compensation or permission, unless prohibited by law.

6. All entries become the property of sponsor, and will not be returned. By participating in this sweepstakes, entrants agree to be bound by these official rules and the decision of the judges, which are final in all respects.

7. For the name of the winner, available after March 22, 2000, send by May 1, 2000 a stamped, self-addressed envelope to Winner's List, Win a Year of Romance from SMP Sweepstakes, St. Martin's Paperbacks, 175 Fifth Avenue, Suite 1615, New York, NY 10010-7848, Attention JP.